PRAIS

TRICKSTI

NATIONAL BESTSELLER

A *Globe and Mail* Best Book of the Year

"The book is full of light and love. Robinson has a loopy and wonderful sense of humour, expressed not just by her trademark laughter but her delightful author's bios." —*The Globe and Mail*

"Crafting such exquisite coming-of-age tales that can bring equal parts tears of sadness and laughter takes a certain kind of narrative genius." —*The Vancouver Sun*

"Robinson balances realist, coming-of-age subject matter against a supernatural horror-fantasy plot with a comic tone. . . . Robinson understands, like few writers do, how comedy (when committed to fully) can enhance and deepen unfunny emotions such as horror, sadness and pain." —*Winnipeg Free Press*

"Canadian Haisla/Heiltsuk writer Eden Robinson has delivered the second in her Trickster trilogy—the first installment, *Son of a Trickster*, was shortlisted for the Giller Prize. *Trickster Drift* is even better. It's an enlightening, entertaining and very funny novel." —*NOW* (Toronto)

"*Trickster Drift* by Eden Robinson is an amazing second entry into her Trickster trilogy. Here we follow Jared, still as coy and as frank as ever, from the small town of Kitimat through to the depths of Vancouver's urbanity. The magic is very much alive here as Jared melts into a life of tricksters, witches, shape-shifters, and monsters that sometimes look all too much like us." —Joshua Whitehead, author of *Jonny Appleseed*

"[A] riveting sequel. . . . Robinson has created a smart, funny and very likeable character in Jared and the reader will yearn for his success and fear for him as the evitable pull to embrace his power is realized." —*Pique*

"The mix of sharp comedy, quick character sketches, and unsettling horror is note-perfect." —*Quill & Quire*

"My favourite book of 2018 is *Trickster Drift*. Eden's amazing writing style shines through brilliantly, once again: The words fly off the page—which allows the reader to experience the characters, scenes and plot vividly because the mechanics of reading don't ever get in the way. Eden's characters are vibrant and real—I actually expect to bump into a few of them the next time I'm in Vancouver." —Darrel J. McLeod, author of *Mamaskatch*, CBC Books

PRAISE FOR

SON OF A TRiCKSTER

NATIONAL BESTSELLER
Finalist for the Scotiabank Giller Prize
Finalist for the Ethel Wilson Fiction Prize
Shortlisted for the Sunburst Award

"A novel that shimmers with magic and vitality, featuring a compelling narrator, somewhere between Holden Caulfield and Harry Potter. . . . Energetic, often darkly funny, sometimes poignant, this is a book that will resonate long after the reader has devoured the final page." —Scotiabank Giller Prize jury citation

"An incredibly engaging, coming-of-age story of an Indigenous teen in northern British Columbia. Eden Robinson's almost magical ability to blend wry humour, magical realism and teenage reality will have you holding your breath for the next in the series." —*The New York Times*

"A unique, genuinely surprising novel from one of Canada's finest writers, a blend of hardscrabble coming-of-age story with mythic fiction at its most powerfully subversive. It's exactly as slippery as a trickster tale should be, changing direction and shape even as you convince yourself you know what's going on and what will likely happen next. . . . This is Robinson at her best." —*National Post*

"[Robinson is] one of Canada's pre-eminent Indigenous writers. . . . Her depictions of the complex interplay between First Nations peoples of varying levels of wokeness and cultural immersion are undeniably funny and subtle." —*The Globe and Mail*

"In its melding of normalized violence, Native myth, gutter talk and ready wit, *Son of a Trickster* readily recalls its predecessors. . . . [A] charmingly chaotic party." —*Toronto Star*

"Robinson has a gift for making disparate elements come together into a convincing narrative, breathing myth, lore and magic into otherwise harsh realities. . . . Jared offers readers, particularly First Nations youth, a comrade in the angst and alienation of their experience. Eden Robinson does much to enhance the growing body of Indigenous Canadian literature." —*Maclean's*

"Eden Robinson is more than funny, more than intelligent, more than a novelist—she's an enchanter. *Son of a Trickster* creates a terrifically believable teenage character who lives both on the rez and in a witchy soup of blood, sex and magic. Harry Potter goes to reform school. Full of sparks, full of pain, full of joy." —Alix Hawley, author of *All True Not a Lie in It*

"Eden Robinson is a writer with a magical touch. Crisp prose, taut dialogue and a cast of maniacal characters you sure as hell don't want living next door." —Thomas King, author of *The Back of the Turtle* and *The Inconvenient Indian*

"Eden Robinson is a masterful storyteller. Shimmering with deft prose, unforgettable characters and haunting truths, *Son of a Trickster* reminds us that sometimes the surest way to solid ground is through believing in magic." —Ami McKay, author of *The Birth House*, *The Virgin Cure* and *The Witches of New York*

BY EDEN ROBINSON

Traplines

Monkey Beach

Blood Sports

The Sasquatch at Home: Traditional Protocols & Modern Storytelling

THE TRICKSTER TRILOGY

Son of a Trickster

Trickster Drift

Return of the Trickster

EDEN ROBINSON

TRiCKSTER DRIFT

VINTAGE CANADA

VINTAGE CANADA EDITION, 2019

Published by Vintage Canada, a division of Penguin Random House Canada
Limited, in 2019. Originally published in hardcover by Knopf Canada,
a division of Penguin Random House Canada Limited, in 2018. Distributed
in Canada by Penguin Random House Canada Limited, Toronto.

Vintage Canada with colophon is a registered trademark.

www.penguinrandomhouse.ca

Library and Archives Canada Cataloguing in Publication

Robinson, Eden, author
Trickster drift / Eden Robinson.

ISBN 978-0-7352-7344-3
eBook ISBN 978-0-7352-7345-0

I. Title.

PS8585.O35143T75 2019   C813'.54   C2018-900469-X

Cover design: Jennifer Lum
Cover images: (city skyline) © David Gn Photography/Getty images;
(geometric pattern) © Tanor & (birds) © art4all, both Shutterstock.com

Printed and bound in the United States of America

2 4 6 8 9 7 5 3 1

Penguin
Random House
VINTAGE CANADA

For John Robinson.
Always in my heart

Coolly and deliberately I let go of Lucucid
Grieve the parking of my original language
And bury it inside my bones.

—Lee Maracle, "I'm Home Again"

CONTENTS

THAT OLD BLACK MAGIC

The clouds finally broke into a sullen drizzle after a muggy, overcast day. Jared Martin flipped up his hood as he turned the corner onto his street. His mom's truck was in the driveway. The house he'd grown up in was two storeys high, white with green trim. The large porch was littered with work gear. His mom rented out two of the rooms and the basement to pay the bills. Most of her tenants were sub-subcontractors, in Kitimat for a few weeks and unwilling to shell out for a pricey furnished one-bedroom or a motel room. Or they were hard-core smokers who wanted to be able to light up in their rooms and found a kindred spirit in his mom, a dedicated two-packer who hated being forced outside.

He paused on the sidewalk, listening. Things seemed quiet. Which didn't mean it was safe to go in, but Jared went up the steps and opened the front door. Not **visiting** his mom before he took off for Vancouver would save him **a lot of** grief, but it would be such a douche move. She'd never let him forget it.

"Mom?" Jared said.

"In here," she said, her voice coming from the kitchen.

The kitchen windows were all open and moths fluttered against the screens. She was frying a pan of meatballs, her cigarette tucked into the corner of her mouth.

Her hair was in a ponytail. She wore her favourite ripped Metallica T-shirt over jeans and flip-flops. He could see all the little muscles working in her face as she inhaled. She was losing weight again. He hoped it was just coke.

Jared put his backpack down by the table and then hopped up to sit on the counter. His mom salted a pot of boiling water and cracked in some spaghetti.

"Nice of you to show up," she said.

Jared swung his feet, staring down at them. "Where's Richie?"

"He is where he is."

Her boyfriend sold the lighter recreational drugs. They used to get along, but Richie seemed suspicious of Jared now that Jared was sober, like he had suddenly turned into a narc. When they were forced together by his mom, Richie wouldn't talk to him for fear of incriminating himself.

Jared watched her resentfully making him dinner. She hated cooking. He wished she'd just ordered a pizza. He tried to think of a safe topic of conversation. His Monday night shift at Dairy Queen was normally dull, but his new co-worker had kept stopping to sob into her headset. "Work was nuts. I had to train my replacement. She does not handle stress well."

"Not many people survive the soft-serve ice-cream racket."

Ball-buster, his dad called her when he was being charitable. His adoptive dad? His dad. Philip Martin, the guy who had raised him when his biological dad turned out to be a complete dick.

She stirred the pasta. "What? No snappy comeback?"

"I'm tired."

"Yeah, looking down on all us alkies and addicts must be exhausting."

"Are we going to do this all night?"

"Get the colander."

Jared hopped down and grabbed the colander from the cupboard above the fridge.

When he handed it to her, she stared at him a moment. Then her lips went thin, the lines around her mouth deepening. "I don't want you staying with Death Threat," she said.

Death Threat was the nickname of one of her exes, Charles Redhill, a low-level pot grower who said it would be okay if Jared bunked in his basement while he was going to school in Vancouver, if he didn't mind working a little security detail in exchange.

"People aren't exactly lining up to let me sleep on their couches," Jared said.

"He's a fuckboy with delusions he's Brando."

"Stel-la!" Jared said, trying to make her laugh.

She ignored him as if he wasn't standing beside her. She took the cigarette out of the corner of her mouth and let the pasta drain in the colander in the sink and then dumped it back in the pot. She poured in a jar of Ragú spaghetti sauce and stirred and then added the meatballs. She crushed the last bit of her cigarette out on the burner and tossed the butt in a sand-filled coffee can near the sink. He carried the pot to the table. She pulled some garlic bread out of the oven.

They ate in silence. Or, more accurately, Jared ate in silence. His mom smoked and picked at a meatball with her fork, slowly mashing it into bits.

"Where's Death Threat's place?" she said.

Jared shrugged. He was hoping against hope that Death lived near his school, the British Columbia Institute of Technology. Didn't matter, though. Nothing beat free.

"Nice. I'm your mother and you don't trust me enough to know where you're fucking staying."

"He's away in Washington State right now. I'm booked at a hostel for the first week. Just text my cell."

"He told you where he lives, right?"

"He'll show."

"He's a fucking pothead. He'll forget you exist. He forgets where his ass is until someone hands it to him."

"I can handle myself."

His mom sucked in a great impatient breath.

"Can we just have a nice supper?" Jared said.

"Can you not live with the spazzy fucktard who calls himself Death Threat?"

"Chill, okay? I just need a free place until my student loan comes in, then I'll find a room or something."

"Buttfucking Jesus on goddamn crutches."

"Mom."

"Don't *Mom* me, genius. This is a crap plan."

"It's my life," Jared said, pushing the plate away.

"Jared, you can barely manage warding. What're you going to do if you run into something really fucking dangerous?"

His mom was a witch. For real. As he had found out definitively, just before he swore off the booze and the drugs. He'd always thought she was being melodramatic when she told him witch stuff. Then he was kidnapped by some angry otters and his shape-shifting father/

sperm donor stepped in to save him, along with his mother. He only lost a toe. Her particular talent was hexes, though she preferred giving her enemies a good old-fashioned shit-kicking. Curses tended to bite you in the ass, she'd told him, and weren't nearly as satisfying as physically throttling someone.

"Who's going to bother me?" Jared said. "I got nothing anyone wants."

"You're the son of a Trickster," she hissed.

"There's a billion of us." On one website he'd found 532 people claiming to be the children of Wee'git. Either Wee'git couldn't keep it in his pants or a lot of people wanted to appear more exotic.

"You think you're so fucking smart," his mom said.

Jared recited the Serenity Prayer in his head. She shook another cigarette out of the pack and lit it off her butt before crushing it out on the full ashtray in the middle of the table. The TV went on in the living room. The recliner squealed.

"I'll be out of your hair tomorrow," Jared said. "You can forget you ever had me and party yourself to death."

"You are testing my patience."

It was always a bad sign when his mom stopped swearing. Jared focused on the tick of the kitchen clock to stay calm.

"You think I don't love you," she said. "Is that it?"

"I don't think I'm high on your priority list."

She got up and stood over him. She took her cigarette out of her mouth and he half-expected to get it in his face. He must have flinched, because her eyes narrowed dangerously.

She grabbed his chin. "You shoulda been a girl. *Wah. Mommy doesn't fucking love me. My feelings. My feeeeeelings.*"

He shoved her hand away. "Get off me."

"Are we done emoting?"

"I am."

She backed up a step. "So I asked my sister if you could stay with her."

Holy crap. Jared was stunned. His mom hadn't spoken to her sister since . . . forever. God. She really didn't want him to stay with Death Threat.

"I dunno," Jared said.

"Mave's willing to put you up," his mom said. "But be careful. She's deaf to magic. Don't bring it up around her. She'll think you're nuts and try to get you on antipsychotics."

"I thought you hated her."

"I do."

She took a piece of paper out of her jean pocket and handed it to him. His throat tightened when he saw the name and number. His aunt, Mavis Moody, had tried to get custody of him when he was a baby, figuring her sister would be bad for any baby. His mom had married Philip Martin to avoid losing Jared. He couldn't meet his mom's eyes knowing how much of her pride she'd sacrificed to find him a safer place to crash. He dropped his head.

"Don't say I never did anything for you," she said.

Jared reached down, rifled through his backpack and gave her his grad picture.

She frowned. "Are you throwing it in my face? I only have grade eight and you're a fucking high school graduate? You think that makes you special?"

"It's just a picture," Jared said. "Toss it if you don't like it."

———

His bed was stripped. Clean sheets were folded on top of the dresser. Usually he had to shake out the used condoms and indiscriminate underwear, reminders of the parties that had gone on in his house while he was couchsurfing. When he first sobered up, he'd tried to ride the parties out, but when he was shaky, the temptation to join in was non-stop. And somehow, being sober alone at a party seemed sadder than being a barely tolerated guest on someone else's couch. Also, as he became more comfortable with sobriety, he got tired of fighting randoms for his own bed.

He studied the changes to his room. The floor was swept and free of discarded beer cans and roaches. His desk was cleaned out, completely empty. All the letters Granny Nita had written him were missing. He rechecked the drawers, just in case. He hadn't hidden them from his mom, but he wasn't exactly waving them in her face, since Granny Nita was the other close relative his mom hated with a passion. Granny Nita had always disapproved of her daughter's hard-living ways and of her choice in men (Jared couldn't argue with that). But Granny Nita had mostly written Jared about her legal woes trying to get compensation for what had been done to her at residential school. It didn't seem like she had anybody to talk to about it— she and Mavis also didn't talk: what was with the women in his family?—so she poured everything into her letters to him. She said there was no paperwork, no surviving evidence that she had been experimented on. Just the scars on her body, the masses in her lungs and her own testimony. She'd gotten compensation for her years of being in the Port Alberni Residential School, but not for her time in the preventorium where she'd been sent for a persistent cough that the doctors had said was tuberculosis. Her legal team was thinking they'd have to start a class action suit. But she worried. She didn't want to sit in court and itemize everything that had happened in public, like she was a sideshow, there for everyone's entertainment. If they were going to go forward on "an individual basis," though, the lawyers wanted her to limit the adjudication to things they had witnesses and paperwork for, like the time the supervisors had burned her hand on the stove or when the doctor had punctured her eardrum with a scalpel.

Sometimes Jared hadn't been able to open her letters for a few days. He'd sit and steel himself to read her neat cursive writing. She wrote these things so matter-of-factly, as if everyone got their eardrum punctured when they came in for treatment one too many times for an ear infection, or had a bunch of women drag them into the kitchen and burn their hand because they wouldn't shut up about what was happening to their cousins, who were getting picked out of bed in the night, leaving her to listen to them scream and scream and scream.

God bless you, Jared, she always signed her letters.

When she wasn't writing about her adjudication, she was talking about her church, her church groups, her friends in God. How her faith helped her through her trials and she hoped one day he'd come to know Jesus Christ, our Lord and Saviour.

Always trying to recruit him—yeah, he could see why his mom had a bug up her ass about Granny Nita. Even if his mom had read the letters, there was nothing damning in them. She couldn't be that mad, right? She would have mentioned it at supper if she was feeling homicidal. He'd have a knife through his hand or the Ragú jar bust over his head. He'd wait till morning to ask for the letters back. If there was a scene, he wouldn't be stuck here afterwards. Still, he wished Granny Nita would learn to text like a normal person.

Rain had begun pattering on the roof. Jared made his bed, then flopped down and checked his cellphone. Three texts: one from Bianca, a co-worker at Dairy Queen who went to the same AA meetings he did, and two from Crashpad, his only remaining friend in high school after he stopped selling pot cookies and giving kids access to his mom's party palace. Nothing from Death Threat.

Proud of you, Bianca had texted him. *Keep it up!*

She'd attached a picture of an animated, dancing cake with a giant "1" candle sparkling like the fuse in a stick of dynamite. He texted back a quick *Thanks!*

Why'd you grad early? Crashpad had texted. *Whoʒ gonna sit wit me @ lunch?*

And then: *This sux. Do your upgrading here! U can park in my room.*

Crashpad's parents could stand Jared for a stretch of about a week, maybe two, before they started asking when he was going home. Or if he had relatives he could stay with. Or what his plans were. He couldn't blame them. He'd probably spent half of this last year sleeping on a camping foamy on Crashpad's bedroom floor, watching his DVDs and Blu-rays of science fiction and fantasy TV series. In part Jared wanted to go to school in Vancouver so he could watch a show where the hero didn't wear Spandex or wasn't battling obvious CGI monsters. Jared knew he was only welcomed back to their house because no one at school picked on Crashpad when Jared was around. Not because Jared had spectacular fighting skills or anything. Just a willingness to mouth off and a high pain threshold. Also, most people knew his mom's reputation.

Survived dinner, Jared texted Crashpad, who texted back immediately: *Dad says need a ride to the bus depot?*

I'll bet he did, Jared thought. *Momʒ driving me. thanx 2 yr dad.*

Dude u shud stay. We conquer Van 2GETHER. BCIT can wait!!!!

When you go 2 film school next year u wont have 2 look 4 a place. U can park with me.

Still sux.

Tired of being the king of couchsurfing.

New show filmed in Van called Continuum. *Therez this cop from da future & she gets sent back in time by a terrorist explosion. Theyre filming a block from ur hostel! Check it out! Send me pix!*

Jared tried not to be annoyed, tried to remember that the dude had never, not once in his life, had to worry about where he was going to sleep or how he was going to eat. *Gonna b busy finding a place before school starts*, Jared finally texted. *Sorry.*

The copz hot, Crashpad texted back. *1 signed headshot & I owe u 4ever. Kk.*

Downstairs, the music suddenly cranked up to a crushing jet-engine rumble, and he could hear his mom laughing overtop of it. Jared moved his dresser against the door. He scrolled through his phone, catching up. From his ex's Instagram posts, Sarah was still in the women's wellness centre on Vancouver Island, mocking the morning yoga sessions, the attempt to cure depression with cultural appropriation. Her Twitter feed was dominated by her flame war with some dude arguing about the effectiveness of Canada adopting the UN Declaration of Indigenous Rights. The subtweets went on forever.

Not that he was creeping Sarah's feeds. Not much anyways. Just . . . checking up.

They hadn't seen each other in a year. She was his first real girlfriend and his first real breakup. She'd lived next door for a few months with her grandparents, the Jakses. They'd mostly started dating because of proximity. She hated Normcore clothes and dressed like she was living in a perpetual Halloween. She'd mocked him relentlessly for his choice in music, specifically Nickelback. She'd have a field day if she ever found out he listened to "Someday" when he was missing her more than usual. He hadn't expected to feel this shitty about her for this long. Mostly he hid it, worried he was some defective loser, the pathetic kind of person who couldn't move on, who played mopey emo music when they knew no one was watching and hated themselves for almost crying every time. It didn't seem to matter that he was the one who broke up with Sarah, after the craziness they created together got out of hand and Sarah had ended up nearly bleeding out on her grandparents' kitchen floor. They both came from magical families, but Sarah was pro-magic and Jared wasn't anti-magic so much as he wanted to avoid the batshit-craziness-that-will-likely-result-in-your-death.

A woman murmured in the bathroom next to his bedroom, her voice amplified by the acoustics. A man's voice mumbled something and then Jared heard zippers coming undone. The wet smacks of the hookup lasted about two minutes. The bathroom door slammed and he heard them stumble down the hallway.

Someone tried his door. He watched the knob turning back and forth, and then the door shook with a hard couple of shoves.

"Occupied!" Jared shouted.

"Sorry," a dude mumbled. "Is there another bathroom?"

"Next door."

"Thanks."

His mom was right. He probably could have planned his exit better. He was mostly winging it, figuring things out on the fly. A part of him was already gone, but a part of him didn't want to leave.

Cold feet. Staring down his future, Jared knew he had rotten luck and nothing backing him up but snark.

Jared woke when his dresser squealed across the floor as it slid with an invisible push to the wall. His mom crossed the room and dropped a shoebox of confetti on him. The street light shining through the window turned all the paper orange. He switched on the lamp. She swayed, nothing but her Metallica T-shirt draped over her thin frame, and shook like it was winter. Her eyes were black, fully dilated, none of the light-brown irises showing at all.

"Mom?" he said, brushing the confetti off. He recognized Granny Nita's handwriting on the torn-up bits of letter.

"Did you start writing her or did she write you?" his mom said. "How did you start this little conversation with the woman who tried to kill you with a blood curse? You do remember that, don't you?"

"I wanted her to know I'm not a Trickster," Jared said. "That's all. That's it. We weren't planning on writing each other—"

"*Lying* to me."

Jared felt the curse in the air, a building charge like thunder grumbling through the clouds before a lightning strike. His arm hair stood up and, suddenly, he shared what his mom was thinking, felt the weight of his betrayal like a stone in his gut. He wanted her out of his head. Out. He wanted his own thoughts, his own feelings. But he felt her soured love, raw like road rash after a spectacular fall. Cold rage over everything. Her fingers twitched. She knew the words that would have him vomiting his guts out by the end of the day. She wasn't ready to say them, but she wanted him to know that she could.

LIFE IS A HIGHWAY

Shortly after dawn that Tuesday, Jared stuffed some of his things into his backpack and picked his way through the debris from the party and around the passed-out partiers, then walked to the highway. Even if his mom came down from whatever she was taking, he didn't want her driving him to the bus station. Not after that. His head ached. He didn't want to think about why it ached; he just wanted to get out of there. Walking helped. Stopped the shaking. He didn't know what his mom was taking that made her that sloppy. The mind-melding thing had only happened with Wee'git. Jared had been pissed when he found out that the Trickster was his biological father and also the snarky voice in his head, a mental peeping Tom who hadn't actually helped Jared in any meaningful way, except that once. He usually knew what his mom was thinking because she was a no-bullshit kind of person, but he'd never done brain sharesies with her and he didn't want to do it again. It was next-level messed up. She must have been more enraged than normal. Granny Nita was a big trigger for his mom, which is why he hadn't told her about the letters. He'd meant to tell her. But there hadn't been a moment when she wasn't pissed at him or high or both.

He expected to be holding his thumb out forever, but within a few minutes a guy in a red Dodge Ram pulled over. Jared jogged to the truck. Some death metal band Jared wasn't familiar with blasted out of the speakers, the subwoofers vibrating the windows. Jared hopped in. The guy had forearm tattoos in black, Gothic ink that read *Spawn* on the right one, *and Die* on the left. The whole forty-five-minute ride to Terrace, the guy shouted fishing stories at Jared, bragging about all the sockeye he'd caught. The dude dropped him off at the bus depot an hour before it opened at 7:30 a.m.

Jared sat on one of the concrete dividers in the rain, wishing he'd brought an umbrella. He could sit here until the A&W restaurant next door opened and then drink coffee and wait until the noon bus showed. Or he could visit Phil, who thought Jared and his mom were delusional for believing all the Trickster stuff. Jared considered the next twenty-two hours—a milk run that stopped at every small town between here and Vancouver. He knew his dad would be up, because he didn't sleep much. Maybe he had breakfast going.

The townhouse wasn't far away. Jared knocked. He heard his dad shuffling to the door. When he opened it, he was in pyjama bottoms and an untied bathrobe.

"Hey, kiddo. Are you leaving for school already?"

"Hi, Dad. Yup."

"I got coffee on."

"Cool."

His dad had been a big guy before he'd got hurt in an accident at work. Now he was on disability and his back had started to curve. He'd gotten himself off Oxy, but he wasn't going to physio. No point, he'd told Jared. His new wife, Shirley, was nowhere to be seen. She didn't like Jared and he wasn't a big fan of hers. He liked her daughter, though, his stepsister, who was now dating a welder from Prince Edward Island who wanted to take her and her son back home when his contract was up. She was thinking about it.

After his dad made them a vat of oatmeal, he broke out the cribbage board and they played a few games. Then they watched the morning news. The townhouse had even less furniture than the last time Jared had visited. Phil told him the rent was going up and the landlord was making noises about renovating. Jared tried to remain detached and let other people handle their own problems. They shot the shit until Jared noticed the time.

"I should head 'er," he said.

"I'll walk you there," his dad said.

"No, that's okay."

"When am I going to see you again, huh? Gotta squeeze in all my Jared time."

His dad put on sneakers with a sole that flopped when he walked and a dusty, cracked windbreaker that looked like it would leak in the rain. He put on a cheery smile, swinging his arms hard in an unconvincing show of vigour. At the last crosswalk before the bus depot, he took too long to cross the street and cars honked at them. His dad touched the brim of his trucker's cap to the honkers. The bus was already parked in a covered area at the depot. Passengers smoked or ate from A&W takeout bags as they waited for the driver.

"You got enough money for the trip down?" his dad said.

"I'm good."

"Got enough for your ol' dad?" He tried to smile, but it was shaky. The corners of his mouth twitched.

"I got enough for a week," Jared said.

"Even a five'll do," his dad said, looking at the ground.

Jared gave him a twenty.

"Thanks. Thanks, Jared."

His dad stayed by him all the way to the door. Once Jared was on the bus, Phil stood under the covered area and waved. Jared waved back. Watching his dad, a still, wet figure in the jumble of departing cars, Jared felt something twist in his gut. He couldn't name it and it took a while to stop.

The rain clouds disappeared as they moved away from the coast, giving way to blue skies and relentless sunshine. The bus driver droned the name of each town as they approached it. An old woman in the back yelled at the driver to put on the air conditioner. People got on. People got off. Jared drowsed against the window, cold air gusting on his face.

At Fraser Lake, where Mrs. Jaks now lived with her brother, the bus pulled into a Petro-Can gas station. Jared looked around hopefully. He'd called Mrs. Jaks right after he booked his ticket, saying he'd be on this bus at this time and if she happened to be around, and didn't have anything better to do, they'd have a short layover and he could buy her a coffee or something. She said she'd try, but she didn't have a lot of energy these days. She'd beaten her leukemia into remission, but it had taken a toll. The driver got out and loaded luggage for a couple of guys. The parking spaces were empty. Jared craned his neck to peek through the window on the other side of the bus, but no one was on the street. No one came out of the gas station.

When he was a kid, Mrs. Jaks used to watch him when his mom went haywire, under the guise of asking him for help with her chores. When she'd gotten sick last year, she'd had to sell her house and move away. Jared missed her. He even missed her husband, who had advanced Alzheimer's. Still, it had been awkward between him and Mrs. Jaks after her granddaughter, Sarah, had tried to do magic herself and ended up bleeding all over the kitchen. Even after she'd almost died, she still wanted to do spells with him and he couldn't go there, so he'd broken up with her. Mrs. Jaks had given Jared her new phone number and address, but she hadn't answered his calls in the last couple of days, so he guessed he wasn't really surprised she hadn't showed.

The bus chugged on. He had a three-hour layover in Prince George. The evening light hung in the air with the familiar tang of rotten eggs from the nearby pulp mills. The sweet smell of money, his dad liked to say. Jared took a walk to stretch his legs, heading to the Superstore, where he bought a two-litre of no-name root beer and bulk nachos. Then he went back and sat outside the bus depot near the smokers, whose stiff body language and refusal to meet anyone's eyes warned of their lack of interest in socializing. Jared yawned. He munched his nachos slowly and sipped his root beer from the bottle, counting down the hours until he could board the bus and be on his way. He was dreading messages from his mom, but the lone text wasn't from her number.

Is Mags wit u? the unknown number had texted.

Death? Jared texted back.

No response.

When the time came to board the bus, Jared wandered to his seat near the back, tucked his pack under his knees and pulled his baseball cap low over his eyes. In the seat behind him, a middle-aged woman was loudly explaining into her Bluetooth headset how she'd trained her dogs to shit in her neighbour's yard.

———

Dawn was the grey of old socks. Jared made a sticky bathroom wash-up at the breakfast stop. He'd slept on the bus in fits, waking each time they stopped and the lights came on. His reflection looked rough, like he'd been on a weekend bender and wasn't totally sober yet.

The bus had half-emptied and then refilled with new faces. The driver wandered down the aisle taking a head count. Jared thumbed through his text messages. Crashpad had included Jared in some threads. His old friends were organizing a bush party in the old quarry back in Kitimat this Saturday. Nothing made him feel like a friendless loner like seeing a former buddy's excited party plans that didn't include him. He scrolled through the chain of back-and-forth texts anyway. Was it masochism? Nostalgia? Plain old nosiness? Didn't matter, he decided. He was leaving it all behind him in the most literal way possible.

His cellphone buzzed.

C'est moi. Still need a place? Death Threat texted.

Ya, Jared texted back.

Txt me yr address. Back tomorrow or next day. Txt u l8r wit deets.

Thanks, Death. Hostel @ 1114 Burnaby St.

Wherz ur mom?

Still wit Richie.

Dude is Mr. Anger Issues.

Wow, Jared thought. Pot, meet Kettle. When pissed, Death shook like an excited purse pooch and would launch into a Tourette's-like spew of profanity usually ending in *fuck ya dead*, ergo his name. He had a high employee turnover because not many people could stand to work for or with him for more than a single harvest, no matter how well he paid.

Ya, Jared texted.

Say hi to ur mom 4 me.

Ok, he texted, although he knew Death Threat had as much chance getting back with his mom as a turtle had of crossing a six-lane highway intact. All she wanted when it came to Death Threat was to take a dull razor and slowly shave off his skin. His mom wasn't the kind of woman who stayed friends with her exes, especially one who left her with his drug debts when she was struggling to pay her mortgage on a part-time waitressing gig.

The closer to Vancouver they got, the more the bus went through unsecured wi-fi bubbles that let Jared check his Facebook wall. His mother had posted a picture of his mattress on their front lawn, a giant yellow stain at the bottom.

Thanks, SONNY BOY, his mother had written. *I love cleaning up your messes . . . whatz 1 more pissy diaper?*

Three likes and a handful of snide comments about some people's lack of respect.

Rot in hell you psycho meth freak, he started typing, but the wi-fi bubble popped.

Let it go. Take your own inventory. Forgiveness not resentment, he told himself. Don't let her rent headspace. What if his mom's sister was like his mother dearest? No—he wanted a new start. He was definitely not calling the older Moody sister, and certainly wasn't going to bother visiting.

Try to remember the good things about your mom, he told himself. She'd raised him and kept him safe until their family fell apart. Even when she was in the depths of her own addiction, she'd come for him when he'd been kidnapped by shape-shifting otters. She came, she cursed them and they died.

Her post was gone by the next stop. He unfriended her anyway and went through his list and deleted all the friends and relatives who still talked to her. He wished life was more like Facebook. He wished there was a button that would let him delete everything.

Near noon, with the sun boiling in the centre of the sky, the Greyhound circled around behind the Vancouver terminal and then sighed into its bay. Everyone crowded the aisle. When the door opened, a slug of hot, humid air crawled into the bus. The line edged forward as people pulled their luggage down and trudged out.

When Jared exited the terminal, the sun beat down on the traffic and a SkyTrain as it whined past. He shifted his backpack on his shoulders and plodded across a dusty square with yellowed grass, feeling sweat drip down his neck. He considered not paying for a train ticket, but he didn't have the kind of luck that would let him get away with it. He plugged the last of his change in and hauled himself up the stairs. The SkyTrain downtown was so crowded, he didn't have anything to hold on to. He pinballed against the other passengers when the train shifted speeds or directions, earning elbows and glares.

He couldn't face any more public transportation, so he hiked from Burrard station to his hostel, where a lineup of sweating, cranky people in the lobby glared at the two clerks. Using the hostel's wi-fi, he texted his dad, Bianca and Crashpad: *Alive & ok in Van. Big bright ball in sky. Think it is the sun. Very hot.*

Will send rain asap, Bianca texted back seconds later.

Film crew shooting Supernatural *near you tonight*, Crashpad texted. *Attaching map & bus routes. Take lots of pix.*

Have you told your gran you're in town? his dad texted.

Jared's temple ached when he thought of Nana Sophia, Phil's mom. Just Sophia, he reminded himself. His dad had his own reasons for getting back on his mother's good side. Jared wanted to stay out of their relationship. That bridge was burned. The possibility of salvaging what they'd had was nil. Zero. Zippo. When she was his Nana Sophia, Jared had been the centre of her world. When she found out Jared wasn't her blood, well, that was the end of that: unlike her son, Sophia believed in magic, and in Tricksters. She'd thought that Jared had known what he was all his life, and that he'd been playing her, but he hadn't known. He hadn't played her. He didn't think she was a mark. But nothing he said was going to fix anything, and the attempt would probably just make them both feel worse.

After twenty minutes, he made it to the front of the line to discover he couldn't check in until three, so he sweet-talked the clerk into letting him use the laundry room while he waited. He dumped all his clothes in one washer. He paused and then took off his hoodie and his T-shirt. He kicked off his sneakers and tossed his socks in. The girl loading the washer beside his raised one eyebrow, much the way Sarah would, disdainfully amused, like Spock when Captain Kirk did something typically, illogically human.

"That's as far as I'm stripping," Jared assured the girl.

"Good," she said.

He sat in an old plastic chair and ate some of his nachos and drank his flat root beer. The need to sleep made him heavy, like he'd landed on Jupiter and was being sucked down by two and a half times Earth's gravity.

After his laundry was done, he went back to the desk, where the clerk gave him a key card. His room was on the second floor, a male dorm with two bunk beds lining one wall and four lockers, a sink and a desk on the other wall. He'd lucked out and been assigned a bottom bunk near the open window. He untucked the blankets and sheets and checked the mattress but didn't see any bedbugs hiding in the nooks and crannies. Relieved, he flopped on his bunk, throwing his backpack on top of the folded towel at the foot of the bed. His stomach grumbled. The nachos were not going to hold him tonight. He also needed to hit a meeting or at least take a shower, but his eyelids felt glued shut.

Later, he woke to a couple of guys laughing as they came into the room. The lights snapped on. He covered his eyes with an arm, and was instantly back asleep.

SARAH, INTERRUPTED

In his dreams, his ex-girlfriend, Sarah, was always in the basement of his mom's house where he used to live. Jared was usually on the mattress on the floor, one arm under his head. Sometimes she was leaning against him, frowning in concentration as she texted. Sometimes she was plucking her eyebrows in the cracked mirror under the barred window. Sometimes she lounged on the sway-backed Ikea chair in the corner, flipping through his mother's *In Touch* magazines, bopping her head to whatever was on her iPhone.

She loved to hotbox when they smoked his js, and they'd make forts out of broken furniture and blankets. She hated the way he rolled, called it fussy. In between the coughing and the laughing and the reek of cheap skunk, they'd make out slowly, starting with her pursed lips, her held breath and her small, crossed eyes as she leaned forward to blow smoke through her kiss.

Tonight, in this dream, she was bleaching her bangs, idly timing the chemicals she'd foiled in her hair. She had an old beach towel around her shoulders, and she posed for herself in the mirror, changing her pout from demure to duck lips. She tried on a grin, and quickly dropped it, tilting her head and putting her hands on her hips to vamp.

The kitchen timer dinged. After she rinsed, her bangs were a stained yellowy white against the blue-black of her long, straight hair. Then she dyed them blue with Kool-Aid.

She danced while she waited, jittering and humming to no music. He'd liked this part of their relationship the best, before things went all dark and weird. They'd drop their outside faces and hang, not doing anything in particular or saying anything deep. In this dream, Sarah lifted her shirt and tucked the hem into her neckline, exposing a strip of her purple-and-grey sports bra, her smooth torso, and the puckered scars of the skin she'd cut near her hips that peeked above her jeans. She lined her belly button with lipstick, turned to him, and made her voice deep and growly while she pinched her stomach to make her belly button talk: "Cookie! Cookie Monster want cookie!"

He laughed. She looked up and their eyes met. He woke.

THE INEVITABILITY OF DEATH THREAT

He squinted, couldn't remember why the ceiling was so close or why it was wooden slats. Light shone at an odd angle, blinding him when he turned his head towards it. Jared could make out a shadow behind the bright light. Right—he was in a bunk bed. The guy across from him was sitting on the edge of a chair, shining his cellphone flashlight on Jared.

"Dude," Jared said, shielding his eyes. "What the hell?"

"Hello, Jared," the guy said.

"Can you shut that off?"

"How's Maggie these days? Still a psychopath?"

Jared went cold, then sat up. The man lowered the phone so it lit his own face from beneath, like someone telling a ghost story around the campfire. Clean-shaven, angular features, dirty-blond hair, blue eyes, a pale linen shirt and khakis, shiny loafers. David always had a preppy thing going.

"You look terrible, Jared."

"You have to leave. Get out. Now."

David raised the phone again so the light shone in Jared's eyes. Jared wished he'd worn a T-shirt. That the sheets were covering him. That the worst ex of his mother's long string of bad exes wasn't parked an arm's length away.

"We have a restraining order," Jared said.

"It expired. They only last a year, dumb-ass."

"Yeah, you would be an expert on that."

"I like watching karma at work," David said. "You and your psycho bitch made my life hell." He sounded sincerely offended and hurt, like he was the innocent party.

"You broke my ribs," Jared said.

"She nail-gunned my feet and arms to the floor and you both left me there, all night, screaming in agony. I have nerve damage. I had to have months of physio."

"You got off on torturing me. That's messed up. What you're doing now is messed up. How did you get in? How did you even know where I'd be?"

"So you're not going to take responsibility for anything?"

"Dude, you seriously need help,"

A pillow whacked David's hand and the light wobbled. The guy from the upper bunk near the door peered over the edge, glaring. "Some of us are trying to sleep! Go outside if you want to talk!"

"Yeah," the other bunk mate growled.

"Sorry," David said. "Jared? Let's go to the dining room."

"Go fuck yourself."

"I recorded that," David said.

Jared gave his phone the finger. "Bye, cray-cray."

"I'll see you later," David said, standing. "And we'll continue our talk."

"Get help."

"With Maggie as a mother, you're the one who needs it."

The light from the cell clicked off and David left. In the dark, Jared reached for the sheets tangled at his feet and covered himself, trying to tell himself he'd been dreaming.

"Can you hand me my pillow?" the guy from the upper bunk asked.

Jared reached over, grabbed it and tossed it to him.

"Thanks," the guy said.

"You're welcome," Jared said automatically. He was embarrassed that there had been witnesses, but at least with the two other guys in the room, David had been more restrained.

He couldn't fall back asleep. Whenever he heard footsteps in the hall, his heart raced and his skin went clammy. The sensible part of him knew David wouldn't do anything to him if he stayed put. But he wanted to go down to the front desk to report him, except David was likely waiting in the stairwell or something.

Head fuck, Jared thought. One massive head fuck.

When there was enough daylight that everything in the room was grey, he got up and got dressed. He jammed his feet into his sneakers, grabbed his phone and hesitated at the door, listening. Silence.

The clerk at the front desk was holding an extra-large Starbucks mug close enough to her face that she could breathe in the steam. Her reddish-brown hair was tightly controlled in two French braids. She smiled at him. "Can I help you?"

It was one thing to have your freakazoid past show up and stalk you, and another thing to explain it to a complete stranger, especially a cute girl with freckles across the bridge of her nose.

"Do you speak English? *Parlez-vous français?*" she said. "¿Hablas español?"

"Low caffeine levels," Jared said.

"Preach," she said, slightly lifting her coffee in a salute.

Maybe he'd give her an edited version. He hated the way people changed when they learned things, the way they looked at him afterwards. That combination of pity and revulsion.

"I . . . a guy . . . when I woke up . . ." Get it together, he told himself. Use your words. "I caught the guy in the bunk above me recording me sleeping on his phone. The guys in the other bunks saw him too. I was wondering if I could change rooms."

"Yikes," she said, putting her coffee down. She typed into her computer. "He checked out a half-hour ago."

So David *had* waited around. Ew, Jared thought.

"Would you like to make a complaint?"

"No," Jared said. "As long as he's gone."

"Creeps. Gotta love 'em," the girl said. "Wanna switch rooms anyway?"

"I'd appreciate that," Jared said.

"No worries. I once had a guy trying to film up my skirt the whole bus trip to work. I still feel slimed when I think about it."

"That's shitty."

She shrugged. "Watcha gonna do?"

Breakfast came free with the room. Jared loaded up, knowing he had to make his money stretch. But he had to talk himself into eating, working past his nausea to swallow. He wondered how David had known he'd be here, and which dorm he was in, which caused him to run to the nearby washroom, where he heaved until stringy yellow bile came up.

He knelt in front of the toilet. The chills kicked in. The old Jared would have gone and gotten hammered. Found a party. Drank and smoked up until nothing made sense anymore. He was days away from his first birthday, the anniversary of his sobriety. He didn't want to remember the shit David had brought to his life.

It wasn't fair. He'd worked through this. The amount of therapy one-on-ones, group work and AA meetings he'd spent talking and feeling and processing amounted to nothing as he fought the flood of raw panic—his traumatized, broken-ribbed, inner eleven-year-old resurfacing with a vengeance. It felt unfair that he was bothering Jared now he was away from his mom. David hadn't gone anywhere near Maggie after she and Richie had paid him enough visits.

The world is hard, his mom liked to say. *You have to be harder.*

In that moment back in Jared's bedroom when Maggie had caught David torturing her son, and she had him screaming on the floor, nailed in place, she had handed Jared the nail gun and Jared couldn't do anything but cry and shake his head. If he could travel back in time, knowing everything he knew now, maybe he'd be colder. Practical. Some guys really didn't know when to stop. You had to let them know you wouldn't put up with their shit.

What had happened was in the unchangeable past. But he hadn't bargained on David ever showing up again. He couldn't think straight now. He had a hard time taking a deep breath. He couldn't put together the steps he needed to take to look for a place to live or go check out the school. But he didn't want to hide in the hostel and stew all day.

He checked the list of AA and NA meetings Bianca had sent him. They were happening all around him, any time he wanted, open, closed, Big Book, men only, women only, LGBTQ, youth. He had his pick.

You get your head right, Jared told himself, and everything else follows.

The day spat rain, hissing on concrete sidewalks and parched lawns, giving the air a fresh scent, the promise of green. The great thing about meetings was that you could sit in the back and cry and it wasn't a big deal. People emoted all the time here. The woman beside him dug around her purse and handed him a wad of tissues. He nodded thanks.

He hit four meetings in a row, living on weak coffee until his stomach could handle the fruit from breakfast he'd stuck in his backpack. Around supper, he found a Chinese restaurant and ordered won ton soup. He sat at the back, facing the door. If David was stalking him, watching him meeting-hop, then he was a sad, weird dude with no life. Jared was going to have to ask his mom to dig around for the restraining order. Even if it was expired, it was there in black and white to show something had happened. People tended to believe the clean-cut white guy over the mouthy Native kid.

His phone pinged. Text from Sarah: *Last night I dreamed we were in your basement hanging like we used to. It was so real. I could hear you laughing.*

Damn it, he thought. Jared had about a thimbleful of magical ability and so did Sarah. But put the two of them together and freaky things like this started happening. He wanted to see her, especially today, but Sarah always wanted to go there, wanted to see what they could do. Jared wasn't willing to let his life descend into weirdness again. Not after they'd literally tripped out of their heads with 'shrooms and went for a walk through the spirit world and brought back a troop of half men, half apes. Jared remembered choking on the thin air as Sarah followed the cosmic fireflies that swirled around her head, seduced by their song. Once they'd come home, he'd pretended the ape men were hallucinations until Sophia sent them back to their own world. Their dabbling in magic was what had attracted the otters. Sarah saw none of that, hadn't been haunted by ape men or chewed on by otter people. She'd just remembered the trip and the fireflies' song.

He hesitated before deleting her text.

He was going to have to deal with it, talk to her, but he didn't want to, and at the same time he wanted to see her again, desperately.

Right now, though, the waitress brought his soup.

He let it steam in front of him until his stomach grumbled. He ate slowly, not wanting to hurl again. The soup stayed down. He finished eating and then, on a whim, decided he wanted to be by the water. He wanted to hear the ocean.

Slanting sunlight streamed through the high-rise apartment buildings as Jared checked his Google map. Wisps of steam lifted off the sidewalk as the sun evaporated the rain. He found the seawall by the bay filled with people. He paused near a bunch of bronze statues of laughing men. People took selfies in the golden light as the sun and its reflection glittered on the water, close to touching. The beach was lined with logs in careful man-made rows. He found a spot and then sat in the damp sand, his back against a log. Seagulls complained overhead. The surf rolled in lazy waves. Little kids ran into the water and screamed and ran out.

He wasn't eleven anymore, Jared thought. David wasn't the scariest thing in his world, not by a long shot. He wasn't running. He wasn't hiding. He wasn't going home to Kitimat. There were always people who wanted you hurt, who cheered when you failed. David wasn't the first and he wouldn't be the last. Normally, he'd be texting his mom by now, letting her handle this kind of shit. But he was almost eighteen; he was striking out on his own. Plus there was her whole pissy mattress post and the fact that she'd ripped up his letters from Granny Nita.

He'd figure out the David thing himself. Probably not tonight. He sat on the sand until the breeze shifted and brought a chill to the early evening and then he went back to the hostel.

The upper bunk wasn't as bad as he'd thought it would be. His new bunk mates had spent their evening bar-hopping, and after they got back, they continued drinking on the lower bunks, laughing about who had hurled first, who'd fallen down the most, who'd danced the worst. They were about his age. He couldn't place their accents. The booze fumes were as thick as cheap cologne. Jared hopped down and they offered him a beer. He begged off and took his backpack to the lounge, where he cracked open his copy of *Living Sober*.

A couple of hours later, he went and checked, and they had all passed out. Lightweights, he thought as he put his things back in his locker. He hesitated at the light switch then left the light on. He climbed up onto his bunk, crawled under the sheets and watched the ceiling until his eyes burned, waiting for sleep that never came.

Jared was walking back to the hostel from a Friday morning meeting when he got another text from Death Threat.

I'm here, Death texted. *U ready?*

Not far, Jared texted. *Be there soon.*

As he rounded the corner, Jared instantly spotted him. Death Threat was tall and still skeletal, but he'd stopped wearing skinny jeans, which was an improvement. The bandana over his long, stringy hair and the ratty leather pants were not. How he made it through customs without a free colonoscopy was a mystery.

"Yo!" Death shouted, waving. "Jared! Over here!"

When Jared got to him, Death Threat gave him a bro hug.

"Kid," Death said. "Only people with male-pattern baldness should have shaved heads."

"How was Washington?" Jared said.

"Overrated," Death said. "It's an extremely reluctant legalization. Their grows are too limited."

"Yeah?"

"Colorado's light years ahead of them. Do you have a passport?"

"No."

"We'll get you one. The future is edibles—'cause you know how squares hate bongs—and we need someone with half-decent culinary skills."

"I'm stuck here for classes."

"Screw your classes. Go get your shit. Come on. Places to be, fortunes to make."

Jared tucked his hands in his pockets. "I thought you said it was just some security."

"Plans change."

"I dunno. I'm, you know, sober now. And I'm going to school."

"The sober part is your big selling point. I know you won't sample."

"Yeah, yeah, I hear you. But I'm not travelling. And I'm not making product."

"Look at you," Death said. "Fucking thinking you're going to get a free ride."

"Hey, man. I'm just being straight with you."

"If you want to park your lazy ass at my place, you are going to fucking do what I tell you to do. Got it? Are we clear?"

Jared nodded. "I hear that. I do. And, you know, thanks for the job offer. But I don't think this is going to help my sobriety."

Death sucker-punched him in the side. Jared folded over, grunting, and Death pulled him up by one of his ears, yanked him close and whispered: "I don't like being played."

Jared kicked Death's ankle and then, while Death was hopping around, attempted to knee him in the groin. He missed and hit Death's thigh. Death tried to punch him in the head. Jared ducked, holding his side as they both stood in the street, panting.

"Screw you," Death said. "You and your fucked-up mom."

"Go to hell," Jared said.

"I was trying to help you, shithead." Death yanked his car door open, got in and slammed it shut behind him. He rolled down the window. "Enjoy homelessness."

Jared gave him the finger. Death squealed out of the parking spot, swerving towards him briefly before he bombed down the street.

Jared looked around to make sure no one had witnessed their dust-up. He limped to the front door and took the elevator up to his floor. He rested his head against the wall, careful not to touch his sore ear.

Not my week, Jared thought. Not my week at all.

5

A BRIEF OVERVIEW
OF VANCOUVER

When you are looking down on Vancouver from an airplane, the mountains form a half-circle around a fan of alluvial plains built up by the Fraser River, which empties into the Pacific Ocean. Bridges cross the river's branches like dental braces. The downtown core is a cluster of skyscrapers with a hitchhiking thumb of green that is Stanley Park. The larger streets make illogical bends and turns where once-distant communities were swallowed into the growing metropolis. Smaller clusters of skyscrapers punctuate the centres of the outlying suburbs, especially where the metropolitan rail system called the SkyTrain has stations.

The indigenous people who remember Vancouver before Contact are centred on reserves dotting the outlying areas of downtown. The Xʷməθkʷəy̓əm (Musqueam) live on the Musqueam Indian Reserve, located south of Marine Drive near the mouth of the Fraser River. The Sḵwx̱wú7mesh Stelmexw (Squamish People) reside on several urban reserves in the city of Vancouver, North and West Vancouver and the municipality of Squamish. The Tsleil-Waututh (People of the

Inlet) live on reserves along the Burrard Inlet. Native Indians, Metis and Inuit from other nations who migrate to Vancouver for work, school or nightlife tend not to move to these reserves unless they have family connections. If they're lucky, they find accommodation in Vancouver Native Housing or Lu'ma Native Housing, societies set up to help low-income Native people find affordable homes, either sliding-scale (you pay a percentage of your income) or market-value (you pay about the same as the equivalent non-Native unit). Most of these rental units are located in an area of Vancouver called East Vancouver.

Between downtown and a suburb called Burnaby, East Vancouver is further divided into smaller districts, the most infamous of which is the Downtown Eastside. You may remember hearing about the Downtown Eastside from news reports about Robert Pickton, the notorious serial killer, or about drug overdoses, sex-trade workers, slumlords or inner-city violence. (Surrey, another suburb of Vancouver, is collectively rolling its eyes right now. They like to say East Van is bad but it ain't Surrey.) Being one of the less prestigious postal codes, East Van was, until the latest housing boom, one of the more affordable neighbourhoods in the city and a magnet for new immigrants, artists and leftists. Recently, it has become a hub for alternative gender activism. If you are interested in eating at restaurants where you can't recognize the language of the menu, or you prefer your protein not to have a mother, take a walk down Commercial Drive, or the Drive as the locals call it.

What East Van lacks in swank, it makes up for in swagger. All of Vancouver is considered left coast, but within Vancouver there are conservative enclaves, solidly working-class enclaves, nouveau riche enclaves, etc., where you are expected to drive a certain kind of car or exercise in a certain brand of clothing. East Van expects you to a) have a freak flag and b) fly it proudly. Which means on any given day on the Drive there is a cultural festival, obscure sporting event celebration or political protest, which usually boils down to a parade of some sort and involves food, loud music, dancing and/or brawling.

And now we return to Jared Martin, who is still in his downtown hostel.

6

THE COMPOUND

Now that Jared was paying attention, he realized that David was actually a shitty stalker, who gave a friendly wave when he was noticed, all smiles and good cheer. Or maybe that was part of the head fuck. A dare. Go ahead. Call me out. See what happens. That Saturday morning David sat in the dining room at breakfast as if he wasn't sticking out from the backpacking crowd, as if everyone else was also in pastel crew wear, like they just got off a yacht. David chatted with his tablemates, and Jared wondered if he was actually back staying in the hostel or had just talked his way in for breakfast. It was kind of infuriating, David behaving like he was going to get away with it, like Jared was helpless.

Jared snapped a picture of David watching him. He uploaded it to Facebook and captioned it *Me & my shadow*. He didn't feel comfortable going into a police station and trying to get a renewed protection order, but if David was going to be this in-your-face, Jared was going to document it. He kind of didn't want his mom to be involved, but David had made his own bed and if he was nailed to it, it was his own damn fault. He wrote, *Day 3 of being stalked by David Thompson my mom's ex. Here he is at my hostel watching me eat breakfast.* Jared added a location tag and then posted.

Holy shit!!!!! Crashpad texted him. *Call cops!!!!*

David reached into his pocket and brought up his phone. His smile dropped. Jared snapped another picture of David that was much less cheerful. He posted it too. David slowly got out of his chair. Jared turned on his phone's video and filmed David walking towards him.

David stood over him. Jared waited for him to slap the phone away or hit him, but David turned, then walked out.

Jared, Sarah texted him. *You have to change your privacy settings on FB. Anyone can find out where you are & what you're doing.*

Noted, he told himself, change security settings. But all the David stuff was going to be public, he decided. No hiding. No backing off. The truth and nothing but the truth, no matter how humiliating. He tried to upload the video but got the swirly of death. When everyone at the hostel was on their phone, the wi-fi speed was rotten. He'd have to find a coffee shop later.

David was parked illegally outside the hostel in a silver Lexus 570, an SUV with an expensive-looking grille. Jared took a picture of his licence plate and then of David ignoring him as he kept taking pictures. David started his car, signalled and drove off.

When Jared returned to the dining room, someone had cleared away his breakfast. He wasn't hungry anymore anyway. He had planned on going to BCIT to see if anyone needed a roommate, but he felt too sweaty and giddy. He knew he hadn't gotten rid of David. But he'd temporarily wiped the smug off Ol' Dave's face.

His cell rang. Georgina Smith, the caller ID read.

Jared listened to his phone ring and ring until it went to voice mail.

Crap, Jared thought. Crap, crap, crap.

Jared took a shower. He went to a meeting. From his dwindling supply of cash, he bought himself a ham sandwich and a root beer. He walked back to the beach and sat in the sand listening to the ocean for a long, long time, staring at his phone. High on the list of people he never wanted to talk to again was Georgina Smith. He'd first met her when he was hitchhiking back from Rupert to Kitimat. She drove up in an older burgundy Caddie and offered him a ride. He couldn't make himself get in the car. She looked like a sweet, kindly old rez grandmother with her large, old-fashioned glasses and floral dress, but Jared could see she had a monster under her face. No one else seemed to notice. She claimed to be his aunt, Wee'git's sister, and she'd arranged it so that she had bumped into him three or four times since then.

He regretted posting now. The fleeting satisfaction was so not worth it. The sandwich was dry. By the time he drank it, the root beer was warm. He didn't even want to listen to Georgina's message, much less call her back. His nerves jangled when he thought of her, loud, like a smoke alarm going off. Bad juju, his mom would say. Some people radiated it.

Every time Jared saw her, he was half-convinced she was going to eat him, but instead, once, she'd taken him out for ice cream and they'd had a chat that he half-remembered. And she'd brought him to his first AA meeting. He'd been pretty hammered. Her kindness had been unexpected.

But she'd also messed with his head. She'd planted a thought during one of his French classes that he wanted pizza, and when he'd arrived at the pizza place after school, she'd been waiting for him, acting innocent. When he'd thought to himself that this was not what he'd wanted to do, her voice had been in his head, telling him it had been his own idea. No one normal did that. No one with healthy boundaries. Even his mom wouldn't pull that shit.

But Georgina hadn't hijacked him in a long while. And he couldn't imagine her on Facebook. Maybe it was a coincidence that she'd called when she had. Curious, he dialed his voice mail.

"Jared?" Georgina's recorded voice said. "Jared, are you there? Why can't I hear him?"

"It went to voice mail, Gran!" some kid yelled in the background. "You're not supposed to talk and drive!"

"Jared, I can hear you. You're somewhere close. Call me back when you get this recording and let me know that you're alive. Jared?" A series of clunks and then the phone squealed. "Did I break it?"

"Stop sign! Gran!"

"How do you hang it up?"

"Give it to me."

"I can hang up a phone. I'm not an idiot."

"No, no, not that one!"

"I don't appreciate your tone."

"This button! This—"

How terrified could you be of someone who didn't know how to hang up a cellphone?

You should call her, he thought.

He was pretty sure it was his own thought. It didn't feel like someone meddling with his mind. Letting her back in his life was a bad idea. He got stomach flutters just thinking about it.

She sounds worried, his brain told him.

She did, but he hesitated. I don't want to call her, he thought.

You do, his brain told him.

He hit Redial and listened to the ringing, half-hoping she wouldn't pick up.

"Hello, Mrs. Smith speaking," Georgina said.

"Hey, it's Jared. I'm okay."

"For heaven's sake, Jared," she said. "I was starting to think this David fellow had killed you and dumped you in a ditch."

"Sorry. It's been crazy."

"My grandson showed me your post on the Facebooks. You must be terrified."

He felt a blush starting, burning his cheeks. Security settings would be changed ASAP. "Um, yeah. I'm okay."

"Come stay with us, dear."

"I'm in Vancouver. I'm getting ready to go to school."

"I live in Ladner," she said. "Didn't I tell you that?"

"Is that close?"

"I could have sworn I told you. This is what happens when your poor old brain is five hundred years old. Are you curious at all about your father's side of the family?"

He'd never thought of it that way before. The possibility of people who were related to him and wanted to meet him made him suddenly lonely and hopeful. Maybe he had cousins he could hang with. This is my cousin so-and-so. We're going to hang.

"I can send someone to pick you up if you're nervous about this David fellow," Aunt Georgina said.

"It's okay. He's backed off," Jared said. For now.

His aunt gave him careful instructions to get to her house, as if Google Maps didn't exist.

"Just a visit, though," Jared said. "I'm looking for a place close to my classes."

"We're having our Sunday barbecue," she said. "Come and eat with us and we'll go from there. How does that sound, dear?"

"Any time in particular?"

"No, not really. We're not formal at all."

"Thanks. Okay. See you tomorrow."

"Be careful."

"Bye."

After he hung up, he looked up instructions for limiting the people who could see his posts to "friends." The David post was getting a lot of comments, mostly advice on how to deal with a stalker. The people from his AA groups and old high school friends meant well, but they didn't know David. They hadn't had him popping up at corner stores and paper routes all through their teens, or waiting for them after school, smiling in a way that never reached his eyes.

The next day, Jared hopped a couple of buses out towards the Tsawwassen ferry terminal to the suburb called Ladner. He listened to music and stared at the traffic, carefully studying the silver minivans, especially the Lexuses. It was a long ride. Even if he wasn't leery of her intentions and wanted to stay with her, it would be a brutal commute.

He got off at the bus stop just before the ferry terminal. He followed the streets on his list as traffic zipped by, racing to the ferries at the end of a long promenade surrounded by sparkling water. Approaching and receding vehicles hummed like angry bees. The day was hot, but the ocean breeze had a bite that made his skin prickle through the sweat. Jared squinted, wishing he'd brought sunglasses, and finally spotted the right number on a post in front of a house with patchy grass.

He recognized Aunt Georgina's burgundy older-model Cadillac in the driveway, surrounded by battered trucks and SUVs. The only part of the main house Jared could see was the roof of dark-green shingles and a gabled window. The place was surrounded by older trailers and jury-rigged, tarp-covered walkways. The trailers were arranged as if they'd come home half-cut and plopped themselves down when they were too tired to move anymore. Jared wasn't sure where to knock. He could hear laughter, some hip-hop beats and kids screaming.

Hello, Jared, Aunt Georgina said in his head.

Don't do that. I don't like it.

I know. I just wanted to tell you I'm sending my grandson, Cedar, to come get you. The Compound can be confusing.

Jared waited. He checked the bus schedule for times for the return trip. He waited. And waited some more. He wondered if he should get out while the getting was good. But then a shirtless little boy came bouncing out from one of the trailers and galloped towards him. The kid wore a pair of Iron Man shorts and sandals. He was tanned, and the tips of his dark, spiky hair were burnt lighter by the sun. His lips were ringed with either barbecue sauce or jam.

"Hey," Jared said.

"You're stupid-looking," the kid said.

"I get that a lot," Jared said.

Manners.

"Gran says you have to come."

It's the sugar. I apologize for Cedar.

Aunty, Jared thought at her. *Please stay out of my head.*

"I had to wear skin for you," the kid said, leading him up a set of stairs then down a hallway with a flapping tarp roof and then down another set of stairs that led to an empty space with dried-out clumps of grass surrounded by walkways and trailers.

They seemed to wander around in circles for a while before they came to a backyard with a gazebo where a large propane barbecue smoked. A couple of men in golf shirts and khaki shorts stood around it, one of them wielding tongs. Georgina Smith—Jwasins, his aunt through Wee'git—was kneeling on a picnic blanket, changing a baby's diaper. The baby in question was a frowning girl, who kicked, excited, as Aunt Georgina sang in a high, quivery voice. Cedar took off running and tackled a beach ball, bouncing to the ground and rolling around on it.

A tall, thin Native woman wrapped in a black shawl with bright-red, traditional north coast formline designs stood regally beside Aunt Georgina, posing as if she expected a photographer to pop up and take her picture. She had a giant-ass raven necklace with what looked like real feathers.

"It is so good to see you, Jared," Aunt Georgina said.

Jared watched the reptilian thing beneath her skin bare its teeth at him, snarling, like a double-exposed film under her gentle granny exterior. He shook his head, then said, "Hi, Aunty."

She struggled to get to her feet, and Jared offered his hand to help her up. She thanked him, then picked the baby up and snuggled her close.

"I," the tall woman said, holding her hand out, "am the daughter of the Trickster, Wee'git. The raven who brought light into the world."

"Okay," Jared said, shaking her hand.

"This is Lilith," Aunt Georgina said. "She's a healer."

Lilith sighed. "I commune with the other side. I consider it a privilege and an honour. But you have no idea the responsibility I carry as a messenger between the worlds."

Jared said, "That must suck."

"Hi, Bob Yeager," one of the khaki-shorts guys said, coming up to them, holding out his hand. "Also one of Wee'git's offspring. I just want to know if I can get a status card. Is Wee'git Native? Does he belong to a registered band? Who do I have to blow to get a status card, haha?"

"Hi," Jared said.

"Seriously, I want to know."

"I really couldn't tell you," Jared said.

"No one has answers," Bob said.

"The blood of gods runs in your veins," Lilith said. "Material goods are meaningless in the face of your existential burden."

"I got a fleet of trucks and getting a break on the taxes would be very meaningful."

"Bob has a towing company," Aunt Georgina said to Jared.

"Your pain is my gain," Bob said, trying to elbow Jared in the ribs. Jared dodged him.

Aunt Georgina hefted the baby onto her shoulder and lightly tapped her back. "Jared is also one of my brother's children—he's your half-brother."

Lilith and Bob studied him. The silence stretched a little too long to make their half-hearted head nods seem anything but extremely reluctant acknowledgement. They were the kind of people he found when he went on the Children of Tricksters Support Group website. He'd checked it out a couple of times, but found the chat rooms both dull and intense, like listening to Richie grind on about football or Sarah lecture him about the real corporate agenda. Jared didn't think being the spawn of some shape-shifting horn-dog made anyone special, but his opinion seemed to be the minority.

"Do try some pie, Jared," Aunt Georgina said. "I made them myself."

He nodded. "Later," he said to his half-siblings.

The other people at the barbecue had facial features that were similar enough that Jared suspected they were family too. He could see the same nose, the same triangular jawline repeated. The group around the barbecue smiled when he came up to them.

"What's your poison?" the guy with the tongs said, pointing to the assorted meats cooking on the grille. Some of the steaks were barely seared. Jared wasn't a big fan of raw.

"Hamburger, please. Thanks."

At a small picnic table, Jared loaded his burger with ketchup, mustard, lettuce and tomatoes. The vat of potato salad was largely untouched. The rest of the table was taken up with pies. Jared smiled at a group of women sitting under a patio umbrella. One of them patted the fold-out chair beside her.

"Hey," Jared said, and sat.

"Howdy," the woman said.

They were comfortably quiet. The kids ran around the dusty yard shouting happy instructions at each other. Jared ate his hamburger quickly then got up for pie. It turned out Aunt Georgina was a master of crusts. He could hear Lilith and Bob still arguing about

the responsibilities of being half-god. The kid who'd led him into the
compound paused in the middle of a game of tag, reached up and dug
his fingers into the back of his own skull, pulled his skin up and then
apart, revealing wet fur and then a snout, a large wolf's head on top
of a boy's body. As Cedar continued pulling his skin off like an
uncomfortable snowsuit, a gangly wolf pup emerged. He shook like
a wet dog as he went down on all fours. Jared felt the food in his
mouth go dry. He swallowed hard. The little wolf yipped as his play-
mates smacked him. Everyone but his half-siblings turned to watch
Jared. He heard growls in his head, warnings, as the people who
were at the barbecue waited to see what he would do.

Lilith and Bob, oblivious, kept talking. He couldn't tear his eyes
away from Cedar, who leapt about, radiating delight. Aunt Georgina
tsk-tsked as she picked the boy's human skin up off the ground and
draped it over her free arm.

Cedar, you need to learn to put your things away, she said.

"Oh, God." Jared stood, dropping his paper plate.

"The river otters that tortured you were deranged with grief,"
Aunt Georgina said. "You can't use them as a yardstick for all animals. It's not fair."

Had he told her about the otters? He must have. He couldn't
remember, what with his adrenalin rising, memories flooding and
panic crawling around inside him like a chest-bursting alien. He wasn't
so sure it had been his idea to come here. He wasn't sure if she was
siding with the otters, the ones that had wanted to snack on him, their
bait, while they waited for his mother, the main course.

One of the women at his table reached up and started peeling off
her human skin as well, revealing first a wolf head and then shaggy,
dark-grey shoulders.

"I have to go," Jared said, and got up to walk away.

"Jared, wait," Aunt Georgina called.

His body became slow as if he was wading through quicksand. Yet he wanted to go, he wanted to leave, he wanted this place in his rear-view mirror. He fought through the heaviness, ignored Aunt Georgina's voice in his head telling him to calm down, as he remembered what it was like to be eaten alive in the most literal way possible. Chewed and raw and bleeding. His vision narrowed until he couldn't see anything but what was directly in front of him. He could hear himself fumbling through tarps and felt the plastic flapping around him.

Suddenly the weight lifted and he could run. He sprinted clear of the compound and kept running, and ran, and ran. He wasn't sure where he was going, only that he could hear someone pacing him and he looked down and found Cedar loping beside him, tongue lolling out.

Stop it, Cedar, Aunt Georgina thought.

The wolf cub sat with a thump, whining as he broadcast an image of Jared in frightened flight, triggering his urge to chase.

Aunt Georgina said, *Jarod, we're not hunting you. You're family*.

He only stopped when he was too tired to run anymore, when his legs shook and his breath hitched. He sat on a bench in a bus shelter and, when his hands stopped trembling, used his phone to find out where he was and how to get home.

He listened, but there was no voice in his head. He scanned the street carefully but couldn't see anyone following him. His guts remained clenched. His body felt light. He was here, physically, but in his memory he could hear the excited chitter of the otters. He could feel the bones on the floor of the cave, could remember crawling over them as if it had happened yesterday. Aunt Georgina was definitely not someone he wanted in his life. She hadn't warned him she was living with a pack of wolves. She'd sprung it on him like some kind of test.

Jared wanted to scrub his brain. He wanted to un-see the compound. He wanted to be blissfully unaware like Bob and Lilith. He wanted the world to be a simple place where animals and humans stayed in their own bodies, where people who claimed to be family didn't turn out to be monsters.

NANA ISSUES

On August 25, one year after his first sober day, Jared sat on one of the lower hostel bunks with his roommates, who'd snuck in back-packs full of beer and had a liquid lunch. Half-cut, they were waiting for the happy hours to start so they could bar-hop again. They said they were from the Hub of the Universe. Here for the pah-tay.

One of them lifted his butt cheek off the mattress and farted. They all laughed like it was hysterical, helplessly teary-eyed.

"Come on," the guy sitting on the desk said. He cracked open a can of Kokanee beer and handed it to Jared. "Why so glum, chum?"

Jared hadn't realized how much he missed the easy friendship of drinking buddies. Mr. Wilkinson, his first sponsor, had been his non-stop sobriety buddy, driving him to and from meetings, send-ing daily texts, and conducting long phone conversations despite the awkwardness it caused with his own son, whom Jared had once considered a friend, a party dude busy rebelling by drinking as much as humanly possible. Then Mr. Wilkinson was laid off and was sucked into work camps, first Fort Mac in northern Alberta and then Labrador on the other coast of Canada. Bianca, his manager at Dairy Queen, had stepped into the sponsor role, but she'd spent most of their time together detailing the ins and outs of her divorce.

These random dudes didn't know Jared'd partied with the hardest of the hard core. That he had supported himself and his family selling pot cookies. That his brain had melted and he'd gone insane and his girlfriend had gone insane. They just saw some sad dude and they wanted him to join their fun and stop being sad.

Jared held the sweaty beer can as the guys traded jokes. He rocked when one of them slugged his shoulder, emphasizing the punchline with a punch.

Beer splashed on his hand. The room smelled yeasty and sweaty. He used to have a few with his mom, watching the boob tube or gaming. She loved first-person shooters: *Call of Duty*, *BioShock*, *Doom*. She hated narration, overly complicated backstories told with earnest computer animation.

"Fucking get on with it!" she'd shout at the TV screen. "Jesus, these cock-teasing geeks and their foreplay."

Why was he doing this to himself? Who was he kidding? Sober Jared was a loser. A friendless, lonely sad sack whom his bunkmates pitied and tried to include in their woozy hop of the bars.

He'd spent the morning under his blanket. Three days left in his hostel reservation and then probably a homeless shelter, if he didn't get his shit together. But he couldn't face the dining room, much less calling strangers and inquiring about rooms.

"Why so blue? Girlfriend dump ya?" one of the dudes said, thumping Jared's mattress.

My five-hundred-year-old aunt married into a shape-shifting wolf pack, Jared thought. I'm being stalked by a dude who likes breaking children's ribs slowly. I may be homeless in three days. And that was just this week. "Something like that."

"Been there, igit. Come on. The first step in healing is getting thoroughly hammered."

So easy to take a drink. Simple lifting of the arm. White crescents against his tan skin. Moon-shaped scars on his arms where he'd been bitten. Like freckles. Stitches. Lots of them.

"I'm in AA," Jared said, handing the can back.

"Poor bastard," one of the guys said. "What's the point of living?"

Jared forced himself to a meeting, but was too shy to ask for a one-year chip in front of so many strangers. Walking back to the hostel, he worried that David would be waiting in the lobby, or in his room, but the person he wasn't expecting to see, not in a billion years, was Nana Sophia.

Not Nana. He had to stop thinking of her as his grandmother. But there she was: Sophia Martin with her hair cut short, finger-waved like a flapper, no longer dyed black and permed but silver-white with a sparkling barrette holding her deep side part in place. She wore a white suit and a silver shirt with a plunging neckline. She didn't smile when their eyes met. She simply waited, ankles crossed demurely as she sat on the lobby sofa.

"Hey," Jared said, not sure what to call her, not sure if he should sit near her. He stood, shifting from one foot to the other, trying to think of something else to say. Sophia Martin also had a creature under her skin, but it wasn't showing right now. He'd only seen it once, when she learned he wasn't really her grandson. That his mother had lied to Sophia and married her son, Philip, under false pretences.

"A rotten little birdie told me you were coming to Vancouver," Sophia said.

"You talked to Dad?"

"My son is not your father," she said.

"Then no one is," Jared said.

Their silence stretched. She smoothed her skirt.

"I didn't expect to see you," Jared said. "You know, ever."

"So David Thompson is back," Sophia said.

"You don't have to get involved. I'm handling it."

"Yes," Sophia said. "Facebook drama solves everything."

"I'm doing the best I can."

"Why don't you sit?"

A crush of teens poured into the lobby, all wearing the same orange hoodies, excited, shouting and shoving. Jared sat beside Sophia. They watched the teens.

"I need you to stop giving Philip money," Sophia said.

Ah. The real reason she was here. "It was twenty bucks."

"I gave you money to strike out on your own, did I not? That was for you, you silly thing."

"He paid his rent with it. That's why he's not homeless."

"Isn't there something in your AA about enabling?"

"He needed some help. I helped him."

"But you aren't helping him, Jared."

"No more helping. Got it."

"That money was for you."

"I didn't think there were strings."

Sophia didn't smile, but her eyebrow quirked. "I expected you to blow it on your mother's unfortunate habits, not my son's."

"Richie's supporting her in the lifestyle to which she is accustomed."

"I've spoken with my lawyer. I'd like to help you get another restraining order on David. I can set the wheels in motion if you want."

Conversations with Sophia were like this. She liked to keep people off balance to get a real reaction rather than a rehearsed one. "Why?"

"I loathe Mr. Thompson. Such an unpleasant man. Why hasn't your mother vaporized him?"

"She tried. Her curses didn't work."

"He probably sold his soul for another inch of penis."

Jared snorted. Sophia Martin had a way of hammering down to the brass tacks.

"Thank you," Jared said. "But I think it would just make things worse."

"Most people would have kept lying to me. You didn't. You told me the truth."

Jared shrugged.

"I have three granddaughters your age," she said. "One of them would be happy to marry you if I bribed them with a fat trust fund. We could be family if you're amenable."

"I missed you, too," Jared said. "But maybe we should start with coffee."

"With me or my granddaughters?"

"You," Jared said. "We're not related, you know."

She laughed, a big, head-thrown-back belly laugh. People in the lobby turned to check them out. "So you're trying to give your mother a heart attack?"

"She'd be your mother-in-law."

"Now there's a particularly daunting version of perdition."

He wanted to hug her. He wanted to kneel down and put his head in her lap and cry. She had been a bright spot in his childhood when everything was dark and he'd say that to her, but she hated it when people got maudlin.

"You'll have to dump what's-his-face," Jared said instead.

"We have a pre-nup," she said. "I want the island."

"Our love is all the island you'll ever need."

She laughed again, eyes sparkling. But then silence fell and caution came back, a hesitation, an awkward pause, and they continued to sit apart, close but not touching.

A man in a black uniform and a cap walked into the lobby and nodded at Sophia.

"My island man awaits," she said. "What about a peace bond?"

He didn't want to drag Sophia into the mess. David would put her through the ringer, and he didn't want to be responsible for any more of her pain. "Thank you, but no. We'll deal with it, me and Mom."

"Hmm. I see that ending well."

"I'm not your monkey," Jared said. "This isn't your circus."

She smiled again, wistfully. "Goodbye, Jared."

"Bye, Sophia."

The room reeked because the party dudes had crammed all their cans into the garbage. Jared brought the cans to the nearby Safeway for the deposit and then bought himself a coffee at a Starbucks. He sat on the sidewalk patio and pulled out his cellphone, typing in the wi-fi password.

Seven messages from his mom. Her cell number had left three voice mails, the maximum his phone plan would allow. He fought the urge to delete them and block her number. He didn't want to listen to them just yet. Messages from Sarah and Crashpad, who had texted: *What happened wit David?*

Jared texted him back. *Dude backed off. Howz trix?*

Teacherz strike still on & skoolz supposed 2 start next week. Mom signed me up 4 a study group 4 home skoolers.

No rest for the wicked, Jared texted him.

Suuuuucks. Every1 gets 2 have fun but me. Did u find a place?

Working on it.

Herez a link to indig youth apts. Mom says hi.

Hi back.

They chatted until Crashpad had to go help with supper. Jared downloaded the application. He'd fill it out and hand it in, but he suspected there was a wait list. Jared stared at Sarah's name on his phone.

U ok? she'd texted.

And then, later, *Jared, come on. Sound off.*

I'm ok, Jared texted her back.

His Facebook wall comments had slowed down, but at the very bottom of the comments about David, a reply from the man himself:

Yeesh. Try to say hi to an old friend. Gotta love drama queens.

David had also sent him a private message: *Do you understand libel, Jared? Expect to hear from my lawyer.*

I'm not eleven, Jared told himself, even as he did a quick scan of the street. Even as he decided it was time to check the texts from his mom. It was always good to have the nuclear option in your back pocket.

Jared Benjamin Martin, his mom's first text read. *U der? Helllllloooo.*

And then: *Painting on my sarcasm lines so u no I don mean nothin.*

Fuck off, he thought.

But then, in her next text: *Dead man walking. I'm on it.*

Her voice mails told him not to worry. To keep his head down and stay in public for the next few days. Public meant witnesses, alibis. His mom was entirely capable of taking it to the next level, to all the levels. His mom in prison? Fine, but not because of David. He'd done enough damage.

I got this, Jared texted his mom.

His phone pinged. Not his mom, but Sarah. *Glad ur ok. Is that the same David?*

Ya.

Fuck. Sorry.

David hasn't shown since the FB-bomb.

That's good. Gran's in Brno. Děda can't remember English anymore. They're staying with his fam. Last minute thing. She told me 2 tell u but I lost phone privileges for 1 week.

Where r u?

7th level of hell AKA self-harm retreat. The folks did an intervention. This or institution.

Holy crap.

Ya. Should have emancipated the 2nd I turned 16. Stuck @ Camp Cutter. My minutes r up soon. Bye.

L8r.

Damn it, Jared thought. They'd slid into casual conversation after a year of not speaking. Directly. The whole shit show of their breakup not mentioned. Well, maybe they were capable of simple friendship. No expectations on anyone's part, his or hers. Maturity, maybe.

Bastardz gone 2 ground, his mom texted.

Jared chugged the last of the coffee. *Don't do anything slammer-inducing.*

Why arent u @ Mavez?

U bit my head off 4 writing ur mom. Not staying with ur sis. Not interested in vomiting up my guts.

Jesus. Sensitive much? I wuz hi. U don't take that shit srsly.

I didn't mean to hurt you, Mom. I'm sorry. I was going to tell you about the letters. I feel really shitty.

The minutes passed and he could see that she was typing a response and suspected it would be lengthy and filled with swears.

Maybe I shud've let Mave have u, she wrote.

A good time to practise detachment, Jared thought. Separate the emotions from the conversation. Treat it like information, because that's all this was. Information.

SCREW U, he wrote.

Not like that MORON. I didn't exctly give u a silver spoon life.

How did she push his buttons so fast? Why did he let her? How come he couldn't be cool about shit like this? Fighting back fury and sadness like a toddler standing in the candy aisle of Walmart, wailing at the unfairness of it all. *You don't seem to like me anymore.*

Ur a lot easier 2 like when u arent here all pious n slogan happy.

Thanks.

I thot we'd run a grow-op 2gether sum day. Then u went n got fuckin sober.

You kill spider plants, Jared reminded her.

Wutever. A pot shack on da rez. You'd make the cookies n I'd handle the AK-15.

You still can. You have Richie.

After a pause, his mom texted *Didn't mean 2 drive u away. U judge me n annoy me but I thot I raised u different but I still drove u away the way Mom did me.*

You didn't drive me away, Jared texted back. *I'm going to college.*

U think that makes u better'n me?

I think that means you raised a kid that's going to college. That's probably the most normal thing we've ever done.

Thatz why it feels so wrong.

Miss u 2 Mom. He hesitated, but decided this was not the time to tell her about seeing Sophia. Or the freaky shit with Georgina. He'd tell her. Of course he'd tell her. Just, you know, not at this moment, when they were barely on speaking terms. Jared then admitted: *My marks weren't good enough. I have to re-take some prerequisites before they'll consider me for medical sonography programme.*

U'll figure it out, his mom texted him. *You r sneaky that way. Always no how 2 game the system.*

Thanks, Hallmark.

I mean it. U have 2 be a smart cookie 2 get through the shit we've survived. U got it in u. Figure out what they wanna hear n you r golden.

A notification popped up. She wanted to be friends on Facebook.

U can text, he typed, *but I'm not re-friending you after your spaz attack.*

But SON how will I no if itz raining on you?

Sarcastic cow, he typed.

Stuckup lil shit, she typed back.

Ttyl, he typed. "Talk to you later": their code for everything's okay.

Ttfn. "Ta ta for now": their mocking way of pretending they were normal.

8

ORCA YODA

For some reason, Jared was on a seiner. He leaned against the railing, watching seals slip below the surface while seagulls screeched overhead. The day was cloudless, the sky a seamless blue. The wind whipped his hoodie and made him squint. Large, dark figures glided under the water. Tall, black dorsal fins broke the surface as the killer whales closed in on the seals, which scattered towards a small, rocky island.

I'm dreaming, Jared thought. I've had this dream before.

"Why, hello," Aunt Georgina said.

She smiled up at him, cheek-dusting glasses and a scaled, reptilian creature with very sharp teeth snarling under her skin. Her flowered dress fluttered around her legs. She sat at a cloth-covered table, drinking from a china tea set with gilt and roses. She turned her head to watch the orcas.

"Why are you in my dream?" Jared said.

"You brought me here," Georgina said. "I was picking apples in my dream. I'm not a big fan of boats. Seasickness, you know."

"You don't have to stay," Jared said carefully.

"You're upset."

"Please go," Jared said.

They watched the shadows under the water pace the seiner and then peel away, causing broad wakes when they dived.

"I'm sorry I didn't tell you I was married to a coy wolf," Georgina said. "I didn't think you could *see* supernatural beings. You've mostly been blind to them unless they're eating you."

"A coy what?" Jared said. "Never mind. I don't want to know."

Her expression lightened, but the thing under her skin studied him, interested. She stood, came over and covered his hand where it rested on the railing with hers. She was warm and solid.

"I'm not human-centric like my brother. My first husband was a deer. Such a sweet man. So gentle. Wee'git got hungry and whacked him over the head with a rock and ate him. After a hundred years, I forgave him because he's my kin, my clan. I was married to a beaver by then. Hard worker. Very cranky. I came home one night and Wee'git was barbecuing my husband's tail over the fire. I decided then that I would only marry someone strong enough and smart enough not to get eaten by my brother."

"I'm not like Wee'git either," Jared said.

She sighed. "My poor, confused Jared. You're upset and lonely. You reached out and here I am."

"Sorry."

"Did you know orcas depend on seal pups the way bears depend on salmon?"

"What?"

"Killer whales gather at the birthing shores. They have a small window of opportunity, when the pups are too naive to know the danger orcas represent, to eat as many pups as they can. Once the pups gain experience, the feast is over."

Jared studied her serene face. She'd be an excellent poker player. "Your point?"

She chuckled, taking her hand back. "Do you think you're a seal pup in this story?"

"I'm pretty sure I'm not an orca."

"Humans don't share dreams like this," she said.

"I said I was sorry."

"I'm not threatening you, Jared. I'm telling you something you aren't ready to hear. When you're prepared to know the things that I know, just call me. I'll come."

She vanished. Jared stood at the railing. His palms were clammy where they gripped the railing, despite the wind. Even in the sunlight, Jared felt his skin crawl. Granny Nita said supernatural creatures didn't think the way normal people thought. Maybe that was it.

The dream went on, and on, and on. Jared wandered around the seiner. He was alone and far from shore. The orcas and the seals disappeared. The horizon stretched away and the seiner surged forward, faster and faster, as the waves became swells the size of hills, walls of winter-green cold topped with foam. Jared took the wheel, but every way he tried to turn the boat, he saw nothing and no one.

9

FORGIVE AND FORGET

The last potential apartment of the day had sixteen people standing in line on the walkway leading up to the door, filling out the rental application as they waited to be interviewed. Most of the rooms Jared had seen were in basements where he'd have to share a bathroom with three or four other students. Access to cooking facilities, it turned out, usually meant a microwave, a cocktail fridge and a hot plate in the room. The girl who took his application was about his age, wearing an off-the-shoulder shirt, leggings and stilettos, her hair a side-fall in a rainbow of carefully curled colours. She frowned at Jared, studying him as if she'd seen poop on her shoe.

"Don't call us," she said. "We'll call you."

"Don't I get to see the room?"

"Next," she said.

The party dudes were having a hangover day. Jared brought them coffee from downstairs and they promised to name their first-borns after him and to give him half of whatever lotteries they won. In his head, Jared could hear Sophia saying something like, Hey, Mr. Enabler 2014, come get your crown. But if David showed again on this last night at the hostel, Jared wanted these guys on his side.

"Did you find a place?" one of them said.

"Not yet," Jared said.

"Good luck, man."

The dudes slept and snored. Jared lay in his bunk. Maybe he should just withdraw from school. Get his tuition back and get a job. His mom was the only person who thought he had enough smarts to make this work, but she was his mom. But once he got sober, even with his job at the Dairy Queen, he had torn through grade eleven and twelve in one year. He'd taken a cue from his classmate Ebony, who took correspondence courses on top of the regular ones. They were free if you were trying to get your high school diploma. He could only take two at a time, but he'd finished online Art and Geology 11 and then 12. Business Ed and Sociology 11 and then 12. Mr. Wilkinson had kept warning him about burying himself in work. Focus on your recovery. Don't just replace booze and pot with another addiction.

No, he wasn't going to quit before he started. But his student loan wasn't going to stretch to cover rent and bills. He guessed he could try Mave's place. Given his recent track record with relatives, he'd probably last a night, maybe two, before he discovered she ate living monkey brains with a grapefruit spoon. His mom insisted she was okay with him staying with Mave, but it was wrong on so many levels. What kind of person tried to take another person's kid? How did you get past that?

His mom held grudges like her life depended on it. His childhood had been messed up, but hers must have been catastrophic. How did you grow up with someone who'd been experimented on? How did you walk away from that as a normal person?

He hadn't even known Mavis existed until last year, when Richie had let it slip that Jared had an aunt. Then Sophia had pointed him to Mavis's author website, warning him that she was one of his mom's biggest triggers. He had no idea why his mom'd decided to stop grinding that particular axe. Maybe if he met Mavis, missing pieces of the Mom puzzle would fall into place. Maybe Mavis had answers.

He checked the time on his phone. It was way too late to call her. He'd leave a text, see if she even remembered he was in town.

Hello, Ms. Moody. This is Jared, Maggie's son. Is the offer still open to stay a few nights at your place? Hope to hear from you soon. Thanks.

On my way, Mavis Moody texted him back. *Throwing on some clothes.*

Night owl, a part of his brain thought. Another part of him wanted to erase the message. He really couldn't deal with any more drama.

But it was Mavis or a homeless shelter. Any port in a storm, he thought.

Is tomorrow okay? he texted back. *I check out at 11 am. I can catch a bus if you give me your address.*

Don't be silly. I'm driving a red bug. You can't miss it. 1114 Burnaby?

Yes.

I'll see you tomorrow @ 11. Night, Jared.

Night.

And that was that.

10

OMINOUS WARNINGS
FROM THE DEAD

The red-headed front desk clerk had her hair braided into a crown. "Hey, Jared. Checking out?"

"Yeah."

"Did you enjoy your stay? You know, other than the creep?"

"Yeah. Thanks."

It wasn't until he was outside and checking the total that he noticed she'd written her number and a note on his checkout receipt: *Nice meeting you, Jared. Call if you need help finding a place, Brianna*☺

He leaned against a wall and scrolled through his messages. As the minutes ticked by, he started to think Mave had forgotten him. He took his ball cap out of his backpack to shade his face from the sun. He looked up available shelters, trying to figure out which one was the closest.

Traffic! Mave texted him at 11:35. *Sorry! I'm almost there!*

Jared went back into the lobby to escape the blistering midday heat. Brianna, the redhead, smiled when she saw him walking back in, lifting her giant-ass Starbucks mug in a salute.

Maybe she was just one of those super-nice people who wanted to help. Jared gave her a little wave, hoping she didn't think he'd come back to hit on her.

She waved back.

He hadn't flirted in so long, he had to run through a mental list of responses. *Go talk to her* seemed appropriate. See if she was interested, if they vibed. Not that he could take her out anywhere. But saying hi couldn't hurt. Hey, Brianna, what's shaking? Hi, yeah, I'd love some help. No. God. He'd forgotten how to be chill.

At that moment, a short-haired woman with a bunch of metallic helium balloons walked into the lobby. His aunt—he recognized her from her author photos. She was tanned. She wore a bright-blue dress and shiny brown heels. Her neck dripped with turquoise beads.

"Jared!" she shouted when she spotted him. "Jared!"

"Hi," he said.

She clutched him. The balloons formed a wobbly cloud over their heads as she burst into tears, saying his name over and over. Brianna, helpful Brianna, smirked. Mavis grabbed the sides of his head and stared at him, her forehead bumping his baseball cap.

"I knew you the second I saw you," she said. "I'd have known you anywhere. Did you know it was me?"

"Uh, yeah," Jared said.

She looked up and then loosened the knot of ribbons. "Give me your wrist."

"Yeah, um, I—"

"One balloon for each birthday I missed," she said, and started crying again. Not wanting to make a bigger scene, he let her slip the ribbons around his hand, feeling a furious blush start. People passing through the lobby paused to stare. Brianna lifted her cell and snapped a picture. Jared grabbed his backpack and slung it over his free arm. Mavis clutched his balloon hand. The ribbons formed a screen of sorts as she led him away. The balloons banged around the door frame as they exited the hostel.

"Is that all you brought?" she said, indicating his backpack.

"Yup."

"My, you travel light. Are you hungry?"

"No. No, thanks, I mean. I'm good, Ms. Moody. Tired."

"It's Mave, just Mave. I'm so sorry I'm late. I told the woman at the dollar store that I was in a rush, but the helium tank made her— Never mind, not important. Do you want to get some lunch or go straight home?"

"Um. Home."

"I can drive you up to BCIT if you'd like to look around before your classes start."

"You don't have to."

"Don't you want to get orientated?"

"I'm just tired right now."

She laughed. "I'm sorry. I'm so excited. Beginnings are all about possibilities, aren't they?"

"Yeah," he said.

She popped the trunk of a cherry-red Volkswagen Beetle with black polka dots and two black, glittery wings on the roof. The headlights had black pupils painted on them and were surrounded with long black lashes.

"Okay," Jared said.

"I wanted an orca or a Darth Vader helmet," Mave said. "But my artist was all hormonal and precious from her pre-op crap."

"Huh," Jared said, half-listening, trying to figure out how he was going to get his backpack in when the trunk was crammed with banker boxes, stacks of books, stuffed grocery bags, dry cleaning and what looked like a hamster cage filled with Barbie heads. "Maybe we should put this in the back seat?"

"You may be right," she said. "I'll ask her to re-pimp my ride after she gets her boobs done. Then we'll get something fierce."

They spent another five minutes stuffing the balloons in the back seat. In the end, he tied them to his backpack. Mave smiled at him. Jared tried to smile back, and then felt stupid, and then felt bad about feeling stupid. He wished she'd stop staring at him. He sat and pulled the door closed, relieved to be looking at something other than his aunt, who slid into the driver's seat. She opened the windows.

"I have a fantastic phone plan," Mave said. She turned to him, putting a hand on his arm. "I bundled it with my cell service and Internet."

"Yeah?"

"Yeah."

"Okay," Jared said.

"So if you want to phone anyone, any time, you can." She rummaged in her purse.

"I'm good."

Her cellphone was in a bright-red case. She waggled it. "I bet your mom wants to know you're safe."

"That's, um . . . yeah. Thanks."

"Are you going to phone her? 'Cause if she's waiting to hear from you and she doesn't, she might freak."

"She won't freak."

"I'd freak."

Jared tried to think of a diplomatic answer.

"I'm amazed she called me," Mave said.

Jared shrugged.

"That's proof she loves you more than anything."

"I guess," Jared said.

His aunt zoomed out of their parking space without doing a shoulder check. Jared pulled his seat belt down quickly. They turned left on a yellow light that flipped red when they were halfway through the intersection. Jared lost what his aunt was saying, watching the oncoming black truck in slow motion. It honked. Mave airily waved and sped up, honking in turn at the car ahead of her.

Buildings rolled in small hills in the distance until they hit the mountains circling the city. Light reflected off the buildings and, despite the open windows, Jared could feel the sweat drip down his armpits and his back, could feel the grunge of his sweaty jeans. The balloons bobbed in the back seat like excited kids.

"So. Your mom tells me you want to get into diagnostic medical sonography," Mave said. "That you're upgrading to get into this . . . technical programme. Is that your passion?"

"What?" He loosened his death grip on the seat belt and the door.

"Is it your dream?" Mave said.

He turned to look at her.

She frowned at him. "You're going to be spending your days looking at people's innards. Sick, grumpy people. It had better be something you love."

"It'll pay the bills."

"I'm just saying that before you commit a whole bunch of time and energy to something that isn't going to make you happy, maybe you should have a little rethink, Jelly Bean."

He thought that nickname had died with his parents' marriage.

"What does your mom think?" Mave said.

"She's, um, you know, Mom."

"There's no judgment here. Just concern. And love."

Jared could see why his mom found her sister irritating. The shelter would be noisy, and there was the possibility of bedbugs, but at least no one would be questioning his life choices.

"I was going to make us something, but it's too damn hot," Mave said. "Let's do a drive-through. What do you feel like? Burgers? Wraps? Fried chicken?"

"I'm okay."

"My blood sugar is so low I'm a road hazard. This'll just take a sec."

"Um, is this a legal turn?"

"Oh, it's Vancouver," she said, thumping over a concrete dividing curb, the love bug's undercarriage groaning like a dying foghorn. "They change the rules all the time. Who can follow them?"

"God. I hope you have a decent skid plate."

"Jared, relax." Mave cut off a banged-up older-model Toyota Corolla as she pulled into the drive-through lane. The Corolla honked.

He poked his head out the window to see if they'd left anything behind. The curb was crossed with layers of smears, probably from other impatient coffee hounds, but none of the smears and scrapes looked shiny and new. "You might want to check your universal joint. And your oil pan."

"What a little worrywart you are."

"Bugs aren't built to four-by-four."

"Oh, you should see the potholes we've survived." Mave pulled out her wallet. "You have a chance to make your life what you want it to be. Open your mind to the possibilities!"

"Can we drop this subject?"

"I'll drop the school talk if you drop the snarky remarks about my driving."

"Fine," Jared said.

Mave rolled down her window and studied the menu board as if it were a secret treasure map. Jared willed himself to unclench his jaw.

"Welcome to Tim Hortons," a young woman's voice droned over the intercom. "How can I help you?"

"I don't think you understand your potential," Mave said.

"I didn't catch that, ma'am. Are you ordering poutine?"

"Potential!" Mave yelled into the intercom. "The possibility contained within you before full realization."

"Good, 'cause we don't make poutine here."

"How did you decide what you wanted to do with your life, if you don't mind me asking?"

The line of cars was growing behind them. A man yelled, "Fucking order already!"

Jared peered in the side mirror. The yelling man was behind them in the black SUV. He laid on his horn. Jared sighed. Trust his luck to finally make it to Vancouver and get shot because he was between some asshat and his caffeine fix.

"I hated retail," the attendant was saying over the intercom. "This was close to my apartment and I don't have to do the night shift. It's kind of boring, but I like being home when my kids get home."

"Order a fucking coffee like a normal person!" the SUV guy shouted.

"He's going to shoot us if you don't order," Jared said.

"Some people," Mave said.

"Amen," the woman said. "I miss real winters. I'd move home if there were any jobs there."

"Where's home?"

"Just a sec, honey," the woman said.

Honk. "What the fuck is wrong with you?" Honk. Another voice chimed in: "Some of us have lives, you know."

The intercom crackled. "Uh-huh. Okay, uh, my manager is going to give you a free coffee if you get out of line."

"What a sweetie! Do you want anything, Jelly Bean?"

"No, nothing. I'm good."

"Don't worry. I'm paying."

"Let's just move."

"Are you too shy to ask for what you want?"

"He sounds shy," the woman said.

Honk. Honk. Honk.

"A grilled cheese panini," Jared said. "Okay? Can we go?"

"Oh, that sounds good. I'll have one of those too."

"My boy loves it with ham."

"That sounds better," Mave said. "One regular and one with ham on multigrain."

He checked his phone, more for something to look at, something to do.

"I worry too," Mave said as they pulled up to the takeout window and a pale blond woman with black rings of eyeliner leaned over and smiled at them.

"Sorry if I got you in trouble," Mave said to her.

"Not a problem. That guy behind you is a regular. His wife left him for his business partner and he's cheesed at the world."

"Hey, add his order to my bill, okay? Tell him I understand heartbreak."

"We've all been there, honey."

They laughed. The blond woman handed Mave a takeout bag and they drove away.

"If you could be anything, absolutely anything, what would you be?" Mave said.

Jared wanted to bang his head against the dashboard. God, she was like a dog with a bone. "I've always dreamed of being an ultrasound guy. It's possibly the most awesome job in the world."

"Really?"

"Yes, it's like being Batman."

"I don't think you're being sincere, Mr. Snarky."

At least she was off the Jelly Bean thing.

"People come in and something's wrong but they don't know what and they want answers. I will help them get answers."

"You want to help people."

"Yes."

"You're not saying that to get me off your back?" she said.

"No."

"Huh."

Mave parallel-parked the love bug four feet from the curb. "Here we are!"

He sort of recognized the street from google-mapping the area. Her apartment was grey with white trim. A kid on the top-floor balcony spat through the bars. One of the ground-floor windows was covered with a Mohawk flag, a warrior in profile against a yellow sun on a red background. Someone had drawn a blunt and stuck it to the corner of the warrior's lips. A memorial pole painted with a black-and-red beaver stood to the side of the wheelchair ramp. Jared tilted his head: *Lu'ma*, the memorial pole read.

"What does *Lu'ma* mean?"

"Lu'ma Native Housing," Mave said, climbing out. She reached into the back seat and grabbed his backpack with the balloons tied to it.

"No, hey, I got that," he said.

"Don't be silly. You're my guest. Take the groceries."

She had six grocery bags. All of them seemed to have bowling balls in them. She held the door open for him and they made their way down a wide beige hallway. They took the elevator to the second floor. Mave hummed, out of tune, a melody that buzzed at the edge of his awareness. Jared shrugged. He stifled a yawn.

"Damn," she said. "Did you remember the takeout?"

"Uh, sorry."

"You go in and make yourself at home," she said, pushing the apartment door open. She dropped his backpack inside. The balloons shivered. "I'll be right back."

The floor of the long hallway was a jumble of her shoes. The walls were painted with a mural of a forested mountain reflected in a flat-calm sea. On the left wall were mountains. At the bottom of one, giant-beaked bird-headed men stood in a clearing on a carpet of human body parts. The monstrous bird men studied a wooden longhouse emerging from a thunderous red-black foam of clouds. On the right wall, the ocean. Near the beach, a giant black bear with a seal's tail snacked on a canoe of screaming warriors in full regalia.

Okay, Jared thought. That's intense.

Jared carried the groceries into the kitchen and set them on the floor. Holy Costco addict, Batman, he thought. The counters were already filled with industrial-sized packages of food—vats of spaghetti sauce, kegs of ketchup, a box of oranges. The kitchen had a window cut into the wall that opened to a large living room where columns of books hugged the walls and clustered in the open spaces. One corner of the living room was stacked with thin cardboard boxes filled with unassembled bookcases. The window overlooked the street and a wall of apartments. The TV was tuned to a rerun of the first episode of the rebooted *Doctor Who*, when Rose was in the basement before the mannequins came alive. Hunched in the recliner was a scrawny Native guy in a fuzzy green bathrobe who glanced at Jared and then turned back to watch the show.

Mave hadn't mentioned a roommate. Or a boyfriend, though this man seemed a little too sloppy to be her type. Maybe a cousin, a fellow couchsurfer.

"Hi," Jared said. "I'm Jared."

The guy hunched into himself, squinting.

"Okay," Jared said.

He had assumed he'd be on the couch, but he could, maybe, clear a spot on the floor. There was a little maze through the books. Some of the columns came up to his waist and some came up to his armpits, but most were around knee height. He bent over: *Saltwater Women. Our Laws Bid Us Protect the Land: Pre-Contact Indigenous Logging Practices in British Columbia. Emergence: Native American Cannery Workers, Unions and Political Resistance.* One pile of books seemed to be all about residential schools. The next one was all poetry. The one assembled bookcase in the living room had collapsed under the weight of what looked like a collection of encyclopedias, which had tumbled around it in a spray of pages.

"You'd think that, as a Capricorn, I'd be a little more anal," Mave said, dropping the bag of takeout on the dining room table.

"But I'm cusp-y. If I'd been born four hours later, I'd be an Aquarius."

"You have a library," Jared said.

"Sorry about the mess," she said. "Edgar sold all *our* bookcases on Craigslist and I haven't gotten around to setting up my new ones."

So Bathrobe had a name. "Have you read all of these?"

"Most of them." She pointed to the takeout bag. "Let's have a picnic on the balcony."

Mave and the bathrobe guy didn't look at each other. So they had a silent-treatment kind of relationship, Jared thought as he followed her through the door that led to a large balcony lined with planters filled with dead plants. It overlooked the front of the building. Mave sat on a metal chair that had been haphazardly spray-painted primary yellow with bits of grey showing through. She pulled the food out of the takeout bag, checked the contents and leaned to hand one of the paninis to him.

"Thanks," he said. He sat on the other chair, still in the original grey with cancerous rust patches. The metal was sun-warmed. Heat from the balcony radiated through his shoes.

"I travel a lot for work," his aunt said, poking a pot on the table. "I think this was basil. I was on a pesto kick."

"Mom kept bringing home spider plants to clean the air," he said, "and they kept committing suicide."

"It's genetic, then."

"Looks like."

"I have to warn you," she said, "your room's weird. Edgar painted it. I meant to repaint it, but, you know. Life."

"Does Edgar mind me taking over his room?"

"He owes me three months' rent. And the damage deposit I'll never get back. Edgar can kiss my ass."

So not a boyfriend—a roommate. Awkward. Roommate fights were never fun when you were caught in the middle. A room in Abbotsford was looking like a good option. Hopefully, his loan would come in soon. He could always get a part-time job to make ends meet.

"I should have got an iced coffee," she said. "Want something cold? I have Diet Coke or orange juice."

"Whatever you're having."

"Back in a flash."

Jared felt sweat drip down his back. He hunched his shoulders, rolled them back. The sun was still high, but the wind shifted, bringing a damp ocean breeze. The skinny trees lining the street shivered. Traffic lurched. Pedestrians ambled in the August heat like zombies. He unwrapped his grilled cheese and as he was taking his first bite, he noticed someone across the street standing completely still, staring at him. David. Jared had a moment of dislocation when the world paused like a DVD, and he was both here and not, in his body on the balcony and above it, looking down from a great distance.

"What's the matter?" Mave was back with two glasses of orange juice. She followed his gaze.

Not David—the man had darker hair, and was wearing high-waisted jeans that David would never be caught dead in. The creepy dude ducked his head when he realized Jared was staring back at him and wandered towards Commercial Drive. Jared had lost track of time. It felt like hours since Mave had left, but obviously it had only been minutes.

"Nothing. Just zoning," Jared said.

"I promised to bring my aunt grocery shopping and then we're going out for lunch," she said. "If you want to meet your great-aunt today, you're welcome to join us, but don't feel obliged."

"If it's okay with you, I'll play it by ear."

"Fair enough. Sorry for the weird factor in your bedroom. The sheets are clean, though." She handed him a set of keys.

"Thanks, Mave."

"You're welcome to stay as long as you want. I mean that."

"Do you mind if I take a shower?" Jared said.

"Scrub-a-dub-dub," Mave said. She checked her watch. "I'm going to meet a friend for coffee. I'll see you later, Jelly Bean."

She kissed his cheek, which made him uncomfortable. A few minutes later, she emerged from the entrance below him, walked crisply to her car then turned and blew kisses. She got in the bug and squealed into the street. In her empty parking spot, Jared saw a suspicious puddle of fluid on the pavement. She probably had damaged something at the drive-through. Jared went inside, leaving the balcony door open. Bathrobe was still parked in the tan recliner in front of the TV.

"Hey," Jared said.

Bathrobe ignored him.

"I'm only going to be here for a few days," Jared said. "I can sleep on the couch if you want your room back."

"Obviously, you've mistaken me for Mavis's previous tenant. But I am not the insalubrious poet, Edgar Six."

"So, what—are you Mave's cousin? A friend? What's your deal?"

"You obviously lack anything resembling brainpower."

"Dude, can you stow the 'tude?"

"My 'tude?"

"If they were selling manners-in-a-can, you'd need to buy a truckload to get to normal."

Bathrobe rolled his eyes. "Oh, and you're a veritable diplomat. My humblest apologies, Ambassador Jelly Bean."

"Whatevs," Jared said.

He grabbed his backpack. He locked the bathroom door, hung his cap from a hook draped with necklaces and stripped out of his grubby clothes.

The water was gloriously hot. He let the shower blast his shoulders where his muscles had cramped. He sniffed through the soaps and chose the one that was the least floral. He scrubbed hard. He towelled off. Dug out a clean T-shirt, underwear and shorts.

He opened one door, onto Mave's room, where a queen-sized bed was a calm spot of carefully tucked blue sheets in the middle of a clothing explosion and more books. He opened the other bedroom door. The window had a black garbage bag duct-taped over it. A large solar system mobile was attached to the light socket, and when he flipped the switch, the sun glowed orange and the planets creaked in wobbly circles, bouncing on their wires, which made the red bits of cloth tied to them flicker. A grey, billowing fog was painted on the walls and ceiling. Suspended in the fog were disembodied heads, lit from below, serene and staring men, women and children. Some of the faces were tiny and far away, but the ones closest to the bed loomed larger than life-size.

Someone had ripped up the carpet, leaving jagged bits of beige around the wall. On the floor was a painted city of skyscrapers that were curled like shells, like coral reefs, like sand dunes as seen from a helicopter looking down. The city painted on the floor was alive with chubby grey people, who, on closer inspection, turned out to be dolphins.

The desk was clear plastic, and Jared could see a stapler, pens and sheets of paper in its only drawer. Which was kind of cool, like having X-ray vision, he thought, except it made the desk a useless place to stash porn. The chair was a grey plastic hand. Jared sat and put his backpack on the desk beside a cat-shaped clock with large cartoon eyes that swept the room with every tick. He swivelled. The twin bed had a steel frame that Jared hoped wasn't creaky and a quilt patched from shades of grey cloth, edged with a black ribbon stamped with white skeletons disco-dancing à la John Travolta in *Saturday Night Fever*, a movie Sophia had conned him into watching when he was a kid by promising all the characters turned into zombies at the end.

His phone pinged in his back pocket.

R u ok? Sarah texted.

He took out his charger and plugged his phone in. He was trying to decide how to respond when he noticed Bathrobe standing in the doorway.

"Your aunt gave Edgar the boot after he painted the hallways," Bathrobe said. "She thinks he went off his meds. But he didn't. He saw the dead and it drove him insane."

"Huh," Jared said.

"I must warn you," Bathrobe said. "This room is haunted."

"Yeah?"

"Not by me," Bathrobe said. "Some of us have better things to do than lurk in the walls like some Amityville reject."

"I'm taking a nap," Jared said. He stood and walked over to the bed, and sat, bounced a couple of times to test the firmness of the mattress. In case Bathrobe didn't get the hint, Jared lay down and closed his eyes. The quilt was soft and smelled like lavender. When Jared squinted at the door, Bathrobe was gone. The solar system creaked in rusty circles.

"Weirdo," he muttered, and got up to flip the light switch off.

DOLPHIN WORLD

Humans evolved as prey and have the sleep patterns of nervous mammals, a measly seven to eight hours of unconsciousness that cycles from light to deep sleep, half-alert and ready to run. Top predators can sleep fifteen to sixteen hours a day, secure in the knowledge that nothing is hunting them. They are the scary thing in the night.

Dolphins never sleep and yet they're always asleep. The two hemispheres of their brains have evolved so that when one side is asleep, the other side is awake. The hemispheres switch back and forth, letting one rest while the other is active.

In the grand multiverse, there is a world where dolphins evolved into land-dwelling, upright, bipedal beings. Their cities are dimly lit. Because their buildings are designed to be acoustically pleasing rather than eye candy, their skyscrapers are fluted and curved, shot through with holes and tunnels to catch the wind, the sounds of traffic and the crowds, turning everything into song. Dolphins never truly sleep, so their cities never rest, an unending overture, a polyphony that shifts in and out of a hundred thousand melodies.

12

CHRONICLE OF A
CRASH FORETOLD

Something banged the garbage bag–covered window, like a bird had flown into it. It banged four or five more times and paused before another flurry of bangs, then went quiet. As Jared raised his head, he caught movement out of the corner of his eye, something black and long creeping along the floor. He pulled his feet under the quilt. He felt like he was floating above the city and thought that he was dreaming but then remembered that Edgar had painted the bedroom floor.

Morning light leaked through tiny holes in the garbage bag. The room was empty. His room, if he wanted it. This apartment was only a couple of short bus rides from BCIT. He could even walk if he had to, but over seven kilometres each way? He'd spend most of the day getting to and from class. Guilt lingered like a bad aftertaste. Was he being disloyal? His mom was the one who had given him Mave's address, but the history between Mave and his mom made him feel like a shitty son.

His phone started vibrating on the desk. He wasn't up to chatting with Sarah. Not before coffee. Not if it would lead her on. God, didn't breakups mean you stopped talking? But maybe she had news about Mrs. Jaks. He reached over and grabbed his phone.

Sophia had messaged him. *Are you still at the hostel, Jared?*

Yeah, if his mom was mad that he hadn't mentioned reconnecting with Granny Nita, she wasn't going to be any more pleased that he'd reconnected with Sophia. He'd have to at least mention it in passing if he didn't want his mom to do more angry brain-bonding. Soon. Ideally, you broke bad news to his mom with a plate of crispy bacon, a fried steak and a baked potato smothered in butter and more bacon. A couple hits of a bong filled with something that gave her a huge body stone so she was less likely to use you as target practice. Or at least it would throw off her aim.

Couchsurfing with Mom's sister, Jared messaged Sophia.

I wasn't aware you had suicidal tendencies.

Mom connected us.

Has she had a stroke?

She got sick of Sober Jared.

Ah. If you really want to rebel tell her you're vegan and ask her to sign your petition for stricter gun laws.

I knew you were trouble.

Please send me your address, Jared. I had my lawyers dig up an old copy of your restraining order. Just in case.

She mostly knew divorce lawyers, but she'd arranged the first restraining order. Jared felt like he'd swallowed a rock and it was stuck in his throat. He couldn't think of anything clever to say. He sat on the edge of the bed and the screen blurred as he fought crying. The relief. The sudden release of tension he hadn't known he'd been carrying.

Jared?

Having a moment. Sorry.

Don't be.

Thank you, Sophia.

Address, please. The courier awaits.

Jared sent the address and thanked her again. Sophia sent an emoji of a smiley face rolling its eyes. She'd hit her warm-and-fuzzy limit. He sent random emojis of an octopus and a monkey.

Goodbye, she messaged.

Bye.

Jared listened for his aunt, but the apartment was still.

"Mave?" he said as he poked his head out of the bedroom.

No answer. Jared went into the kitchen and rummaged around for something to eat. He picked up a mango. You could seriously rub people the wrong way if you helped yourself to their food even if they'd invited you into their home, even if they had a full pantry and fridge. Or, in Mave's case, even if you were auditioning for a hoarding show. He put the mango back. He rinsed out a cup and ran the tap. Vancouver water had a metallic tang.

The TV was still on in the living room, but Bathrobe was gone. Was he a roommate? Was he an overly friendly neighbour? Mave didn't seem to be talking to him, yet she hadn't kicked him out, either. Jared dug through the couch for the remote and watched the news for a few minutes. But people could be weird about their TVs too. He shut it off. He went back to his room, dug around his backpack and pulled out the bag of crumbling, stale nachos. Breakfast of champions, he thought.

Jared woke again, confused, not sure if it was night or day in the dimly lit room. He checked his phone for the time. Damn it. He'd meant to rest for a few minutes, but closing his eyes had turned into an all-day nap. His stomach complained, loud and urgent. He needed something more substantial for supper. He went to get his hoodie and tried out his apartment key. It worked. He wandered around the block, found a convenience store that sold watery coffee and instant cup of noodles in a brand with very little English on the label and bought two for a dollar, Spicy Shrimp, simulated flavours. He chugged his coffee on the way home. The small plastic key fob opened the entrance door. He took the stairs two at a time and dug through the kitchen for a kettle. He made both the cups then brought them back to his room. He sat at the desk, finishing his first cup by tipping it into his mouth. Just the right amount of MSG. The second one he ate more slowly, considering Sarah's message.

No BS, his mom would say. Straight to the point. Grab some balls.

I don't think we should get back 2gether, he texted Sarah.

Duh, she texted back.

Then wutz wit the txts?

Bored. Patronizing anti-intellectual body positive re-education camp sux. Plus I thot u were being stalked. Got concerned. My bad.

How long r u @ Camp Cutter?

Sweet deflect. 2 bad u dont play hockey.

Hey. Me friend. FR-End.

Ya u n this super chipper army of pastel-wearing pharma pushers. I swear by the gender-neutral deity therz uppers in the water.

Immunity must b ur superpower.

Ur hi-larious. Where r u?

Mom has a sis. Couchsurfing 4 a few days.

She kool?

Dunno. She wanted 2 adopt me when I wuz a baby. Her n Mom had a big fite. I didnt even no she existed til last year. Mom gave me her # but still h8tz her.

Shitty. Anywhere else u can go?

No. Classes start Tues. Loan haznt cum in yet. Blew my wad on tuition n hostel. Cant afford 2 start anything wit her but damn.

2 sides 2 evry story. Confront her. Clear the air. I have friends u can stay wit if it goes tits up.

Ya?

4 realz. Gotta go for supper. We must all eat together like good lil robots. TTFN.

TTYL

He took his ancient laptop out of his backpack and plugged it in.

Confront Mave. Not yet. Maybe never. He didn't know any of Sarah's friends, but the likelihood that they were normal was pretty low.

The laptop screen finally whirred to life. He'd taken off as many programmes and files as he could to speed it up, but it still clunked and hissed. Labour Day was this Monday. Classes on Tuesday. If he'd had any money at all, he'd have gone up to BCIT and bought his textbooks. He'd been relying on Death fronting him a week's pay to cover the books, but that was shot to hell. He had the weekend to figure things out. Maybe they had the textbooks in the library. Maybe he could sweet-talk someone in class into letting him photocopy the first couple of chapters and assignments.

One day at a time, he reminded himself. Lately, it had felt like one crisis at a time. He hadn't thought to ask Sophia when the courier was coming. Tomorrow was Friday, so they probably wouldn't be delivering until Tuesday.

He was busy looking up possible rentals when he heard the front door open, and voices coming down the hallway. His first instinct was to close his bedroom door and pretend to be asleep, but he reminded himself that he was a guest. Poking his head out to say hi was the least he could do.

The hem of Mave's skirt was smeared with black grease and her knees were scraped. Her eyes were puffy from crying and her mascara had migrated, giving her a raccoon-like mask. She straightened and wiped her eyes when she noticed Jared. A lean, dark woman with shoulder-length black hair kissed Mave's cheek then wiped the lipstick off with her thumb. She had a prominent Adam's apple. A buff Native guy who looked as chiselled as a Greek statue stood behind them. Buff dude wore a security guard's uniform. He glowered, typing into his phone.

"What happened?" Jared said.

"M-m-my car died when I w-w-as . . . we were going . . . Aunt Agnetha and I, t-t-t—" Mave said.

"Shh. We're home, Maamaan," the woman said. "Everyone's safe."

"Is this Jared?" the guy said, looking up and scowling at him.

"Oh," Mave said, swallowing hard. "Yes, this is Maggie's boy."

Buff dude said to Jared, "Who's this David that's stalking you?"

"Hank," the woman hissed. "Not now."

"We need to know what we're getting into," Hank said.

"Go check on Agnetha, Hank," the woman said.

"I could have picked Gran up," Hank said.

Mave cleared her throat. "Aunt Aggie said you've taken enough days off, Hank. The groceries, though. We couldn't get the trunk open. They're still in the trunk."

"You should have called me earlier," Hank said.

"I was closer," the woman said. "Your gran is safe. We towed Maamaan's bug to my school. I'll have my students look at it in the morning, but it looks like a leaky oil pan. Easily fixed."

"If the engine didn't seize," Hank said.

The woman shot Hank a cold look as Mave hiccupped in a failing attempt not to cry again. The woman jerked her head and mouthed, "Go." Hank's shoulders hitched up.

"Your bug will be fine," the woman said to Mave.

Jared shoved his hands in his pocket and tried to be invisible.

"It just stopped," Mave said, swallowing hard, "in the middle of a turn. We. We were rear-ended. Twice."

"Thank goodness neither of you were hurt. And we pushed it to safety like the goddesses we are," the woman said. "Traffic be damned."

"How long since you had a snack?" Hank said.

"I—I don't remember," Mave said. "We had lunch before . . . we, the car . . ."

"Check your sugar levels, Aunt Mave. Now, before you faint." Hank stomped into the kitchen.

The woman smiled at Jared and held out her hand. "I'm Justice Moody," she said. "What a pleasure to meet you. Maamaan says all manner of lovely things about you." She had a firm grip and warm hands.

Jared tried to smile.

"Would you like to join us for tea?" Justice said.

Mave came over and hugged him. She rested her head on his shoulder and sighed.

"You okay?" Jared said.

She said, very quietly, "Thank you for not saying, 'I told you so.'"

Hank put the kettle on. Justice followed him into the kitchen. Jared could hear them murmuring. Mave kept holding him. The hug went on and on. Jared patted her back. Justice came back. She peeled Mave off Jared.

"Let's get you cleaned up, Maamaan." They disappeared into the bedroom.

Hank opened and closed cupboards, then yelled, "Where's the sugar?"

"Figure it out!" Justice shouted from the bedroom.

"What a mess," Hank muttered, picking the flat of mangoes off the counter. He looked around, and then put it back where he'd found it, sighing. The kettle whistled. Hank poured the hot water into a teapot. He raised his head and looked at Jared. "I hope you like your tea black."

"Need any help?"

"There's not enough room in here for two people. Go sit."

Jared went and cleared a spot on the couch. Hank brought four mugs and a box of cookies into the living room on a silver tray, put it down on a stack of books and handed Jared a mug. Hank sat in the recliner, perched on the edge, hands wrapped around his own cup.

"Does David have any military training?" Hank said. "Any weaponry?"

"Yeah, hi. My name is Jared. I'm fine. How're you?"

"Quit goofing around."

Jared sipped the tea. Hank waited as if he expected Jared to start talking.

"I'm on it," Jared said. "It's not your problem."

"If it affects Aunt Mave, it's my problem."

"I won't be here long enough for it to be your problem, okay? Chill."

"What's that supposed to mean?"

"It means relax."

"I thought you were staying here."

"That's not the plan, okay?"

"So? You're just going to wander around Vancouver with a stalker on your ass?"

"I guess bugs can't four-by-four," Mave said, emerging from the bedroom in a Canucks jersey over some shorts, her face scrubbed clean.

Justice followed her and they sat on the couch with Jared, Mave in the middle.

"He says he's leaving," Hank said.

"Dude," Jared said.

"Jared," Mave said, patting his knee. "Keep my keys. Come back any time. My door is open. I'll save the room for you."

"He's going to get himself killed," Hank said.

"I think we can all agree that I was a horrible sister," Mave said.

Justice and Hank exchanged a look but said nothing. Jared was very aware of how close he was sitting to Hank, of Mave beside him, looking tired.

"There were circumstances, but they don't excuse anything." Mave flopped back. "When you want to hear what I have to say, I'll tell you anything. In your time, Jared. Not anyone else's."

In the lengthy silence that followed, Jared could hear the traffic outside, the happy patrons at a nearby bar, people laughing in the street.

"Glad you're okay," Hank said.

"Thank you, Henry-kins," Mave said. "You're always there for me. I appreciate it."

"Night, Aunt Mave."

"Good night."

When the door closed and Hank was gone, Justice said to Jared, "Don't mind Hank. He's a pit bull, but he's your pit bull. That's how he shows he cares."

"I feel like you're always cleaning up after me, Justice," Mave said.

"Nonsense," Justice said. "You are the sun in my sky."

"Oh, I love you so much, my darling girl."

"Love you more," Justice said.

"I'm going to rest up for tomorrow," Jared said.

Mave caught his hand as he stood. "Leave any time you want, Jared, but please don't leave without saying goodbye. Deal?"

"Deal," Jared said, and she let him go.

13

PROMENADE SENTIMENTALE

"Wakey, wakey," Mave said. "Eggs and bacon. Come on, brunch is ready."

Mave wore a pink, nubby suit with a matching hat that made her look like she was going to be riding in a convertible in Dallas later. Jared moaned and pulled the quilt over his head.

"Mmm, egg whites and low-salt turkey bacon," Mave said, nudging him, and then poking him when he didn't move. "Did I mention coffee? There's coffee."

"Tired."

"Come on. We're burning daylight." She tugged the quilt off him and threw it over the desk. She stopped face to face with one of the painted heads. "Blech. I don't know how you can sleep in here."

"It's a lot easier when I'm alone."

"Aren't you creeped out?"

"Ignore them."

"You really aren't a morning person, are you?"

"Is it morning?"

"Barely. Eleven-thirty in the a.m. Come on. Up, up, up!"

Jared curled around the pillow, squeezing his eyes shut and willing Mave to leave. Her heels clicked across the floor and went quiet once she hit the rug. He considered the space between his bed and the desk, and decided the quilt was not worth the effort of moving. He drifted, breath slowing.

Mave's heels clicked back into the room and the bed sagged as she sat on the edge. Her pearl necklace thwacked him as she leaned over and yanked out an eyebrow hair.

"Ow! What the hell? God."

Mave drew the tweezers back, frowning. "Hold still, Mr. Unibrow."

"Have you ever heard of personal space? Get off me." He covered his forehead with his hands.

"You big baby. Wait, I have some wax in the bathroom."

"No! I'm up—can you please leave my face alone?"

"Are you getting up or saying what I want to hear to get me off your back?"

Jared swung his legs over the edge and sat, tasting his mouth. "I'm really tired."

She put the back of her hand on his forehead. "Are you ill? You've been sleeping since you got here."

How to explain the last week of insanity? He really couldn't. "No. Just tired."

Mave stood, held her hand out. Jared ignored it but got up. He'd meant to take off his clothes but fell asleep before he could. He picked up the quilt, and then rummaged through his backpack. He checked the room.

Mave put her hands on her hips. "Your breakfast is getting cold. A growing boy needs sustenance."

"Do you see my phone? I can't remember where I put it."

She bent over and reached under the desk. "Is this it? My. I haven't seen a BlackBerry in ages. I have an iPhone 4 if you want it."

Jared paused. "How much?"

"Oh, don't be silly. It's just sitting in my drawer. When I renewed my plan, it came with an iPhone 5. I hate to throw out a perfectly good phone. So wasteful."

Jared frowned. It wasn't something you would offer a stranger. A relative stranger. He worried about the invisible strings, the quid pro quo, but an iPhone, even an old one . . . "You can sell it on Kijiji for a few hundred bucks," he said, "or Craigslist."

She made a face. "With the 6 coming out soon, I don't think I'd get much for the 4."

"I dunno," Jared said. "Are you sure?"

"I'm positive."

She seemed serious. Jared said, "Thank you."

"You're welcome. Now come on. Let's eat."

His plate was on the kitchen table. She brought him a coffee and then sat across from him and watched him while he ate. She smiled. He wolfed down his food, partly because he was starving, partly because he didn't like being stared at.

"Simon Fraser University has an Aboriginal Pre-Health programme," she said. "You'd be a perfect fit."

"The programme I want to get into is at BCIT."

"The credits are transferable."

"I'm going to stick with my plan."

"Do you realize a collection of T-shirts does not a wardrobe make? We can freshen your ensemble. I'm part owner of a clothing co-op. I'd get you a discount."

"All this makeover stuff makes me uncomfortable. Really, really uncomfortable."

"I'm not trying to make you over," Mave said. "I'm trying to make amends."

Jared shrugged. "I appreciate you wanting to help, but, um, it's okay. I can handle this."

"Of course," Mave said. "But if there's anything, anything at all that you need to help you with school, please let me know."

Jared immediately thought about his textbooks and then wished he hadn't.

"I mean it," she said.

"I—" he started, then took a breath. "I wouldn't mind borrowing some money for my textbooks. Just borrow. I can pay you back when my loan comes in."

"You don't have to pay me back," she said.

"I do," he said.

Her smile faltered and her expression crumpled. She sipped her coffee, holding the mug in front of her face as her eyes watered.

"Never mind," Jared said.

"I'll call a cab," she said, forcing a smile. "Let's go get you some books."

They stood in line at the bookstore forever. Mave paid for his books on her credit card.

"Let's see if any of your profs are around," Mave said.

"I'm still kind of tired," Jared said.

"Come on," Mave said.

The physics prof wasn't there. In the biology department, a tall guy wearing a fluorescent green windbreaker was chatting with the department secretary when they walked in. He sat on the edge of her desk, gangly legs in black biker shorts. His brown hair was sweat-curled around his forehead. The secretary chewed the end of her pen, and her eyes travelled up and down Cycle Guy's body when he turned to see who had come in.

"I'm looking for Professor Struan Moore," Mave said. "Is he in today?"

"Speak of the devil," the bike guy said. "And here I am."

They laughed. The secretary smiled tightly.

"Hi, I'm Mavis Moody and this is my—"

He shot up, his expression shifting to shock. "*The* Mavis Moody? *Landscape Porn* Mavis Moody?"

"Yes, that's me," she said.

He grabbed her hand and pumped it. "Christ! I'm— Crap, excuse the sweat! If I'd known I was going to meet you today, I'd have— I mean. Hello! What a pleasure! I mean an honour! This is, uh, um, Cecily? It's Cecily, right?"

Mave laughed. She pulled her hand out of Moore's and held it out for Cecily, who gave it a limp shake then sat back, widening the smile that never touched her eyes. "Struan doesn't have office hours until next week," she said.

"I wasn't even going to come in today!" Struan said. "Can I buy you a coffee? I included *Landscape* in my master's thesis and, well, I just, I can't, I mean— Christ, I'm sorry for the babbling."

"What was your thesis about?" Mave said.

"Sediment dynamics and pollutant flow mobility in the middle and upper reaches of the Fraser River system and their effect on Coho salmonoid maturation."

"You're kidding!" Mave said. "Oh, the Mount Polley mine tailing pond dam breach was so heartbreaking."

"Are you free for dinner? Tonight? Tomorrow?"

"Hold on a minute—I'm here with my nephew. This is Jared Martin, who'll be in your biology class."

"Hi," Struan said, grabbing Jared's hand briefly, eyes fixed on Mave. "So, dinner? Sometime? Any time? Or coffee. Yes, let's start with coffee."

"I'd love to go out for dinner sometime. And I know about a hundred people who'd love to read your thesis. Is it downloadable?"

"Give me their e-mails," Struan said. "Just let me get a fresh shirt."

"Honest sweat is never offensive," Mave said.

Struan beamed down at Mave. She lowered her head, smiling coyly through her eyelashes.

"Don't go anywhere," he said. "I'll be right back."

The second he left, she dropped her purse on Cecily's desk and rummaged through it. She flipped open a compact and started dusting her face with powder. She ran gloss over her lips and fluffed her hair with her fingers. From Cecily's murderous expression, if she could have blown up brains with the power of thought, Mave would have been headless.

"Do I have anything on my teeth?" Mave said.

"Is he single?" Jared said to Cecily.

Her expression soured further. "Yes."

"Your teeth are fine, Mave."

"Oh, Jelly Bean," Mave said.

———

Jared didn't want to be a third wheel while they went for coffee, but Mave refused to let him bus back home without her. So they stayed in the office where Mave and Struan gabbed about his thesis forever while Cecily typed furiously on her computer and Jared flipped through his textbooks. After Mave asked Cecily to call them a cab, it was another hour before it showed. Another day shot and he was no closer to finding a new place to park, Jared thought, as he stared out the taxi window. When they entered the apartment, Jared heard the TV going and thought it was going to be the annoying bathrobe man, but Hank sat in the recliner, frowning at his phone.

"How're you doing today, Aunt Mave?" Hank said.

"Wonderful," Mave said. "Thank you for asking, Hank."

"Any word on your bug?"

"They're working on it next week."

"Hey, Genius," Hank said, looking at Jared.

"Hey, Henry-kins," Jared said.

"Boys," Mave said. "Play nice."

Jared retreated to his room and put his textbooks on his desk. He tried to turn his new phone on, but it stayed dark. He plugged it in and hoped it was just out of juice.

After a while, he heard Justice's voice. "Hel-lo, First Lady Mave. You should wear pink more often. Look how you glow!"

Jared sighed. After a few minutes, Mave knocked on his bedroom door. She opened it, even though he hadn't asked her to come in, but she stayed in the doorway.

"Are you hungry?" she said. "Justice brought barbecue pork skewers and a rice noodle salad."

"I'm good," Jared said.

"I promise everyone will behave," she said.

"I just need some space."

"Fair enough," she said. "But if you get hungry later, my kitchen is your kitchen. Help yourself to anything."

The apartment buzzer rang. He heard Hank answer the intercom and then shout: "Jared! Delivery for you!"

When Jared came out of his bedroom, Justice was sitting at the dining table and Hank was near the intercom holding a skewer. "It's from someone named Sophia Martin."

Ah, the copy of the old restraining order.

"Scary Sophia," Mave said to Justice and Hank. "The only person alive who intimidates my sister."

"Sophia's not scary," Jared said.

"Oh, Jelly Bean," Mave said. "She's one dead husband away from her own *America's Most Wanted* special."

The delivery guy who arrived at the apartment door was heart-attack red and sweaty. His board was sticky. After Jared signed the paperwork, the guy handed him an envelope that had not only a notarized copy of the restraining order but also a set of keys, motor vehicle transfer papers and a short note on thick, creamy paper:

A little memento. Yours, Sophia.

"Your scooter's being unloaded," the delivery guy said. "Where do you want it?"

"I'm not, um— My what?"

"Come on down."

Mave, Justice and Hank all came down with them. The delivery van was double-parked and cars honked in irritation as they squeezed by.

His partner had finished unloading Sophia's powder-blue Vespa on the sidewalk. The matching helmet and goggles hung from the handlebars.

"Do you remember Jean-Jacques Beineix's *Diva*?" Mave said. "Oh, I loved that movie. We need to get you a blue jacket, Jared. And a postman's cap."

"The postman rode a moped, not a Vespa, Maamaan. A Motobé-cane."

"Don't be such a literalist, my darling girl."

Jared touched the handlebar. He remembered all the "toodles" he and Sophia had taken, the engine whining up and down the hills of Prince Rupert. He supposed he could use it to get to school, but his mom would have conniptions if she found out city living had turned her son into scooter trash. For a dedicated Harley-Davidson fan like her, that would be like bringing a tofurkey to the Rod and Gun Club potluck. Selling it might get him a few bucks, but Sophia didn't make sentimental gestures often. He noticed the wonder in Mave's eyes, her longing. She was keeping a roof over his head and had just bought him textbooks and offered him her old iPhone.

He held out the key for Mave. "Want to give it a go?"

"I couldn't," she said.

"We don't even know if it works," Justice said.

"Try it out," Jared insisted.

"Does it have gas?" Hank said. "Do we need insurance?"

"Really?" Mave said to Jared.

"Really."

Mave squealed then hopped on, handing Jared the helmet and goggles as Justice and Hank both started giving her instructions. Mave happily ignored them both, started the Vespa and took off. Her little pink hat fluttered on her head like it was trying to take off. She reached up to hold on to it with one hand, bombing along the side-walk, swerving around pedestrians who shouted at her.

"I don't think that's legal," the delivery guy said.

"Off the sidewalk!" Justice shouted.

Mave veered onto the road, cutting off a car that was turning onto Graveley from Commercial Drive. She let go of her hat and it whipped away. A series of irritated honks echoed up and down the street as she wobbled into a turn then zipped back towards them, honking as she passed, her face lit with a blissful smile as she narrowly avoided smacking into the delivery truck.

"Take my picture!" she said.

"Watch where you're going!" Hank yelled.

"She's going to kill herself," Justice said.

"Go, go, Jackie O," the delivery guy said.

14

MY BOO

First thing the next morning, Mave announced they were in dire need of agave syrup. Jared looked up from his laptop, sipping a coffee. She wore a mustard dress with blue tights and rust-coloured boots that she'd probably chosen to coordinate with the scooter.

"You can ride the Vespa any time," Jared said. "You don't need an excuse."

"Shall we get you a new SIM card for the iPhone today?"

"I'd like that," Jared said.

"The nearest store opens at eleven. Consider it done." She flipped her scarf over her shoulder then lowered her giant white sunglasses. "Ciao!"

"Later."

He heard her boots clicking down the hallway. She'd cut up about a hundred mangoes and left them in a large bowl beside him on the dining room table. Jared slid some onto a plate. He was wondering if he wanted to squeeze in a meeting before she got back when the TV clicked on. Jared slowly turned around, but he knew no one else was home. The balcony door was open and the apartment was filled with intense morning sunlight. Dust sparkled in the air. The

TV flipped through the channels by itself. Maybe, Jared thought, someone had the same TV as Mave, and their remote was turning on her set. Old-time transporter sounds from the original *Star Trek* filled the apartment as the TV stopped on the science fiction channel. The scrawny man wearing a ratty green bathrobe emerged from the wall and plopped himself in the recliner.

"Finally. I thought she'd never leave," Bathrobe said.

Crap, Jared thought. He's a ghost.

"The *Doctor Who* marathon starts soon," Bathrobe said. "Feel free to make yourself scarce."

"You . . . you're a . . . you . . ."

"Aha. So you finally realized I'm not fully in your 'dimension'?" Bathrobe said. "I suppose I could wear a name tag: *Hi, I'm Dead.*"

Jared couldn't find any words.

The ghost grimaced. "Your slack-jawed silence is even more annoying than your self-involved blather."

Jared walked over to the television and unplugged it. Bathrobe howled.

"I have nothing against the dead," Jared said. "But if you don't leave this apartment, I'm going to cleanse it."

"That isn't fair!" Bathrobe said. "I was here first!"

"Go haunt someone else!"

"I'm not haunting you! Sweet TARDIS! The hubris of you!"

"This isn't personal. I have zero tolerance for ghosts, spirits or magic."

"Hubris is when a dumb-ass like you thinks it's all about him!"

"Get out!"

"I just want to watch *Doctor Who*!"

"Go watch your lame show somewhere else!"

The ghost flickered furiously. The lamp by the recliner flared to life and the bulb popped. All the lights in the apartment sputtered. Jared hunted through Mave's mess of things for sweetgrass, sage, tobacco, anything. One of her books flew through the air and smacked into the wall. Jared stomped into the kitchen. He found a tiny bottle of dried sage in the spice rack. He got his aunt's ceramic diffuser from the top of the fridge and mixed the herb with some cooking oil, then lit a tea candle and placed it in the diffuser. He watched the ghost expectantly, hoping Bathrobe would vanish. The resulting aroma reminded Jared of all the Thanksgiving turkeys his mother had resentfully plunked in the oven, declaring the bird would be done when she said it was done, so don't fucking bug her about it during the football game.

Bathrobe crossed his arms over his chest. "Your ghetto-smudge won't work."

Jared went up to Bathrobe and stuck his hand through Bathrobe's face, wiggling his fingers. They tingled from the cold.

"Stop that," Bathrobe said. "Stop it."

Somehow, his mom had made this look easy. When she touched spirits and ghosts, they went poof, like burst balloons filled with smoke. Dispersion was a matter of will, she'd told him. Bathrobe stepped back and Jared followed him, willing him to disappear. Bathrobe sighed heavily and started to float. Jared got a broom. He started whacking Bathrobe like he was an otherworldly pinata.

"Fine," Bathrobe said. "I'm leaving. But if you want to avoid the supernatural, you need to leave this apartment. It is an inter-dimensional nex—"

"Get out!"

"I warned you!"

And with that, he popped out of existence.

Jared blew out the tea candle. He waited, but the ghost in the bathrobe stayed away.

Dealing with the dead is a sucker's game, his mom liked to say. If the needy fuckers won't go into the light themselves, you have to punt them.

Jared went to a meeting. When he got back, Mave was home and wanted to take the scooter to the cellphone store.

"I'm not riding bitch-seat on a Vespa," Jared said.

She laughed and suggested they walk instead.

The store was barely ten minutes away. Once the new SIM card was in, Jared chose a new phone number. The clerk offered to transfer his files. When that was done, Jared sat on a bench with his new-to-him phone while his aunt and the clerk discussed oppressive immigration limits and the rise of the Temporary Foreign Worker Program.

Jared texted Crashpad: *If ur happy & u no it . . .*

Crashpad replied: *Ur probably overmedicated. Who's this?*

Jared laughed. *Jared. Howʒ tricks?*

Silly rabbit, tricks r 4 politicians. What's with da new #?

I got an iPhone!

H8t u.

Still got a shitty phone plan but hey thatʒ y therʒ coffee shops.

Haha. Crap. Hitlerʒ mad I'm ignoring her lecture. C u

L8r

His mom's text simply said: *txt me back shithead.*

Hey, Jared texted her. *I'm breathing. This is my Vancouver #.*

He sent out a mass text giving his contacts his new phone number. He checked his Facebook account. Mave wanted to be friends. On her wall, she had about a billion selfies of herself on the Vespa from last night and this morning. She didn't mention Sophia, but it didn't mean she wouldn't. Jared didn't know if his mom and his aunt were Facebook friends or what they could see about each other. Maybe his mom wouldn't recognize the Vespa. Nope, better to bite the bullet just in case. Come clean. Talk like grown-ups. Jared squinted as he texted his mom: *FYI—Sophia dropped by the hostel. Worried @ David.*

No response. As the minutes ticked by, Jared thought maybe it wouldn't be such a big deal. Maybe his mom was having fun and too busy to notice that he'd been chatting with her ex-mother-in-law. Maybe his mom'd had a heart attack when she read his text and was on the floor clutching her chest, stunned at the stupid way he clung to people who showed him the slightest bit of affection. Not surprised, though. That was the problem with becoming self-aware: your own patterns became glaringly obvious. One of the people in the meeting had been sharing today, recounting all their horrible choices in relationships, and Jared had felt a twinge of recognition.

"Ready?" Mave said.

When Jared looked up, she was smiling at him.

"Thanks again," he said, waggling the phone before he put it in his back pocket.

"What did you think of Struan?" Mave said.

"I think he liked you."

"My sarcastic little bean."

"I met him for, what, three minutes? Four?"

"First impressions."

"He also seems to like salmonoids."

"You don't think he was, I don't know, young?"

"I'm super, super uncomfortable discussing your dating prospects."

"He's invited me to dinner tonight."

Jared said, "None of my business."

They walked together. Midday was boiling, but he had worn his shorts and his lightest T-shirt. Mave skipped over a broken part of the sidewalk and sidestepped a couple who were arguing as they turned onto Graveley Street.

"Would you mind if I burned some sage and sweetgrass in your apartment?" Jared asked.

"Of course not."

"Thanks."

"I have a drawer full of sweetgrass braids and sage bundles. Help yourself. Are you feeling all right?"

"I just need some grounding." And to keep Bathrobe away, Jared thought.

"Change is always disorienting," she said.

The apartment was still hot, so they opened all the windows. Jared had to peel the garbage bag off the one in his bedroom to get it open. The duct tape left a grey ring around the moulding. The room had a heavy coating of dust. Mave showed him the kitchen drawer filled with braids and bundles. He picked out the freshest-looking sage. She brought him an abalone shell the size of a small turtle and a fan made of so many eagle feathers it looked like a wing. The handle was beaded with a thunderbird. Jared happily walked through the apartment burning sage until the smoke detector in the hallway went off.

"There's smudging and then there's fumigating," Mave shouted, holding her ears against the noise.

"Sorry."

"Get me one of the tea towels from that drawer."

When he brought one to her, she waved it under the alarm until it stopped bleating. For a moment, one of the painted figures, a little chief, seemed to be moving, but surely it was just the smoke and a trick of his eyes.

"What's with the murals?" Jared said.

"Edgar. He said there was something living in the walls and it would come out at night and attack him. Painting the walls was supposed to keep it out of the apartment."

"Ah."

"If he comes around, go get Hank. He lives next door in apartment 201. I suppose we should get the locks changed."

"Is Edgar dangerous?"

"Goodness, no. Just very confused. A little sad. He's back in his mother's house. He's talented, isn't he? I feel bad. I know these are the Tanis stories, but I find these murals so creepy. Remind me to pick up some primer."

"Tanis?"

"The winter dances about the Man-Eater at the North End of the World and his four Man-Eating Birds that guard the four corners of the world. The one you're staring at is Hok-hok, the skull splitter—have you heard the songs? I have a CD Barbie's dance group made."

"I'm good," Jared said. When he'd seen the creature that lived under Sophia's skin, it had made that sound—Hok! Hok!

Jared swept his room and wiped down his desk. He turned his laptop on and then went to get a bowl of mangoes. Mave was standing in his bedroom when he got back, studying one of the faces.

"We can paint over these too," Mave said.

"I don't mind them."

"Not that I was snooping," Mave said. "But I have a box of laptops in my room. None of them are the latest models, but any of them would be more recent than the one you have."

"Why do you have a box of laptops?"

"I collect other people's castoffs and bring them with me when I do workshops in the more remote reserves. The kids like to bang around on them."

"Is that your job?"

"Sometimes. I'm mostly an adjunct at English departments—creative writing, indigenous lit, ecology—but I got a grant, so I'm taking a sabbatical to finish my book this year."

"Oh," Jared said. He guessed she meant she taught, but he didn't want to look stupid, so he nodded like it made sense.

"Come on."

A silver MacBook Air was among the cast-off laptops. He snatched it up, and then looked at her to make sure it was okay.

"I was going to use that one for travel," she said. "But it has limited memory and I loathe cloud storage, especially when I'm out in camp for a few weeks. It's yours."

She dug the power cord out of the tangle of cords for him and they fired it up at the dining table. She went into her bedroom and brought her own laptop to the table.

"Could I have your wi-fi password?" Jared asked.

"Didn't I give it to you?" she said.

"No."

"Sorry, I thought I gave it to you. 1234Moody. I'm the D-Link 7831 network."

"Thanks."

Her wi-fi ran slower than a coffee shop. She'd left the wi-fi admin functions shortcut on the Air, so he checked her network map. "You've got twenty-three devices hooked up to your router. Are they all yours?"

"Really? Where do you see that?"

He turned the laptop so she could see the screen. "We can boot everyone off, change your password and reconnect just us," Jared said.

"I would really appreciate that," Mave said. "How wonderful to have tech support in my own home."

"Some of Mom's tenants would move out but park on our block and mooch wi-fi to download songs or movies. I had to change the password all the time or she'd be out there with a shotgun using their tires for target practice."

"That sounds like Maggie."

Jared glanced up. Mave was smiling wryly. He said, defensively, "She never shot any of them."

"Dad gave her a slingshot for her sixth birthday and she almost took his eye out with it. He was a mean drunk. He tried to be mad, but she was his little Maggie-pie."

"She never talks about him," Jared said.

"She wouldn't."

She looked sad, so Jared let it drop. Mave made coffee while Jared changed the router settings. Once all the moochers were off, everything sped up. She brought her French press to the table and, after a while, poured them each a mug of coffee. They surfed together in silence occasionally broken by street sounds.

Adjunct, his web search read. *Something added to another thing but not essential to it. Examples: Parts of a sentence that are used to elaborate on or modify other words or phrases. Also it is an abbreviation for a professor employed, usually part-time, by a college or university for a specific purpose or term.*

"I can watch Netflix again without the swirly of death!" Mave said. "You are a miracle worker."

"De nada."

His phone pinged. Message from Mom. Jared took a deep, calming breath.

Ur my kid alrite, his mom had texted him. *Cant tell u nothin. Sophia is dangerous u idiot. Ur gonna hafta figure it out 4 urself I guess.*

Sorry, Jared texted back.

Dont b sorry. B smarter. & dont go running off wit Death. Stay wit Mave til Davidz outta our hair.

He hasn't shown again.

Hez like herpes. U cant get rid of him & u never no when hez gonna pop up & ruin ur day.

Jared laughed. *Miss u.*

Weirdo.

TTYL

TTFN

Which reminded him to text Sophia. It seemed like they'd made peace, despite what his mom thought.

Thank you for the Vespa, Sophia. You didn't have to. Drop by for coffee any time.

She didn't message him back, but she didn't go online as much as other people. He closed up his laptop and brought the coffee press back to the kitchen. When he tried to empty it, the garbage was overflowing, so he took the bag out of the can and asked Mave where to dump it.

"How are you still single?" Mave said.

———

Justice dropped by to help Mave pick out an outfit for her date. They disappeared into the bedroom. Their laughter pealed through the apartment. Beyoncé belted out "Drunk in Love" while Justice warbled along and Mave sang the Jay-Z parts. Mave had given Jared her Netflix password, so he was flipping through the selection of movies on his laptop when the intercom buzzed.

"Hello," he said.

"Is this Jared Martin?" a woman's voice said, tinny through the intercom.

"Yes," Jared said.

"This is Meredith Jaks," the woman said. After a lengthy silence: "Sarah's mother."

"Oh." Good gravy. Even David would be more welcome.

"Can I speak to you?" she said. "For just a few minutes. I promise I won't take much of your time. Please, Jared."

"Um. Okay." Jared buzzed her up. They didn't have the friendliest relationship. She'd threatened to call the cops on him the last time they'd met. Jared glanced around the apartment and wished it didn't look so cluttered and hoarder-y.

A light knock. Jared held his breath, recited the Serenity Prayer as he walked down the hallway and opened the door.

Sarah's mom had her black hair in a neat swoop and wore a navy pantsuit with flared bottoms that hid her shoes. She smiled tightly, but pleasantly, at him. He could see where Sarah had gotten her high cheekbones and her tall, lean frame. Her face looked Photoshopped flawless.

"Thank you for seeing me," she said. "Can I come inside?"

"Sure."

He didn't offer her a beverage. He didn't want to give her ammo if she wanted to throw something in his face. Not that she would. She was all business as she strode down the hallway and parked herself on the couch, ignoring the stacks of books everywhere and Beyoncé telling dudes if they like it then they should've put a ring on it. Her shoes were red and very pointed. Jared sat on the recliner.

Meredith cleared her throat. "Sarah left her self-harm retreat Thursday night. Has she tried to contact you?"

"We just started texting again last week," Jared said. "But she hasn't sent any messages to me since Thursday"

"Did she tell you her plans?"

"No."

"Do you know where she is?"

"No. Sorry."

"If Sarah contacts you again, please tell her I'm worried. We won't send her back. I'd like to see her. Talk to her."

"She's pretty stubborn," Jared said. "Once she makes up her mind, she's a bull."

"She thinks the world of you."

"She's lonely."

Jared couldn't make out whether her expression was anger, sadness or frustration. "Sometimes I work eighty hours a week. My husband does the same. We're trying to give her a good life."

"I'm not judging," Jared said. "I'm saying she wouldn't have gone out with me if she hadn't been lonely."

"She was at a protest and she threw herself between a police officer and a man she didn't even know. She has a record now. Assaulting a police officer."

"It's a juvie record," Jared said. "She'll be fine."

"I thought Dad could handle her. He was always so tough. I thought that's what she needed. I didn't know. I didn't."

"Mr. and Mrs. Jaks don't like to ask for help," Jared said. "They're proud."

She looked at the floor. "Mother explained how much they relied on you, towards the end."

"They helped me, too," Jared said. "It's okay. We're good."

Something in the bedroom thumped. Mave and Justice burst out laughing again and they could hear them happily blaming each other—*You did that! No, you!* Sarah's mom clenched her hands. They shook. She unclenched them.

"I think I need to say I'm sorry," Jared said. "The sh—stuff I said to you when Sarah and I were breaking up, I really wanted to say to my own mom. We weren't in a place where we could be honest with each other. A lot of that was about us, not you."

Meredith blinked faster. "I appreciate that, Jared. That's . . . very generous of you."

Jared nodded, not knowing what else to say.

Meredith swallowed loudly. "She's out there, alone."

"She's smart," Jared said. "And she's tough."

Meredith reached into her purse and pulled out a business card. "Call me. Any time of the day or night. Any news. Anything you hear."

Jared took the card. "She'll be okay."

"It's not a kind world."

"It's not," Jared agreed.

———

Have u heard from Sarah? Jared texted Crashpad, on the off chance they were still in contact.

Jared had given up on sleep and was parked at his desk, staring at his phone and his laptop. Sarah had gone radio silent. Her recent posts gave no clues. She'd taken some selfies of her feet, started a thread about settler tropes in popular TV series and posted a meme of Hot Felon Meeks. Jared messaged one of the friends she retweeted endlessly and he'd written back:

Fucking pig. Don't think I don't know what you're doing. The law is on MY side. Oink, oink, muthafucka.

Crashpad texted back: *Ya she wuʒ in a self-harm retreat on Van Island & hated it. Told me she was leaving, but wouldn't say where in case they confiscated her phone.*

She'd told Crashpad she was rabbiting, but not him. He was the ex, but damn.

Can u tell her to txt me? Jared wrote.

Will do.

He heard the front door open. Mave's heels clicked down the hallway. She knocked on his door.

"I'm back," she said.

"How'd your date go?"

"We danced and danced," she said. "My feet are killing me, but it was so worth it. See you in the morning."

"Night."

He heard Mave humming as she got ready for bed. He was tired, so it irritated him. He wished Sarah'd drop him a line, even to tell him to fuck off, and let him know she was okay.

15

DYSFUNCTIONAL
COPING MECHANISMS

Jared heard the TV turn on late Sunday morning and thought it was going to be the annoying bathrobe ghost. But Hank sat in the recliner, flipping through the channels. Jared was pretty sure Mave'd locked the door when she got home—he'd heard the lock click. Hank was wearing his security guard's uniform, so maybe he was building staff here, but more likely Mave had given him a key to her apartment.

Hank looked up and his eyes locked on Jared. "Still here?"

"Hey," Jared said.

"You need insurance for your scooter."

"Good to know."

Jared went into the kitchen and started another kettle for coffee. He wasn't fond of French presses. He hated the fluorescent lights in the kitchen, their flicker and buzz. He rinsed out the press. He heard the recliner squeak as Hank stood. His boots clunked over to the kitchen, where he loomed in the doorway.

"Do you have a plan for dealing with this David guy?" Hank said. "You know, aside from whiny bitching on social media?"

"Dude, you don't even know me," Jared said.

"I know enough," Hank said.

Jared decided he didn't really need coffee. He tried to leave the kitchen, but Hank wouldn't budge from the doorway. Jared considered Hank's bulk, his scowling face. He stood close enough to feel Hank's breath on his face and said, "Your parents were addicted, workaholics or just took off."

"What?" Hank said.

"Control makes you feel safe. Thus your control issues."

Hank looked like he wanted to grab Jared by the neck and wring, but he simply jabbed Jared in the chest. "At this point, I'm rooting for your stalker."

Mave's hand whipped out and smacked Hank upside the head. Hank turned around and she motioned for him to move. She grabbed Jared's shoulder before he could retreat to the bedroom. Hank rubbed his ear, glaring at Jared.

"Hank and I need to discuss some things privately," Mave said.

"I'll grab breakfast somewhere," Jared said.

"No, no, no," Mave said, grabbing his shoulders and steering him. "Just go onto the balcony. I want to talk to you too. Okay?"

Jared allowed himself to be aimed towards the balcony. Mave gave his back a pat before she let him go. He picked his way through the maze of books and turned at the balcony door to see Mave smiling fake-pleasantly and Hank Hulking-out. Jared stepped into the full heat of summer and shut the door behind him. He could hear Mave and Hank get into it instantly, an angry murmur. The hum of traffic blocked out their words. Jared sat on the rusty, badly spray-painted furniture and took his cell out of his back pocket. Still nothing from Sarah.

Mave opened the balcony door. She brought him a glass of

orange juice and sat in the chair beside him. "You are most definitely Maggie's boy."

"He started it."

"So you used your powers of observation for evil."

"I don't like being cornered."

"Two of you put together don't make one of Hank's leg, so if he was a different person, you would be a stain on the floor, Jared."

Jared shrugged. If Hank had wanted to make Jared a stain, he would've done it by now.

Mave nudged his foot with hers. "You just need to get to know him."

"Wait," Jared said. "If he's your nephew, does that mean I have other aunts? Or uncles?"

"He's really a cousin of ours. But I changed his diapers and baby-sat him, so he's been calling me aunt since he was a fan of *Teletubbies*."

A picture formed in Jared's mind of Hank scowling at a TV screen while Tinky Winky, Laa-Laa, Dipsy and Po frolicked through grassy, bunny-filled meadows.

"Wow," Jared said.

"His grandmother is my aunt, and your mother's too, so she's your great-aunt. She lives in a seniors' complex eight blocks from here," Mave said. "He's on the graveyard shift so he can help her get to her medical appointments. He's not a bad guy."

"I never said he was."

"You don't have a poker face," Mave said.

Jared felt his temples begin doing a low-level throb.

She reached over and grabbed his hand. "I want your mother back in my life. I want you back in my life," Mave said. "I'm willing to grovel."

They watched the street. Jared tugged his hand a bit and she let him go.

"I can't afford insurance for the Vespa right now," Jared said.

"I can pay that," she said.

"Or parking. Or gas."

"Done."

"Mom loves hogs. She'd probably die of shame if her only son rode around in public on a Tonka toy. But if I sold it, that would hurt Sophia's feelings."

"We can store it in my parking garage," Mave said.

"Or you can use it until your car gets fixed."

Mave was momentarily taken aback, frowning, and then she chuckled. "I've never been manoeuvred into accepting a favour before. What an odd boy you are."

"Mom doesn't like feeling obligated. You have to make it seem she's doing you a favour."

Mave laughed.

Jared had an idea. "You should offer to take Hank—"

"Aunt Mave!" A little girl wearing a light-blue satin dress waved at them from the sidewalk. An older Native woman followed her, wheeling a shopping cart full of groceries.

"Oh, you look amazing, Princess Eliza!" Mave called.

"Did you remember my party?" the princess said.

"Wouldn't miss it. Do you need help setting up, Darlene?"

"That'd be a relief," the woman with the cart called up. "Olive was supposed to pick us up an hour ago."

"Kids, huh?" Mave said. "Hey, this is my nephew, Jared."

"Where's your costume?" Princess demanded. "It's a costume party. You have to wear one."

"Only the kids, sweetie," Darlene said.

"But it's a fancy party!"

"Do you have your keys?" Mave said.

"Somewhere in this mess," Darlene said. "Would you mind buzzing us in?"

"Sure," Mave said, popping up and heading inside.

"So you're Maggie's boy, huh?" Darlene called up to him.

"Yeah," Jared said.

"I haven't seen your mother since we were greenhorns together at BC Packers. Gosh, it's been ages. How's she holding up?"

"She's good."

"Say hi fo—"

"Are you coming to my party?" Princess interjected.

The buzzer bleated.

"Grab the door, sweetie," Darlene said.

"If you come," Princess said to Jared, "you have to dress up and give me a present."

"This bossy cow is my granddaughter, Eliza."

"Oh, Kokum," the little girl said. "It's rude to call people names."

They disappeared inside.

Mave rushed back to the balcony. "I need your help."

"What's up?"

"I forgot about Eliza's party. I was supposed to get the cake. Damn it. *Damn* it. I don't even have a gift." She texted someone and then tore back into the apartment. Jared followed her.

Hank knocked on the door as he came in. "What's the emergency?"

"Oh, Hank. Can you please find me a *Frozen* cake? Ideally one with Elsa on it."

"An ice cream cake?"

"*Frozen*, the Disney movie about the ice princess that Eliza loves. The one she watches over and over. You know, the one with 'Let It Go' and—"

"Got it," Hank said.

"I've got a couple of twenties here."

"I said I got it."

"Hank!"

"Stop pushing me, damn it," Hank said.

"You're a lifesaver. I owe you."

"Yeah, yeah." He slammed the door behind him.

Jared paused in front of the bunch of Mylar balloons still bobbing around in the corner. "Why don't you give her these balloons?"

"But those were a gift for you."

Jared grabbed the knot of ribbons to pull them down. "You know I'm almost eighteen, right? Balloons are great, but they aren't really my thing."

"You can give her the balloons if you like. Can you help us set up?"

"Sure."

"Oh, you are the sweetest, Jelly Bean."

"No one's called me that since I was in diapers."

"Privileges of being an aunt and your elder."

"You're not an elder—"

"See? You're sweet."

"And I'm not a baby. I would really appreciate if you didn't treat me like one."

"Poor Jelly Belly."

"Wow. I didn't think you could make it worse."

She laughed and led him down the stairs to the ground floor then down the hallway to the amenities room at the back of the building, where a propped door stood open. Katy Perry warbled about last Friday night from a tinny boom box. Princess bounced around a ring of chairs. Kokum Darlene banged around the kitchen to the left of the door, hunting through the cupboards. Princess came to a thundering stop, staring at the balloons.

"Happy birthday," Jared said.

Princess squealed, jumping up and down. Jared winced. He held out the knotted mass of ribbons. She snatched them. In a burst of manic speed, she circled the room with the balloons trailing behind her.

"And this is before she's had cake," Kokum Darlene said, standing in the kitchen entryway.

"Help me with the tables, Jel—Jared," Mave said.

They pulled the tables out of the corner and unfolded their legs, making tidy rows until the room was full. Mave gave them a scrub with disinfectant wipes. Princess settled in the middle of the room, carefully undoing the knot of ribbons and letting the freed balloons drift to the ceiling.

"This one's for Skylar, and this one's for Mary-Ellen, but I'm not giving one to Riley 'cause she's mean."

"Eliza," Kokum Darlene called from the kitchen. "Be nice."

"But she's mean!"

"Fill your heart with forgiveness, Eliza."

Princess glowered.

They unrolled a spool of blue plastic tablecloth over the tables and cut it to fit. Princess rummaged through the plastic bags by the door and pulled out tubes of silver, heart-shaped glitter, which she splashed over the tabletops. Jared unfolded and arranged chairs. Mave set out paper plates and plastic cups while Princess licked pieces of glitter and stuck them on her face.

At last Mave said, "We've got the rest," waving him off. "I'll come get you when the food's ready."

"Are you sure?"

She kissed his cheek. "Thank you."

He flopped on the couch in Mave's apartment. Crashpad had sent Jared pictures of the lame outfits his mom wanted him to wear to his next study group meeting on Tuesday.

Countdown to hell, Crashpad had captioned the picture.

Nothing from Sarah.

Jared had meant to make amends to Sarah. He could have chosen a better time to break up with her, any time actually, than the one he had. But Sarah wanted to trip the light fantastic, join the swarm of fireflies above her head and go God knows where. Jared wanted to stay in this world. He wanted a normal, sane life where ghosts did not stick their heads through the wall and make a face when they saw you on the couch.

"You're not even watching TV," Bathrobe said.

Don't engage, Jared told himself. Don't encourage.

"Other ghosts haunt this place," Bathrobe said. "And they aren't nice like me."

Jared went to the kitchen and opened the smudge drawer. But when he turned back to the living room, Bathrobe had disappeared. He lit a braid of sweetgrass anyway, waving it around the TV before leaving it to smoulder in the abalone shell, which he'd left on the TV stand. He settled back on the couch.

His messages and texts remained Sarah-less. He put an arm over his eyes. He wouldn't even know where to look, what part of Vancouver Island she'd disappeared from.

He must have fallen asleep, because the next thing he knew, Mave was sitting on the couch beside him.

"Eliza would really like it if you came to her party," Mave said.

"Who?"

"The princess you just gave your balloons to."

"Oh. I'm kinda tired."

"There's food."

He followed her down the stairs towards waves of laughter and screaming kids.

The adults were clustered in the corners of the amenities room. The kids had formed a running gang of assorted superheroes and princesses, and seemed to be playing a game that wasn't quite tag but involved running and bouncing the balloons tied to their wrists off each other's heads. Kokum Darlene had an electric fryer going and was cooking bannock, as she joked with another woman. She waved Jared over and handed a bannock to him.

"Jam's at the other end of the food table," she said.

"Thanks."

The food table was to the left of the door. If everyone had eaten, they hadn't made a dent in the piles. His stomach grumbled. Someone had brought deep-fried seaweed, which he hadn't had since he was a kid. He ignored the chow mein, hamburgers, lasagna, pork chops and seal, and loaded his plate with barbecued moose sausages and coho fillets. He added potato salad and some carrot slices and then globbed some jam on his bannock.

"Jared!"

He turned and looked down at a young woman in denim shorts and a Transformers tank top holding a toddler on her hip. She had her long hair in braids, tied off with pink elastics that matched her sneakers. "Hi," he said.

She reached up and squished his cheeks together. "Oh my gosh. Jelly Bean! What a big boy you are! Do you remember me? I used to babysit you."

"Sorry, I don't," Jared said.

"I'm Barbie," the woman said. "This is my baby, Rayray. My husband, Doug, is out for a smoke. I'll introduce you when he comes in." She put her hand on his jaw. "Oh, I love this squishy face. Don't you just love this squishy face?"

"Ow."

"Barbie founded the Urban Heiltsuk Traditional Dance Group," Mave said.

"We practise right here in the amenities room every Sunday," Barbie said. "Except for days like today when it's booked."

"Okay," Jared said.

They waited as if expecting him to volunteer or something. As the silence went on, he hunched his shoulders. He looked around.

Princess tugged at his shirt. "Kokum says I have to say thank you."

"You're welcome."

"Do you want to be the monster?"

"Um."

"He's eating, Eliza-cakes," Mave said.

"Bye!" she said, lifting her hem and racing after the other kids.

"Let's find a table," Mave said.

They headed to one by the door to the deck. Jared wouldn't have approached it by himself. Three Native guys, early twenties maybe, already sat there. One guy had a neck tattoo of a bear in stylized black-and-red Native formlines. The other two looked enough alike that they could be twins.

"Hi, boys," Mave said.

"Hi, Aunt Mave," they chorused.

"This is Jared."

"Hey," Jared said.

"These two rascals are the Starr brothers, Patrick and Robert."

"They're my brothers," Barbie said. "And they're staying with me. We're just up the street if you get lonesome and need some company."

"And this is Dakota," Mave said, "who's bunking in with Hank."

"Just Kota," the guy with the neck tattoo said.

"Aw, don't be like that," Robert said. "We like your stripper name."

"Shut up, Sponge," Kota said.

The Starr brothers snickered, and Kota hucked pieces of his bannock at them.

"I'm going for some fresh air," Kota said, pushing away from the table and getting up.

"Can I bum a smoke off you?" Sponge said.

"Go to hell," Kota said.

"Aw, did I hurt your widdle feelings?"

"Quit being a cheap fuck and buy your own smokes."

The Starr brothers exchanged glances and got up to check out the desserts. Mavis and Barbie sat, and Jared took the seat beside them, tuning out as they started talking about people from Bella Bella whom he didn't know. Jared didn't realize he was snarfing his food until he noticed his aunt and Barbie staring at him.

"It's good," Jared said.

"There's lots," Mave said. "Have all you want."

Jared cleared his plate and went back for seconds. A girl peeked at him from behind one of the couches. She'd bucked the princess trend and was full zombie, with an impressive makeup job on her cheek that showed yellowed bone, and a threadbare grey costume that floated when she moved. She held a wooden whistle to her lips and played random notes.

"*Walking Dead* fan?" Jared said.

She tooted and then hid behind the couch again.

"Me too," he said.

"Can you see her?" Princess said, coming up behind them.

"What?"

"Her name is Shu," Princess said.

"It's a good zombie costume," Jared said.

"I'm like Princess Elsa," Princess said.

"Yeah?"

"Are you one of— Hey!" Princess suddenly shouted. "Those are my presents! Mine! Get away!"

She ran off to confront the kid carrying off presents and Zombie Shu followed her. He loaded up on fried seaweed and more coho and walked back to the table, avoiding the kids flying around. As he sat down again, he saw Hank come in with the cake and be immediately swarmed by the kids. Kokum Darlene kissed him and took the box. Hank paused when he saw Jared, and then came and sat beside Mave.

"Hey, Jelly Bean," Mave said. "Hank is driving Kota to a youth meeting on Kingsway. Are you up for it?"

"A meeting?"

"An AA meeting."

"You know about . . . my meetings."

"I'm going to round up Kota," Hank said. He got up and left.

Once Hank was safely out of earshot, Jared said, "I'd rather find my own meetings."

"Hank's not going to the meeting, he's just driving you there. He thought it was a good idea if someone showed you around."

Jared did not believe Hank thought that. "I don't think it's a good idea."

"Just give him a chance."

"Mave . . ."

"Please."

Jared stuffed a few more mouthfuls of food in as Hank and Kota made their way back to them, saying their goodbyes.

"Are you coming?" Hank said.

"Sure," Jared said.

"My car's out front."

Kota flipped up his hoodie when they went outside, even though it was still hot. Kota took shotgun, bent down to get in, and then suddenly stopped and turned to the building.

"Are those my smokes?" Kota yelled.

Jared turned to see what Kota was mad about. One floor up, the Starr brothers were puffing on the balcony beside Mave's.

"Keep out of his stuff or find another place to Xbox," Hank called.

"Yes, Daddy," the brothers chorused.

"You owe me two fucking packs, Sponge," Kota said.

"Pat fucking smoked some too," Sponge said.

"Language," Hank said.

"Yes, Daddy," the brothers chorused again.

"I'm going to murder them," Kota said.

"Do it quietly and clean up after yourself," Hank said.

Hank's car had an obsessive neatness. The upholstery was vacuumed spotless. The plastic was spit-polished shiny. The carpet was protected with dirt-free all-weather mats. Kleenex boxes were tucked into each door holder and each tissue that poked out of the boxes was exactly the same length.

"Seat belt," Hank said, looking at Jared in the rear-view mirror.

"He won't move until you put it on," Kota said.

Jared pulled his seat belt down.

They drove in silence. Hank held the wheel like the car was going to run off the road if he let go of the ten o'clock position. Kota stared out the passenger window.

The sun tilted towards the horizon. The traffic had become even more snarled. At last they pulled up to a church and Hank shut off the engine. Jared was used to being the youngest person at any given meeting, but some of the people going in didn't look like they'd hit puberty yet.

"It's a closed meeting," Kota said.

Hank shrugged. "I'll wait."

"Don't."

"I'll pick you up after," Hank said.

"I'll grab a cab."

"What about the kid?"

"I'm not a kid," Jared said.

Kota hit the dashboard. "Fucking show me some trust, man.

And if you 'language' me again, I'm going to shove your fucking face through the fucking windshield."

"I'm hearing that Kota needs some space," Jared said.

They both turned to give him beady eyes.

"Thanks for the ride," Jared said, and quickly exited the Honda.

"Jared, wait for Kota!" Hank yelled as Jared shut the door.

"What, so you're hiring guards now?" Kota said.

"He's Mave's Jelly Bean, dumb-ass. If he gets hurt on our watch, we'll never hear the end of it. Make sure he doesn't get in trouble, and don't make him cry."

"You're leaving me to wipe his fucking ass? Nice."

"Uh, guys?" Jared said. "The car isn't soundproof."

As Hank drove off, Kota cupped his cigarette to light it and sucked in deep.

Jared crossed his arms and then uncrossed them, trying not to seem confrontational. "You don't have to babysit me because Hank says so."

"It's annoying as fuck, right?" Kota aimed his smoke upwards, watching it drift up. "I don't know about you, but I'm walking back."

"I'm heading in."

"Hold up for a second. I need a nic fix and if anything happens to you I'll have Hank *and* your aunt on my ass."

"It's a meeting, not a crack den."

"Sucks to be you."

"I'm almost eighteen. I can take care of myself."

"Almost eighteen." Kota snorted.

Jared tried to think of words that described the level of frustration he felt, but his brain decided it wanted to watch the traffic. Kota sucked his cigarette down to the filter in three deep inhales.

"So your mom's Maggie, huh?"

Jared studied Kota. "Yup."

"She was here last spring. I met her and Richie in a booze can in Surrey. They sold me some shit."

"Yeah?" Jared had wondered where they'd gotten to when they'd disappeared. They'd been gone for a few months.

"She's pretty hard-core."

Jared shrugged.

"Solid, though. I knew if things went haywire, she'd have my back."

"She would," Jared said. "And then she'd break a bottle in your face for looking at her wrong. Especially if you're her ungrateful kid who joined a sobriety cult."

Kota snorted and stomped out his cigarette. "Yeah. Well. Dad kicked the shit out of me when I told him I was gay and said he'd kill me if I ever came back. I had to move in with Hank's gran to finish high school."

"Sucks to be you," Jared said.

Kota gave him a friendly shove. "Come on. Let's get this show on the road."

16

HEX KEY THERAPY

Sarah walked out of the woods in a white dress, feet bare. Like a time-lapse movie, the sun whipped overhead and set. The moon rose equally fast and the stars wheeled through the sky. Shadows crawled through the underbrush behind her. Her eyes were all black like she was possessed. She smiled. Then Jared jerked awake, startled by a bang as loud as a gunshot. He woke in time to see a fuzzy shape disappearing from his bedroom window. Bat. Early morning bird. Extraterrestrials driving their spaceship under the influence. Some loud-ass thing.

He yawned. He must have dozed off while texting because his phone was dead when he picked it up off his chest. Sleep wouldn't come back. He pushed the quilt off. Brought his phone to the desk and plugged it in. One of the faces painted on the wall winked at him. He rubbed his eyes. The face was serene again, and he decided coffee was more important than brushing the gunk from his teeth.

In the hall, Jared stubbed his toes against a stack of books and hopped around, biting his lips. The apartment was like a cave spiked by stalagmites. He picked his way to the kitchen and opened the fridge. The meat compartment had no bacon, but a large, expensive bison roast was hovering on the edge of expiry. Jared pulled it out and gave it a rinse in the sink. He let it sit while he chopped then browned onions in a frying pan and hunted for a roasting pan. Even better, his aunt had a slow cooker.

He checked out her cupboards, pulling out ingredients for pot roast. All of her flours were gluten-free, which meant she was celiac or trendy. He decided on an all-purpose gluten-free flour blend and then salt and peppered the roast. He kneaded it automatically, then dusted it with flour. He grabbed a plate and used the edge to beat the flour into the roast.

"What're you doing?" Mave said, standing in the doorway with her eyeshades pushed up on her head. She was wearing a Canucks jersey and a pair of shorts.

"Sorry. Didn't mean to wake you."

Mave sat on a stool. "Why're you making supper at this ungodly hour?"

Jared shrugged. "Your roast is going to go bad."

"I meant to cook that sooner, then it got hot. You don't have to cook for me, Jared."

"I can't just sit around. I get restless." Jared moved the onions out of the frying pan and then seared the roast. He popped it in the slow cooker, topping it with the onions and some broth. "Potatoes?"

"I'm off white starches," she said. "Sweet potatoes are in the bin in that cupboard."

They were small, hard, organic sweet potatoes. She had blue heritage carrots in the vegetable bin, which would probably not hold their colour but would be a break from all the orange. He scrubbed and chopped and dumped them in, then put the lid on the slow cooker. He cleaned the coffee press and filled it with coffee. The kettle boiled in less than a minute. They watched the grounds colour the water a rich chocolate brown. He poured them both cups.

"Where'd you learn to cook?" she said.

"I had a neighbour who used to watch me. She loved to cook."

The sun broke over the mountains, washing the sky soft pink and blue, promising another scorcher. Jared sipped his coffee and considered his day. Probably another meeting to settle in. Maybe a jog to get the stiffness out.

Mave yawned. "You can't be getting much of a student loan if you're only going part-time."

"I'm going to get a job."

"Wouldn't it be better to focus all your attention on school? If you really want to get into that programme, I mean."

Jared shrugged.

"My writing grant is paying my rent and bills until January," Mave said. "But after that, I'll need a roommate."

Jared studied her, waiting for her to ask him to leave so she could rent his room.

She sipped her coffee. "I was your age when I went out on my own. Mother and I had . . . differences. I made mistakes I regret."

Jared studied his coffee cup.

Mave said, "What did the Heiltsuk band council say about funding?"

"Mave."

"Did you even talk to them? To Bernie, the education co-ordinator?"

"They don't know me."

"Jared."

"It's . . . I dunno."

"You'll get funding, Jared. Maybe not while you're upgrading, but next year." She reached over to touch his hand. "You could stay here rent-free and then, next year, when you get funding, you can pay rent, okay? I wouldn't have to look for a roommate. So you'd actually be helping me. No obligations at all." She grinned. "Think about it."

She grabbed two eggs from the fridge door and peeled them. She handed him one. They'd been boiled a while ago and had a tell-tale black ring around the yolk. He salted and peppered heavily.

She raked her hair with her fingers. "I'm going to do a load of darks. Do you have anything?"

"That'd be great," he said.

Jared went to the bedroom and emptied his jean pockets. He added his T-shirt and socks, but couldn't make himself put his under-wear in the mix; he'd give them a scrub when she was out. He tucked them under his backpack. One of the faces on the wall opened its mouth. Jared moved in to stare, and then shook his head. Lots of fluids today, he thought. Maybe get his eyes checked. He carried his laundry out to Mave.

When she came back, they sat at the dining table and surfed, but it was a holiday and no one was posting anything interesting. Jared felt cooped up. He didn't want to spend the whole morning inside.

"Going for a jog," he announced.

"Mmm," Mave said, staring at her screen. "Have fun."

He threw on some shorts and a T-shirt and sprinted down Graveley Street, which slanted downhill away from Commercial Drive. The streets were lined with small bungalows in between large, older apartment buildings. He hit a busy intersection and turned right, planning on making a large square route. But then he found a park with giant maple trees. He liked the big, leafy trees and the spotty grass, the red swings and the sunny sky. He thought about doing some crunches, and lay down. Then he put his hands behind his head and looked through the branches and sighed. He hadn't lived in a city before and he thought he could put up with it for school, but he had never expected to like it. Maybe in December, when it was dark and grey and had rained non-stop for a few months, he'd sour on it.

The jog back was all uphill, and he slowed to a brisk walk. He yawned and wasn't sure if he was going to shower or soak. He turned the corner onto Graveley and stopped dead.

David's silver Lexus was parked directly in front of the Lu'ma apartment building. David held his phone up, probably recording Jared. He wished he wasn't standing there like a dummy. David started his car, signalled and drove away.

Move, Jared told himself as David drove past him, smiling and giving a happy wave.

Fucker, Jared thought.

Shaky anger. All the emotions. Had David been there the whole time and Jared had missed him? A big fat middle finger of an appearance. *You and your Facebook drama. Ha. This is what I think of that.*

His feet finally unstuck from the spot where he'd been caught like a mouse on a glue trap. He fought the urge to run back to the safety of the apartment, made himself walk like a normal person.

"Was that your stalker?" someone said.

Jared looked up. Above the entrance, just to the right, Kota leaned against the balcony railing, pulling a drag off his cigarette. Because, of course, nothing completed the whole embarrassing scene like a witness.

"He was across the street until you ran by him," Kota said. "He moved his car and then waited for you to notice him."

Jared couldn't think of anything to say, couldn't make words form.

"That kind of stupid gets you stomped," Kota said.

"It's early," Jared said. "I've only had one coffee."

"His stupidity," Kota said. "Not yours. Between Hank and your mom, that dude's going to end up an organ donor."

"Amen," Jared said.

"I'm doing a meeting in an hour. Are you in?" Kota said.

"Sure."

He took the stairs two at a time. The apartment door was open. His aunt had left a Post-it sticker on his laptop: *Off with Justice! Back for supper.*

His phone buzzed beside his laptop. Message from Unknown Number: *Great seeing you again! We'll chat soon. I owe you, Jared. I'm going to pay you back every single thing you and your mom gave me.*

He meant to take a shower, meant to change his clothes. He started when he heard a knock on the front door. The clock on the wall said an hour had passed, but he couldn't remember it. He was standing over his laptop with his phone in his hands. He had no idea how David had his new number. The sweat had cooled and dried on his body. His eyes felt dry. He blinked and blinked.

The knocking became pounding. Kota called, "Jared! Shake a leg!"

"Coming!" Jared said.

Kota had shared at the meeting, and now, as they walked back to the apartment building, Jared didn't know what to say. When he saw people in Kitimat that he knew from AA meetings, it was weird because you knew things about them, things they probably hadn't even shared with their partners, but you had to act like you didn't. In a small town, though, you had to do that with everyone. Kota was a stranger, so to speak. Jared now knew that Kota was feeling like a frequent flyer, fifth white chip in two years, fifth go at sobriety, fifth 90 in 90, the initial ninety days of at least one AA meeting a day. But all his friends were texting him, calling him, inviting him out to the parties. He resented all the fun he was missing.

Hank's balcony door was open and they could hear ominous music, sounds of rapid machine-gun fire and then hoots.

"Just what I need," Kota muttered. "Heckle and Jeckle. Hank says he doesn't want them around, but he bought an Xbox he doesn't play and stocked the kitchen with Pat and Sponge's favourite snacks."

"You can hang at Mave's place."

"Thanks, but she's got the whole crazy hoarder thing going."

"Yeah. Well, if you've got nothing to do later and no plans for supper, I'm making a pot roast. It should be ready by six, maybe seven tonight."

Kota side-eyed him. Jared kept his expression as blank as he could, knowing what it felt like to have someone pity you.

Jared stepped over Mave's shoes and came to a stop at the end of the hallway. Bathrobe hovered near the TV.

"You can't get rid of me that easy," Bathrobe said, crossing his arms over his chest.

Jared got a bundle of sage from the kitchen. Bathrobe sighed heavily, disappearing through the wall. Jared left the sage burning in the living room while he went into his bedroom and checked his phone. No messages. Not a single word.

He felt strange. Disconnected. He knew he was supposed to be feeling something, especially since he knew David knew where he lived.

The ghost walked through the closed door of the bedroom. Jared was taken aback because the air still smelled like sage but the ghost seemed to ignore it.

"I wasn't even bothering you!" the ghost said.

Jared dug out his iTouch, stuck in his earbuds, cranked his tunes and closed his eyes. When he opened them, the ghost was gesturing wildly, mouth moving like he was shouting.

He went to the kitchen and grabbed a glass. Turned on the tap and filled it with water. He glanced around. No yakky ghosts. He washed the dishes. He found a garbage bag and emptied all the leftovers. Took the garbage to the Dumpster.

When he got back, the ghost stood forlornly in the living room. Jared ignored him, sorting the bulk items on the counter into the cupboards. Behind a monster box of lentils he found a DeWalt twenty-volt MAX Li-ion drill. A zip-lock bag of bits and tips was taped to the grip, each bit and tip with a handwritten label taped to it. His dad was a diehard DeWalt guy. Jared pulled off his earphones so he could hear the drill whirr. The battery indicator said it had a ninety-seven-percent charge.

The ghost took his fingers out of his ears. "Are you done?"

Jared pumped the drill, searching the apartment for something to try it on.

"You're such an ass," the ghost said.

Jared remembered the stack of unassembled bookcases. The job was mind-numbingly dull but required enough focus to be distracting.

He cleared an assembly spot, grabbed one of the boxes and then carefully used a paring knife to slice the tape open. He grabbed a stack of bowls from the kitchen, a Post-it pad and a marker. Jared studied the parts lists. The only written instructions numbered the fiddly parts and used the numbers to tell you which part went where. The rest of the steps were depicted by pictograms.

"All I want to do is watch the new series," the ghost said, parking himself on a nearby stack of books. "They say it's like the old *Doctor Who*. Scary. And this Doctor isn't some pretty boy. He's an actor. Come on, Jared. It's not like I'm asking for a beating heart, is it?"

Jared lined up the parts in a tidy row. He pulled off all the plastic and Styrofoam, and separated the recyclables, which went onto the balcony, from the garbage, which went by the door.

"Do you want me to beg?" Bathrobe said. "Please. Please, Jared. Pretty pleeeeeeease."

Ten boxes equalled ten bookcases, which looked like they would neatly wrap around the living room Jared took one of the boards and laid it along the wall, wishing he had a pencil, eyeballing the measurements.

The ghost said, "You're a very cruel person, Jared Martin."

Jared laid out the pieces on the floor in order of assembly. He worked steadily through the afternoon. He spent most of his time shoving books out of the way so he could lift the bookcases over them and plant them in position against the walls.

The box on the bottom of the pile showed a picture of a desk that attached to the bookcase. Jared was studying the parts list when someone cleared his throat. He assumed it was the ghost, so he ignored him.

"Hey," Kota said.

Jared glanced up. Kota and Hank were staring at him from the hallway. "Hi."

"Is dinner ready?" Kota said.

"Help yourself," Jared said.

"You did this?" Hank said.

"Santa Claus and his elves dropped by."

Hank studied the bookshelves, giving one of them a shake. "You should brace these."

"I don't know where she wants them," Jared said. "And I don't have a stud finder."

"I don't see where else she could put them," Hank said.

"Hey," Kota said from the kitchen, "this ain't bad."

"Yeah, it's a good cut," Jared said.

"Were you born in a barn?" Hank said. "Get a plate!"

Kota banged through the cupboards.

Hank and Kota ate at the counter. As Jared worked on the final piece of the bookshelves, his phone buzzed in his back pocket. Text from Sarah: *You still hum like power lines. I hear you everywhere I go.*

The feeling of detachment evaporated. Everything hurt, all at once.

Where r u? Jared texted back. He got up, went into the bedroom and waited for her to respond. The cursor blinked and blinked.

"I'm not the one haunting this room," Bathrobe said, peering in from the door. "I'm the good guy."

Jared pretended to scroll through his messages.

Kota walked through the ghost, sucking sauce off his fingers. He stopped. Eyeballed the walls with a grimace. "What a fucking freak show."

"It's okay," Jared said.

"Dude, it's right up there with clowns painted by serial killers."

Then Hank walked through Bathrobe, who sighed heavily and blinked out of existence. Hank stood beside Kota and examined the room.

Jared tried not to be annoyed. "Please. Come in."

"Edgar was a troubled guy," Hank said.

Kota snorted. "Total whack-job."

"Is the stuff by the door for the Dumpster?" Hank said.

"I can bring it down," Jared said.

"We got it," Hank said.

"I love the way you volunteer me for shit," Kota said.

"I've got the recyclables on the balcony," Jared said. "Is there a place for them?"

"I'm taking ours to the recycling depot tomorrow," Hank said.

"Thanks," Jared said.

"See?" Hank said to Kota. "It's that simple. That's how you say thanks."

"Suck-up," Kota said, giving Jared a shove.

Hank shoved Kota, and then Kota shoved him back. He could hear them laughing as they gathered up the crap in the hallway. Pat and Sponge's voices joined in from the hallway.

The ghost wasn't in the living room or the kitchen. The slow cooker was splattered where Kota had simply pulled out some of the meat, and he'd dripped the sauce all over the kitchen floor. Jared plated the roast and dug out the vegetables, automatically arranging them.

He kept checking his phone. He willed Sarah to text him, to say more.

"Hel-lo," Mave sing-songed as she walked in. "Someone forgot to close the door— Oh, my God."

She dropped her bag and put her hands to her heart.

"Mave?" Jared said.

She was still for so long he thought she was having a heart attack. Jared put his plate down and shoved his hands in his pockets. "They were just lying there," he said.

Mave came over, wrapped her arms around him and rocked them both. "It's exactly the way I pictured it. Exactly. It's like you read my mind."

"Okay. Glad you like it," he said. The hug went on and on until he finally said, "I'm really uncomfortable right now."

Mave was giving him quick, light pecks all over his face when all the guys came back. They chorused, "Aw."

She stepped back, holding on to his hand, while she wiped her nose with the back of her other one. "Isn't he sweet?"

"Vancouver is a high-risk earthquake zone," Hank said. "We need to brace the bookcases."

"Yes," Pat said, "because when the big one hits, we'll all be concerned about Aunt Mave's bookcases."

"They could fall on her," Hank said.

"Hank, we'll be busy drowning in the Pacific."

But Hank went back to his place for his stud finder and a step-ladder. Mave retrieved her good knives and carved the roast, while the Starr brothers rummaged through the fridge for drinks, shoving each other. Mave reached over them and closed the fridge door. Kota went for seconds, hopping up to sit on the counter, holding his plate close to his mouth and shovelling the food in. Hank returned, and Jared offered to do the measurements for the braces, but both Mave and Hank ignored him. Hank set up his stepladder and began pencilling in stud locations while Mave dusted and cheerfully ordered and reordered her piles of books. The ghost emerged from the wall. He walked over to the TV and sighed. He looked longingly at the recliner. Jared loosened the drill chuck and was going to put in a bit when Hank stepped in front of him and put his hand out.

"That's okay," Jared said. "I got it."

"You were standing there staring at nothing," Hank said. "I think you're done."

"I'm fine."

"Oh, Jelly Bean, give him the drill," Mave said.

"But—"

"Go eat," Hank said, taking the drill from him.

"Mmm," Pat mumbled through a full mouth. "You're going to make someone a damn fine househusband, Jelly B."

"Up yours," Jared said.

"Chew with your mouth closed, Patrick," Hank said.

"You aren't the boss of me," Pat said.

Hank lowered his head and gave Pat a flared-nostril squint, his enraged-bull-about-to-charge look. The brothers subsided until Hank turned back to the bookshelves. Then they rolled their eyes in unison. Kota grinned.

"Inconsiderate Neanderthals," the ghost said, popping like a grumpy soap bubble.

After they'd demolished the pot roast, the guys hinted loudly that they'd like dessert, but Mave only had leftover ice cream cake from Princess's birthday party. Hank braced the bookcases, lined up the shelves and then forced the other guys to drag the recyclables to his car. After they did that, the guys retreated to Hank's place without Hank. Soon gaming sounds were coming through the living room wall.

Hank and Mave didn't seem bothered by the noise. They decided that, rather than simply going alphabetical or Dewey Decimal, they'd use a sliding scale of book usage based on Mave's height: the middle shelves would be reserved for her most current research and favourite authors; the lower shelves for resource material, which tended to be heavier and oversized; and, finally, the upper shelves could house light reading. Each shelf would then be alphabetical, by author's last name. It sounded complicated. Jared suggested that they put everything onto the shelves and deal with it later. Hank and Mavis both paused to consider him, then exchanged a look.

As they sorted through the piles of books, they had a weird shorthand Jared couldn't break:

"So?"

"I dunno."

"Yeah?"

"Better."

Mave wrapped Jared in another hug and told him to go to bed. Please. Jared sat down, annoyed, and was trying to form enough words to tell her off when he realized he was face down in the couch. He felt Mave tuck a blanket around his legs. Or at least he assumed it was Mave; Hank didn't seem like the blanket-tucking type.

Jared drifted, comfortable but too wired to fall completely asleep. The stacks of books on the floor slowly migrated to the bookshelves, and after a gap in time Mave vacuumed some expensive-looking rugs that had been hidden beneath the stacks.

When she was done, Mave nudged Jared awake. She put a throw pillow under his head and then perched on the arm of the couch. Hank brought Mave a glass of red wine. Their conversation turned to politics and what they thought of the recent fracture in the Assembly of First Nations and who they thought had the best chance of bringing the organization back together. Jared thought about going to bed, but he was too tired to move.

"All your base are belong to us!" Sponge roared the victory chant of *Zero Wing*, a throwback to the ancient nineties, followed by boos from his brother and Kota.

"Shut it down!" Hank yelled.

"Yeah, yeah, yeah," they chorused.

"Idiots," Hank said, getting up. "I should get Heckle and Jeckle to put their junk food away or they'll be covered in flies by morning. Night, Aunt Mave."

"Night, Henry-kins."

Hank stomped down the hallway and out the door. Mave gave Jared's shoulder a shake.

"Hey, Jelly Bean," Mave said.

"Hmm," he said.

"Thank you for putting my bookcases together."

"Mmm."

"Sweet dreams."

He heard her rummaging around the bathroom and then he heard a bang. His eyes opened. A part of the floor slithered. The apartment lights were off and he couldn't hear his aunt anymore. He sat up, groggily wondering how long he'd been asleep. The sky had a faint pearl-grey shimmer where it met the mountains, but it was still summer, so that could mean it was late or early. In the corner of the room, in the darkness, he felt something watching him.

That's paranoia, he told himself.

He lifted his feet off the floor, feeling silly doing it but doing it anyway, tucking his legs under him on the couch.

Maybe I'm dreaming, he thought.

As his eyes adjusted, he thought he could make out a figure crouching in the corner, a slightly darker shadow that shifted, studying him the way he was studying it.

A bang at the front window drew his attention. His eyes slid off what they saw. On the other side of the pane, a face, a crazy-ass bodiless face with twisted lips and boggled, excited eyes, flew loopy dips and zipped up and sideways like a hummingbird. Jared decided that he was stuck in a weird dream, even as the head banged itself against the window some more.

Jared stood, and the head paused, hovering, and then dropped sharply out of sight. He walked to the window and looked down, expecting to see it splattered on the concrete deck below. The head peered up at him, shyly rising like a balloon until they were eye to eye. It was the size of anyone's head, a normal adult, but its features were warped into a grimace on one side and a goofy smile on the other. It had dark-red skin and green lips. If it had wings, they were moving too fast for him to see.

"Hey," Jared said.

The head bobbled back and forth, like it was waving "hi" back.

So. This is what it felt like to go insane. Surprisingly comfortable. Other than feeling like he was being watched. The head plunged and banged at the bottom corner of the window, like it wanted to get in.

From the corner of his eye, Jared saw the shadow of a man crawl into the wall. His mouth went dry. The hair on his arms and the back of his neck went stiff and his heart hammered in his chest.

I can hear you, a familiar voice said inside his head.

His biological father, Wee'git, the Trickster, who hadn't spoken to him since the incident at the cave with the otters. Sure, that time Wee'git had saved his life. But before that, he'd also discovered, Wee'git had been a witness to every shitty moment in Jared's life and had not lifted so much as a feather to help. Jared swallowed. *Stay out of my head.*

Listen, you giant headache—you're somewhere in East Van. You're frightened and you're broadcasting feedback screams on all frequencies. Way to call attention to yourself. See if I save your ungrateful ass again when something dangerous comes to eat you.

Jared retreated to his bedroom and turned the lights on. He sat on the bed, breathing deeply and slowly. The flying head peeked in, pressing its lips against the glass and blowing out its cheeks. The floating heads painted on the walls started tumbling in the painted fog, rolling themselves up and down, flying through the painted city on the floor and billowing fog across the ceiling. Jared burst into laughter, part hysterical, part surprised. He lay down, watching the heads float like mutant goldfish. When the one outside the window dropped out of sight, the painted heads snapped back into place, frozen and quiet. The solar system revolved around the light fixture, creaking rustily.

I am so cleansing this apartment, Jared thought. Even the dust mites are going to choke on smudge smoke.

17

FIRST DAY OF CLASS

Thankfully, the heat wave broke as rain came down in buckets all night and into the morning, making Mave's offer to scooter him to campus null and void. Jared SkyTrained, then caught the 130 bus to BCIT. He hung on to a pole as the bus rounded a corner. He kept an eye on traffic through the window at the back of the bus, but no silver Lexus trailed them. At the next stop, a black jaguar slid up the steps and brushed Jared's leg as it passed by. The jaguar wore a collar of hammered gold coins that matched its golden eyes. It took a space by the back doors and looked up at the advertisements. No one seemed especially disturbed by the jungle cat, and Jared had decided to ignore the supernatural creatures that ignored him. Pick your battles. Live and let live.

After he arrived on campus, he found his building and sat in the back of the classroom. He set up his laptop, got his textbook ready, and rummaged through his pack for his notepad and pen. While he was waiting, he wrote Granny Nita. He'd meant to do it earlier:

Dear Granny Nita,

Hi from Vancouver. Hope you're okay and your case is going well. I'm sitting in my first class as I write this. Things didn't work out with my friend, so I'm staying with Mave until I find my own place. Wee'git's in Van somewhere. Any tips?

Bye, Jared.

He scrolled through his phone.

God has a really twisted sense of humour, Crashpad texted along with a selfie of himself with a girl in French braids and a sweater vest from his home-school study group. They smiled, making their fingers into peace signs.

Hey, Sonny, his mom had texted him earlier. *Richie'z having family drama. Thinking of a road trip.*

While Jared was texting his mom and Crashpad back, fellow students filed into the class and sat in clumps avoiding the front row of seats. Jared was not about to tell his mom and Crashpad about the ghostapalooza at Mave's place. Crashpad would think he was nuts and his mom would grind on about how she'd warned him he'd need to learn protection spells.

A Native guy sat down in the seat one over. He wore an oversized baseball cap and put his feet up on the chair in front of him. He had long, wavy hair and a T-shirt with a picture of a beaded breastplate. "Are you nish? Anishnabe?"

"Excuse me?" Jared said.

"Are you a skin?"

"What?"

"Pfft," the guy said. "Don't even know what you are, man."

"He's asking if you're First Nations," a bleached-blond chick said from the seat in front of Long Hair, not looking up from her cell. She was chubby and had ink from her wrists to her neck and across her chest. Tattooed angel wings sprouted from her shoulder blades.

"Oh," Jared said. "Heiltsuk."

"I don't know that one," the guy said.

"Island in BC, doorknob," the chubby blonde explained. "I'm Tahltan," she said to Jared. "Evan here is from Winnipeg."

"North Eeeeeend."

"Please," Tahltan said. "Your dad's a chiropractor. You're about as 'hood as me."

"Jared," Jared said.

"Evan."

"Rayne," Tahltan said. "Not the fucking weather; not the fucking queen. R-a-y-n-e."

"Okay," Jared said.

"Don't mind her," Evan said. "She on the rag."

"By your fucked-up attitude, you're always on the rag," Rayne said.

"Pfft."

"Well, hi," Jared said.

"This is bullshit," Rayne said. "I got a B-plus and I still have to retake this shitty course."

"I scraped by with a C," Jared admitted.

"First-timer," Evan said. "Biology virgin."

"Ev, you're gross."

"Heh, heh," Evan said.

"I take it you guys know each other," Jared said.

"Not on purpose," Rayne said.

Struan Moore wandered into class in a blazer and jeans, putting his briefcase on the large desk at the front of the room. He'd tamed his hair by cutting it very short. He printed his name on the dry-erase board, scanned the class and gave Jared a wave. Rayne turned to study him. Evan put his feet down.

"Welcome," Struan said. "I'm your professor, Struan Moore. Call me Struan. Professor Moore is my mother."

No one laughed.

"Tough crowd," Struan said. "Let's get started, shall we? This is your syllabus. Jared, can you help me pass these around, please?"

Rayne and Evan side-eyed him as he walked down to the front and took the stack of papers from Struan, who gave him a wide, happy smile. Jared shrugged and said hey. Evan made a kissy face when he handed him a syllabus.

"Suck-up," Rayne muttered.

Awesome, Jared thought.

Instead of roll call, Struan asked if they could all introduce themselves. Jared mumbled his name and nation and figured he was done.

"And his aunt is Mavis Moody!" Struan added. "The poet! She wrote *Landscape Porn*. Has anyone read it? Anyone? Well, it's life-changing. It's amazing. You have to read it. I could sit here all day and talk about it, but I'll let Jared fill you in if you want to know more."

Jared felt himself turning violently red.

At the break, Struan came up the aisle and sat on Jared's desk. "Hey, buddy. How are you?"

"Good," Jared said.

"How's your aunt?"

"She's good."

"Did she mention me?"

"Dude," Jared said, "I'm, this is, um . . ."

"I'm being that guy, aren't I?"

"You know . . . I mean . . . no."

"She said she had a great time, but she hasn't returned any of my calls. Or texts. Or e-mails. Sorry, sorry. I'm not trying to put you in the middle."

"I appreciate that."

"Well."

"I'm going to hit the head," Jared said.

"You do that," Struan said.

In the bathroom, Jared leaned against the counter, googled the course lists on his phone to check if there were any other biology sections open. He put his name on a wait-list. He sighed, checked the time and then went back to class. Struan kept trying to make eye contact through the lecture. Jared buried his head in his laptop.

Struan waited for him at the end of the class, rocking on his heels as the other students filed out. Jared packed everything into his backpack slowly, deliberately. He glanced up. Struan smiled a tight smile.

"See you next week," Struan said.

"Later," Jared said.

Rayne and Evan were smoking at the bus stop. They stopped talking to watch Jared approach. He could feel the dirty looks sticking to him. Fortunately, they caught a different bus. He hunched into his hoodie. He'd expected the good weather to hold and hadn't brought a decent rain jacket. First things first, he thought. Let's hop off the crazy train.

He bought loose-leaf tobacco from a place on Oak Street and then took a bus out to the University of British Columbia. He guessed the parks around there wouldn't be as busy as downtown Stanley Park, so he'd have some privacy. He followed the map on his phone app to one that promised it had old cedars.

Jared was going to hit up the first random tree he came across. He found himself on a trail. Rain dripped through the treetops. An occasional jogger brushed past him. Birds moved in the underbrush. He hitched his backpack farther up his shoulder. The trail was so wet it squished under his feet.

His hoodie was soon soaked, and he was chilled but not freezing. He wasn't drawn to any tree in particular. He didn't hear voices. No finger poked through the clouds and guided him.

Some dudes in rain jackets passed him, carrying a couple of cases each of beer. Jared turned onto a path with signs that pointed to Wreck Beach. Near some stairs that went down endlessly, an old, old red cedar shimmered. The dudes had passed the tree without reacting, so he knew he was the only one who could see it, and he had never seen anything like it.

The tree didn't speak to him, though, and he was grateful for that. The weirdness level was high enough with the cedar being there and not there. As magically ignorant as he was, he knew that this was where he had to get his branches. He let his backpack slide off his arm. He brought the tobacco out and laid it down, introducing himself and making an offering. Normally, he would have felt silly explaining his ghost problems to a tree, but here, with this tree, he knew it was the thing to do, and so he did. When he'd finished, he went home and again he smudged, this time with the help of the ancient cedar.

Mave made grilled cheese sandwiches and tomato soup for dinner. They ate at the dining table, ignoring each other.

"We need to get you new clothes," she said when they were done eating.

"On it," Jared said. "I'm going down to Value Village."

"Admirable," Mave said. "I respect your commitment to re-consumerism."

"It's more of a commitment to my bank balance."

"I have a counter-proposal."

"A what?"

"Why don't you come to my shop? I could get you a discount."

"No."

"All the clothes are locally made," Mave said. "No sweatshop children. Fair—"

"No."

"Jared." She peered at him over her glasses. "My stubborn little bean."

"I don't like being dressed. I don't like it when Mom does it."

"Think about it," she said. "Please?"

"Okay," Jared said.

"It's extra sage-y in here today," Mave said. "Were you smudging again? How much grounding do you need?"

"Sorry."

"No, no. Just wondering how your first day of classes went."

"Well, Struan had a wonderful time and he wanted me to tell you that."

"Hmm," Mave said. "He's texted me twenty-seven times. The voice mail is full. Facebook pokes and comments all over my wall. If carrier pigeons were available, I'd have a flock pooping on my balcony right now."

"Can you guys leave me out of your relationship?"

"We had one dinner and danced a bit. That's hardly a grand affair."

"Just sayin'."

"Noted. Would you consider taking a look at the clothes?"

"No."

"I could strangle you."

"As long as you don't dress me, go for it."

She gave an exasperated sigh. "Fine. By the way, your roast last night was excellent. Have you considered becoming a chef?"

Jared shrugged. "Too much drama."

"Sweetie," Mave said. "Health services are all about the drama."

"Not the technicians."

"Maybe not the lab work. But any time you deal with people, especially sick people, you have drama."

"Mave."

"I'm not allowed to have an opinion?"

"You're not allowed to beat me over the head with your opinion."

She laughed. "You're surprisingly witty."

"Um, thanks."

"Sorry. I was raised with backhanded compliments and can't seem to break the habit. I meant to say you're funny." She went back to her laptop and he went back to his cell.

The ghost in the bathrobe walked through the wall as if Jared hadn't spent an entire afternoon trying to ghost-proof the apartment. Jared gritted his teeth and wondered if he'd done something wrong with the warding or if it was just his supreme lack of magical ability. His mom would not be surprised. Embarrassed, maybe. Bathrobe pointed to the TV and then lifted the sleeve of his bathrobe and impatiently tapped his watch. Jared gave his head a little shake. Bathrobe mimed despair, falling to his knees and raising his hands like a preacher.

"Khan!" he shouted. "Ahan, an, an!"

"What are you staring at?" Mave turned her head and scanned the room.

"Just thinking," Jared said.

"About?"

"You know, stuff."

"I'm missing season one, episode twenty-two, 'Space Seed,'" Bathrobe said as he got up and wandered over, "with Ricardo Gonzalo Pedro Montalbán y Merino, the first appearance of Khan. Come on, Jared, it's eight on my top ten original season *Star Trek*s!"

Jared bent his head over his phone and typed: *Emote somewhere else, Captain Kirk.*

"Yeah, you're a riot," Bathrobe said, peering over his shoulder at the screen. "A real frakken' comedian."

18

HOLE

On Thursday, Intro to Physics was a large class with a professor who wasn't dating Jared's aunt and so didn't try to make awkward small talk. Their first assignment was about roller coasters. Random, Jared thought. He looked up the lab schedule and chose one on the same day as the physics class so he wouldn't have to make extra trips out. He signed up for a biology lab three hours after his Tuesday class. He wished he knew which lab Rayne and Evan were going to so he could avoid them. He'd really thought college would be less like high school. He wanted to print off some resumés in the library but needed to buy a swipe card first. When he went to the ATM to get money, he noticed his bank account was down to double digits.

Ping. Sophia texted: *You're welcome. It seemed like a waste to just leave it in the garage. Enjoy.*

Ah, Jared thought, the Vespa.

He could hit Sophia up for money and she would give it to him, but then he'd feel like a heel and she'd likely stop responding to his texts. Which would be a simple way to kill their relationship. His mom kept telling him Sophia was someone he should be more careful around.

YOLO, Jared thought. He'd done the things he'd done. You learned and you moved on. Or you lied to yourself and kept repeating the same old, same old. He had a hard time distinguishing between the two. They sounded a lot alike in his head.

The balcony was one of Jared's favourite places in the apartment, even on rainy, miserable days like this one. None of the ghosts liked it here and he could still get a wi-fi signal, but he could also people-watch. He wasn't expecting David—he had to have a job, right? a family? hobbies?—but Jared scanned the street as soon as he sat on the rusty iron patio chair. If the weather warmed up again, he'd borrow a grinder and redo the set. At least prime it before winter rusted the legs completely through.

The apartment face was cubed, with the living room sections jutting out so you couldn't see around them to the other tenants' patios. Jared could smell Kota's cigarettes, but he couldn't see him. If Kota wasn't calling out hello, Jared didn't want to barge into his cousin's alone time. Kota said the Starr brothers escaped their sister's basement suite (and her kids) by hanging out at Hank's place. They gamed with headphones when Hank was sleeping, but Kota was left with his bedroom and the balcony to do his thinking.

Jared took a deep breath and texted: *Hey, Mom. Having a lil ghost issue here. Warding didn't work. Can u walk me thru it again?*

Well, well, well, she wrote back immediately. *Mr. Fancy College Education can't handle a simple lil ghost. Ha. Told u so. Knew u'd cum crawling 2 me 4 advice.*

The gloating went on for the next few texts. Jared sipped his coffee. Information. It's all just information. I'm not annoyed about hearing information.

After ragging on him forever before outlining the basics of warding again, she asked: *u ok if I go wit Richie?*

The road trip to his hometown, she meant. *Paint wit all the colours of the wind,* he texted.

Sumtimes I wanna smack the sarcasm outta ur blowhole so much it hurtz.

Mommy dearest u put the crank in our family car crankshaft.

Sonny boy that makes u the shaft.

Imma complicated man & no1 unnerstands me but my momma.

Ur 2 old 2 b sucking my tit this hard.

TTYL Hallmark.

TTFN lil bastard.

Jared stared at his phone, wondering if Sarah was okay. Then he texted, *Ur mom wuz here. Wants u 2 no shez worried.*

Blinking cursor, blinking cursor. Maybe her mom wasn't her trigger the way his was for him. Maybe Sarah had mastered detachment, had left her cares and worries in her rear-view mirror. Hasta la vista, bitches.

Mave's freezer was full to bursting. At the very top she had three organic free-range turkeys. Their stickers said they were eighty dollars each and had been packaged six months ago. You could keep a frozen turkey for three years, Mrs. Jaks had told him, but past seven months the flavour suffered. They were pretty scrawny for the price, more like gangly chickens than the traditionally chunky gobble-gobbles. He pulled out two and brought them to the kitchen. He cleared out a bunch of wilted veggies from the lower fridge shelf and put the turkeys in to defrost. He chopped up the salvageable vegetables and made a pot of chili.

"Now what are you cooking?" Mave said, coming into the kitchen. She had her noise-cancelling headphones dangling around her neck. She squinted over her half-moon reading glasses as she lifted the lid and sniffed the contents.

"Hey, Mave. How's writing?"

"You aren't my personal chef," she said. "You know that, right?"

"I'm procrastinating. I don't get my physics homework."

"Sorry, Jelly Bean. Can't help you with physics."

"YouTube solves everything."

Mave made herself tea, retreated to the bedroom, where she was writing, and came out a couple of hours later to grab a bowl of chili. She nodded at him and then disappeared again. He flipped through instructional videos and landed on one where the guy wore an Einstein wig and punctuated his lecture with fireworks.

"How can you be having problems with Newtonian physics?" Bathrobe said. "That's like having problems with the alphabet."

Jared could feel a chill where the ghost was standing close to him. By the time he walked into the kitchen, opened the drawer with the sage and sweetgrass, and then turned around, the living room was empty again.

Justice dropped in with fresh bread, hot from the oven. She brought it into the kitchen, attacked it with a bread knife and then handed Jared a couple of slices slathered in margarine. He hopped up on the counter as she wrapped the loaf in a plastic bag. Justice said, "Is Maamaan writing?"

"Yeah, she's been going hard since this morning."

"Thank God. This is her first go at a novel and she's been a bear."

"Want some chili?"

"Is it veggie?"

"Mostly."

"Sorry, I don't eat meat. Thank you for the offer, though. You're very thoughtful."

Jared shrugged. "It's just stuff from the fridge."

"We all meant to help Maamaan with her bookcases, but you actually put them together. Her apartment looks sane again. That's all you, Jared."

Jared swung his feet.

Justice cleared her throat. "Did Maamaan tell you she leaves for her conference in Banff on the nineteenth? The Starr brothers are helping me move an armoire into her bedroom while she's gone. We could use another pair of arms—will you still be here?"

Jared shrugged.

"It's very heavy," Justice said. "It's one of those monstrous antiques I inherited and it's just sitting in my storage locker. My grandparents redefined ostentatious."

"How big is this thing?" Jared said.

"Big," Justice said. "I've cut it in half and shortened it so it will fit up the stairs."

"How're you bracing it?"

"You sound like Hank's mini-me. Next you'll be asking me about load-bearing walls."

"Hey," Jared said.

"Trust me. Hank grows on you."

Jared fought not to roll his eyes.

He dozed on and off through the night, uneasy. Normally he would have gone for a run to blow off some steam, but he didn't want to risk an encounter with David. But his insomnia was more about Sarah being missing, about where she was, about his inability to do simple homework in the first week, the sixty-five dollars left in his bank account, all of it together, none of it, his own frustration and his strong desire to just chuck it in the fuck-it bucket. Stop trying so hard to be something he obviously wasn't. Jared sat up and reached for his phone.

The corner of the room darkened. All the painted heads on the wall blinked at the same time then turned to stare at the corner. They mouthed words Jared couldn't hear. His body felt heavy, as if he'd swum a long way in the ocean and was trying to pull himself out. He had an urge to hide under the quilt like a kid, but he couldn't. The stain, a dark-grey shadow, took the shape of a bony arm. The fingers tapped the wall as if testing for a weak spot. The heads vibrated, blurring.

"Jelly Bean," Mave said from outside his door. "Are you awake?"

The shadow retreated. The heads stilled.

What the hell is that? Jared wondered.

"Jared?"

"Come in," he said. He couldn't move yet.

She paused in the doorway.

"Can you turn the lights on?" Jared said.

She reached over and flipped the switch. Jared squinted and then he could move. He sat up, breathing hard.

"You okay?" she said.

"Bad dream."

"I'm going to do the morning shift at the Sartorial Resistance and then I'm on the teachers' picket line this afternoon. Text if you need anything, okay?"

"'kay."

She smiled at him. "I made coffee. It's on the counter."

"Thanks."

"Mwah," she said, blowing him a kiss.

She left and he went over to the corner. A black dot was on the wall. He had no desire to touch it, so he went and got a ruler from the desk. He scraped at the wall, but the black dot didn't budge. It shivered. He leapt back. The painted faces all frowned at the same time. The thing in the wall poked a finger through the dot.

The warding really hadn't worked. Jared watched the shadow finger wiggling like a worm.

He picked up a bundle of cedar branches from the other corner of the room and placed it over the black dot. The shadow shivered then pulled back from the wall. Jared went to the junk drawer for a hammer, banged in a small nail and hung the cedar branches over the dot. The painted face nearest to him tumbled happily, smiling and winking.

"Can you talk?" Jared said.

They remained silent. But as he stood there, he felt a wave of warmth, like seeing someone you love, a pleasant afterglow. They liked him, he thought. They wanted him to know he was welcome here. Then the faces on the wall went still.

Yeah, he thought. I don't know what to do with that.

———

As he was sitting on the balcony with his homework, he saw a little boy stop below him on the sidewalk. He recognized the spiky, burnt hair and very tanned skin: Cedar, Georgina Smith's wolf-in-training grandson. Cedar scowled up at him.

You made Granny cry, Cedar thought at him. *You're mean. I don't like you.*

Jared looked up and down the street, but no adults seemed to be with Cedar, who was probably five, maybe six.

I can hunt alone, Cedar thought.

Let's see what your gran says, Jared thought at him, lifting his cellphone.

Mom's here, stupid. She lets me go out by myself. I'm a big boy.

I don't see her.

She's bringing my sister to the doctor.

Jared's mind was filled with images. He felt Cedar's impatience with his mother and his baby sister, screaming in a baby buggy— his mom wanting him to come into the bathroom with them to change her diaper. Cedar had kept his fingers in his ears and refused. The baby had pooped so much the smell filled the waiting room and people moved away from them.

Jared recognized the walk-in clinic around the corner. He felt the explosion of fear as Cedar's mother realized he was gone. Her panic made her baby screech.

He's here, Jared said in his head, hoping she could see Cedar on the sidewalk.

She screamed, *Come to me now*, and Cedar took off running.

Tattletale, Cedar thought at him.

Jared closed his textbooks and went inside. His hands were shaky from contact with Georgina's family, from Cedar, from his mother and her panic.

They aren't in your life, he told himself. That's not your crazy.

He wore his best T-shirt and jeans to hand out resumés. The frazzled-looking manager at the Donut Hole sat him down in the corner, asked him a few questions and then phoned his reference, Bianca, in front of him. The guy was old, hunched and sweaty. He didn't offer his name. He wore a battered gold name tag that said *Manager*.

After he hung up, the manager said, "I can train you for the doughnut fryer position at 3:30 a.m. tonight."

"That's it?"

"Minimum wage. Three nights a week, Wednesday, Friday and Sunday. Six hours a shift. No overtime. No benefits. I need someone right now. Take it or leave it."

"Am I being paid for the training?"

"Yeah. Of course. I'll see how you do tonight and we'll go from there."

"Great. I'll be here." Jared hadn't expected to find a job right out of the gate.

Mave was in her bedroom with the door closed when he got home. He checked the turkeys defrosting in the fridge. Still pretty frozen.

His reflection in the bathroom mirror was pasty. He left the light on in his room when he crawled into bed. It didn't feel like even a few minutes later when his alarm went off. He made himself coffee and left Mave a note, giving her his work address. He went to the balcony and scanned the street before he went downstairs and walked to work.

The manager didn't want Jared coming through the front door; he had to go around the back and ring the buzzer to be let in. The job was mostly lifting sacks and buckets of ingredients into industrial mixers. The manager seemed to think the process was complicated, because he kept explaining things. But the recipes were straightforward. It wasn't like Jared had never deep-fried food before. Glazing and sprinkling took no brainpower whatsoever. You found a rhythm and kept going until the batch was done. But he nodded, listened and kept his mouth shut. At the end of his shift, the manager paid him in cash.

"Let's keep this under the table," he said.

Jared passed out on his bed in his work clothes. He woke Saturday near supper and went to heat himself a bowl of chili. He checked the turkeys, which were almost thawed. He'd brine them tonight before he went to bed and roast them tomorrow.

Mave was watching TV. She inhaled deeply as he passed. "You smell like deep-fried heaven."

"Mmm," Jared said.

"If you need a job, we have a stock-boy position at the Sartorial Resistance."

"No, thanks."

"My stubborn, stubborn bean," she said. "Fine. Fry your life away."

Later in the evening, he checked his phone and discovered Sarah had texted him.

Sucka, she'd texted. *Momz playin' u, hates ur guts. Not telling u where I am, dude. U can't keep a secret 2 save ur life.*

Well, she's alive, Jared thought. *If u need anything, txt me.*

A few minutes later, she texted back: *U ready 2 fly the friendly skies?*

Get high and use magic, she meant. Trip with each other. Travel to worlds where ape men and fireflies ruled.

U no the answer, Jared wrote.

We're on different paths, Nickelback. Tired of every1 telling me what I shud think. Found a witch who's willing to teach me.

He wanted to tell her to be careful, but he figured she'd take it the wrong way. *@ 1640 Graveley, 202. Drop by if u feel like.*

C u around.

19

OH, FULL OF SCORPIONS
IS MY MIND

Crashpad changed his Facebook relationship status to "It's complicated." His new profile pic included the blond girl from his home-school study group, who was giggling, giving the camera a nostril shot. Crashpad gave the peace sign, smiling so hard his eyes were slits. They'd only known each other for a week, but Jared couldn't really judge because he'd fallen into the sack with Sarah the night they met.

Barbie wants U @ her Dance Group, Pat messaged him. *5-7 2nite, amenities room downstairs. B there or b noogied.*

Ignore, Jared thought.

An unknown number had sent him pictures of himself walking from Mave's apartment to the Donut Hole. No messages. No captions. Just grainy night shots of Jared strolling along with his hoodie up and his earbuds in.

Get a life, Jared texted.

He considered posting the pics to Facebook. But his mom was finally getting out of Dodge and he didn't want to stir up the whole stalking thing. Mave would probably insist on getting a bodyguard, which would turn out to be Hank. He'd be more alert on his way to work. David was trying to mess with his head. Jared could get all bent out of shape or he could get his shit together. He realized he hadn't gone to a meeting since school started. Seven days without a meeting had made him weak. Well, six, he thought, counting back, but the slogan still held.

Kota answered when Jared knocked on Hank's apartment door. Kota seemed pretty hung: shirt buttons done up wrong, hair in crazy spikes and eye-watering fumes about him. Jared hesitated before asking if his cousin wanted to come to a meeting with him. After a long, long pause, Kota shrugged, rummaged around for his jacket in the hallway closet and stuck a cigarette in his mouth while he patted down his clothes for a lighter. As they left the apartment building, Kota lit up.

"Had a lil break from the grind," Kota admitted as they walked. "Fucking one more white chip. Day fucking one, one more goddamn motherfucking time."

"Easy does it," Jared said.

Kota said, "I really want to punch you right now."

"People keep saying that. Maybe I'm not the annoying one. Maybe everyone else is cranky."

"Nah," Kota said. "I'm pretty sure it's you."

After the meeting, Kota stacked chairs and a blond woman with purple-tipped ends helped Jared tidy up the refreshment table. She wore a loose plaid shirt and ripped leggings that disappeared into a pair of battered, black Doc Martens. Her name was Lex and this was her third Day One this year. Her poison was anything she could get her hands on. She'd gotten up to Day Sixty, but her friends kept calling, and being sober was boring. They all sounded like they were having a blast and so she went with them and in her mind she was going to just have sober fun but she felt left out and what the hell, you know?

"There's a couple of youth meetings around," Jared said. "Maybe you need sober friends who do stuff."

She smirked. "Like hiking and shit? Pfft. Fuck that."

"There's—"

"Jared!" Kota shouted. He pointed to his wrist even though he didn't have a watch.

"Is he hammered?" Lex asked.

"Yeah," Jared said. "But he's aiming for Day One."

"Are you his sponsor or boyfriend?"

"Cousin."

"Ah. Messed-up-family shit."

Jared laughed. "Yup. Later."

"Later."

Kota said he needed a break from Hank yelling at him, so they walked to Café Calabria. Kota ordered a double shot of espresso and Jared ordered a coffee. Then he remembered that he had cash in his pocket and asked for a white chocolate chip cookie with macadamia nuts. Kota opened his wallet and sheepishly asked Jared if he could front him. Jared paid for both their orders.

"No worries. Next round's on you," Jared said, putting some change in the tip jar.

"Deal," Kota said.

They sat on the patio so Kota could smoke. He lit up the second they sat down, his leg jiggling impatiently. The sun flickered between the clouds, giving a watery light. Traffic hadn't slowed down on Sunday. A guy bolted across the street and irritated drivers honked at him as he ran.

"That was embarrassing," Kota said. "Sorry."

"S'okay."

"No. No, it's not. I used to make twenty grand every four months. Twenty-one days in Fort Mac, ten days of partying hard here."

"Yeah?"

"I couldn't make a recovery stick, and eventually people stop giving you chances. Now I'm taking handouts from annoying dipshits who make it to their first year on their first try. Are you even a boozehound? Or are you just doing AA to hit on crazy chicks?"

Jared sipped his coffee. He ate his cookie and watched the people, watched the traffic.

"Sorry," Kota said. "That's the hangover talking."

"I don't have another recovery in me."

"Don't slogan me."

"No slogan. Last year my skull cracked open and my brains fell out. I was seeing shit no one else saw. It took a long time to crawl back. If I go there again, I think I'm done."

"What were you on?"

"Booze, mostly. I think it was 'shrooms too. I can't really remember."

"Sanity's overrated," Kota said.

"That's easy for you to say," Jared said. "You've never lost it."

"We're all crazy, fuckface. It's not a competition."

"To crazy," Jared said, lifting his takeout cup.

Kota clinked his paper cup with Jared's and then concentrated on lighting another cigarette, his hands shaking.

"Why am I such a loser?" he said.

"I love you and your higher power loves you and there's nothing you can do about that."

Kota squinted, giving Jared the stink eye. "Now I want to punch you again."

"Some of us are sicker than others."

"You're irritating as fuck."

"We all have our gifts."

Kota leaned over and started to slowly bang his head against the table. Jared finished his cookie. His cousin suddenly got up and ran a few feet and then hurled into the gutter. Jared wasn't sure if he should watch him or not. Kota wiped the back of his mouth and, without looking around, headed down the street towards their apartment building. Jared left his cup on the table and followed him.

They walked without speaking. Kota lit another cigarette. He dry-heaved for a few minutes but kept smoking.

"I can't deal with Hank right now," Kota said.

"My couch is your couch," Jared said.

Once they were inside, Kota ran straight for the bathroom. Mave's bedroom door was open and she wasn't there. Jared walked to the kitchen, took the middle rack out of the oven and then greased two small roasting pans. He found a bag of squishy lemons at the back of the fridge and chopped them up. They were full of seeds. He scrubbed some of the tiny, hard sweet potatoes and some wilted carrots as he listened to Kota hurl and hurl, pause and then hurl some more. He took the turkeys out of the fridge, pulled them out of their pots and stuffed them with lemons.

Kota emerged from the bathroom and asked to borrow a T-shirt.

"Help yourself," Jared said. "They're in the backpack on the desk."

"Thanks."

"Are you expecting company?" Kota said, as Jared put the turkeys in the oven.

"Bored," Jared said.

"Mind if I take a shower?" Kota asked.

"I'm going to insist," Jared said.

"Yeah, fuck you," Kota said with no heat.

Jared scrubbed out the pots. He turned them over on some tea towels. He heard the shower start. When Jared went to get his textbooks, he discovered Kota had dumped his clean shirts on the desk and thrown his own vomit-stained shirt on the floor. Jared lifted the stinky shirt carefully and rinsed it out in the kitchen sink. He went back to his desk and flipped open his biology textbook. Have faith, he told himself, but the practical side of him was wondering how much of his tuition he could get back if he dropped out now.

"Upgrading, are we?" The ghost in the bathrobe hovered over the desk. "I gather we spent a little too much time enjoying ourselves at the expense of our education. Colour me shocked."

Jared thumped his book shut, picked up the pile of textbooks and walked out, slamming his bedroom door. The ghost walked through it, following him.

"I spent most of high school hiding," Bathrobe said. "Stuffed in lockers. Duct-taped to walls. Tripped. Punched. Magic-Markered."

Jared went into the kitchen and got some sage.

Bathrobe hovered near the dining table where Jared had left his textbooks. "My, my. How could you possibly flunk high school biology? How drunk were you?"

"I didn't flunk."

"So you're upgrading for the fun of it, are you?"

Don't engage, don't engage, don't engage, he reminded himself as he lit the sage and let it smoulder in the abalone shell. The ghost blinked out of existence as Kota emerged from the bathroom wearing one of his T-shirts.

"Is that all the clothes you have?"

"Yeah."

"I have some shirts if you want them."

"That's okay. My motto is *keep things portable*," Jared said. "You never know when people are going to get sick of your shit."

"You could murder hoboes in her bedroom and Aunt Mave wouldn't kick you out."

"There's the things people say and then there's the things people do." Jared lit the sage and then blew on it. "Boob tube?"

"Do you have any Gravol?"

"Front pocket of my backpack."

Kota went back into the bedroom. Jared turned on the TV. He flipped up and down the channels but wasn't interested in watching anything. Kota walked past him and went into the kitchen. Jared heard the cupboards open and close, the tap running. Jared held up the remote when Kota came back, but his cousin put a cigarette in his mouth.

"Need company?" Jared said, shutting the TV off.

Kota shrugged.

They sat together on the balcony watching the street. Their silence was comfortable. Kota closed his eyes and sighed. Jared remembered his first sober days, the open-sore rawness of everything, the head-pounding, throat-aching, stomach-churning need. Listening to his mom's party raging on all around him, he'd curled up in bed like he was adrift in a lifeboat, dying of thirst surrounded by an ocean.

———

Jared frowned at his laptop, his feet up on the balcony railing. Kota asked to borrow a twenty to get some cigarettes.

"Just cigarettes, right?" Jared said, pulling a twenty out of his wallet.

"Bye, Mom," Kota said, getting off the patio chair.

"Dude."

"Later."

Jared felt like an idiot, but he couldn't exactly run after Kota and stop him from doing anything. He could hear Sophia calling him the Great Enabler. But it was hard to say no, especially to his dad. Kota he could say no to. You know, next time.

Mave buzzed past the apartment on the Vespa. She'd added a wicker basket to the front and filled it with flowers. She was wearing the blue helmet that matched the colour of the Vespa and a red rain jacket. When she honked and waved, the scooter wobbled. Jared watched her turn onto Commercial Drive without signalling. A few minutes later she buzzed back, waving and honking again before she pulled up to the curb.

"Come for a ride!" she yelled up at him.

"I told you," Jared called down to her. "No bitch-seats."

"Stick-in-the-mud," she said. "You don't know what you're missing!" With that, she took off down the street again.

Jared got up and went inside. He basted the turkeys. Finished off his biology homework. He was thinking of taking a nap when Kota came back, holding up two packs of cigarettes and waving them around. His cousin stomped to the balcony and shut the door behind him hard enough to make the blinds rattle.

Jared sighed. He stared at his physics textbook and was waffling between watching YouTube or channel surfing when Hank burst through the door. Jared jumped up and blocked him from tearing to the balcony.

"Woah," Jared said. "Dude. Chill, okay?"

"This doesn't have anything to do with you."

"You can't stop someone from drinking by yelling at them."

Hank shoved Jared's books off the table. They landed in a cascade of thuds. Jared looked up at Hank. He recognized the anger and the frustration and the worry, but he didn't want to be the one Hank took all that out on, so he stayed very still.

Someone pounded on the front door.

"Jared!" Pat shouted. "Come on, Barbie's waiting for you!"

Hank punched the wall.

"What's up, Daddy-o?" Sponge said as Hank opened the door and pushed past the brothers.

They all watched Hank slam his own apartment door open and shut. Kota opened the balcony door and peered in at them.

"We've been annoying Hank since we were in diapers," Pat said to Jared. "But we bow to the master."

"We're not worthy," Sponge said, literally bowing.

"I don't think that was all me."

"So modest," Pat said. "I've never seen anyone get under his skin the way you do."

"You're like eczema," Sponge said.

"Persistent, oozing, steroid-resistant eczema."

"Come on," Sponge said. "Barbie's thrilled you're joining her Urban Heiltsuk Dance Group."

"Hank annoys me, too," Jared said. "No one seems to care about that."

"Let the Wookiee win," Sponge said.

"I have turkeys in the oven," Jared said. "I have to study. I don't have time to go to Barbie's thing."

"You really don't want to cross Barbie," Pat said.

"Yeah," Sponge said. "She comes off all sweet, but if Hank's a Wookiee, she's Darth Maul in pigtails."

"What about Kota?" Jared grumbled.

"He sings like a crow," Pat said.

"Dances like one too," Sponge added.

"Ah, fuck you both," Kota said. "I'll watch the stupid turkeys."

Sponge led them down the first-floor hallway. A group of twenty or so people were gathered in the amenities room. The dancers were going through a set of steps in one corner while some drummers were hammering out the beat in another. Shu danced around tooting her recorder, still wearing her zombie costume. Barbie was conducting some kids in a welcome song. Eliza waved furiously when she saw Jared. Barbie looked up and then broke into a smile.

"Oh, I love this squishy face." Once more Barbie squished his cheeks together while Sponge and Pat hooted.

"Ow," Jared said.

Eliza ran up to him. "Hi, Jared!"

"Hi."

"Can I come watch TV at your place after?" Eliza said.

"You'll have to ask Mave," Jared said. "It's her place."

"See you, Jared!"

Eliza ran off, with Shu behind her.

"Get one of the spare drums, Jelly Bean!" Barbie said. "Have fun!"

"Come on, Squishy," Pat said.

He felt like a phony, following along, not knowing any of the music, but he stood and drummed. Eliza and Shu came and danced in front of him.

When they were done, Jared put the drum back in its bag, said goodbye to Barbie and slunk back to the apartment. Kota had moved to the recliner, and was staring blankly at the TV screen. Jared sat on the couch, vibrating. When the timer went off, he got up and took the turkeys out of the oven. They were resting on the counter when Mave came home.

"Jared," she called from the kitchen. "We still have a giant pot of chili in the fridge. How are we going to eat two turkeys!"

"Sorry," Jared said. "I should've asked. But we can cut them up and freeze them."

"No, no, it's not that," Mave said. "You have to stop trying to feed an army. Okay?"

She came into the living room, still wearing the Vespa helmet, and saw Kota.

"Hi, Aunt Mave."

She peeled off her helmet and put it on the table. "Can we talk?"

Kota pulled the recliner handle so he was sitting. "About what? Hank?"

"He's upset."

"You would take his side," Kota said. "See you later, Jared."

"Kota," Mave said. "Wait!"

He grabbed his jacket and was gone out the door.

"Jelly Bean," she said. "Let them sort out their issues, okay? It's between them."

She didn't seem to see the irony of what she was saying, so he nodded, biting his tongue so he wouldn't bite the hand that housed him. Mave stomped down the hallway and out the door, and he could hear her loudly saying, "Hello," as she entered Hank's apartment and then Mave, Hank and Kota in furious conversation through the wall. Jared sat on the couch. Feelings churned inside him. Or *feeeeeelings* as his mom would say. He had work in a few hours and he didn't want to think about maybe encountering David on the walk there, so he carved the turkeys. He'd meant to save the carcasses for soup, but before he knew it he'd already chucked them, tied the garbage bag and taken it to the dumpster.

Some days you couldn't win for losing.

20

SPOOK

Consider a leaf.

Not a terribly exciting thing. Green, generally. Leaves can be pointy, like the needles on your average Christmas tree. Or they can be flat like paper. Some leaves change colour in the fall, and when you were in kindergarten you probably pressed some maple ones between wax paper to make art that you taped to your refrigerator.

In biology class, you learned about photosynthesis, the process by which a leaf takes sunlight, water and a few minerals and makes the earth a habitable place for oxygen breathers. Your leaf captures light photons in its chlorophyll molecules— the molecules that give leaves their green colour. Light hops through a forest of chlorophyll molecules straight to the cell's reaction centre, where it is stored as potential energy.

While most of the solar panels on people's houses are inefficient, hovering around 14 percent, your leaf stores 99.9 percent of the light it captures. Light, you see, doesn't behave like a localized particle travelling along a single route. In your average leaf, light behaves quantum-mechanically, like *a spread-out wave that samples all possible routes at once to find the quickest path.*

Consider the posted speed limit of our universe: 299,792 kilometres per second.

Or about 186,000 miles per second, for those of you who prefer not to dabble in the metric system. Nothing travels faster than this, the speed of light.

Before Albert Einstein, mass (the amount of matter an object has) and energy were considered two separate entities. In 1905, Einstein published his special theory of relativity, which permanently tied mass and energy together in the simple yet fundamental equation, $E = mc^2$—energy is the equivalent of the mass of an object times twice the speed of light in a vacuum. It takes an enormous amount of energy to make a tiny amount of mass. His equation also predicts that nothing with mass can approach the speed of light or move faster than it.

But in the world of the tiniest particles we can detect, the world of quantum mechanics, things are not so neat. One of the more peculiar qualities is the idea of entanglement. If, for instance, two photons interact, they are changed. After they've touched, when one photon is positive, the other is negative. When one changes, the other instantaneously changes to the opposite frequency, even if they are light years apart, seemingly in violation of the universe's speed limit. Einstein dubbed this behaviour "spooky action at a distance."

The limitation of light speed, it turns out, mainly applies to objects with mass. Photons can approach light speed because they have no mass. The void, being empty, also has no mass and can expand infinitely instantaneously, as it did during the big bang.

Such a simple thing, a leaf, which relies on a complicated biomechanical quantum process to eat light. You are far from simple. You are a little universe. You are the wet and pulsing distillation of stars, a house of light made bipedal and carbon-based, temporary and infinite. You are also the void.

Cartographers used to write on maps, "Here be dragons," when they reached places beyond their known world. When humans touch the void, they say, "Here is magic."

21

SOMEONE I USED TO LOVE

When he got home from work Saturday morning, Jared collapsed and slept until noon. His shift had passed uneventfully. The Donut Hole manager had left him alone for the last hour. Jared had worked faster without the old dude hovering. He still hadn't told Jared his name.

Jared puttered through the apartment. Mave wasn't around, but she usually did a weekend shift at the clothing store or went brunching with Justice. He didn't feel like cooking anything. His sense of time felt off. Graveyard shifts were brutal. He made a run for a bagel and large coffee at the Tim Hortons around the corner. On the way home, he found himself scanning the street for David, but what he wasn't expecting was to see a swarm of fireflies. They glowed, a large cloud above the entrance of his apartment building, circling just under Mave's balcony, sparking and crackling like northern lights. Sarah.

She sat on the edge of the concrete retaining wall in front of Mave's building. He would know her lean frame anywhere. That and her giant-ass Sailor Moon shirt. Her long hair was black except for two small, buttery-pink buns curled on the sides of her head.

Shit-kicking boots with black marker hiding the scuffs. Her short plaid skirt and the white tights she used to hide the scars from her cutting. She was watching her feet as she kicked them back and forth. Above her, the fireflies sparked and spun.

He let out a breath that he hadn't known he was holding. She was safe. She was alive and she was here. He felt light-headed. Knee-shaking excited.

She looked up as he came down the sidewalk.

Jared stopped in front of her. "Hey."

She smiled at him and her up-tilted eyes sparkled. "Hey."

"You okay?"

"Are you?"

Jared crossed his arms over his chest. "Where you staying?"

"Is that all you have to say?"

The fireflies crackled. He forced himself not to look at them, hoping they wouldn't start spouting poetry or snarky remarks. As far as he could tell, no one else could see them, except Sarah when she was with him and they were stoned or drunk enough. Not even his mom, who was pretty powerful.

She stood. She touched his hand and, when he didn't pull away, brought it to her cheek. "I almost died and that's the moment you chose to dump me," she said.

He pulled his hand away. He wanted to deny it. And there had been circumstances. But she was here and she was the person he needed to make amends to the most and she was waiting for him to say something. "That was one of the shittiest things I ever did. I'm sorry, Sarah. I was scared. I don't know what I can do to make it right, but I'm willing to try."

She moved close enough that he could feel the heat of her body, her breath on his cheek. Her pupils were wide black pools and he wondered if she was tripping.

"'And though I have the gift of prophecy,'" she said, "'and understand all mysteries and all knowledge, and though I have all faith, so that I could remove mountains, but have not love, I am nothing.'"

"I can't go there, Sarah. You know I can't."

She tilted her head so she looked down her nose at him. "Chickenshit."

"We fried our brains. We almost died."

"We were amazing, Jared. When you're ready to admit it, drop me a line. Later!" She twirled, waving cheerfully, which made him furious.

"We won't go there!" he shouted as she skipped away from him. "Because we're done!"

"Love you, too!"

"We're so done!"

"Toodles!"

He couldn't think of anything to shout at her and he really, really wanted to shout something satisfyingly ugly, but all he could think of was repeating *we're done*, which was lame.

"Exes, huh?"

Above the entrance, just to the right, Kota leaned against the balcony railing, pulling a drag off his cigarette. He was flanked by Patrick and Sponge, who were still holding their Xbox controllers, gaming headphones pushed off their ears.

"What was amazing?" Patrick said.

"It was kinky, perverted sex, wasn't it?" Sponge said. "Sex so dirty you're ashamed you liked it."

"Crazy chicks, man," his brother said.

They laughed and bumped controllers.

"Ignore them," Kota said. "They're horny, desperate and probably still virgins."

Jared felt his face flush. "You were spying on us?"

"Dude," Patrick said. "You guys were loud."

"Heh, heh, yeah, I bet they were," Sponge said.

Jared yanked the entrance door open.

Sponge and Patrick were waiting for him outside Mave's apartment. "You had a ménage, right? But I bet it was guy-guy-girl and not the right way, girl-girl-guy, right?"

"I bet it was bondage," Patrick chimed in. "She looks like she'd like topping."

"Can you get out of my way, please?"

"I bet you begged," Sponge said.

"That's enough," Kota said, coming over and shoving the brothers. "Get inside, you nimrods."

Sponge made his voice high: "Oh, Sarah, stop!"

"I'm doing a meeting in an hour. Are you in?" Kota said to Jared.

"Yes." He unlocked Mave's apartment door.

"*We're done!*" Patrick said. "*We're so done!*"

The brothers howled their way back into Hank's place.

"I won't ask," Kota said, hovering in the doorway.

Jared kicked off his runners. "Thank you."

"But we're only as sick as our secrets."

Jared shut the door in Kota's face.

"So we're still on?" Kota called through the door.

Jared knocked his forehead against the wood a couple of times, listening to Sponge and Patrick yukking it up. "Yeah."

"Okay, see you later," Kota said.

———

He wasn't hungry anymore. Thoughts ran like greyhounds, retreading the same ground quickly and pointlessly. He had managed to say sorry to Sarah. She'd sort of accepted his apology. She looked healthy for someone who'd run away from home and for all he knew was homeless. She hadn't told him where she was living, but it couldn't be far if she was skipping away so casually. He'd promised to phone Sarah's mom if he had any news. If his daughter was missing, he'd want to know she was okay. But he didn't want to deal with it, any of it.

Yeah, and he'd been worried about David. Worried about school. He was making a mess of things. Or things were a mess. He was a mess and that's why he couldn't make anything work. To top it all off, he smelled like greasy doughnuts and he had meant to take a shower but now he didn't want to move. He gave up on the day and went back to bed.

Sometime later he heard someone knock on the apartment door. He didn't want to go to a meeting anymore. He didn't want to answer the door. He didn't want to get out of bed. Ever.

The front door squealed open. Did I lock it? Jared wondered. I thought I locked it.

"Jared!" Kota said. "Shake a leg."

Maybe if he didn't answer, Kota would go away. He listened to Kota's footsteps coming closer until Kota knocked on the bedroom door.

"Go away," Jared said.

Instead of leaving, Kota came right in. "You coming?"

"No."

Kota parked himself on the desk chair. "I've got the twenty bucks I owe you."

"Keep it."

Kota sighed. The chair squeaked as he swivelled. "I'm not taking twenty bucks from a kid with four shirts."

"I'm tired."

"Yeah. We can go to a meeting later."

"Can you give me some space? Please?"

Kota put his feet up on the bed. Jared pulled the quilt over his head. Kota didn't take the hint. "You haven't even finished puberty," Kota said. "And I dumped my grown-ass problems all over you. I'm sorry. Not my golden moment."

"I'll go to a meeting if you'll shut up," Jared said.

"Deal," Kota said.

Kota was too embarrassed to go back to Café Calabria, so after the meeting they went to a different coffee place. He ordered Jared a cookie and a latte, saying, "You add enough milk, you might as well drink the real thing."

They sat on the patio. The latte was good but too expensive. Jared almost wished he hadn't tried it. Going back to regular coffee was going to be hard. Kota turned his Day One white chip over in his fingers.

"Even half a dozen. Maybe I'll make them into a necklace," Kota said.

"One day at a time," Jared said.

————

Mave was washing dishes when Jared got home. She turned to him. "Can we talk?"

She peeled off her rubber gloves. They went to sit at the dining room table. Jared waited for a lecture.

"Kota said you've brought him to a couple of meetings."

"Yeah."

"Thank you. Hank and I were wondering if you could talk to him about a treatment centre. I have a list here of gay-friendly facilities. We think it could help him over the initial hump. Really get him on track."

Jared touched the flyers. "You know, they have meetings for family of alcoholics. It's called Al-Anon. I have a list of times and we can find one that works for you. I'll even bring you there. We'll tackle your issues together."

She stared at him. Her mouth opened, and then closed, and she seemed like she was about to say something, but didn't.

"That's what it feels like for Kota," Jared said. "People aren't puppets. You can't work the steps for them."

She turned to look out the window. The silence continued until Jared pushed back his chair, remembering that she could boot him out any time.

"Sorry," Jared said.

"Never be sorry for speaking the truth," Mave said, grabbing his hand as he got up. "I'm not mad. I'm processing."

"Oh. Okay."

She let him go. "You're so thoughtful. And so annoying."

"That is the popular opinion," Jared said.

22

THE SARTORIAL RESISTANCE

The mailman buzzed up as Jared was stuffing his feet in his sneakers, already flustered and angry at himself for having slept through his alarm. He was going to be late for class, and didn't really want to sign for a package, but the mailman said it was for him and it needed a signature. The package was heavy. It felt like a book. Sophia always sent things that needed to be signed for, so he signed, grabbed the package and ran for the bus, which pulled away just as he got to the bus stop. He looked down Commercial but couldn't see another bus coming, so he jogged nine blocks up to the SkyTrain station, wishing he'd left the stupid package in the apartment. Especially once he'd jogged up the escalator, shoved his way into a waiting car and then found a seat, panting as he finally read the return address:

Mrs. G. Smith, Ladner.

He shook it. Not a bomb. Not clothes. Definitely a book. He didn't want to have anything to do with her. He didn't want to accept anything she was offering. It was so creepy that she knew his address. Cedar's little visit, he guessed. At his stop, he stood and left the parcel on the seat. But at the door, he couldn't do it and ran back for it, almost getting stuck in the door on his way out. What would she be sending him, he wondered as he waited for the bus that would take him to school.

Jared was twenty minutes late. All the seats in the back were taken, so he was stuck with a seat in the front row. Struan stopped talking when he noticed Jared, so everyone watched him fumbling through his backpack for his laptop, his textbook and their first assignment. He blushed and he couldn't look up, concentrating on his laptop screen until Struan started talking again. At the end of class, when Jared handed in his assignment, Struan forced a smile and said thank you, but didn't ask Jared about Mave. Which was a relief.

While he was waiting for the bus, he texted his mom. *Hey. Howʒʒit goin?*

Richieʒ bro died, his mom texted him a few moments later. *We're in the Peg. His mom shot his bro — she thot he was her ex. Magic fite gone nuclear. I thot our family wuʒ fucked up.*

Holy, Jared texted back. *U ok?*

Yuppers. Total shitstorm here. Nothing I can't handle. Richie sayʒ hi.

Hi to Richie.

Howʒ Mave?

Bossy.

Ha. Hasnt changed then. Gotta go.

B safe.

U 2.

TTYL

TTFN

He had two unanswered messages. Kota asking which meeting he wanted to hit. An automated reminder that he needed to top up his phone minutes. Nothing from Sarah. Nothing from Crashpad.

A girl asked him if she could sit, so he picked up the package and put it on his lap. It couldn't hurt to take a peek. If it seemed hinky, he could dump it in the nearby trash bin. She'd taped it so much he couldn't rip it open and was slowly peeling the tape when the girl sitting beside him offered her nail file.

Georgina had sent him a copy of *Alcoholics Anonymous: The Story of How Many Thousands of Men and Women Have Recovered from Alcoholism*. The Big Book. Jared had it on his phone app, but he'd never had a physical copy of it. Tucked inside the book was a blue envelope with his name written in careful cursive. She'd taped a one-year sobriety chip to the back of the envelope and surrounded it with hearts.

He handed the nail file back to the girl and mumbled thank you. He stuffed the book into his backpack and then peeled the chip off the envelope. Georgina had remembered. Despite his mistrust, he was touched. He put the chip in the back pocket of his jeans.

He turned the blue envelope over and over in his hands. Buses came and went. People sat beside him and left.

The paper she'd written on was pale yellow and delicate. Her writing slanted right in neat rows. She'd included ten crisp hundred-dollar bills.

Dear Jared,

You left before I could give you the chip, the Big Book, and the money. Congratulations! One year is quite the accomplishment. I have 67 sober years. Each year is a challenge but none of them were as hard as the first. When you live as long as I have, everyone dies and you are left alone so many times. I know the pity ditty well—poor me, poor me, pour me another drink. The money is for your schooling. This doesn't obligate you to me and you don't need to pay me back. I give this to all my nieces and nephews and grandchildren for their first year of post-secondary education. If you are uncomfortable accepting it, do pass it along to someone who needs it.

I'm sorry we scared you. I didn't think you could see as well as you do. Most humans can't. We will leave you alone. You will never hear from us unless you initiate the contact. I promise.

On that note, please don't think me presumptuous, but I'd like to offer my assistance if you ever need it. Magic can get you drunk too. You lose the ability to function without it. You lose sight of what's important and you use until you are spent, and then you borrow. I borrowed. I was indebted to creatures and people and beings you can't even imagine. If you ever find yourself in that position, please don't hesitate to call me. You have my phone number. You don't have to fight it alone. I'm here if you ever need me.

Yours,

Mrs. Georgina Smith

Jared stepped over the women's shoes and came to a stop at the end of the hallway. Bathrobe blocked the entrance to the living room.

"Oh, good gravy," Jared said, turning back and walking straight to the kitchen. The last thing he wanted to deal with was the ghost.

"Entry-level biology is mostly memorizing," Bathrobe said, appearing in front of the smudge drawer, blocking it as much as a ghost could. "When they assign you a chapter, make a list of all the bold-faced vocabulary then go to the glossary for the official definition. Then write the term and its definition five times. Then put it on a notecard and review every night before you go to bed."

"Why are you here?" Jared said. "What do you want?"

"I'd really like to watch the new *Doctor Who* series."

"They don't have TV in heaven?"

Bathrobe grimaced. "So you're one of those, are you?"

"Can't you go watch it somewhere else?"

"I like it here," the ghost said.

"Why?"

"Who else is going to tutor you for free?"

"You . . . want to tutor me. That's insane."

"Interdimensional time-space is a causality funhouse. The rules are a mishmash of whatever universes are overlapping at the moment. I'm not locked in one place, but it's very easy to get lost."

"Go into the light," Jared said.

The ghost crossed his arms. "Thanks, Carol Anne."

"Who's Carol Anne?"

"You've never watched *Poltergeist*?"

Jared considered how fast he was burning through the sage and sweetgrass and how it didn't seem to be doing any good anyway. Granny Nita said you couldn't trust the dead. His mom said it too. Their thoughts were strange—death changed them. Still. He hadn't figured out his physics homework and it was due Thursday morning. "What about physics?"

"So simple," Bathrobe said. "I would use small words and go slowly."

"I can't think today," Jared said. "But I wouldn't mind some help with physics tomorrow."

"Done."

"Can you promise me some privacy?"

"Turn the TV to the science fiction channel and I swear by the great and mighty Time Lord you will not even know I exist."

"No floating into my bedroom without asking?"

"Like I really want to be in that cesspit of temporal dynamic instability."

"What?"

"Never mind. You won't believe me and explaining basic physics to you promises to be a Herculean task, without getting into chaos theory."

Jared went into the living room. He plugged the TV into the wall and turned to the science fiction channel. The ghost walked through the wall to stand in front of the recliner.

"So we have a deal?" the ghost said.

"If you get weird on me, the deal's off."

"You're the strange attractor, not me."

"What?"

The ghost plopped himself in the recliner. "Shut up and go away."

"So who are you, anyway?"

"I'm Dent, Arthur Dent."

"Arthur Dent."

"Not Arthur Dent. *Dent, Arthur Dent.* I had it legally changed when I was sixteen because of my deep love of the *Hitchhiker's Guide to the Galaxy* series."

"Dude," Jared said, "you are so weird."

"The living are *so* annoying," Dent muttered. "What part of 'go away' did you not understand?"

Jared's alarm woke him at three. He dug around the fridge for a quick and easy snack. He found the bagel he'd left there yesterday. Dent's eyes were still glued to the TV and he completely ignored

Jared even though he was only a few feet away. He wasn't sure what he'd expected from a ghost, but it wasn't this. Jared was putting the wrapper in the garbage when Kota knocked on the door and told him to shake a leg.

After their meeting, they grabbed a coffee and a cookie, and then sat on a sidewalk patio a couple of blocks from the apartment building. Well, Jared grabbed a cookie. Kota stuck to his espresso and the single square of dark chocolate that came with it. Jared couldn't make himself switch to lattes. He'd repaid Mave for the textbooks and she'd asked if his loan had come in. He'd offered to pay a bill or two and she'd said when he got funded, they'd revisit their arrangement. Jared'd stuck the remaining seven hundred dollars under his mattress. He was looking at another three or four hundred for textbooks next semester.

Jared squinted at the sky. A smattering of trees on the mountainsides had turned golden yellow. Fall was coming. He realized Kota was talking.

"—bought Hank that car when I was flush," Kota said. "I wanted to help them out. And, you know, rub it in my parents' faces. *You coulda had this. This coulda been you.* I paid for Gran's move. Set her up with new furniture. The best mobility equipment. Only decent things I did with my money. Only things I don't regret. All the assholes I tried to impress. Christ. None of them would look at me once the money ran out."

"Sorry," Jared said.

"Yeah."

"Hank and your gran—they'd still want you in their lives even if you don't buy them things," Jared said. "If they stuck by you through the last few years, I think—"

Kota's eyes went beady. "Shut it."

"—you're more than a paycheque to them."

"Holy fucking Christ, you just don't know when to quit, do you?"

Jared finished his cookie. He sipped his coffee and watched the world go by while Kota stewed.

"I talk to you more than I talk to my sponsor," Kota said eventually.

"Yeah?"

"Maybe you should be my sponsor."

"You just want someone you can push around."

"No, you actually listen. And you don't try to shove your opinions down my throat."

"Have you told him that?"

"See? You listen." After a while Kota added, "Maybe I should try the camps again. I don't want to mooch off Hank anymore and I don't want to work with him on security."

"Hard to take a pay cut?"

"Shut it."

"I made buttloads of money selling pot cookies," Jared said. "It was a big comedown working at Dairy Queen. All my party buddies came and made fun of me and my hairnet. I was always broke, living paycheque to paycheque."

"You aren't selling regular jobs."

"I did what I had to do for my sobriety."

"That's not the way it works. We live in a—" Kota's cell warbled. He checked it. "Aunt Mave and Hank are coming to pick us up."

"What?" Jared said.

"Aunt Mave wants her Jelly Bean and her Henry-kins to get along. She's got something planned and it's supposed to be a surprise."

"Bye," Jared said.

"Jared."

"You can't force people to like each other just because you want them to."

"Welcome to the clan."

"What?"

"Fucking sit your ass back down. Sit. You're doing this. If I have to hear about you and Hank fighting anymore, I swear to God I'm going to shove a pen through my eardrums."

Jared sat and gulped the dregs of his coffee. After a few minutes of sulking he saw Hank's anonymous grey Honda Civic pull up and parallel-park in front of them. Mave rolled down the passenger window and waved to catch their attention.

"Yahoo!" she said. "Jared! Kota! Fancy meeting you here! Hop in!"

Free rent, Jared told himself as he got up. Free rent, free rent.

"Hi," Jared said as he got in the back seat.

Hank glanced at him in the rear-view mirror but didn't turn around. Kota got in the seat behind Hank. Jared remembered the seat belt rule.

"How was your meeting?" Mave said.

"Good," Jared said. "What's up?"

"I thought we could go out for a little supper," Mave said. "My treat!"

"I'm kind of full," Jared said.

Kota reached over and gave the side of Jared's head a warning slap. "We're in."

"Have you ever been to Banff, Jared?" Mave said.

"No."

"It's so lovely this time of year. So many places to hike. I'll be working all weekend, so my hotel room will just be sitting there. Empty."

Mave went on about the things you could do in Banff and Jared got the feeling she was hinting around that she wouldn't mind some company, but she didn't want to ask him directly. He looked out the window, trying to figure out where they were going. They were still in East Van, but had dipped down to one of the side streets and seemed to be circling, looking for free parking.

At last they parked. When they got out, Mave grabbed his hand and held it, like he was a toddler. Jared swallowed his resentment. Kota smirked. Hank kept checking his watch. Mave let go of his hand when she opened the front door of the offices of the Lu'ma Native Housing Society.

"Hi, Mave," the receptionist said, lifting up some papers. "I see you have the whole gang with you."

"Have you met Jared?" Mave said.

"I'm Blanche. Pleased to meetcha."

"Hey," Jared said.

"Mave asked us to put you on the rental agreement and make everything official, which means—you guessed it—paperwork." She handed him a clipboard.

Jared stared at the clipboard.

"A little birdie told me you were feeling a tad insecure about the informality of our arrangement," Mave said.

Jared glared at Kota, who mimed surprise.

"You don't have to," Jared said to Mave.

"He's like a personal chef," Mave said to Blanche. "And he's really good at killing spiders."

"Can't let that go," Blanche said.

Jared wanted a moment alone to absorb things, so he went and sat on one of the chairs and bent his head over the paper, pretending to read it.

"Just sign it already," Hank said.

He did.

They had dinner at White Spot. Afterwards, Kota and Hank argued about the fastest route home all the way back to the Drive. Hank missed the turnoff for their street and parked in front of Mave's store, the Sartorial Resistance.

"And now, the pièce de résistance, if you'll excuse the pun," Mave said. "New clothes!"

"No," Jared said, trying desperately to open the car door.

"Child-locked," Hank said. "They have to be opened from the outside."

"Screw you," Jared said.

Hank grinned at him in the rear-view mirror. "Better you than me."

"Double screw you."

Hank and Mave got out of the car.

"Fucking relax," Kota said. "Let her buy you some weird-ass shirts, wear them a couple of times and stick them in the back of your closet like the rest of us did."

Hank stood by his door. "Tick-tock, Jared."

"You have epic control issues."

"I'm going to count to three."

"He will drag you into Aunt Mave's store," Kota said.

Hank pressed a button on his key and Jared heard all the locks unclick. Kota got out and moved into the front passenger seat, pulling out his phone and scrolling through it.

"I hate you all," Jared said, getting out.

The Sartorial Resistance had an *Entrez, Nous Sommes Ouverts* sign on the door. A chime went off as they came in, a strange, off-kilter, gong-like sound. A very tall, very thin woman in a plain black dress with a jagged hem paused in arranging a rack of clothes to look over at them. The store was spare. Clothing racks hung from the ceiling on wires. The floor was industrial grey with sparkles. Jared sighed. Sparkles in the floor were never a good sign.

"Holy crap," Jared said, suddenly noticing a framed poster featuring Mave wearing a deep-blue gown, half her hair plastered to her scalp by blood. She stood with one hand on her hip, staring directly at the camera, lit by a burning car as cops and protesters clashed around her, a mist of billowing tear gas softening the skyscrapers in the background. *The Sartorial Resistance*, the poster read. *Fashioning the Revolution.*

"I know," Mave said. "But Timothy's an old war photographer and he wouldn't stop focusing on the fighting."

"Is that real blood?" Jared said.

"It was a head cut. They always look dramatic."

At that moment Hank said, "We're going to head 'er."

"Thank you, Henry-kins."

"Later," Hank said.

Jared watched him get in the car, and then watched him and Kota arguing as they drove off, wishing he was going with them.

"This is Gwen," Mave said. "Gwen, this is Jared."

"Charmed," Gwen said.

"Is Justice here tonight?" Mave said.

"She's on a vape break."

"Ah," Mave said. She took some T-shirts off a rack, checked the tags and handed them to Jared. "Try the Secret Cyborg line." She gave him a heavy stare, then turned to Gwen. "I know he'll appreciate your work because he's always trying to unbrand himself."

"I loathe our billboard culture," Gwen said. "Clothes should scream your style, not corporate logos."

"Go on," Mave said. "Try them on."

The dressing room was flat black. A single basketball-sized bare bulb hung from the ceiling, which vanished in the darkness. The T-shirts fit and had lots of room in the neck. They weren't too fancy or weird, but he couldn't find any price tags.

"I'm passing you some jeans," Mave said. "We also have some dressy-casual pants for job interviews. Back in a sec!"

"I have a job," Jared said.

Skinny-legged jeans were not his thing, but the pants were okay. Again, no price tag. Jared picked a T-shirt and the pants. He heard Justice and Mave laughing in the store. He put his own clothes back on. When he walked up to the counter, Justice and Mave smiled at him.

"I see you liked them," Mave said.

"Yup," Jared said.

"Hello, Jared. How's school?" Justice said.

"'s okay."

"I can never get him to shut up," Mave said. "Chatter, chatter, chatter."

They laughed again and Justice rang up the clothes.

"Do you want to come back to my place for tea when you finish?" Mave said.

"I'm driving Gwen home," Justice said.

"Ah, well," Mave said. "I'll see you later, my darling girl."

"Sweet dreams, Maamaan."

They air-kissed.

Justice handed him a purple bag with silver tissue wrapping the clothes. She winked. As Jared and Mave walked home, the lampposts flickered on. Mave linked her arm in his.

"You could come to Banff if you wanted," Mave said. "I have enough frequent flyer points to bring you for free. I'd be out all day and you'd have the room to yourself."

"I'm just getting the hang of school," Jared said.

"It's only for the weekend."

"I have studying."

"So very earnest," Mave said. "As Maggie said you would be."

"You guys talk?"

"She texts. She's worried about this David character. Otherwise, her and Mother want nothing to do with the baby-stealer." Mave was leaving herself open to questions that Jared wasn't ready to ask. She let his arm go when they reached the apartment entrance.

Dent, Arthur Dent was watching TV when they came in. Mave sighed, picked up the remote and shut off the TV.

"Hey!" Dent shouted.

"Edgar was the TV fanatic," Mave said. "He's programmed the damn thing to turn on and I can't figure out how to stop it. Would you mind if we got rid of the cable?"

"We had a deal!" Bathrobe said. The living room light flickered.

"I can pay it," Jared said.

"Don't be silly," Mave said. "Fine, we'll keep it. But could you try to figure out how to stop the idiot box from blaring nonsense at all times of the day and night?"

"I'll give it a shot," Jared said, as Dent glared at him.

When he was sure Mave was writing with her headphones on, Jared phoned Sarah's mom and told her he'd had a Sarah sighting but couldn't get any information out of her and she wasn't answering his texts anymore.

"Tell her Mother's come home," Meredith said. "She left . . . *left* Father with his family in Brno. She . . . she . . . I . . . can't. She's refusing . . . treatment . . ."

He listened to Meredith crying. After a while she whispered, "Everyone's leaving me."

The line clicked and Jared heard dial tone. He had accepted Mrs. Jaks's death a long time ago. She told him more than once that this year was borrowed time. He held the phone and listened to hum, to static, frozen. He should text Sarah.

We're all alone in the end, he thought. Whether or not people care about us or don't. But he wished with everything in his being that Mrs. Jaks would be okay even when the evidence overwhelmingly said that she wouldn't be.

23

OPEN DOORS

"How can you not get this?" Dent said. "The acceleration is minus 9.8 metres per second squared. It's dead simple."

Jared took a large swig of coffee. He'd made it extra strong. He'd woken up ready to tackle his physics homework, trying to work himself out of his melancholy mood. But nothing was staying in his head. "Is that the g?"

"Of course it's g. Acceleration due to gravity equals g."

"Why is it negative again?"

"Oh, my God! Acceleration is downwards! How hard is that to remember?"

"Shouting isn't helping, okay?"

"Jared?" Mave said. "Who are you talking to?"

She stood outside her bedroom door, her headphones pushed down around her neck. He could hear her music, solemn drums and mournful voices. He was at the dining table with his physics homework open in front of him. Dent sat in the chair beside him, arms crossed over his chest.

"Sorry," Jared said, scrambling to think of a reason he was talking to the air.

"Tell her it's your process," Dent said.

Mave came over and lightly touched his shoulder. "Are you okay?"

"Yeah, it's just a tough section."

"You're just not focusing," Dent said. "Tell her it's *your process.* Or not. Let her think you're nuts."

"Talking it through—it's, um, my process?" Jared said.

"Ah," Mave said. She sat in Dent, who gave a frustrated sigh and jerked away. "I dated a playwright who sounded out his dialogue. Great way to get your own seat on the bus."

She laughed and he laughed with her, although he didn't get the joke.

"I was just about to take a tea break when I saw you talking to yourself and got worried," she said. "Edgar used to do that."

"Didn't mean to bug you," Jared said.

"You could never bug me, Jelly Bean. Are you doing anything this afternoon?" She checked her watch. "I'm going to do a shift on the picket lines with the Grandview teachers. Could you help me carry some coffee?"

"Sure," Jared said.

Dent rolled his eyes, drifted back to the TV and sat in the recliner. A break would probably do everyone good.

She wandered back into her bedroom. The kettle whistled on the stove. Jared got up and poured hot water into the mug she'd left on the counter. He brought the tea to her in her bedroom where she was sitting cross-legged on the bed, frowning at her laptop. He waved to get her attention. She pushed her headphones off her ears again.

"It's a good thing it's just tea and not a nuclear warhead," Mave said. "Ugh. This stupid novel will never end. Kick me hard if I ever decide to write one again."

After Jared finished his physics assignment, they walked to Tim Hortons. Mave bought the teachers a box of coffee and doughnuts. He carried the coffee and she carried the pastry boxes and a bag of sugar packets, whitener and stir sticks. The school wasn't too far away. The teachers waved as they approached the picket line. Mave posed for a bunch of pictures and they sat in lawn chairs with signs. She gossiped with the teachers about people Jared didn't know. The traffic bombed by with the occasional honk.

"Get back to work, you freeloading bums!" one guy shouted as his car whizzed by.

"Nice," one of the teachers said. "I wish him head lice three times a year."

"And scabies," another added.

The afternoon grew hot. By four, they were all drooping and Mave promised to bring iced tea the next time around. Jared hauled away the empty coffee box and cups. When they got back home, Mave wanted to ride the Vespa while the weather was still good, and took off.

Before he went in, Jared looked up and noticed Kota sitting morosely on Hank's balcony. He lifted a cigarette in a half-hearted salute. Jared waved back.

The apartment door was open. Jared gritted his teeth. Only one person besides him and Mave had the apartment key: Hank.

He took a slow, calming breath and then walked down the hallway. Eliza looked up from the couch, hugging a stuffed snowman with goofy teeth. He almost didn't recognize her without her princess costume.

"Hi, Jared," she said. "Do you wanna watch TV?"

"Are you supposed to be here?" Jared said.

"Aunty Mave said I could. Daddy sold our TV and DVD player. Momma kicked him out. We changed our locks, but Kookum says that's like closing the barn door after the horse's ass pawns your stuff."

"Oh."

"It's okay," Eliza said. "It's just stuff."

"Do you have a key?"

"The door was open."

Jared patted his basketball shorts and found the keys. He was sure he'd locked the door but couldn't really remember. He felt uncomfortable alone with a kid he didn't know that well. "Does your mom know where you are?"

"Momma's asleep now. She cried all night. Don't wake her, okay? She'll just cry again."

"Do you know your phone number? I'll text her to tell her where you are."

"I know my phone number," Eliza said. "I'm not a *dummy*."

"Sor-ry."

They texted Eliza's mom. Jared brought Eliza a breakfast bar. She looked at it suspiciously.

Jared took a bite to show her it was edible. "Justice made them. It's like a granola bar, but with honey, dried blueberries and ground-up hazelnuts and stuff."

"Ew."

"You can dip it in jam if you want."

"Do you have Nutella?"

"We have a case of Nutella. Help yourself."

"Have you ever seen *Frozen*?"

"No."

"It's only the greatest movie. Ever. You can watch it with me."

"I gotta take a shower."

"I'll start it again when you get out." Eliza took the bar from him.

Jared grabbed some clean clothes from his bedroom and made sure he locked the bathroom door behind him. He took a long shower. He brushed his teeth. Flossed them. Dressed very, very slowly. When he opened the door, he heard Eliza talking to someone. He hoped it was Mave, but it didn't sound like her.

The woman on the couch had long black hair that tumbled down her back. She wore a crumpled navy blazer and matching pants that were too big on her. Eliza's mouth was a giant smear of Nutella. She dipped her bar in the jar and tried to feed it to the woman, who turned her head as Jared walked into the living room. She had a pointy chin, like a fox.

"Hi. You must be Jared," the woman said. "Thanks for the message. I'm Olive. You left Eliza's party before I got there. She loved the balloons, by the way."

"Yeah?" He bet he was lighting up like a stoplight.

She tickled Eliza's belly. "Someone isn't supposed to wander out of the apartment. Someone was supposed to be napping."

"I don't need a nap, Mom."

Olive smiled wryly at Jared. "I'm so sorry—how many times has Eliza made you watch *Frozen*?"

"No worries."

"Nom, nom, nom," Eliza said, dipping the bar again. "Nom, nom, nom, no—"

"Eat the bar, Doodle-bug. You can't just use it as a Nutella delivery system." Olive's eyes were puffy and red from crying, but they crinkled at the corners when she smiled. "Thank you for feeding my little diabetic in training."

"She was no problem."

"Okay, kiddo, we should motor," Olive said to Eliza. "Pizza won't order itself."

"But my movie's not over!"

"You've seen it a billion times. Come on."

Eliza clutched the jar of Nutella as she leapt up and thundered down the hallway. He heard the front door whack the wall. Olive yelled at her to bring the Nutella back, but Eliza was already gone. Jared insisted it was okay—they had a case no one was eating. Olive bent over and grabbed the DVD out of the player.

"If Eliza wanders over here again, just bring her back to me or her grandmother. We're down the hall in 208."

"Not a problem."

"You're a lifesaver," she said. "Bye, Jared."

"Bye."

Dent seemed to have vacated the apartment. Jared wondered where the ghost went when he wasn't watching the sci-fi channel. He went to his room and scrolled through his contacts. He paused at Mrs. Jaks's number, hesitated then dialed. No one picked up. They didn't even have voice mail. It rang and rang. He wondered if they had call display and were avoiding him. More likely they were caught up in medical drama and weren't home.

He'd said his goodbyes when they thought Mrs. Jaks wasn't going to make it through the first round of cancer treatment, and then the second. Jared was a neighbour, not family. Sometimes moments like this were too painful to share. Especially with people who'd dumped their granddaughter and refused to consider dating her again.

———

His night shift was welcome because he hadn't been able to sleep. Mave's bedroom light was still on, but he didn't want to interrupt her writing if she was on a roll. He bounced down the stairs and out onto the street, turning up to the Drive. Traffic was sporadic. He hoped the manager wasn't napping. If he was, it took him a long time to unlock the back entrance and Jared had to stand around in the alley, which stank and was badly lit.

As Jared turned into the alley, Shu flickered into existence near the back door of the Donut Hole. The tendrils of her fraying clothes moved to an unseen wind. Jared's mind skittered over the realization that Shu was a ghost, slipped past it not wanting to believe it. She pointed to something behind him. Jared heard a vehicle speeding up and ran to the safety of a doorway. He didn't stop to look back. As he neared the door, he heard tires squeal and he was hit, a glancing blow, his backpack pulling on his shoulders, a fiery pain radiating from his funny bone as he was propelled into the wall.

The truck sped off down the alley, its driver-side door flapping a few times before the driver pulled it closed. It was hard to tell the colour, a dark truck in a dark alley, older, regular cab, open bed, no rear licence plate. The driver only visible from behind, baseball cap in profile for a moment. Still, he knew who it was. Jared limped to the Donut Hole's doorbell. The backpack had taken the brunt of the blow, but his elbow tingled like it was asleep and now painfully coming to life.

Shu reached up and put her hand over his and it went cold. She looked up at him and her flesh was full of holes, bones shining yellow beneath.

We could curse him.

The thought didn't come from Jared, but he didn't let go of Shu, didn't push her away. Some things were so unfair, you got payback where you could. The cold crept up Jared's arm and numbed his tingling elbow, his tight shoulders where the backpack straps had dug into his flesh. You could see the appeal, Jared thought. A touch of instant karma in a world where stalky assholes got away with drive-by truck-door hits.

He was full of cold power from the ghost of a little girl. Power, if he wanted it.

"Thank you, Shu," Jared said. "You saved me."

She became shy then, taking her hand away from his. *My duty,* he heard her voice say in his head. She skipped down the alley, giving him a little wave before she vanished.

He took another moment before he rang the doorbell. He reminded himself that the life he wanted had a price. He couldn't drink. He couldn't be with Sarah. He couldn't indulge this hot surge of fury. Besides, if his mom couldn't curse David, Jared doubted that he could make a curse stick, even with the help of a ghost.

But Shu had come to warn him. Through the fog of aches and bruises, he knew that meant something. He pushed the doorbell again, made himself not turn that thought over in his head. He waited for the manager to open the door like any normal person in a normal, shitty job. Fake it till you make it.

24

GHOSTAPALOOZA

A week later, Jared's newly assigned physics lab partner returned to their table with another coffee. The dude had some of the worst acne Jared had ever seen and seemed to be trying to hide it by letting his long black hair hang over his face. He didn't say much. They had decided to work on their lab report at a Tim Hortons near the school. When they were done, they exchanged phone numbers.

Jared caught the bus home, keeping a wary eye on the traffic. He still had bruises where the pack's straps had dug in, his elbow ached and his back twinged whenever he tried to bend or turned too fast. He also had a bruise on his forehead. All a reminder that David had always been great at dishing criticism but not so fond of receiving it.

When he got home, Mave and Justice were packing in her room. He threw his backpack on the desk and then took a long, hot bath in borrowed Epsom salts. He'd been racking his brains. If David kept escalating, and Jared didn't say anything, things could get Emerg-worthy.

He couldn't tell his mom. He didn't want her blowing into town and meeting Mave when she was already in the middle of Richie's family drama. Mave, God. He'd tell her if he had to, but she already treated him like he couldn't cross the street on his own; he didn't want her getting all riled up. Which left Sophia, whom he mostly trusted. She also had access to lawyers, though he didn't want her to pay for anything else, especially if he couldn't pay her back. He sniffed himself. Even after his bath Jared still smelled vaguely of doughnuts and grease.

Justice had made lentil soup and biscuits for supper. They ate in the living room, watching a DVD of a bunch of hyper puppets called *The Muppet Show*.

Out of nowhere, Mave said, "If you won't come with me to Banff, maybe Justice can stay with you while I'm gone."

Jared paused mid-sip.

"Maamaan," Justice said.

"Not because I don't trust you, Jared," Mave rushed to say. "I just worry about your stalker. Has David bothered you since you've been here? You seem spooked."

Jared studied his bowl. He wanted to lie to make the awkwardness of the moment go away, but it kind of went against the honesty he was aiming for in AA.

"Has he?" Justice said.

"I don't need a babysitter," Jared said.

Mave looked at him over her glasses. "I'll have Hank keep an eye out."

"Justice can stay here," Jared said.

"Hank likes you," Mave insisted. "He does. He's just not good at expressing himself."

"I'll hang out this weekend," Justice said.

"So it's settled, then," Mave said, patting his hand. "I promised your mother I'd watch out for you and that is what I'm going to do."

"Yay," Jared said.

Sarah had texted: *I saw the fireflies today! Brite as day just for a minute! Still can't hear them, but I saw them!*

Jared lay in bed and wondered if Sarah knew her gran was back in Canada. She had to know. Right? Maybe her mom was exaggerating how sick Mrs. Jaks was to get Jared to tell her where Sarah was hiding. To do her legwork.

Crashpad and his new girlfriend, Muriel, had moved their show to Instagram, where heavily filtered pictures displayed meadows, sunsets and water shots.

My love for you, Crashpad captioned one photo, *is like the stars in the sky: vast and unmeasurable.*

You are my ocean, Muriel captioned another of their pics, *wild, powerful and endless.*

Get a room, Jared thought.

He thought about charging his phone, but the desk was too far—the Advil hadn't kicked in yet, so he ached everywhere. He could hear Justice and Mave laughing in the living room. His earbuds were in his jacket pocket, which was slung over the chair. If he got up and walked a few steps, he could listen to his music until the battery ran out. He meant to do that, meant to take his clothes off, meant to brush his teeth, but the second his eyes closed, he was out.

———

The apartment was quiet that Friday without Mave. Dent lived in the recliner, glued to the science fiction channel. Jared and Kota attended an afternoon meeting together, and then hung out for coffee. Tonight, Kota was off to the dry dance in North Van. He invited Jared, who had no interest in going. That smacked of drama.

Elk! Mave texted him, attached to a picture of elk grazing on someone's lawn.

Strike over. Classes start Monday, Crashpad texted, making a frowny face. His girlfriend frowned beside him, cheek to cheek. *We're sad*.

Miss u Shithead, his mom texted him. *Fkn txt me*.

Alive, Jared texted. *Hi 2 Richie*.

Jared took a shower, and then flopped on the couch and ran through his biology notecards. The cranky-looking Time Lord on the TV screen was frowning into the industrial distance. "Which series is Matt Smith?"

Dent narrowed his eyes. "Don't tell me you're a floppy-hair fan."

"Dude, just because Smith wasn't all Hamlet about shit doesn't mean he wasn't a good Time Lord."

"You can't even remember which season he was in. You don't get a say in which incarnation was superior. He was girl-bait."

"He was okay."

"'Okay'? What kind of analysis is that?"

"I liked him. He was funny."

"Oh, sweet TARDIS, give me strength."

"I can't have an opinion?"

"You can't defend your opinion!"

"So?"

"So this is an argument! You have to argue!"

"We're arguing? Why're we arguing? I just wanted to know what season Matt Smith was in."

"Then google it. Stop ruining *Doctor Who*."

"You watched this one last Sunday. You already know how it's going to end."

"You don't know how to be a true fan, do you?"

Jared unparked himself from the couch and went to check on the cast iron patio set. It had taken a lot of effort to scrape off the rust and Mave's half-hearted attempt to paint them yellow. The new, red paint was dry, so he sanded, vacuumed and shook the spray paint can and gave the chairs and table a second coat. The patio set glistened. He'd put down cardboard and plastic to keep the paint from staining the balcony and it looked like someone had been murdered and the murderer had fled the scene before cleaning up.

He heard a knock on the front door and then the lock clicked.

"Hello!" Justice called. "Jared? It's me, your weekend roommate."

"On the balcony!" Jared said, exasperated.

"I've brought Maamaan's bug back from repairs," Justice said, rolling something that sounded suspiciously like a suitcase down the hallway. "I'm leaving the car keys on the kitchen table."

"Okay," Jared said.

High heels clicked and then Justice poked her head out on the balcony. "Maamaan wants to know if you need anything."

"I'm good," Jared said.

"Want to see the bug?"

He was tired but curious. They went down to the basement parkade. Mave's Volkswagen Beetle had been re-pimped into the colours of the Canucks hockey jersey—blue, green and black. Its logo, a stylized orca, breached on either side, chomping on a broken hockey stick mid-leap. Johnny Canuck, with a giant V on his chest, skated over the hood. The seat covers and steering wheel had additional logos, and two Canucks flags flapped from the rear windows. The new vanity plates read, BLD BLU. Oh, good gravy, Jared thought.

"Want to take a spin?" Justice said.

"I don't think I'm a big-enough Canucks fan for this ride."

Justice laughed. Plus, Jared thought, Hank would have conniptions if he knew he was driving Mave's bug.

"Did you know Mave legally adopted me?" Justice said.

Jared turned to look at her. "Yeah?"

She smiled carefully. "When I was twelve."

"Oh. So . . . she's your mom?"

"Yes. Maamaan has her faults, but she has the biggest heart," Justice said.

Jared wasn't sure what to say. He didn't think he was that easy to read.

Justice cleared her throat. "Come. The armoire awaits."

Since Justice insisted he only help from a distance, Jared held the lobby doors open. Pat and Sponge glared at him as they sweated and grunted to angle half the massive armoire—inlaid with glittering birds and flowers—through the front door. Jared lifted a corner when they started hauling it up the stairs. Hank was supposed to be going to work and was in his security uniform when he joined them. He booted Jared off his corner of the armoire.

"Get," Hank said.

"Safely out of harm's way," Justice said.

"This thing weighs a ton," Pat said. "Let him help, for fuck's sake."

"Mave will go nuclear if her Jelly Bean gets hurt on our watch," Hank said. "Get."

Jared let go of the armoire and climbed up to the apartment, wedging the door open. He sat on the couch, listening to them shouting instructions at each other, and to the assorted thumps and swearing as they struggled.

"I think it's made out of neutronium," Pat said as they huffed down the hallway.

"Or your butt," Sponge said.

"Ha. Ha ha. You're so funny I forgot to laugh."

"Stop messing around," Hank said.

"Yes, Daddy," the brothers chorused.

They set it down outside Mave's door then went downstairs and, after a long time, returned with the other half. Jared sat up to watch them muscle the pieces into Mave's bedroom and then lay back down on the couch, wondering where the remote was and if Dent would mind a break from the nerdfest.

"Hold it!" Hank said.

A nail gun thumped.

(The world is hard.)

— *holding the nail gun and his mom—tense and jumpy, telling him David was going to never, ever let them go if he didn't—*

Pop.

Jared found himself in the apartment hallway. Not all of him, though. He'd left his body on the couch. The hallway light was dark blue. He was cold like he'd just stepped into a freezer. He exhaled, expecting to see a cloud of chilled breath, but there was no cloud because he was having some weird episode, like an epileptic fit. He pushed into the wall, electric zaps hitting him. The mural moved, the painted clouds billowed as a longhouse lowered itself from the sky. The bird men swivelled their heads around as they chewed human body parts. On the other side of the wall the half-bear, half-seal creature roared and chomped through the screaming chiefs. Jared figured he must have fallen asleep and was having an epically weird dream.

Dent stood over his body on the couch. "Jared? Jared?"

"Here," Jared said.

Dent startled. "Holy crap. Jared. Are you, um, you know . . ."

"Dead? No. I just need to get back in my body."

"Oh. Well. A little astral projection, then. Well. Well, well, well. Not disconcerting at all."

They stared at each other. Dent was fraying. His bathrobe was fuzzier and he had spots where you could see right through him. On the couch, Jared's body was perfectly still except for his chest rising and falling. His eyes were open but his stare expressionless. Jared sat on his body. Little sparks zapped around the areas where his real body and his dream body touched. He yipped and hopped off. He rubbed his butt.

"Well?" Dent said.

"This is weird."

"Have you done this before?"

"Yeah. Not willingly. I was being tortured at the time."

"Oh. Well. How did you get back in last time?"

"My neighbour, Mrs. Jaks, kind of guided me back." He thought of her and the walls shimmered, and then everything blurred and—

Pop.

He was in a hospital room. The lights were turned low and machines beeped. Mrs. Jaks lay in the bed, a blanket pulled high on her thin body. Her face was swollen, her skin shiny and tight. A thin nurse was sponging her legs.

"Mrs. Jaks?" Jared said. He didn't want to be here. He didn't want to see this. He wanted—

Pop.

He was back in the apartment behind Dent.

"Dent," he said.

Dent spun around. "Not funny!"

"Sorry," Jared said. "Didn't mean to scare you."

"Where'd you go?"

"I don't know. I thought about Mrs. Jaks and then I was with her in a hospital room."

He heard the guys thumping around in Mave's bedroom, shouting instructions at each other. They sounded like they were underwater. Jared wished he'd gone to the dry dance with Kota. He really had to get some headwork done. If he was going to freak out and hallucinate every time he heard a nail gun, things could get awkward.

Something hissed like a snake.

"Uh, Jared? Don't . . . disappear," Dent said. "Okay? It can't hurt you."

A body crawled out of his bedroom. He assumed it was a man because it was bald, with a few straggly hairs on its shiny scalp. He wore some kind of cloth around his privates but was otherwise naked, skin yellowish-white like a halibut belly, like a chain smoker's fingers. Every bone in his body poked through his skin. The guy shivered, eyes closed, sniffing the floor.

"What the hell is that?" Jared said, backing up.

"It's the thing in your wall," Dent said.

It followed him as he backed away and then lunged, and he felt its cold mouth through his socks sucking his toes.

"Ew," Jared said, shaking his foot. "Get off me, you freak!"

"That's all it does," Dent said. "Kind of a fetish thing, I think. It drove Edgar nuts trying to get rid of it. That's when he started painting the walls and putting up wards. That's what started this little ghostapalooza."

"Get it off me!"

Pop.

Jared was back in the hallway, in the same spot he'd jumped to before. He heard a hiss, and realized it was the sound of the guy as he slid over the phantom ground. He tried to back into Hank's apartment but was zapped like he'd run into an electric fence. He yelped.

Dent poked his head through the apartment door. "We can't go in there. Some kind of force field."

Jared backed down the hallway. The thing slid in and out of the walls, trying to sneak up on him.

"Stop it!" Jared shouted. "Stop it right now! Stay!"

"It's not a dog," Dent said.

"Make it stop!"

Jared pushed his way through the wall and ended up in someone else's living room. The hiss followed him. He ran through the wall, past a bedroom and into another living room.

"Jared?" Eliza said. She was wearing her princess dress again.

The living room was empty except for some toys scattered on the floor. It didn't look like anyone was living here. Jared noticed Shu was floating near the ceiling, slowly coming down like a deflating balloon.

"Crap," Jared said. His hallucination was getting weirder and weirder.

"Wait!" Eliza said. "Jared, wait!"

His feet became stuck to the floor like he'd been glued to the spot. "Something's after me! I have to go!"

"Did you die?" Eliza said.

"I'm sleeping," Jared said. "This is a dream."

"I'm awake," Eliza said.

"You're awake in my dream."

"Now you're being a big silly," Eliza said.

The zombie ghost girl tooted her wooden recorder.

The thing slipped through the door and wiggled across the floor straight for Jared's toes. The zombie girl's mouth opened, but in a way mouths shouldn't open, like her jaw had come unhinged. Her tongue lolled out like a wet carpet. Her teeth were double-rowed like a shark's.

The thing paused, half in and half out of the wall.

"Bad thing. Go home," Eliza said.

The thing blurred and then was sucked away, disappearing.

"Thanks," Jared said.

The zombie girl tooted her recorder. She whispered in Eliza's ear.

"Jared, Shu says you should get back in your body," said Eliza, "or the thing in the wall will keep you in the spirit world."

"What is it?"

"A bad spirit."

Shu tooted. She held up her hand.

"She won't hurt you," Eliza said.

Shu's hand was unexpectedly warm. It had been freezing when she saved him from David. Jared's feet came unstuck. She led him through the front door, down the hallway back to Mave's apartment. Eliza followed, locking her apartment door behind her and then tucking her keys in her purse. She skipped down the hallway behind them.

Mave's door was still propped open. The painted creatures on the walls of the hall replayed their roles like a GIF, messily devouring people.

Assorted thumps and more swearing came from Mave's bedroom. Dent was standing over Jared's body. He looked up when they came in. He put his hands on his hips. "Oh, for the love of TARDIS. What are *they* doing here?"

"Mean old man," Eliza said.

Shu opened her mouth in her creepy, unhinged way.

"Be nice," Jared said. "Everyone be nice."

"He doesn't like us," Eliza said.

"They're both little nightmares," Dent said.

"He hogs the TV."

"One can only watch *Frozen* so many times and remain sane."

"Your show is stupid. And you're stupid, you stupid old poopy head."

"Well, your show is romantic drivel."

"Enough trash talk," Jared said. "Can we focus on getting me back in my body? Please?"

"How did you get out of your body?" Eliza said.

"I think I'm dreaming," Jared said.

The walls shimmered then throbbed. Something hummed like a power line.

"You're not dreaming," Eliza said. "The thing is back through your wall again."

"It's a pest," Dent said.

"It's bad," Eliza said. "We should call Huey. He'll take care of it."

"Who's Huey?" Jared said.

"Fantastic," Dent said. "Let's invite all the neighbourhood weirdos in to interrupt my *Doctor Who* time."

"Huey!" Eliza shouted. "Huey, come here!"

The thumping in Mave's bedroom stopped. Justice came into the living room.

"It's just Eliza!" Justice shouted. She bent down to the little girl. "Does your mother know you're here?"

"She's crying in the shower," Eliza said. "Daddy's friends took our furniture. He owes them money."

"Oh, poor dears. Do you want to watch *Frozen*?"

"Yay!" Eliza said.

"Noooooo," Dent said.

The thing crawled out of the bedroom, creeping along the baseboards.

"Ew," Jared said. He tried to hop onto the couch and ended up standing on the ceiling, head pointed to the floor. Shu kicked at it, but it dodged her foot. The thing circled the spot directly below him.

"Crap," Jared said.

"Where did Maamaan move your DVDs?"

"Jared left his body," Eliza said. "He's stuck on the ceiling."

"Oh, that's nice," Justice said, rummaging through the media cabinet. "Is he playing with your imaginary friend, Sue?"

"She's *Shu*."

"Shoe? What kind of shoe is she?"

Something banged on the window. The thing from the wall skittered sideways, hissing. Jared swallowed. The large red flying head battered itself furiously against the window.

"Huey!" Eliza said.

"Hurray, indeed! Here we go!" Justice said, sliding in the DVD.

"Help," Jared said.

Huey flew in the balcony door and chased the thing around the living room. It screeched as Huey bounced off its back, biting its pale skin. It rolled and wriggled, but Huey kept bouncing off it like it was a trampoline. Justice frowned at the remote. The DVD started and Eliza plopped herself in the recliner.

"I'll phone your mother and leave a message that you're here," Justice said.

"Hey!" Dent shouted. "Turn it back! Turn it back right now!"

"Thank you, Justice," Eliza said sweetly.

"Don't wake Jared. No more shouting," Justice said. "Okay?"

"Okay," Eliza said.

Huey chased the thing back into Jared's bedroom. Eliza stuck her tongue out at Dent as Justice went back to wrestling the armoire. Jared looked down at his body. He sighed and wished he was on the floor. He wished very hard. Shu floated up to him and played him a song on her recorder.

"Yeah," Jared said. "That's nice, Shu. Can you help me down?"

"You don't want to go on the floor," Eliza said. "Or you'd be here already."

"Thanks, Yoda," Dent said. "Now get out of my chair."

"It's not your chair. It's Aunt Mave's chair. And you're dead, so you don't need a chair."

"Wa wa waaaaah," Dent said. "I hear a big, whiny baby."

"Guys," Jared said.

"I'm watching *Frozen* a hundred times. Stand there and rot, you old meanie."

Jared jumped, hoping to catch the couch and pull himself back into his body, but the ceiling sucked him back. His hands were so cold he couldn't feel them anymore. He opened and closed them, trying to get circulation back.

The flying head rolled upside down so they were looking at each other eye to eye.

"Hi," Jared said.

The head waggled hello.

"I'm stuck. Can you help me?" Jared said.

Huey rammed himself into Jared.

"Ow!"

But Jared came unglued from the ceiling and fell with a plop all the way through the floor to the apartment below. The old woman who lived there glared at her ceiling. Huey came through it and bounced off him, hitting him with the force of a baseball. Jared snapped awake in his body, feeling his legs and arms tingle back to life. His eyes were so dry, they watered. His heart trip-hammered. He coughed. His big toe was numb.

"You watch TV all day!" Eliza said.

"Go home, you brat!" Dent said.

"Thank you," Jared whispered to Huey, who hovered above him. He dipped shyly before zipping out the door and disappearing.

"Must be nice napping while we slave," Sponge said, peering over the back of the couch.

"Dude," Pat said. "Did you know you sleep with your eyes open? It's so wrong."

"Yeah, you freak," Sponge said. "Close your eyes like a normal person."

25

ALWAYS SOMETHING DIFFERENT GOING WRONG

Jared came home from his Friday night shift and slept despite his brain's best efforts to tangle itself in knots about his increasingly weird life. He woke to the scent of coffee and something baking that smelled very honeyed. The painted heads smiled at him as he walked past them. He smiled back, and then realized how bizarre that was, but it seemed rude to do anything else. They liked him and they had been his first warning against the thing in the wall. It couldn't hurt to be polite.

Justice had made more breakfast bars. She wore a flowing red pantsuit and heels so high and pointed they could impale a gopher. She cradled her cellphone between her ear and her shoulder. "Morning," she mouthed, gesturing to the bars.

"Hey," Jared said.

Justice scrolled through her iPad as she listened to a loud voice on the other end of her phone. Jared poured himself a coffee and grabbed a plate for a couple of bars. He sat at the other end of the table and checked his own phone.

"But if he doesn't show on Monday, I'm not holding his spot," Justice said into her phone. "Look, I haven't seen him in weeks and I have other kids who actually want . . ."

Nothing from Sarah or his mom. Crashpad was posting sad emojis and broken hearts along with his undying love for Muriel, who posted pictures of herself with a filter that made her eyes creepy-large and tear-filled.

Justice windmilled her fingers in a wrap-it-up gesture. "Uh-huh. Uh-huh. Well, you're the boss, boss. I'll give you my written notes by Tuesday. Is that all right? Okey-dokey. Bye." Justice banged the cellphone against her forehead.

"You okay?" Jared said.

"Micromanagers," Justice explained. "I have to leave for the store soon. Could you wrap the breakfast bars when they cool?"

"Yup."

"Maamaan's arriving at 2 p.m. on Monday. Would you be a dear and pick her up? I said I would, but something's come up."

"Sure."

"Fantastic. Flight info is on the calendar. The tank is full. I left some money under the keys for parking."

"'kay."

"You're so sane," Justice said. "It's so wonderful."

"You have a really low bar for sanity."

She laughed. "Maamaan's roommates are usually *artistic*. All right. I'm going to dance off some frustration tonight, so don't wait up."

"Later."

She stood and smoothed her pantsuit. "Call if you get in trouble."

"Bye."

Jared went to Mave's room. The new armoire dominated an entire wall, but all her clothes were hidden and the room looked calm and organized. You couldn't even tell where Justice had chopped it up to fit it up the stairwell. Jared turned on his aunt's printer. The password was the same for the printer as it was for her router. He made a copy of his old restraining order against David that Sophia had couriered to him. He could probably get away with a peace bond. David would contest it, though, and shit would get real. The alternatives were more Facebook drama or his mother—one being kind of useless results-wise and the other holding the possibility of him being charged as an accessory to murder. He folded the copy of the restraining order and stuffed it in his back pocket. If someone found him in a ditch, it would at least point in David's direction.

Dent slouched in the recliner, moving reluctantly when Jared asked for help with his physics homework. The lesson was easier this time and Jared felt better once he finished his homework. Dent floated back to the TV afterwards. The ghost tutoring was weird. Of course it was weird. His mom's stories of the dead all ended with souls being eaten or curses that enslaved you. But he couldn't afford a living tutor and Dent seemed content with their arrangement. Jared wrapped the breakfast bars in parchment paper and put them in the fridge.

He needed to do something about David, but he didn't know what. He sucked at fisticuffs. And David never fought fair anyway. He was a sneak-attack kind of guy, as with the truck in the alley. He'd lay low until Jared forgot he existed and then show up again. It bothered him, the waiting. He couldn't control what David was going to do.

The deep unease settled in his guts, like a smoke detector going off in a distant room. David had picked Jared as a target. David was escalating. Jared sat at the table and considered his options, tumbling them over in his head like worry stones.

Well, chasing his mental tail wasn't doing him any good. Time for a meeting.

Jared was trying to decide if he'd stay and sit through another meeting or if he wanted to go back to the apartment and study some more, when someone nudged him. He turned to see the girl with blond hair with purple tips, wearing a blue T-shirt and black cargo shorts.

"Hey," she said.

"Hey," Jared said.

"Where's your cousin?"

"Dunno." Lex, Jared remembered.

"You wanna get a coffee?" Lex said.

"Sure," Jared said.

Lex lived in an older apartment building. Her bed was a lumpy futon mattress on the floor. She had a red sleeping bag and no sheets. Her Batman lamp figurine had fruity scratch-and-sniff stickers on his feet and butt. She brought him a mug of coffee, black because she'd run out of sugar and milk. She scrolled through her phone and plopped it on an ancient, well-loved red Beats pill speaker. After a single guitar exploded into many, the vocals were scream-y and tortured.

"'Tears Don't Fall,'" Jared said. "Me and Mom used to play *Halo* after I got home from school and she'd sing along every time this came on. Wow, that brings me back."

Lex said, "Fucking sellouts. Jesus, now I have to delete every single Bullets for My Valentine song from my library."

"It was a pretty cool game."

"Fuck nuggets." She reached up and flipped through her playlist. Guitars rose and fell like someone struggling to get off the floor and sliding back down. The intro went on and on. "Destruction Unit. Were they ever in your lame-ass games?"

"No," Jared said.

"Good."

Jared watched her take off her shirt. She flung it towards her laundry basket and flopped beside him, naked from the waist up. Her breasts looked like they would fit in his mouth and he really, really wanted to see if they would. She touched his crotch, cupped him.

He traced an old scar up her arm and then put his hand on the back of her neck and pulled her in for a kiss. She felt up his ass. The kiss went on until she tilted her head up, sighing as he slid his hands down. He thought they were going to jerk each other off, but she unbuttoned his jeans.

The last time he'd been laid had been—what? God. God, her skin, her mouth travelling down, warm. She reached under the mattress and pulled up a condom. Holy fuck, he thought when she tried to help out, holding his cock. He surged, her fingers, her breasts, and he came, urgently, instantly, like a kid jerking off for the first time, and Lex swore. Her Batman lamp had a clumpy spray of semen across the black lampshade. He felt himself going bright red and they both collapsed back to the futon, panting.

"It's been a while," Jared said sheepishly.

She punched him. "You loser. Fuck."

"Here," Jared said. "I'll bring you up to speed."

Lex's roommates came home early in the morning, banged on her bedroom door and told her to turn it down. She cranked the music to deafening levels before she lowered the volume. They listened to her roommates loudly calling Lex down.

"I wish you could screw yourself sober," Lex said.

"That would be a very popular programme," Jared said.

Jared and Lex were at the breakfast table. Her roommates ignored them—other than pointed side-eyes—while they made an omelette and argued about some soccer thing. Lex was wrapped in her sleeping bag. Jared had put his clothes back on. He borrowed her charger to check his phone.

Gran's in a coma, Sarah had texted him late last night. *Can't stop crying.*

Jared texted her back. *Where r u?*

"Girlfriend?" Lex said, sipping her coffee.

"What?"

"You've got guilt-face."

"Oh, no. Yes. My ex. But we're friends. Her gran's dying. It's shitty."

"You're one of those," Lex said, lighting a cigarette.

"One of what?"

"I like to keep things disposable," she said.

Jared emerged from Lex's apartment after a night of loud death metal bands on replay, no-name instant noodle cups and screwing. She didn't ask for his phone number. He didn't offer it.

He walked home. A little bruised, lots of tender spots that didn't like being rubbed against his clothes. Pleasantly tired, ready for a day of napping. Which was pretty much the kind of hookups he'd had before Sarah, but back then he'd been either plastered or stoned.

Sarah still hadn't answered his text.

Everything about this hookup had been familiar. Comfortable. He hadn't given a rat's ass about school or work. Ghosts. Spirits. Stalkers. And it had been easy.

So he wasn't sure what was bothering him now. He couldn't pinpoint the blossoming guilt. He didn't really want to go back to Mave's apartment. He didn't want to find Sarah there. Maybe he still wanted to get back with her and had just fucked up everything. No, he thought, no, he'd been on this merry-go-round so many times. Just no. He liked her gran. Mrs. Jaks was a good person. He wanted to stop feeling guilty about her dying, about not visiting her more often, about not being at the hospital right now. Sarah was a constant reminder of things he wanted to forget, human and magical. He wanted to party like a normal kid and not have his life fall apart afterwards. He wanted to not miss the one person who'd been with him through his parents' divorce, through the horror show that had been David, and his mom nail-gunning David. Mrs. Jaks had been a homey constant, a bright spot. And now he wasn't bothering to show up for her end.

You have a real talent for sucking the joy out of everything, said a familiar voice in his head. *You didn't murder a hobo. You got laid. Teenagers. Yeesh.*

Piss off, Jared thought at his biological father. *Stay out of my head.*

Your constant whining ruined Vancouver for me, you know that? I'm not in your head. You're broadcasting again. This is worse than the summer you were obsessed with "The Ketchup Song."

Jared's heart trip-hammered, embarrassed, thinking of every-thing he'd done lately and hoped he hadn't accidentally shared with Wee'git. And then he realized that he'd been five, maybe six when he'd loved that song. He could only play it when he was alone because his mom kept threatening to break his CD if he played it again.

Wait a minute, Jared thought. *Weren't you buried somewhere when I was five? Or was that a lie too?*

I heard you through the veil, Wee'git said. *That's how annoying you were. You and your off-tune, half-remembered Spanglish singing made me want to die harder.*

Their relationship had not improved with age. Part of the problem had been that Jared hadn't known he was talking to his biological father and not a voice in his head. So one of the least-involved fathers in the world felt free to make snarky remarks about Jared's life from childhood to now, like it was a reality TV show he didn't really like but was too lazy to change the channel on. The other problem was his tendency to get in the pants of Jared's female relatives. Like his mom. And his gran. When he was wearing other people's faces. People they loved.

I saved your ungrateful ass, Wee'git thought at him.

Once.

Believe me, I won't make that mistake again.

Yeah, go back to ignoring me.

Done.

The drizzle sparkled as the sun broke through the clouds. Jared could see his apartment building now. He stopped in for a coffee, adding a cookie. He listened to his thoughts, wondering if Wee'git was still there.

Stop thinking about me, his bio-dad said.

Are you still listening in?

I'd rather have your mother shoot my head off again than spend another second in your head.

I can arrange that.

I'm not the bad guy! I'm protecting you from the bad guys!

Why?

Silence. More silence. Someone cleared their throat and Jared realized he was holding up the line in front of the sugar-and-cream station.

"Sorry," he mumbled.

He sat on the patio and thought about his sobriety, how he'd fought for it and how close he'd come to losing it so many times. When his thoughts tried to wander over to Sarah, or David, or Lex, or the absentee father who was listening in because he happened to be close by, Jared thought about the things he wanted in life: A steady job in a town big enough to have brown people but small enough not to have too many traffic problems. Someone sober in his life who didn't take themselves too seriously, but seriously enough. A small, easy-to-heat house with a wood stove, a vegetable plot and cold frames. Maybe kids. You know, later, when he was more grounded. A dog—a big, friendly pound mutt. A newer car for work and an older truck to bushwhack the back roads on the weekends.

Wow, Wee'git thought. *I'm out. If we never meet again, enjoy the dullest life ever.*

Buh-bye, Jared thought.

Jared took the lid off his coffee cup to get the last dregs of caffeine to soothe his throbbing headache. The sun played hard to get. The traffic got heavier as the morning went on. He let it go. He let the bastard go. He forgave and forgot. Wee'git wasn't renting head-space. Not in his head. His phone pinged.

Jared, Kota texted him. *U home soon?*

Ya, he texted Kota. *I'm close.*

K.

Jared crushed his coffee cup against the table and then tossed it in a trash can as he walked home. Kota was sitting with his back against Mave's apartment door. He had his earbuds in and was mood-ily staring at his cell. His eyes were bright red, sleepy and puffy. He reeked of skunk. Jared waved to get his attention.

"Mind if I hang?" Kota said, taking out his earbuds. "I'm not ready to deal with Hank and his fucking pious bullshit."

Jared could hear the Starr brothers trash-talking each other through Hank's closed apartment door. "Sure. Come on in."

"Thanks," Kota said. He struggled to stand, trying to push him-self off the floor and falling over. Jared held out his hand and hauled him up. Kota giggled.

Jared unlocked the door and Kota followed him down the long, shoe-filled hallway. Dent sat in the recliner. He rolled his eyes when he saw Kota.

"What's *he* doing here?" Dent said.

"Wanna crash in my room?" Jared said to Kota. "I've got a shift tonight, so the bed's up for grabs."

"Your room's fucking creepy," Kota said, flopping on the couch face first.

"You okay?"

"I'm not drunk," Kota mumbled into the couch cushion. "Jus' baked."

"I know. I'm going to take a shower. Need the bathroom?"

Kota giggled again. "Yeah, go wash off your dirty weekend, Jelly Bean."

"You can't just leave him here!" Dent shouted as Jared shut the bathroom door.

After his shower, he took his dirty clothes down to the laundry room, put in some soap and then went back to the apartment and pulled out his textbooks again. Kota snored on the couch.

Did Wee'git talk to all 533 of his kids? a part of his brain wondered.

He wondered then what Granny Nita knew. He'd only written her a short letter to say hello, I'm okay. She seemed fairly willing to talk, but maybe not about Wee'git, Jared suspected. Wee'git had lied to him—outright lied about how long he'd been listening in on Jared's broadcasting or thoughts or whatever they were. Why would he do that?

"If I keep the partying to the weekends," Kota mumbled to himself, "I can handle it."

Jared got up and filled the kettle. He rinsed out his aunt's Bodum and ground some coffee beans. While he was waiting for the water to boil, Kota staggered to the bathroom.

"Take him to a meeting!" Dent yelled.

The lights flickered.

He listened to the kettle for a moment and then filled the Bodum. His cousin returned from the bathroom with his hair combed. His eyes were still sleepy, but he'd washed his face. Jared pressed the coffee. Kota came into the kitchen, expression wary. He watched Jared as if he expected a lecture, leaning against the counter faux-casually, too posed to be natural.

"Coffee?" Jared said.

"Sure."

Jared suggested they go to the balcony. Kota hugged his mug, and stared at the newly painted patio chairs. Then he sat, and smoked and brooded, staring off into the middle distance. Jared watched the street. An hour passed, the time marked by the number of cigarettes Kota butted out in the dead planter on the table. Jared checked his phone every few minutes, but no one tried to call or text him. Or made snarky remarks in his head, pretending to be his thoughts. He asked Kota if he wanted more coffee, and then went down to the laundry room and put his clothes in the dryer. When he came back to the apartment, he started the kettle again, rinsing out the Bodum.

Things seemed crazy right now. He could react and react and react. Or he could let go of the unfairness of his life, the looming possibility of failure. The looming death of Mrs. Jaks. His disposability to his parents. His stalker. All anyone ever had was the present. He had supper. A place to stay. A bed. A little nest egg under his mattress. A small but growing total in his savings account. He had meetings, as many as he wanted to attend.

"Is he leaving soon?" Dent said, poking his head through the wall.

"Probably not," Jared said. "But no one's going to fight you for the TV."

Dent floated back to the recliner. "You're the biggest chaos magnet I've ever met."

"Wait'll you meet my mom," Jared said.

26

FIREFLIES REDUX

Early Monday morning, Jared was wired from all the coffee he'd drunk to stay awake at work, so he dragged the freshly painted cast iron patio set over to Olive's apartment so they'd have something to sit on. Eliza's kokum, Darlene, answered the door. She clapped her hands when she saw the chairs and table. They set them up in the living room, where there was an old-school tube TV the size of a small freezer sitting on the floor, currently tuned to *The Young and the Restless*. Eliza snoozed on a sleeping bag on the living room floor, arms wrapped tightly around her stuffed snowman. Shu hovered near the ceiling, facing the wall.

"It took seven men to get that damn TV in here," Kokum Darlene said. "Let 'em try to steal that."

At lunchtime, Kokum Darlene brought him a paper grocery bag full of freshly fried bannock. Jared didn't have the heart to tell her he couldn't look at anything deep-fried without feeling slightly nauseous. His pores were still oozing fryer fat from his Sunday night shift.

He took out a few pieces for Kota, who remained passed out on the couch. He put a few aside for Justice in case she dropped by. The bannock was still warm and there was still enough to feed an army, so he decided to take the rest of it over to Barbie's place. The address she had given him led him to the basement suite of a house just a few blocks away.

Barbie's oldest daughter, Bernadette, was home and bored, baby-sitting the two younger kids, who weren't in school yet. She talked his ear off as she brought out some maple syrup, telling him Barbie was at work at the Vancouver Aboriginal Friendship Centre and her dad was driving shuttles for a TV series currently filming in Richmond. Bernadette was taking night courses to become a dental technician. She told him Pat and Sponge were tech support at a computer store. Jared was surprised. They never talked about work. He'd assumed they were still in high school. Their twin mattresses were propped up against the living room wall. The kids flopped them down and hopped on them, spreading maple syrup all over the sheets. The brothers had plastic totes beside their beds marked *Robertʒ Clothʒ —touch and DIE you bratʒ*, and *Pat's unmentionables: Open at your own RISK!!!!*

After claiming he needed to study, Jared stopped at Café Calabria and treated himself to a latte. When he checked his phone, his mom had sent him selfies with her new-found in-laws on horses, on ATVs, at the hospital. Mave had sent him pictures of her writing cabin, with its excellent view of elk and the fall forest with its gold-and-rust leaves against the dark-green spruce and pine.

Miss you, she'd texted. *Can't wait to see you this afternoon!*

Jared squeezed in a meeting. He spotted Lex coming in and nodded hello. She sat beside him, casually, like they were strangers. Her hair was green today, spiked in uneven, short braids. She had matching eyeliner. She wore a green jersey of a sports team he didn't recognize.

"Hey," Jared said afterwards.

"Hey," Lex said.

"You wanna hang later?"

"Ugh," she said, getting up to leave. "Don't smother me."

Jared brought his biology notecards to the airport and flipped through them while he sat on a bench near the carousel destined to spit out Mave's luggage. Either he was getting the hang of studying or he was delusional. He almost felt ready for the first quiz tomorrow. He'd never felt ready for a quiz before. He heard Mave before he saw her, a piercing shriek. He saw her hand waving above a crush of rumpled passengers.

"Jared!" she shouted as if they were on different mountaintops.

"Hey," Jared said as she ran in for a bulldozing hug.

They rocked. She pecked his cheek. "How was your weekend?"

He shrugged.

"I hear we have an asylum seeker."

"What?"

"Kota."

"He's just crashing. He's not moving in or anything."

"My sweet Jelly Bean. We need to chat about who you are responsible for and who you are not."

"There's your suitcase."

It was hard to miss. Someone had painted her black suitcase with a giant red ovoid eye and glued an abalone button on it for a pupil. It also had red pom-poms around the edges. He grabbed it and wheeled it to Mave, who linked arms with him as they walked towards the parking.

"You missed a great trip," she said. "You'll have to come next time."

"We're on level three."

Once the elevator doors opened and she saw her refreshed ride, Mave uttered a piercing scream that rang through the parking lot. Mave skipped. She immediately had to go for a spin. She honked the horn before they got out of the garage, and the horn played "Na Na Hey Hey Kiss Him Goodbye."

On the highway, other Canuck fans honked enthusiastically as they passed. When Mave honked back, they went nuts, a noisy parade of two. They grabbed drive-through coffee and cruised up and down the Drive.

"I know it was supposed to be a surprise, but Justice also put up an armoire in your room," Jared said, in a plot to get them home.

More screaming when they reached the apartment. Kota groggily hopped off the couch to watch Mave bounce up and down in front of her new-to-her closet.

"I love it!" she screamed, temporarily deafening them.

"Neighbours," Jared said. "Lots of neighbours." To Kota, he said, "There's bannock in the kitchen."

"Oh, my God, look at it!" Mave ran her hands over the inlaid wood. "Look at it."

She insisted on taking him out to dinner to celebrate. She then invited Kota, who said he had to take care of some shit. Mave tugged on Jared's sleeve and they left. They parked in front of a small red house that was divided into smaller apartments. Mave cried as soon as Justice opened her door, and then Justice cried. She lived in a bachelor suite with the oven and sink beside her daybed. Her window overlooked the backyard, an untamed jungle of trees, vines and birds. Justice wore a flouncy dress the colour of lemon curd. She had oversized sunglasses perched on her head. They held each other like one of them was dying. Jared jammed his hands into his pockets and rocked on his heels, wishing he'd stayed home.

"Really, Maamaan," Justice said, holding Mave at arm's length and studying her yoga pants.

"Travel gear, darling."

"That's all well and good, but why on earth are you still wearing it?"

"I had to thank you immediately. I love my new closet. I adore my Canuck bug."

"Ah. Good. I was worried it was the first signs of incipient insanity."

After supper, Mave dropped him off at the apartment so she could take Justice out for mimosas. He went upstairs and unplugged his phone from its charger, flopping down on the couch. Kota was gone, along with one of Jared's shirts and a note saying he'd bring it back. Dent was back on the recliner with the TV tuned to the science fiction channel.

Jared made himself coffee. He brought the mug to his bedroom and cracked open his books when the intercom buzzed.

"Hey," Sarah said.

"Come on up," Jared said.

He waited at the door for her, heart trip-hammering, palms clammy. Sarah's hair was braided into a crown and she wore a jumpsuit that looked like it had been designed by grannies tripping on acid. Her glittery makeup had a smeared lightning bolt over one eye. Her dark lipstick had feathered and run beyond her mouth. This Sarah didn't have any fireflies, though. The only other time he'd seen Sarah without fireflies was when he was actually looking at a shape-shifting otter who was using Sarah's form to try to lure him into the woods. That had ended in a cave, with him being used as a chew toy, his toe bitten off and eaten in front of him.

They were both silent.

"Who are you?" Jared said.

"Britney Spears," this version of Sarah said.

"You're not Sarah."

"It's me," she said. "Jared. For fuck's sake, stop playing around."

He looked up to see if the fireflies were in the ceiling or something, but he couldn't hear their telltale hum. "You're not Sarah."

"They're gone," Sarah said. Her shoulders heaved and she leaked tears. "He ate them and then he left me."

Jared crossed his arms over his chest, refusing to let her inside the apartment until he was sure it was Sarah. "Who ate them?"

"He said he was a medicine man. I couldn't stop him. He disappeared and he took them. I felt them leave." Her face contorted, and then she took a few deep breaths. "Are any of them left?" Sarah said, suddenly looking away. "Can you see any of them?"

Jared watched her. "No."

She bent over, sobbing. Jared reluctantly led her inside and sat her at one of the kitchen chairs and then sat beside her. He didn't feel like she was a fake Sarah, but it was weird seeing her without her fireflies.

"I killed them," she whispered. "I got them killed."

Eventually, Jared reached over and she crawled into his lap and cried into his shoulder. He held her as waves of her grief washed over him. Dent made an annoyed sound and popped out of the room.

———

Her body was warm and heavy against his. They lay in his bed, curled together under the quilt. He wiped the snot from her nose with the hem of his T-shirt. Sarah blew her nose hard.

"Missed you," she said.

"Missed you, too," Jared admitted.

Her eyes looked up to the ceiling. "Are you sure they're gone?"

"Yes."

"He seemed like a good guy," Sarah said. "I thought he was my friend right up to the moment his jaw unhinged and he started eating them. He put the rest of them in some kind of bag and disappeared. Poof."

They were quiet. The traffic outside was a steady rumble. Having Sarah beside him was comfortable. Jared drifted. He felt his cellphone buzz, but he was too tired to check who was texting him. He wondered if the fireflies had suffered. If they felt pain the way humans felt pain. He didn't like them, but he didn't want them eaten. If any of them were alive, he hoped they found their way back to Sarah. He hated to see her suffer like this.

The painted heads on his bedroom wall shivered. A spot of light above the bed began to glow and then sparked like bulbs exploding. Suddenly, about a dozen fireflies hung in the air above them, faint and silent.

Sarah sat up. She raised her face, staring blindly. "Are they back?"

"Just a few of them," Jared said. "They seem pretty weak."

"What did you do?"

"I didn't do anything," Jared said, not wanting to get into the whole painted heads and ghosts and spirits conversation with her. "They just appeared."

"You did something," Sarah insisted.

"I didn't. I really didn't."

The fireflies rose, until they were circling half-through the ceiling.

Sarah pushed the quilt off her legs and rolled out of bed. "Are they saying anything?"

"No. "

"Thank you," the fireflies said.

"I didn't do anything," Jared said.

The painted heads had done something. They had read his mind. Or the fireflies had just come back. It wasn't him. He wasn't responsible. He didn't even like the pompous little asses.

Sarah lay back down beside him, her makeup smeared more than ever, and rested her head on his arm.

"Thank you," she said. "I knew you could help us."

Jared made coffee. Sarah was asleep in his bed. He was too wired to do homework. He checked the freezer and brought out a pack of ground hamburger. He defrosted it in the microwave. He boiled some sweet potatoes and mashed them, throwing together a pan of shepherd's pie. He needed to keep busy, to not think too hard about what it all meant. The oven timer clicked.

Jared walked into the bedroom and watched Sarah sleep. The fireflies were a dim glow. The timer went off in the kitchen. Jared hadn't been conscious of time passing, but he went and took the shepherd's pie out of the oven. Kota walked in and helped himself.

"I found another place to stay," he said. "Everyone can calm the fuck down about me falling off the wagon now. I'm not your fucking problem anymore."

"Dude," Jared said. "Chill, okay?"

Kota dropped his plate on the counter. "Suck-up. You'll say anything for free rent."

Jared turned the oven off. He watched Kota stomp away and heard the apartment door slam. He heard a telltale slither and from the corner of his eye saw something moving in the wall.

"Huey!" Jared called.

The slithering stopped. Jared covered the shepherd's pie loosely with tinfoil. He didn't know when Sarah would wake. He went back to his room and crawled into bed beside her. She made an annoyed sound, then flung an arm over him. The fireflies had perked up and were spinning faster, brighter. The painted faces in the wall watched the fireflies suspiciously.

He liked having Sarah here. He didn't even mind the fireflies. They glowed. His eyelids shut and he listened to her breathing. He heard Justice and Mave come in, their laughter. He drifted. When he woke again, Sarah was checking her phone beside him.

"What time is it?" Sarah said.

"Dunno."

"Blanket."

He pulled the quilt from the bottom of the bed where it was crumpled. He covered her and she kissed his hand.

Sunlight poured through the blinds, warming Jared's face. He slid his arm out from under Sarah's head. She stayed asleep as he carefully crawled over her. His arm was numb, tingling to life. He used the bathroom. He brushed his teeth, staring at his reflection.

Jared made coffee. He chopped up some fruit for a salad because he knew Sarah liked that for breakfast. He took his coffee to the couch and blankly watched the morning news with the volume turned low.

"I thought I heard voices," Mave said, coming into the living room.

"There's coffee."

"I love you." Mave banged around the kitchen and came to sit beside him with a mug and a small bowl of fruit salad. "Who is she?"

"Sarah," Jared said. "My ex-girlfriend."

Mave's eyebrows went up. "Oh?"

"It didn't work. We want different things."

"And you're still friends?"

Jared shrugged. "She dropped by. We started talking. We fell asleep. We didn't, um, do anything."

Mave yawned. "That really isn't any of my business, is it?"

Jared stared at the TV. He hadn't dated since he broke up with Sarah. He'd been pretty ripped up about everything, and then he'd spent a lot of time getting sober, couchsurfing and working. Plus all the girls he knew were into partying. The sober girls were from square families who didn't want their daughters dating someone so hard-core he'd needed AA to straighten up. And, if he was forced to admit it, he'd gotten used to arguing with Sarah. She didn't agree with him just to get along. She wanted to know what he thought about shit like Idle No More and indigenous identity and she razzed him when she thought his opinions were shallow. He missed that.

He heard the fireflies humming louder and winced. Mave stood and held her hand out for his mug. "Want another?"

"Sure. Thanks."

Sarah came out of the bedroom, squinting.

"Good morning," Mave said. "I'm Mavis Moody, Jared's aunt."

"Morning," Sarah said. "Sarah. Sarah Jaks. The ex."

"Would you like some coffee?"

"Sure. That'd be great."

Sarah came and sat beside him on the couch, bringing her knees up to her chest and hugging them.

"She's deaf to magic," Jared said quietly.

Sarah side-eyed him again. "And?"

"She'll think you're nuts if you try to tell her about it."

Mave came back and handed Sarah a coffee.

"Thanks," Sarah said.

"Ziggy Stardust?" Mave said.

"It's better with the wig," Sarah said, "but the wig's itchy."

"I adored Bowie's *Space Oddity* stage. Those shoulder cut-outs are lovely. Did you have the jumpsuit altered or did it come like that?"

"The suit's vintage. I did the cut-outs myself."

"Such exquisite piping. Most people would have just used fabric glue."

"Mom used to knock off designers when she couldn't afford the clothes she wanted. We were a little sweatshop of two."

"Fast fashion is all the rage these days."

"Her days of seizing the means of production are so done."

Mave laughed. "I thought Marx was passé among young radicals."

"He's still relevant. Our government is the executive committee of the One Percenters who hoard their wealth offshore while the rest of us are indentured to cheap credit to survive."

"Then don't use credit cards," Jared said.

"That's wasn't my point!" Sarah said.

"Well," Mave said, turning to Jared. "You have impeccable taste in women."

Jared and Sarah looked at each other for a moment, and then Sarah ducked her head and pulled her knees closer.

"If you don't mind me asking," Mave said, "who else have you read?"

Sarah shrugged, then said, "*Recolonization. The Birth of Biopolitics. Feminist Theory: From Margin to Centre*—"

Mave nodded. "Hooks, good, good."

"Words themselves are doors," the fireflies suddenly intoned, their voices ringing slightly out of unison like church bells tolling across town. "Metaphors leading to and from comprehension for *un esprit enfermé dans la langue*."

Oh, good gravy, Jared thought.

He slowly realized that Mave and Sarah had stopped speaking and were staring at him. He'd pressed his hands over his ears, even though he knew it was impossible not to hear the fireflies. The women were silent.

"Sorry," Jared said, releasing his hands.

"Language coheres with itself, not reality," the fireflies continued, oblivious.

Would you shut it, Jared thought at them. *Please*.

"Are you all right?" Mave said.

"Headache," Jared said.

Sarah looked up, her eyes sliding blindly past the cluster of fireflies.

"Words or language," the fireflies said, "as they're written or spoken, don't play any role in the mechanism of thought. Tell Sarah we can't go home if she doesn't find her path. We need her help."

"I'm going to lie down," he said. "You guys keep talking."

"Are you okay with that?" Aunt Mave said.

"Yeah. Philosophy bores the crap out of me."

"*Politics*," Sarah said. "Not philosophy."

Jared glanced up at the fireflies. "Whatevs. Later."

He stood and Mave gripped his hand, squeezed it and let him go. The fireflies swarmed Sarah and she glowed, lines of energy sparking between the cloud and her head.

"This is how we live in a world run by thugs," the fireflies said mournfully as they followed him to the bedroom in a gloomy, glowing cloud, "who think a mind is just a weapon."

The walls of Jared's bedroom trembled, like the horizon on a hot day, like the air above a fire. The faces painted on the mural blinked, began to vibrate and then spun madly, as if they were possessed and about to spew bile. The fireflies flattened into a single layer. They hovered just below the ceiling. The faces on the walls screamed all at once.

"What the hell?" the fireflies said.

Jared went over to his desk and opened his copy of the Big Book, which was generally referred to as the Big Book because of its size. He turned to Chapter Five, stuck his fingers in his ears and read about the Twelve Steps.

"'We admitted we were powerless over alcohol—that our lives had become unmanageable,'" Jared read out loud.

"We want to go home!" the fireflies shrieked.

The painted faces suddenly went silent. Jared cautiously took his fingers out of his ears and turned. The fireflies had left. He could hear them back in the living room snapping like mosquitoes hitting a bug zapper, but at least they had stopped trying to talk to him. The faces bobbed around the wall.

"Thank you," Jared said.

The faces blinked all at once and then were still.

Jared listened carefully, but his aunt and his ex didn't seem to have picked up on the screaming and screeching that had just finished. He could hear them talking excitedly, sometimes running over each other's words, finishing each other's sentences. He slowly let out a breath.

He felt safe in this room. Jared wasn't sure what that meant. He wished he could talk to someone, but he wasn't sure who, or what he'd say. Some things were so insane, the only thing to do was ignore them as stubbornly as humanly possible.

Sarah wandered into the bedroom, holding a plate of shepherd's pie. She hopped on the desk and munched away, staring at her plate. The fireflies circled above her, slow and quiet.

"This is Gran's recipe," Sarah said with a full mouth.

"She taught me a lot about cooking."

Sarah took another forkful, studying the room. She was close enough to touch. At the same time, the weird-ass jumpsuit was causing snarky remarks to bubble up in his head. He knew if he said any of them, she'd mock his Normcore clothes and his unblinking adherence to the great god of sobriety clubs.

"Your mom sounded wrecked," he said. "But I don't know her."

"You really don't."

"You can stay here if you want."

Sarah stopped chewing and studied him.

"As friends," Jared said. "Strictly friends."

"I'm thinking of hitchhiking up to see Gran."

"I have money under my mattress," Jared said. "Take it. Fly up. Bus up. Don't hitch, please."

"I don't want your money."

"I don't want you dead."

She hopped off the desk and stood beside him again. She seemed near tears again.

"Are you okay?" Jared said.

She shook her head.

"Do you want to talk about it?"

"How I screwed up? Again?"

"We all screw up. We're human," Jared said, thinking that he should tell Sarah about Lex, but then, they weren't even together.

"He said we could put a love spell on you. You'd be helpless and would teach me anything I wanted." She sighed and stared up at the ceiling. The fireflies said nothing now, spinning sluggishly.

"I assume you didn't?" Jared said.

"It was kind of rape-y. So I couldn't finish it. Probably wouldn't have worked 'cause I don't have any juice."

"I've never stopped loving you," Jared said. "That was never the problem."

Sarah's lip curled and she gave him the side-eye she always gave him when she thought he was getting too emo. Some things didn't change. She could try to put love spells on someone but couldn't talk about love itself because that was emotionally controlling or some bullshit.

Jared sighed. "Mom put heavy-duty warding on me. The second you finished the spell, you would have activated it."

"I wish your mom liked me," Sarah said. "You know, enough to teach me some stuff."

His mom wasn't going to waste her time babysitting Sarah through her first spells. Mostly because she found Sarah annoying.

Jared lifted his bare foot. "See the missing toe?"

Sarah looked down.

"That's what happens when you don't have a lot of power and you mess with magic. You get eaten alive. Or your fireflies get eaten alive."

"You're such an ass," Sarah said.

"I like breathing, so I'm not going anywhere near magic. The end."

"Can you still see them?" She looked up to the ceiling.

"Yes."

"Are they saying anything?"

"No."

"Why you?" Sarah said. "Why not me?"

"I don't know."

She reached into her pocket and scrolled through her phone. "There's a seven-thirty flight. It's pretty pricey."

"Take the money," Jared said. "I have more in the bank."

"Sometimes I think I love you. Part of me does. The rest of me wants to push you off a building."

"Ha. I knew this was really about the fireflies."

"*Such* an ass," Sarah muttered.

"I didn't ask to see them."

"Okay, Epic-y McDenial, let's pretend you didn't just save my fireflies from whatever the hell was eating them. Let's say you're just a normal Joe Blow. How do you explain your bedroom?"

"What about it?"

"The cave of creep?" She looked around. "Yeah, totally normal. Jesus, Jared. I have goosebumps being here. Something's in this apartment. It's close. It's dangerous."

"It's a ghost," Jared said. "He's okay. Kind of a TV hog, but he's fine."

Dent called out from the recliner: "She's talking about the thing in the wall, you moron."

"Jared," Sarah said. "How can you be so clueless?"

He decided to switch the topic. "What's your mom going to say when you show?"

Sarah said, "I'm hoping having family around will stop her from making a scene. As long as she can pawn me off on someone else, we're golden."

"Testify," Jared said.

"Don't make this about you," Sarah said.

Mave lent them her bug and he drove Sarah to the airport. They waited in a series of lines, close but not touching or speaking. When she finally got in the security line, she put her hand on the back of his neck and drew him in for a long, slow kiss. Her mouth, her tongue, the warmth of her, the familiarity of it all and the sense he got that this was a goodbye kiss, an end.

"Be safe," he said.

"When you embrace your truth, let me know," she said.

He stood behind the roped area and watched her shuffle through the line until she unloaded all her things onto the X-ray machine. She turned and gave him the peace sign. He waved, and then she was gone.

Sarah texted him later that night. *Arrived @ hospital. Doc called the family in. Momz in a hotel. I'm with the uncles.*

Sorry. Wish I could come.

Wish you could 2. Gotta go. Doc is here.

Jared got up and made himself coffee. He wasn't going to sleep anyway. He took his mug onto the balcony. His phone chimed and he saw Kota's name.

Mind your own fucking business, Kota texted. *Spoiled fucking brat. Go fuck yourself.*

Dude. What did I do?

Stop fucking texting. Im busy asshole. Some of us aren't fucking coddled suck ups. Fake as fuck, thatʒ wut u r.

Jared put the cell down. The message alarm dinged, and dinged, and then dinged again before it went silent. Jared drank his coffee, holding the mug tightly. The last twenty-four hours had felt unhinged. He picked up the phone. Apparently, Kota had a list of things he didn't like about Jared and he seemed to be in the mood to share. Jared decided to delete the rest of the texts without reading them. He could take his own inventory. He didn't need Kota's help.

Someone knocked. Jared couldn't be bothered to answer. He heard Hank stomping down the hallway, crossing the living room. Then the balcony door opened. Hank was in his security uniform.

"Did you hear from Kota?" Hank said.

The message alarm dinged again.

Jared flipped the phone over. Still Kota. "There's coffee on the counter."

"This is literally a bad move, really bad," Hank said.

"It's his choice."

Hank looked out over the street. Jared listened to the message alarm dinging and dinging. Hank left without saying anything else. Jared sat on the patio chair until his butt went numb. Then he went inside and watched TV. Eventually, Dent popped back into the living room and Jared switched from news to the science fiction channel. Jared was glad for his company.

27

I DIDN'T CHOOSE
THE MOD LIFE

When Jared got home from school that Thursday, an old truck with its hazard lights blinking was parked in front of the apartment building. Random computer and gaming gear was piled haphazardly in the back and on the sidewalk. In the hallway on the second floor, Pat and Sponge were fighting a twin mattress out of a crammed elevator. Hank's apartment door was propped open and more moving boxes were piled randomly down the hallway and in what Jared could see of the living room.

"Hey," Jared said. "Are you guys moving in?"

The brothers paused, exchanging a knowing look.

"Hey, Casanova," Pat said. "Is the weirdo ex still here?"

"That was *quite* the outfit she was wearing," Sponge said.

"Bye," Jared said, unlocking Mave's apartment door. So Hank was replacing Kota with the Starr brothers.

"Bring more bannock!" Pat shouted through the door.

Awesome, Jared thought. Just peachy.

Dent was in his spot on the recliner. He didn't look up when Jared dropped his backpack on the table. "How'd your physics quiz go?" Dent said.

Jared shrugged. "Seemed fine."

"You're welcome."

Jared flopped on the couch. "What's on?"

"Use your gift of sight."

"What crawled up your butt?"

Dent shushed him. Jared checked his phone. Crashpad had posted about a billion photos of Muriel. Their love must be shared widely. No news from Sarah, Kota or his mom. A new message from an unknown number. He hesitated before opening it. Pictures of himself on the bus home today, hanging on to a strap, staring at his phone.

Jared raised his head instantly when he heard something rustling. Dent blinked out of existence. The thing in the wall slithered around the living room floor like a lumpy snake.

"Don't even," Jared said to it. "I'm not in the mood for your bullshit."

It came close then disappeared from sight under the couch.

Jared poked his head over the side and saw it blinking up at him with black eyes, no whites, like a television demon.

"I'll call Huey," Jared said. "Get. Get out."

The thing slithered back to the wall and crawled in, a dark lump of sadness. Jared felt his own waves of loneliness and abandonment. He let the feelings sit in his gut. The thing watched him, waiting.

And that was the great irony of his life. People he hated, the ones who wished him harm or users who wanted something from him—those he couldn't shake. While the people he actually liked vanished like a mirage shimmering in the heat, a hopeful oasis that disappeared as soon as you got close.

Someone banged on the apartment door and then opened it.

"Jared!" Pat shouted. "We need a third for a pickup game!"

"I'm studying!" Jared lied.

"Come on!" Sponge said. "Take one for the family!"

He wouldn't mind a break from the apartment that wasn't meetings, work and school. He grabbed his hoodie and followed them down the hallway. Sponge shoved Pat out of the apartment. His brother shoved him back. They snickered and shoved each other until they got out of the stairwell, where they took turns shoving Jared down the first floor hallway.

A nearby school had some basketball courts and they played three-on-three with some dudes the Starr brothers seemed to know but didn't introduce. Jared hadn't played basketball since tenth-grade gym class, he'd been more of a track and field guy, but no one here played really well and when everyone got tired, it devolved into tripping and pushing.

Jared stopped dead when he noticed the silver Lexus was parked in direct sight of the courts. David studied him, sipping a takeout coffee.

The other basketball team scored and the brothers shoved Jared around, cursing him for being a speed bump. David raised his cup. Jared suddenly understood his mother's love of guns, the great equalizers. All he wanted was to play a pickup game without having some shitty excuse for a human being smirk because he'd ruined Jared's night.

"Sorry," Jared said to the brothers, glad they hadn't noticed anything.

"You cooking anything?" Pat said.

"I've got some leftover shepherd's pie," Jared said.

"Forgiven," Pat said.

"Come on, Space Cadet," Sponge said. "Dinner waits for no man."

Back at the apartment, once Jared unlocked the door, they pushed past him in a snickering tumble like puppies.

"Hey, Aunt Mave!" the Starr brothers said.

She looked up from her plate at the table. She wore a deep-blue blazer with a long scarf. "Hello, boys. I hear you're my new neighbours. Barbie must be heartbroken to lose her roomies."

"Yeah, she's all torn up she can't dump her rug rats on us any time of the day or night," Sponge said.

"What happened with Kota?" she said.

"You missed the big showdown," Pat said. "Kota's hanging with the party people again. Him and Hank had it out in the lobby when Kota came to get his stuff."

"Hank's feeling is hurt," Sponge said.

"Oh, dear," Mave said.

"We heard you have ingredients assembled into food-like substances," Pat said.

"Help yourself," she said. "Wash your dishes when you're done, please."

"Yeah, yeah," they chorused.

"Wanna come over to Grandma's house after supper?" Sponge said.

"What?" Jared said.

"From his selection of furniture," Pat said, "we believe Hank is secretly a ninety-three-year-old grandma."

After supper, Jared followed the brothers over to Hank's apartment, which was filled with mismatched second-hand furniture. The couch was heavily floral and worn through on the edges of the cushions. A fifty-inch Samsung TV sat on a clunky thrift-store end table. Beneath it, cables sprawled like a black nest to laptops and game consoles. Beside a virgin Xbox One, a tricked-out Xbox 360 burned blue when it was turned on, like the neon underglow of a street racer. Sponge handed him a controller with obvious DIY modifications.

"Yeah, I'm not a modded bitch," Jared said, handing it back. He'd never liked people who used cheat modes to win and had no intention of being one of them.

Pat deepened his voice to Vader depths: "Come to the dark side, Luke. We have jitter mode."

Their *Grand Theft Auto V* opened normally, but instead of seeing the game from the point of view of Michael in all his menacing and muscled glory, in his place was a giant brown Care Bear with a picture of a cupcake on his chest.

"Woah," Jared said. "How'd you do that?"

"Barbie's a total Nazi," Sponge said. "We had to mod the crap out of *GTA* so we could play it in front of her kids."

"What does that mean for the strip club?" Jared said.

"Things get furry," Pat said.

"There's a trampoline," Sponge added.

Mave's bedroom door was closed when he got home and her bedroom light shone under her door. Writing mode. Jared broke out his biology textbook and reread this week's assigned chapters on the couch. Dent ignored him. He weighed his options over and over. How do you get your stalker off your back? He didn't have an answer that didn't make his life worse. His phone pinged and he glanced at the display. Sarah had sent him a picture of her hand over her gran's hand.

Gran's a tough old bird, she wrote. *Still kicking. Unconscious but not giving up.*

Glad you get 2 say goodbye.

Mom says hi.

Hi 2 your mom.

Olive phoned him, asking if he could watch Eliza while she went grocery shopping.

"I don't want to drag her out to Metrotown on the SkyTrain at night if I don't have to," Olive said.

"Mave's got her bug back," Jared said. "I'm sure she wouldn't mind if you borrowed it if you put back the gas you use."

Olive hesitated. "Really?"

"That little terror can't watch *Frozen*," Dent said.

"I'm sure," Jared said.

Mave looked up from her bed when Jared poked his head in her room. She pushed her noise-cancelling earphones down around her neck and then said it would be no problem if Olive borrowed her car. She waved him away, and then put her headphones back on, staring intently at her laptop.

Olive carried Eliza over. Her daughter had her stuffed snowman in a death grip. Jared gave Olive the keys. Eliza ignored Dent and curled into a corner of the couch. Olive kissed her, and said she'd be back soon, then tucked one of the throw blankets around her daughter.

After Olive left, Jared asked, "You okay?"

Eliza nodded.

"You want to talk about it?"

She shook her head. Her eyes welled up and her lips trembled. God, he had no idea what to do. "Wanna watch *Frozen*?"

She pulled the blanket over her head and Jared could hear her sniffling. Dent's shoulders crawled up to his ears. "Put the damn movie in," Dent said.

Shu appeared, eyes boggled and angry. She only calmed down when Eliza poked her head back out and propped it on her stuffed Olaf so she could watch the TV. The zombie ghost girl sat on the couch near Eliza then. Dent flickered. Shu touched his hand and he solidified.

"Thank you," Dent said.

When Olive got back, she and Eliza lounged around the couch. Shu and Dent held hands as she guided him through the floor, sinking slowly out of sight. Dent laughed, flickering, but Shu zapped him and the ghost stabilized. Jared considered taking a shower, but the distance between him and the bathroom seemed vast. Screw it, he thought. He wasn't going to die if he stank for a night.

Olive stroked Eliza's hair. "I forgot what it was like to look for parking. But it was very hard to lose Mave's Canuck bug."

Jared laughed. "I didn't know she liked hockey that much."

"Oh, *like* is such a weak word for what Mave feels about anything." Olive looked down at Eliza. "Would it be okay if we spent the night?"

"Sure," Jared said. "Is everything all right?"

She smiled unconvincingly. "Nothing you need to worry about."

He could hear Mave and Olive whispering in Mave's bedroom, but not what they were whispering about. Jared sprawled on top of the quilt, considering his phone. He wanted to see if Sarah had written anything more about Mrs. Jaks, but he didn't want to deal with Kota's messages yet.

Shu and Dent slowly emerged headfirst from the ceiling above Jared's bed.

Dent's eyes were wide. "This is so freaky."

"Can you get out of my ceiling?" Jared hissed.

"My God," Dent said. "It's full of stars."

28

SUPER FLY

No one followed Jared to or from his Friday meeting. No one he could see, anyway. When he got back, Mave's hallway was filled with unfamiliar shoes and he could hear urgent voices. He sighed. All he wanted to do was take a shower. He was not in the mood to meet or talk to anyone.

Well-dressed people crowded the living room, having dragged the kitchen chairs to form a circle with the couches. Some of them were white, some were Native, some of them were face types he had no idea how to categorize. He didn't recognize any of them except Gwen from the Sartorial Resistance, who sat in the recliner, scowling. All the people looked equally grim.

"No. Absolutely not," one of the white dudes said. "I'm tired of hiding behind indigenous rights. This is about the complete and total denial of our carbon footprint on this—"

"We get that! God," Gwen said. "But we need to have one strong, unified voice!"

"So shut the fuck up?" the guy said. "Is that the subtext? Keep your flaky-ass opinions about the Anthropocene to yourself?"

"Stop making this personal. I'm saying we—"

"Good evening, Jared," Mave said. "Everyone, this is my nephew."

Jared was in the middle of trying to tiptoe to his bedroom. The people in the living room swung their heads around and he froze.

"Hey," Jared said.

"This is the co-op board for the store," Mave said.

People muttered hello then started talking amongst themselves. Mave got up and came over to him.

"Sounds tense," Jared said.

"The revolution needs snacks," Mave said.

Jared grabbed some clean clothes from his bedroom. When he caught a glimpse of himself in the bathroom mirror, he paused. His hair was plastered down on one side and spiking up on the other. Had he been walking around like this? He hadn't realized his hair was getting so long. He went back to his room and got his clippers, then carefully buzzed his head over the sink.

He let the shower pound his back, the spot between his shoulder blades where he held his tension. He scrubbed his head to make sure all the little hairs were off. He stood under the water for a long time.

When he emerged from the bathroom, Mave was alone, staring out the window. Jared joined her on the couch. She took his hand and held on.

"You okay?" Jared said.

"Thinking," Mave said.

"About what?"

"The things we do for what we believe."

"Is everything okay?"

"There's a protest camp starting up soon. I'm probably going to get arrested. Civil disobedience. Catch-and-release. I might be sued."

Jared laughed, sitting back. "Man, I thought I was done bailing people out of jail."

"Oh, I think I have more arrests than Maggie."

"Pleeease don't tell her that," Jared said.

"What a family," Mave said.

When Jared checked his marks online, both the physics and biology labs hit the low nineties. As a thank-you, he pirated the first season of a British science fiction show called *Red Dwarf*, which Dent had mentioned a couple of times. After Mave retreated to her room to write, Jared plugged the flash drive with the pirated episodes into the TV. He told Dent he could do a marathon if he wanted. Dent became very shy, fading until he was a wisp. Then he solidified and happily sat on the recliner, ignoring Jared for the rest of the night. Dent's occasional snicker echoed through the apartment.

Kota texted him: *So hung. & not in the good way.*

Jared stared at the message. He tried to feel detached and instead felt annoyed.

Sorry, Kota texted him.

And then, after a while: *Not my shining moment.*

Kinda mad at you, Jared finally answered. *WTF, dude?*

Sorry.

U ok?

Sober 1 hour & 6 minutes. Feel like death. After a few minutes: *U still there, Jared?*

Still here.

Sorry. Again.

We all have crap moments.

Pissed at Hank. Took it out on you. Amends? Has to be cheap or free.

Someone knocked on the apartment door. It was Barbie dropping by with freshly made bread. She squished Jared's cheeks and thanked him for the bannock. "Come to dance practice this Sunday."

"I'll try," he said.

"I'll send the boys to remind you," she said.

"It's not really my thing."

"Your culture is important. Make it a priority," she said. "I promise there'll be snacks."

Pat and Sponge clomped down the hallway with Barbie's kids clinging to their legs. She told her children to get off their uncles and they said they needed to go and hop on their beds, like old times. The kids ran out and after a few minutes they heard Hank, his voice carrying through the walls, yelling at them to behave. The brothers dug through Mave's fridge and started assembling sandwich ingredients on the counter. Barbie rolled her eyes.

"You're welcome back at my place any time," she said to her brothers. "I hate to see you scavenging like this."

"Yeah, thanks but no thanks, Hitler," Sponge said.

"We're enjoying our carefree bachelor life," Pat said.

"Goodness, you boys would try the patience of a saint," Barbie said. And then, as the brothers carried their sandwiches towards the door, "Come back here! *Now.* Clean up your mess! Don't make me raise my voice!"

The rest of the evening passed uneventfully. At the end of his shift, the Donut Hole manager offered to put him on the books.

"I dunno," Jared said. "It'd be hard to wait for cheques."

"Suit yourself," the manager said.

That Saturday morning, Jared was making himself an omelette when Olive phoned him. She was at a garage sale up the street and needed help carrying a kitchen table back to her apartment. He said no problem and turned off the burner, shovelling down his eggs before he headed out the door. At the end of the street, Jared paused in surprise. Dent and Shu were hopping over trees. Which would look a lot more Matrix-cool if they weren't shrieking like kids in a bouncy castle.

"I'm ignoring the ground!" Dent shouted.

At the garage sale, Eliza was stoked because she'd found a grimy, kid-sized *Frozen* fold-out foamie chair, which she clutched like a baby. Jared balanced the rickety, rusty, metal-legged table on his head. Olive carried two chairs, stacked. Dent and Shu leapfrogged over parked cars. On Commercial Drive, Dent took a tumble and landed in the middle of the street. A bus bore down on him and he held his hands up and screamed. The bus passed through him.

"Oh, yeah, I'm dead," Dent said.

Shu danced into the street and they joined hands and did a silly jig together while the traffic went through them. Jared noticed a jogger on the other side of the street who wore a loose sweatshirt over a yellow jogging bra and yoga pants. She looked Native, had classic high cheekbones and large, dark eyes. Jared thought she was staring at Dent, but she jogged through him when the light changed. Sweat followed the curves of her body. As she passed, she eyed the table, then Jared. He turned his head slightly to watch her jog away until the table started sliding. Olive paused to hoist the chairs back up.

"Kokum got me a Blu-ray," Eliza said, puffing a bit as she carried her chair. "Want to come watch *Frozen* with me?"

"Maybe later," Jared said.

"We're washing that chair," Olive said.

"No! You'll wreck it!" Eliza said, clutching it tighter.

They argued down the street, through the lobby and up the stairs. Jared dropped the table in the dining nook and Olive helped him move the cast iron patio set back to Mave's balcony.

"I'll go back to the garage sale and get the other chairs," Jared said.

"Oh, no," Olive said. "No. I couldn't let you. No."

Jared waited.

"I'd really appreciate that," she said.

"Right back," Jared said.

"Are you avoiding the *Frozen* marathon?" Olive said.

Jared laughed. "You got me."

"Lucky, lucky, lucky," Olive said. "Some of us do not have that option."

Outside, Huey the flying head had joined Shu and Dent's game of traffic leapfrog, spinning excitedly between them as they Superman-posed over cars, trucks and buses.

He was watching Huey head-butt Dent as Dent flailed his arms and Shu grabbed his bathrobe, when someone yanked him off the street and into an alley. The jogger in the sweatshirt and yellow sports bra pressed a small knife against his throat.

"Hello, Wee'git," she said.

29

NEEKA

Jared blanked. He wasn't sure how long he blanked, but when he was back in his head, the jogger had shoved him up against the alley wall. She flicked the knife against his cheek and tasted his blood. She grimaced.

"Witch," she said. "And Trickster. So, are you one of Wee'git's children?"

Jared nodded, touching the cut on his cheek.

"You have his stench," she said.

Words wouldn't come. He nodded again, swallowing. Dent flew over them, hooting. Shu cartwheeled by. Huey bounced off the alley walls like a rubber ball. The woman squinted up at them and then back at Jared.

"Where's Wee'git?" she said.

"I don't know," Jared said.

"Don't protect him."

"I'd hand him over in a heartbeat if I knew where he was. The last I heard, he was here in Vancouver."

"Is that why you're here?"

Jared snorted. "No."

The woman crossed her arms over her chest. "Wee'git has something of mine. I want it back."

"Yeah, he's a douche. Good luck with that."

"Who are you?"

"My name is Jared. I have to go," Jared said. "The garage sale is over soon and I need to get my neighbour's chairs."

"You're going to a garage sale."

"No, my neighbour went to a garage sale. She bought a kitchen table and chairs."

"You're getting furniture. For your neighbour."

"Yeah."

She cocked an eyebrow. Jared thought they were done, and tried to leave, but she brought out the knife again.

"She doesn't have a lot," Jared said. "Her ex keeps stealing her stuff."

"Do you like her?"

"She's a cousin."

"Family," the woman said, nodding. "Fine. Let's go get your furniture."

"Uh, I can, you know, get it myself."

"We'll talk more. Move."

"Listen, that's all I know. That's everything."

"Move."

When they got there, the people running the garage sale smiled at them and handed Jared the chairs. The woman walked beside him as he carried the chairs back to the apartment. She got a lot of stares and the occasional whistle, but was either unaware of them or didn't care. She held the lobby door open for him and then rode with him up the elevator to the second floor. Olive answered his knock, startling when she saw the woman.

"Oh, my," Olive said. "Jared. Who's your friend?"

"I'm Neeka," the woman said.

"I'm Olive. Pleased to meet you." She smiled at Jared then, taking the chairs from him. "Thank you for being so helpful. I don't know what I'd do without you. He's a gentleman, all right. You could do a lot worse."

Jared felt his face flaming red. Olive made a terrible wingman.

"Come watch *Frozen*!" Eliza shouted.

"Have fun," Olive said, closing the door.

Neeka put her hand on Jared's elbow. "Move."

They walked down the hallway to Mave's apartment. Jared pulled out of her grip. She stuck the knife against his side, slicing easily through his shirt and touching his skin. He unlocked the door and she followed him in. She toured the apartment, keeping the knife pressed against him, prodding him when she wanted him to move. She paused at his room, taken aback.

"What is this?" she said.

"I call it my bedroom," Jared said. "I sleep here. See? It has a bed."

"What spell did you use?"

"Paint. And it was the guy who lived here before me who painted it. Some dude named Edgar Six."

"It corrupts the air."

"Okay."

"And you sleep here?"

"I do."

"Reality bleeds here."

"It's not that bad once you get used to it."

"Are you a shaman?"

"That's a little personal. But no, I am not a shaman. And before you ask, no, I am not a witch. No, I am not a Trickster. I am a human dude."

She was taller than him, so when she turned him around so she could look him in the eye, she had to bend her knees. She studied him for so long, he felt himself growing both uncomfortable and aroused.

"Your horde of familiars gives you away, shaman," she pronounced. "No normal human has so many spirits following them."

"Okay. Whatever. What do I need to do to get you to leave?"

"Come." She turned abruptly and walked to the living room, where she sat on the recliner. She waited for him, sitting regally, like a queen.

Jared swallowed his annoyance. He sat on the couch. He considered asking her if she wanted a glass of water, because she was still glowing from her jog. Normal people looked oily, but she shone like she'd been buffed. She was very much out of his league. Plus, the cray-cray factor seemed pretty high.

"Who's your mother?" Neeka said

"Who's *your* mother?"

"Do you want to drag this out or do you want me gone?"

Jared slouched on the couch, glaring out the window where normal people were going about their normal business. "Maggie Martin. She's from Bella Bella. She's a witch. You're probably smelling her protection spells. She says I'm 'special needs' magic."

Neeka frowned. "How did she meet Wee'git?"

"He slept with my gran. He slept with my mom. He tricked them both by pretending to be people they loved."

"Is your mother Wee'git's daughter?"

"Ew. No."

"Are you sure?"

"Why don't you go taste my mom for yourself? I'll give you her address."

"Can you hear him? Does he talk to your mind with his?"

He considered lying about it. But decided to go with an edited version. "Not anymore."

She closed her eyes. *Can you hear me?*

"Stop it," Jared said. "I don't like that."

Tell him we want our skins back.

He shifted slightly away from her. "What are you?"

"Otter."

He sprang from the couch and ran. He was halfway to the door when he ran into an invisible swamp and couldn't push through. He could hear her coming down the hallway. He could sense her behind him. He couldn't make his legs move. He was stuck.

Go, go, go, go, go, go, go, his mind was telling him.

"We have no interest in you," Neeka said. "Just Wee'git."

The cave, the cave, run, the cave, he saw bones, he felt them crunch as he crawled down the tiny entrance, blind, the darkness, the cave, the half-human, half-otter bodies, his blood, his screaming, the cave.

"Calm," Neeka said. "Calm yourself."

His body turned to face Neeka. She frowned at him. He walked past her, unwillingly, and sat back on the couch. He remembered getting his toe chewed off. He remembered one of them holding a lighter to his flesh. He wanted not to see it anymore. He wanted to wipe the memory from his mind. Neeka sat on the recliner again.

"Those were river otters," Neeka said.

Otters. Otters like her. Otters in human form. But in the cave, they mashed things up. Human limbs sat randomly on otter bodies.

"We belong to the ocean," Neeka insisted. "They belong to the river."

He wanted to hurl. Neeka handed him the garbage can from beside the recliner. He took it and felt his breakfast crawling up his throat. He generally avoided thinking about the otters. He avoided thinking about that night. Little flashes of memory stole back in his dreams or unguarded moments. But they flooded back now.

She got up and then he could hear her in the kitchen, opening cupboards, and he hoped she wasn't going to get another knife. He hoped this didn't turn into a knife thing, where he lost little bits of himself, bled all over Mave's carpet.

"I'm making tea," Neeka said.

She's reading my mind, Jared thought.

"You're very loud at the moment. It's like trying not to hear a jet engine."

He did hurl then. He lost his omelette and kept retching until bile came up. He rested, feeling hollow. His hands shook. Adrenalin. Light-headed. He wished his mom was here. She had no patience with the supernatural bulldozing into her life. She had hexes and curses. She'd tried to teach him, but it didn't make any sense to him. Magic was another language and he had a tin ear. He barely made it through French classes and everyone told him if you spoke English, learning French was a snap. Something about the structure being similar. Or their origins. The ancestors of languages. Was that a thing? Did languages have ancestors? His throat burned. He wondered if they had any Pepto-Bismol left.

Neeka handed him a cup of tea.

He hesitated before reluctantly reaching up and taking the cup, setting it carefully on his knee.

"It's camomile," she said.

"What do you mean, you lost your skin?"

She sat in the recliner. "I thought you had secrets. But you don't, do you?"

"Not really. I'm not good with magic, so I tend to avoid it."

"But your life is full of ghosts."

"Isn't everyone's?"

"No. Not literal ghosts."

"What about the Long Island Medium?"

"The what?"

"You know. That chick on TV who has the hair and goes around hearing the dead."

Neeka stared at him for so long, he wondered if she was okay. She finally blinked. "I realize you spoke, but the words don't make any sense."

"That's pretty well how I am with magic. And French. And Heiltsuk. The languages, not the people. You know?"

"Now I'm annoyed."

"Uh, hello. *You* invited yourself in. *You* barged in and got all talky."

"Talky."

"It's a word."

Jared sniffed his tea. He didn't want to offend her, but he didn't really trust her, so he fake-sipped it. She watched him like a cat, an unreadable expression that could be boredom or disdain.

"So are we done?" Jared said.

"No."

"I don't know what else I can tell you."

"You can tell me everything."

"Why? Why would you want to know anything about me? There's

a website full of people who'd talk your ear off about their ol' dad Wee'git. Go bug them."

"We know all of the 532 people claiming to be or rumoured to be Wee'git's offspring. You, Jared Martin, we've never heard mentioned. Not once."

"So?"

"We've talked to all of them. Every single soul. And not one of them has ever heard Wee'git in their mind. Not one of them answered me when I talked to them mind to mind."

Jared didn't like the conclusions she seemed to be drawing. "I'm human."

"Maybe it's a witch thing," Neeka said. "Maybe you're a baby Trickster. Or maybe you are human. Regardless, you are the closest we've gotten to Wee'git in a long time."

"He won't come," Jared said. "No matter what you do to me, he won't come."

"I don't expect him to. He's a horrible father. Irresponsible. Negligent. He lives for his own pleasure. But he is a curious being and he has odd moments of conscience."

"So . . ."

"So we talk. We get to know each other."

"And then?"

"Do you have a cellphone?"

Neeka stood, bent over and patted his shorts. Jared fought to move, but couldn't. He couldn't even twitch his fingers. She took out his iPhone and sat beside him, her thigh against his.

"Password," she said.

He tried not to think of it, but it became irresistible. As soon as he thought of it, she typed it in and began browsing through his texts.

"You know what's, like, super rude?" Jared said. "Snooping through someone's phone in front of them. And kidnapping. But mostly the snooping. Seriously. How is this okay in your books? How do you justify this?"

"Maybe you should go to sleep," she said.

And he did.

She woke him at suppertime. She'd brought the quilt from his bed and put it over him. His neck had a crick from sleeping on one of the fat throw cushions. He noticed his laptop open to his Facebook messages on the side table by the recliner.

She invited him to the table. She'd made pork chops and mashed potatoes with a side of green beans. She poured him a glass of apple juice. She puttered around the kitchen. He stared miserably at his plate. You weren't supposed to eat food given to you by unfriendly witches, especially the non-human ones. Spells and poisons, his mom liked to say, are easily delivered through your stomach.

"Eat," Neeka said.

The chops were very tender. Juicy. Just the right amount of salt and pepper. The mashed potatoes had the perfect amount of garlic. She sat across from him and put a napkin on her lap. They ate in silence. Tonight, the pub at the corner of their street was raucous, the sounds of merrymaking echoing loudly.

She stared at her own phone, typing responses. He thought about all the people he'd texted, all the messages she'd seen. He felt naked. He finished his plate and automatically took it to the sink and rinsed it. A large bowl of fruit salad was on the counter.

"How long are you staying?" Jared said.

"Bring the fruit salad," she said. She carried her own plate to the sink, scraped the bones into the garbage.

Jared carried the bowl to the table. She brought two dessert bowls and two large spoons. She served them and they ate. Jared couldn't remember the last time anyone had cooked for him. When he didn't cook, Mave nuked herself gluten-free non-dairy burritos. She had a case of them in the freezer.

Neeka washed the dishes. Jared dried them and put them away.

"You're loyal to your family and your friends," Neeka said. "I like that."

Jared waited for the rest.

"My sister says your mom is infamous," Neeka said. "She's not like other humans. I like her."

"Not many people do," Jared said. "She's an acquired taste."

"Did she really blow off Wee'git's head with a shotgun?"

"Yeah, that's Mom."

"So that's why he vanished for all these years. She must have buried him deep. We owe her."

"She's into pepperettes more than fruit baskets."

"She's powerful. Her spells around you are flawless. You have older ones too. This Sophia, she's Halayt?"

Jared nodded.

"And you pissed her off and lived. Amazing. Even more amazing, she left her protection on you. The combination of their protection and the remoteness of your hometown kept you off the radar. Until now."

Jared hadn't realized Sophia had put protection on him too. Or that she hadn't taken it off. It made his throat tight, thinking about it. Things would be so different if she really was his grandmother.

He felt Neeka watching him. He hated emoting in front of strangers.

"What do you want?" Jared said.

"These are the end times," Neeka said. "We want to go back to ocean. We want to die in our home."

"I can't help you. I can barely help myself."

"Wee'git must give us back what he took."

"So you want to use me as bait," Jared said. "That's what the other otters wanted. How are you different?"

"We want to be your friends."

Neeka turned out to mean this literally. First, she became Jared's Facebook friend. Then she added her cell number to his phone. She trimmed his fingernails and tweezed a few of his hairs and put them in a small cloth medicine bag on a leather string around her neck. He did not want her to do that, but she said it was a finding, not a binding, spell. He knew what his mom would say to that. She would be a very unhappy camper.

Neeka went through his clothes, pulling the occasional thread and adding it to the Jared collection in her medicine bag. He protested, but she said she wasn't disturbing any of his mom's spells. She studied the faces in the bedroom wall suspiciously. "And they haven't hurt you?"

"No," Jared said. "They float around. It's cool."

"They float through the room?"

"No. Just in the fog in the painting."

"That's disturbing."

"They're kind of like goldfish."

"Do you see them moving now?"

"Do you?"

"So they don't always move?"

"No. There's this thing in the wall that sucks toes. It's like, you know, Gollum, from that Hobbit movie, except it's mostly a shadow. They warn me when he tries to crawl out. We don't like him."

Neeka stepped away from the wall. "This is horrifying."

"You get used to it."

"No, this is the path to madness. This is magic run amok."

"For someone who claims to be an otter, you have a really low weirdness bar."

One of the painted cars on the floor turned its headlights on and off, and she jumped.

"That's new," Jared said.

"It's spreading," Neeka said. "Like a contagion."

"Ooooh, scary headlights."

"You need to take this seriously."

"Okay, okay. I like them, though. I don't want to paint over them."

"You *like* them."

"They're not—they aren't hurting anyone. I don't want to hurt them."

"You don't want to hurt painted faces in the wall."

"They keep the toe-sucker away. I'm totally cool if you want that one dead. He's a creep."

Neeka shook her head. "You have a very strange life."

"Yeah," Jared said. She was just the whacked icing on his weirdo cake.

I heard that, she thought.

I know, he thought back.

30

WHEN FURRY AQUATIC RODENTS RULED TURTLE ISLAND

Once upon a time, the continent of North America glittered like a disco ball. Large ponds, small ponds, mega ponds as large as lakes shone like a million tiny mirrors in the sunlight as the world spun. The ponds were created by over 100 million beavers who toiled to build dams, to build their dens and raise their children to transform the landscape as their ancestors had before them.

But then, in much the same way a butterfly flapping its wings in China can cause a tornado in Texas, a fad for furry hats in Europe caused the near extinction of beavers in North America. From 1550 to 1850, felt hats made from beaver fur were valuable status symbols that told the wearer's story of wealth, rank and privilege to the casual viewing eye, much the same way a luxury car does these days.

First, beavers were hunted to extinction in most of Europe. When the fur traders arrived in North America, the Great Hunt continued here. Today, beavers have rebounded from near oblivion to ten million strong. Other fur-bearers like the otters generally loathe humans for the genocide they perpetrated and will take human form to lure the unsuspecting to their death.

Though beavers have the ability to transform, they have no interest in shape-shifting to exact guerrilla retribution.

Ordinary beavers, like this young couple who are putting the finishing touches on their food cache at the bottom of their new pond on the outskirts of an urban park, work long into the night even as they await their first litter.

"The Creator bid us build, so we build," the male beaver says.

"Don't encourage the damn Trickster," the female beaver says. "Just ignore him until he goes away."

The male waddles up the shore, dark eyes glittering in the moonlight. The female ducks behind him, protectively smoothing the fur over her belly.

"Her name is Waterlily," the male says. "And I'm Aspen."

"Shut it, you ass," Waterlily says.

"He's narrating our lives. He might as well get our names right."

"You! Trickster! Piss off, you troublemaker," Waterlily says. "Can't you see we're working here? Clueless human-lover."

"Hormones," Aspen says.

How can they forgive? How do they continue to live as if nothing happened after so much wrong has been done to them? How are they not consumed by hate like everyone else?

"Are you mocking us?" Waterlily says.

"I think he's drunk." Aspen stands up on his hind legs. "Yeah, I'm going to have to ask you to leave, buddy."

Such strength. So noble. The noble beaver.

"I'm this close to slapping you," Aspen says, raising his tail.

31

THROUGH THE VEIL

Jared studied his biology text on the couch while Dent watched his show, bits of him drifting in an invisible tide. Jared's phone pinged. His mom sent him a picture of a dog. He wasn't sure whose dog it was or why she felt like sending it to him. He didn't want to interrupt her trip, but he didn't like being moved around like a puppet by Neeka. It was bad enough with David prowling around, waiting for an opportunity to be an asshole, but now otters were back in his life. Maybe it was time for the nuclear option.

Hey, Mom, he texted her. *How's Winnipeg?*

She responded instantly. *Thinking of selling house. Movin here. Whaddya think?*

Really?

Richie's family likes me. They want me to stay.

She must like it there a lot, he thought. 'Cause she loved her house. She'd fought for that house. She'd sacrificed for that house. He wasn't so attached to it, but it would be weird without the place he'd spent most of his childhood. He'd planned to ask for some help with Neeka and David, but if she was finally in a good place after so much hell, maybe he needed to deal with his own mess.

If it makes you happy, Mom, u shud do it.

TTYL

TTFN

Mave wandered out of her room with her headphones on, her music bleeding through. She stood in front of the bathroom door for a long time, frowning, before she turned and went into the kitchen, eventually meandering back to her bedroom munching on an unpeeled carrot with the leafy part bobbing, reminding Jared of Bugs Bunny.

"So weird," Dent said. "If she didn't have such a great cable package, I wouldn't be here."

"Can't you just, I dunno, put yourself in the TV or something?"

Dent rolled his eyes. "That's not how it works."

"Really? Can't you go to the end of the series and binge-watch *Doctor Who* from there?"

"Being dead doesn't make me a Time Lord, you Muggle," Dent said.

"How did you die?"

"I was eaten by Tribbles."

"Nice."

"Jared, get lost. Please."

He read some more of his biology text, and then asked Dent, "If you were me, what would you do about your stalker?"

"Tell Hank," Dent said.

"Really? Even though he annoys the crap out of you?"

Dent let out a frustrated sigh. "It's simple. Hank wants to help you but in a way you don't like. David wants to run you over. Your call. For the record, you can't haunt this apartment. We're full up with ghosts and spirits."

"Fine, fine," Jared said. "I'll talk to Hank."

Jared went to the nearest convenience store to grab a breakfast sausage bun. He didn't see David following him anywhere. No pictures appeared on his cellphone. Maybe David was getting bored. Or it was too early. Maybe he was slowing down and would lose interest. Maybe Jared wouldn't have to do anything.

When he returned home, he heard Justice laughing in Mave's bedroom. When he poked his head in to say howdy, she tried to convince him to go to brunch with them. He begged off, saying he had to study, and went to his bedroom. The dolphins were having a traffic jam. The painted heads in the wall talked soundlessly to each other, like neighbours, except for one of the child heads, which tumbled happily, following Jared as he dumped his backpack on the desk, plugged his phone into the charger and then flopped in bed. The kid stuck his tongue out.

"Hey," Jared said.

The kid rolled away. Jared had no idea what to do about Neeka. She didn't seem to want to hurt him, despite the whole puppet thing. Maybe if he was super boring, she'd lose interest. Or maybe he could tell her he loved her. That seemed to do the trick when it came to him and women.

He would talk to Hank if things got worse. The thought of asking him for help made his shoulders hunch. There had to be another way. You know, other than the police or Mave. He had to come up with a better plan. One that didn't involve Hank.

Jared broke out his textbooks again and studied at the table. He ran through his notecards and worked through some equations. Dent was supposed to help him with a practice mid-term this morning, but his ghost friend had left the apartment.

How'd it go with Neeka? Olive texted him. *She's so pretty!*

Our fearless leader wants U @ *her Dance Group 2nite*, Pat messaged him.

The apartment buzzer rang.

"Hello, Jared," Neeka said when he pressed the intercom.

Good gravy. "Seriously? You just left."

"Buzz me up."

When he opened the apartment door, she handed him a latte and a white chocolate macadamia nut cookie. The part of him that was pleased she'd gone to the trouble was drowned out by the part of him that knew she'd read his mind.

"What are we doing today?" Neeka said.

"I don't know if you know this about friendship, but there are boundaries. And you're stomping all over mine."

She came right up to him and stood nose to nose. He could feel her breath on his face.

"You'll forgive me," she said. "That's what you do."

"Are all otters this aggro?"

"Give me your phone."

He glared at her, but handed it over before she froze him and took it. "This is not how friends behave."

Neeka tapped in his PIN and then scrolled through his texts. "Why didn't your mother bury this David Thompson?" she said.

"Not that it's any of your business, but she'd be the first suspect. She has priors."

"Have you told her what he's been doing since you posted about him on Facebook?"

Jared fumed. He wanted his phone back. Now. And he wanted Neeka not to tell his mom anything, but he didn't know how to stop her.

"It's a dangerous world for a baby Trickster." Neeka grinned.

"Not funny," Jared said. "Really not funny."

Neeka made salmon patties and wild rice for lunch. After they ate, she continued to nose through his phone, poking through his private business while he pretended she wasn't there.

Dent drifted through the ceiling, yawning and stretching. He stopped when he saw Neeka.

"Woah," he said. "Who's the hot chick?"

"Dent, this is Neeka. Neeka, this is Dent."

Neeka looked up from his phone. "Your spirit familiar is faint today."

"Holy Time Lord," Dent said, tightening the belt on his robe then running a hand through his hair. "She can see me?"

"Yeah," Jared said. "She can see you."

"You hear him," she said, raising her head to look at Jared. "You hear the dead."

"You can't?" Jared said.

"No," Neeka said. "He's beyond the veil."

Jared squinted. "He's wearing a bathrobe."

"She's being metaphorical," Dent said. "It's a layman's term for interdimensional space."

"What?" Jared said.

"What did the spirit say?" she said.

"He thinks you're hot," Jared said.

"For the love of— Don't tell her that!" Dent shouted at him.

Neeka put his phone down on the table. She'd been reading Kota's messages. Jared took a deep breath and held it, but didn't feel any calmer when he let it out.

"The only way to hear the dead is to exist in this world and in the land of the dead. Very, very few beings can do that."

"Mom can hear them," Jared said defensively.

"Can she?"

"It's not a big deal."

Neeka considered him and then Dent. "Do you understand the implications of this?"

"Whatevs. I have a mid-term coming up and I have to study. How much longer are you going to be here?"

"Study away," Neeka said. She picked his phone back up.

Jared went to the bathroom. He sat on the toilet and held his head, massaging the headache that flowered at his temples. He knew she was making a point about him being different. He didn't like what she was hinting at. He wanted her to go away now.

Are you going to hide in there all day? she thought at him.

Don't do that.

Dent floated through the door. He checked his hair in the mirror.

"Can I have some privacy?" Jared said.

"Neeka, huh? Neeka who?"

"She's an otter in human form."

Dent glanced at him, then continued studying his reflection. "I meant are you dating her?"

"Dude, she's an otter."

"She can be a can of peas for all I care."

"You're dead. She's crazy."

"Sounds like a match made in heaven."

Dent shouted at him a lot less with Neeka around. He stood beside Jared while Jared studied, looking all sage and wispy, like Obi-Wan Kenobi on his day off. When Jared's brain was full, he said he needed a meeting and Neeka grabbed her purse. Dent trailed them all the way to the church, eyes riveted to Neeka like a magnet to steel.

The meeting was open and in a basement with water-stained, industrial-grey concrete walls. He liked the grunge of it, the realness. The day felt a little less insane there, even with Neeka sitting beside him.

His mom could take care of her. His mind skittered away from that thought. He wasn't going to get anyone killed if he didn't have to. He continued to hope that once Neeka saw how boring he really was, she'd lose interest and stop coming around.

Dent sighed and popped out of the basement. Jared realized he hadn't been listening, wrapped up in his own problems. He tried to focus on the reading a monotone man was giving, his confession of relapse after relapse, which made him think of Kota. Kota hadn't told him how close he was to slipping. Maybe Kota hadn't realized it himself.

Mr. Wilkinson had said the difference between sympathy and empathy was the difference between getting in a hole with someone or getting a ladder so they could climb out of the hole themselves. He wasn't sure if he was the one in the hole or if Kota was in the hole. Maybe they were both in deep, dark pits and that's why they couldn't help each other. And then there were the psychos who saw you struggling in the hole and started shovelling dirt over you.

After the meeting ended, Neeka sipped a tea and chatted with some of the guys, holding Jared in place by putting her arm through his. When she finally decided to leave, the guys looked Jared up and down, resentfully. She held his hand up the stairs, and then put her arm through his again as they walked down the sidewalk. The day was drizzly. His hoodie was damp. The drizzle clustered in her hair, where it sparkled.

"My sister's in and out of NA," she said. "We haven't seen her for weeks."

Jared glanced at her. He suspected she was playing him, because her expression was so calm. Or she was way better at detaching than he was. "Can you talk to her, you know, mind to mind?"

Neeka shook her head.

His phone buzzed in his back pocket, but he ignored it. When they approached the apartment, the Starr brothers were leaning on the rail of Hank's balcony.

"Jared!" Pat shouted. "Come on, Hitler awaits!"

"Damn it," Jared grumbled. "It's a dance practice. You don't have to stay."

"Move," Neeka said.

The group gathered in the amenities room was smaller this week. One of the dancers was showing the intricacies of a particular turn, while the drummers warmed their drums. Shu danced around tooting her recorder as Dent hung on to her shoulder, staring at everyone. Eliza waved furiously when she saw Jared. Barbie looked up and then broke into a smile. The Starr brothers galloped into the room to stand beside Barbie, staring at Neeka with awe.

"You made it!" Barbie pecked Jared's cheek, then she said to Neeka, "Are you in school with Jared?"

"We're kin through his father," Neeka said.

"We haven't done any tests," Jared said, uncomfortable with the casual lie. "It's not official."

"I'm Neeka."

"Welcome, Neeka. I'm Barbie. Are you from around here?" Barbie said.

"Neeka," Jared said, trying to distract Barbie from more questions, "these are Barbie's brothers, Pat and Sponge."

"Robert," Sponge corrected.

Pat bobbed his head shyly.

Eliza ran up to him. "Hi, Jared!"

"Hi."

"Can I come watch TV at your place after?" Eliza said.

"Sorry," Jared said, very conscious of Neeka beside him studying Shu and then Eliza. "I have to study."

She pouted at him, but Shu whispered in her ear. They ran off. Dent wavered as he followed them, shimmering and flickering like a TV tuned to bad station.

"Get a couple of the spare drums, you two!" Barbie said. "Have fun!"

Neeka went and got herself a coffee from the kitchen. Barbie shoved a drum into his hands and a beaded beater, watching Neeka make conversation with people. Eliza and Shu locked hands and started spinning. Dent blinked out.

After about twenty minutes, Jared made his escape, Neeka following him.

At the apartment door, she kissed his cheek. "See you later, Baby Trickster."

Jared said, "Don't call me that."

Good night. She walked away.

In the apartment, Dent clung to his recliner, staring at the blank TV screen, fainter than he had been this morning.

"You okay?" Jared said.

Dent nodded. Jared turned the TV on and then flipped to the science fiction channel.

"Thanks," Dent said, shoulders unhunching.

"You're welcome," Jared said.

Near midnight, a small spot in the air near Jared started to glow. He put down his textbook, bracing himself for more weirdness. The glow lit the living room, intensifying until it was like a spotlight beamed through the window. Jared squinted, turning his head. A figure emerged in the centre, a bright core of radiant light like the filament in an old-fashioned bulb.

Dent popped out of the room, disappearing from the recliner. The TV picture rolled, fragmenting into static.

Everything drained from Jared, all the sorrow and anger and fear and worry. The figure darkened and he saw a young Native woman with her black hair in two braids. She wore a plain flowered dress. She smiled at him and he was filled with love, so much love there wasn't room for anything else. He knew her now, this younger version of Mrs. Jaks. Sarah's grandmother had finally died. His neighbour, his friend, his teacher had passed away and he waited for the grief to hit him. It never came. She touched his face, smiling at him with such tenderness, warmth poured into him like sunshine.

32

DETACHED

When he was walking home from his Sunday night shift, he saw David cruising down the Drive. Jared waited for the fear to wash over him. Instead, he made mental notes about the time, the pressed white shirt David was wearing, his Matsuda sunglasses, like the ones Linda Hamilton had worn in *Terminator 2*. David had had those glasses forever and he was careful with them.

The light changed and the Lexus drove off.

The mess of emotions he'd been feeling recently were gone. He calmly watched the Lexus driving away in the rain. Then he continued his walk. At one stoplight, the man who stood beside him wore only a tank top, water beading and rolling down his bare arms. In the place where Jared would normally feel sympathy for the man's shivering, he felt nothing. Jared's message alert dinged.

Gran died, Sarah texted him. *Last night. We were all there.*

You ok?

No. Mom wants to leave after the funeral. I'm staying. Fighting about it. I'm hiding in a coffee shop.

Sorry.

Sarah went quiet for a long time. And then wrote: *My great-aunt is here. I'm going home with her.*

Take care.

You, too.

He had a new Gmail notification. His student loan had finally showed. He waited in a coffee shop until the bank opened, filled out his paperwork and popped it into his bank account. He could afford to find his own place now, but it would be either a crappy apartment he shared with others or a closet in someone's basement. He had to admit to himself he liked living at Mave's.

Back at the apartment, Jared took off his wet hoodie and changed into sweats and a dry T-shirt. He made himself a sandwich. He drank a tea. He studied for his biology mid-term. Though he noticed that Dent wasn't back and the TV was off, he felt no curiosity about the ghost's whereabouts.

The floating heads in his room had faded. The skyscraper city painted on the floor had developed a fog that made it hard to see anything. He sat on his bed. He tested the memory of Mrs. Jaks, gingerly, like poking a sore tooth. He could remember her slightly exasperated tone as she told him the difference between types of tomatoes. This one was good for sandwiches. This one was for sauce. This one grew well in sandy soil.

A shadow stained the corner of the wall. Jared turned his head to watch a bony finger poke through, wiggling in the air. The shape climbed out of the wall and crept across the floor. The place where he felt fear was empty. He remembered being disgusted, but he didn't feel that anymore. Jared flicked his hand and the thing that lived in his wall flew back, tumbling ass over teakettle until it disappeared.

That meant something, but he had no curiosity about it. Jared considered David, who loved things and appearances. Maybe this was how he felt, Jared thought. Removed. Numb. You couldn't appeal to David's sympathy because he didn't have any.

Even in this cold state, Jared didn't want to hurt anyone. It didn't excite him to think of David suffering.

His Lexus, on the other hand, was fair game. David was behaving inappropriately and he needed to know there were consequences. Jared could key it or pop the tires. Or set it on fire. Throw something combustible under the gas tank.

He got up and rummaged through Mave's storage closet and found her empties. He chose a screw-top bottle of wine and scrubbed off its label. He then handled it with dishtowels so he wouldn't get his fingerprints on it. He took some tubing from Mave's junk drawer and put the bottle in his backpack, cushioned with brown paper bags.

He rode the Vespa out of the underground parking lot, manoeuvring it the way Sophia had showed him so many years ago. When he found a deserted park, he stopped and siphoned some of the Vespa's gas into the bottle and screwed the cap back on. His mom was more a fan of grenades, but they'd set wasp's nests on fire with Molotov cocktails.

Just before you release, flick your wrist slightly for a nice tight spiral, she'd told him.

As he contemplated setting David's Lexus on fire, he knew something was wrong with him. But he didn't care enough to stop.

The fly in the ointment was finding the car. He couldn't scout the neighbourhood without calling attention to himself. Standing on the balcony, Jared was unable to spot the silver Lexus or David either. Maybe all his planning was for nothing. Maybe David was just commuting through the area.

Shu had saved him and had been willing to curse David. Jared thought of her and she shimmered into view, staring up at him. She held out her hand. Jared took it. The longer they held hands, the colder he became.

He pictured David and his vehicle in as much detail as he could remember, explaining to Shu that he wanted to set it on fire. Shu let go of his hand and popped away. Jared saw her on the sidewalk. She skipped down the street, playing her recorder. She popped away again. He heard her music distantly, but couldn't see her. Jared went inside and flipped through his notecards on the couch while he waited.

When he had given up on her, she popped back beside him, she touched him, and he saw David at the pub on the corner. His mother's ex was leaning over the pub's second-floor balcony with a baseball cap pulled low, sipping a beer, watching the front of Jared's apartment building. Then she showed him the silver Lexus.

Jared got his stuff together and slipped out the back door that led to the alley and the Dumpster. In the shadows of the alley a block away, Jared put on a black, disposable rain jacket and latex gloves. David had parked in an empty lot, four blocks from Jared's apartment. The gloves squeaked against the bottle as he held it and lit the gas-soaked rag. The bottle tinkled as he rolled it under the Lexus. He walked quickly away, stripping off the gloves.

He glanced back. The dishcloth soaked in gas stuck in the top of the wine bottle burned merrily, lighting the undercarriage. He ducked down another street, stripped, and then stuffed his gasoline-smelling outer clothes in a plain plastic grocery bag before tossing it in a rank Dumpster. Then he rinsed his hands in a puddle and pulled on the clothes he'd tucked in a large zip-lock bag.

The rain quickly soaked his hoodie. He zigzagged back to Commercial. He stopped in a park, empty except for teens smoking up, to look back. The smell of skunk wafted everywhere. No explosion. No fireballs. Disappointed, Jared headed back to the apartment.

A car alarm went off, whining in the distance. As Jared turned down the alley, fire trucks screamed past. Shu appeared beside him and in his mind he saw the Lexus burning like a campfire. Shu popped away again.

When he came in, Mave was sitting on the living room couch. "Were you at a meeting, Jared? Some guy was shot just up the street and there was a car bomb."

"Don't worry. I'm okay. All I really need right now is a nap."

Mave hadn't seemed to notice a gasoline smell, but he put the clothes he'd changed into in the washing machine and then took a long shower, scrubbing with the most floral-scented soap he could find.

In the morning, he went down to the laundry room with his biology text and washed his clothes two more times then threw them in the dryer. Hank came in and they ignored each other until Jared's dryer beeped. Hank went and stood in front of it. Jared looked up at him.

"Have you heard from Kota?" Hank said.

"Not recently," Jared said.

Hank shook his head. "You don't give a rat's ass about anyone but yourself, do you?" He looked like he wanted to say something else, but instead he left in a huff. Jared took his clothes out of the dryer and went back upstairs.

Jared studied some more for his mid-term on the bus to school. He finished early, so he slowly flipped through the test. He went through it twice, but didn't change any of his answers. After a few people had gone up and handed in their tests, he went up too.

That evening, the light was on in Mave's room but she didn't respond to Jared's knock. The apartment buzzer rang.

"It's me," Neeka said when he answered.

She came in with a latte and a cookie. She stopped in the doorway of his bedroom, staring at the walls. The painted heads had stopped rolling. The walls were almost ordinary walls again. Neeka studied him.

"What happened to your painted people?" she said.

"Mrs. Jaks died," Jared said. "She came to say goodbye and they all faded."

"Did she come in person or spirit?"

"Spirit."

"Ah. You have a wall up. It's not very strong, but it's palpable."

"It's what?"

"Here." Neeka put the latte and cookie down on the table, and then reached out to him. Her hand glittered as it came close. One moment he was fine; the next, something was trying to claw its way out of him, ripping through his guts and his chest.

Jared heard himself howling, but it was as if it wasn't really him. The sounds coming out of his mouth weren't his sounds. Neeka lowered him with her to the floor before he collapsed. He curled into himself. He was on fire. He'd swallowed gasoline and now it was lit, burning inside him.

The floor became uncomfortable. He was too tired and too embarrassed to move. He worried that Mave had heard the commotion and would come out of her room, but her door remained closed. Neeka didn't seem bothered by him emoting all over her lap. She lifted his head off her and reached up to his desk for some Kleenex. Jared took the tissues she handed him, sat up and blew his nose. He couldn't meet her eyes. He hadn't expected to fall apart. Again.

"Tea?" Neeka said.

"Please," Jared said.

"Even when you're expecting it, death is a hard transition," she said. She held her hand out and pulled him to standing.

While she puttered around the kitchen, he sat on the couch. He felt as hollow as a chocolate Easter bunny. He stared out the window. The night was coming earlier, especially since the rainy season was in full force. The street lights flickered on.

She brought him a weak tea with lots of sugar and milk. She turned the TV to the news and sat beside him. Jared sipped his tea. Neeka ate an apple.

Grief made him heavy. It felt like a dream, a horrible, horrible dream that he'd set David's Lexus on fire. He'd asked Shu for help. When he was as cold and logical as Spock, it had all made sense, but now he was filled with dread. He wanted to check his phone and see if there was anything on the news, but he didn't want to do it in front of Neeka in case she took it from him and nosed through it.

Someone knocked on the door. Neeka turned her head and quirked her eyebrow. Jared shrugged. The lock clicked and the door opened.

"Jared," Hank called from the front hall. "Are you home?"

Fantastic, Jared thought. A visit from Hank was just what he needed to make this day perfect. "In here."

He heard Hank's heavy tread coming down the hallway. Jared sat up, putting the mug of tea on the coffee table.

"Listen, I didn't mean to ta—" Hank came to a full stop when he saw Neeka, like a cartoon of someone realizing they've stepped off a cliff and gravity is about to take over. Hank swallowed. He shuffled, moving from foot to foot like a little kid who needs to pee.

"Should I leave?" Neeka said.

"No," Hank said.

They stared at each other for so long, Jared became annoyed. "What do you want, Hank?"

"Oh," Hank said, not taking his eyes off Neeka. "Hi."

"Would you like some tea?" Neeka said.

"Yes," Hank said.

Hank followed Neeka into the kitchen. Jared listened to Hank explain where the teacups were. And the good tea. And the teapot. He offered to lift the kettle. Jared blew his nose. He went to the bathroom and checked his reflection. It looked like mosquitoes had been feasting on his eyes. He had snot crusted around his nostrils. Jared washed his face. He could hear Hank laughing, an uncool hee-haw.

When Jared returned, Hank's expression darkened. He couldn't be more obviously jealous if he painted himself green.

"Are you two together?" Hank said.

"His dad went out with my mom," Neeka said. "We could be siblings."

"Oh," Hank said.

"I know," Neeka said. "Messed up, huh?"

"No, no. Not at all. No." Hank's face scrunched in concentration and Jared would have bet anything that he was examining the family tree to see if that meant Hank and Neeka were cousins of some sort. He suddenly looked relieved, and straightened, smiling. Hank obviously thought Neeka meant Philip Martin.

You lied to him, Jared thought at her.

He'll be nicer to you if he thinks you have a hot sister.

He went into his room and lay down on his bed. The floating heads in the wall were still. The mobile of the sun and planets creaked. He heard his message alert ding, but was too tired to check who was texting him. He wondered when Mrs. Jaks was going to be buried. He wondered if she would visit again, or if that was the last time he was going to see her.

At the grocery store the next morning, David appeared beside him and casually picked up a bag of grapes. He didn't seem angry, the way you would expect of a normal person who'd just had their car blown up. Jared had a moment of doubt, about what was real and what he'd dreamed. David paused. Jared hadn't ever expected to feel this detached, this aloof. But he wasn't, not really. Underneath everything, he wanted to shove David's head through the wall. The longer David lingered beside him, the angrier Jared grew. He was sick of David's shit. Sick of being stalked, of living in dread. In the distance, Jared heard a slither.

"Good luck with your physics mid-term on Thursday," David said.

"Thanks," Jared said.

The thing that lived in his bedroom wall squirmed in the shadows of the store. Jared could feel its stare.

The thing gurgled. Jared remembered all the ways David had made his life hell. The hairs rose on his arms. He was angry and he felt the thing agree with him. David was bad. David needed to go away.

Eventually, David headed for the line at the cashier. The thing crawled beside Jared, its bony back rippling as it followed him like a dog.

Jared heard rustling and expected to see Mave, but Neeka was waiting for him in the apartment, nosing through his bedroom when he walked in.

"What the hell?" Jared said.

"Hank let me in," she said. "He's checking up on your aunt. She's up on some mountain for a protest."

"Can you give me some space?"

"I did."

"This isn't space. This is the opposite of space."

She cocked an eyebrow. "If you'd listened to your mother and learned some basic protection spells, this wouldn't be an issue, would it? You're lucky I like you. A lot of beings take issue with Wee'git. They'd happily hurt you in his place."

The threat hung in the air. She waited, watching him.

"What do you really want?" he said.

"My mother is a witch too," Neeka said. "But she isn't powerful like your mother. She would take little bits of my soul to power her spells."

Jared stood uncomfortably, wishing he wasn't having a conversation about witches stealing their children's souls. "I'm sorry."

Neeka's smile disappeared. "I don't need your pity."

"Okay."

"Sit."

Jared sat on the desk chair before she made him. She sat on his bed.

"I can't hear you today," Neeka said.

"I didn't say anything."

"No." She tapped her temple. "Here. Sometimes you're loud and clear like a siren. Most of the time you could be any one of the human herd."

"Thanks."

"My mother would kill for your power."

Jared shrugged.

"And you pretend you have nothing."

"I don't. I can't make it work."

"You don't want to."

"You can take it," Jared said.

Neeka was very still. Jared thought she'd want to take everything, and he half-hoped she would so he could be a human, plain and simple.

"You don't know what it would do to you," Neeka said.

"Would I be normal? A normal human?"

"No. No, you would not." Neeka sighed. "You're lucky, Jared Benjamin Martin, that I am not my mother."

They sat for a long time. Neeka stared into the distance, scowling. He could see spots of her memory: a green seiner with white trim; a black fish with an oily rainbow sheen cupped in small hands; a delicate woman with brown hair and large, nervous eyes. Her dress covered her from neck to ankle and her hair was curled in tired ringlets. Neeka was coldly furious. She saw a drop of her own blood on the blue table. The kitchen cupboards had no doors. The nervous woman stirred a large steel broth pot, glancing over at Neeka.

"Stay out of my head," Neeka said.

"You're in mine," Jared said.

They had a loop of irritation going, hers, his, hers, his, until they Vulcan mind-melded and he wasn't sure if he was feeling his feelings or hers.

"You need so much help," Neeka said, then she stomped out.

"You barged in on me!" Jared shouted at her retreating back.

Jared massaged his temples where a headache threatened, wishing furiously that he'd never met Neeka.

Hank popped in later, trailed by a mud-splattered Mave, who announced she needed a shower. Hank's hair was suspiciously groomed, his face shiny, and he was wearing a clean, ironed T-shirt and new jeans. "What did Neeka say?"

"She's a serial killer," Jared said. "She wants to kill me. Thanks for letting her in the apartment, asshole."

Hank's eyes were as glossy as if he was stoned. "Your half-sister is amazing."

"Oh, good gravy," Jared said.

33

SNACKS ARE A MANY-SPLENDOURED THING

When Jared got home from his night shift, Mave made him break-fast, scrambled eggs and chopped fruit. She poured him a coffee. "How's Jared? You seem very subdued this morning."

"If you get arrested for your protest stuff," Jared said, "I can take a bill or two off your hands. My student loan came in."

"I might take you up on that if my bail is high, but for now, save it for your incidentals and quit your job."

"Why would your bail be high?"

She sipped her coffee. "That isn't your worry."

"Don't do anything slammer-inducing."

"You have a colourful way of expressing yourself."

"Aunt Mave."

Suddenly, her eyes welled up and she reached across the table to grasp his hand.

"You okay?" Jared said.

"You've never called me Aunt before. Bring it in. Come on, gimme hugs."

"Can we not make a big deal?"

"No. Deals will be big."

She got out of her chair and stood beside him, squeezing him in an air-limiting hug. When she cried on his shoulder, he patted her back.

"Love you," she said.

On the bus ride to school for his physics mid-term, Jared checked his phone. Sophia had messaged him yesterday: *Hooligans set Mr. Thompson's car on fire while he was visiting your neck of the woods. Such a dangerous neighbourhood you live in.*

And then, a few hours later, *The Lexus belonged to his father, a communal car for the help. His daddy owns a number of luxury properties that David squats in when they're vacant.*

The last message, early this morning: *If you don't answer me, I'm going to assume you're in a hospital bed somewhere and come find you.*

Hey, Sophia, he messaged back. *I've been busy with school. Sorry. Haven't been checking my messages! I'm okay!*

Dindins? she messaged back.

I have physics mid-term today.

Tomorrow then. Clear your Friday night schedule. Pick you up at 6!

Jared thought about Sophia and her cleansings when she had come to visit. His mother had dreaded them. Jared hadn't understood until much later that Sophia was scrubbing the house of everything supernatural, making snide comments about his mother's "house-keeping" all the while. Back then, he'd thought she was old-fashioned and loved the smell of sage, cedar, sweetgrass and tobacco.

The thing crawled around the floor of the bus in anxious circles, like a nervous dog turning before it lay down. It dropped through the bus floor and disappeared just before his stop.

Jared and his lab partner met up at Tim Hortons for a quick study session before they went to class. He wanted to get this over with, get it done.

The physics mid-term seemed very easy. Jared finished before everyone and caught the bus.

Mave was gone when he got home. He spent the rest of the afternoon on the couch. He dozed, still all emo about Mrs. Jaks. She had suffered and now she wasn't anymore, but she was dead and, not being the kind of person who overstayed her welcome, she seemed to have permanently moved on to the next stage of life. Death. Afterlife. Wherever she was, she had popped in to say bye and that was that.

Dent drifted near the ceiling, suspended in an invisible ocean. His colour was so faint, he was more an impression of Dent. Maybe that's how ghosts slept, Jared thought, not sure if he should wake his friend.

His friend. Was it weird that he was friends with a ghost? Did that make him delusional? A mark? He knew what his mom would say about needing to think with his head, not his heart, but Dent was solely responsible for his mid-term marks being respectable. Jared's phone pinged.

Are you free? Olive texted him. *Finalizing divorce papers with lawyer. Need someone to watch Eliza for a few hours.*

He wasn't sure if he liked being a resident babysitter. But Eliza mostly watched *Frozen* and he was already moping on the couch. Company couldn't hurt.

Sure. Come on over.

Thank you, Jared.

Hank dropped by before work to see if Neeka was visiting and then he poked around as if he didn't believe Jared wasn't hiding her somewhere. Jared hoped Neeka wouldn't show up while he was babysitting.

Olive knocked and they chatted while Eliza thundered down the hallway to the TV with Shu skipping happily behind her, tendrils of her clothes floating around her like worn silk threads in water, the flesh of her cheek bloodlessly pared to the bone. She waved excitedly at Jared as she passed.

"Thank you, thank you, thank you," Olive said.

"No worries," Jared said.

Olive smiled, waiting until Eliza was out of view to whisper, "It's awkward asking Darlene. She's been wonderful, but Aiden is her son."

"Sorry."

"No, no. Big-girl panties. Putting them on. Here I go." She took a long, slow breath. "See you in a bit, Doodle-bug!"

"Bye, Momma," Eliza shouted back.

Eliza and Shu played on the living room rug. Dent bumped against the ceiling like a stick in a stream bumping against the bank. Shu lay on her back and pointed her toes, pretending to bicycle. Eliza laughed, rolling like a log through Shu, over and over.

He didn't know anything about Eliza's dad. But he watched her goofing around with Shu and he felt bad for her. Shit was coming, and she didn't know about it yet, so everything in her world was fine. Jared remembered when his parents had told him they were getting divorced. They had driven to a steak house and Jared'd thought they were celebrating. He'd hoped his dad had found a job. Maybe, he'd thought, they were moving. They'd waited until dessert. Jared had

had a bite of cheesecake in his mouth and he hadn't been able to swallow it.

He should have guessed. His parents had stopped screaming at each other and the house had a stillness that was more nerve-racking than the shouting. That should have clued him in, but he was a kid. Eliza had to know her parents weren't going to get back together. Eliza's dad wasn't even living with them anymore. His friends had stolen their furniture.

Shu was suddenly in front of Jared, tilting her head as she studied him.

Family, Shu said, and Jared's mind was filled with images of Eliza and Shu playing together. Shu saw Eliza when she was a baby in a crib. Shu saw Olive when she was a baby in a bassinet. Shu saw Olive's mother in a cradleboard.

"It'll be okay," Jared said to Shu.

Eliza said, "Can we make cookies, Jared?"

Shu saw her own body on a cedar mat in a longhouse. Her face was unrecognizable because of the sores, blistered and swollen. Her body was curled into her mother's, which was equally as rotten. Flies hummed in the weak daylight filtering in the smoke hole. Clouds made the sky a grey sheet. The longhouse was full of shadows. Nothing moved but the flies and their maggots. Her mother's spirit waited for Shu, standing in the bow of a canoe offshore, calling Shu's real name, telling her it was time to go.

"Let's get ice cream instead," Jared said.

A man entered the longhouse in Shu's memory. When he bent over her body, the little skulls in his long, matted hair clinked together like shells fringing a dance dress. He looked up and saw Shu's spirit. When their eyes met, she felt dread. He smiled at her spirit and his teeth were filed to points.

Why haven't you left? the man asked Shu, mind to mind.

Don't want to, Shu said to the man in her memory.

Can't you hear your mother calling you?

I want to stay.

"Please?" Eliza was saying. "Pretty please?"

"What?" Jared said, trying to shake the images Shu was sharing. The man picked up her body, ignoring the larvae that dropped off her, the slime and the ooze from her decomposing flesh. The smell of all the bodies in the longhouse didn't bother the man. They walked through the forest behind the village, following a deer trail into the mountains. Shu helplessly followed him, tethered to her body by unseen strings.

"One balloon," Eliza said. "That's all I want."

"Sure," Jared said.

"Yay!"

Great evil walks the land, the man with pointed teeth said in Shu's memory. *I can't protect my family by myself. If you help me, I'll keep your bones safe.*

Jared didn't want to see any more and the images stopped. Shu was trying to tell him something, but he wanted no one in his head but himself. Shu touched his hand and it sparked as if she had dragged her feet along a carpet while wearing wool socks.

Protect my family.

At the dollar store, Eliza hit him up for marshmallows and chocolate bars on top of the balloon. They went to the café and stood in line for gelato. Jared got himself an espresso. Eliza held hands with Shu and they skipped to the park. Jared sat on the bench while the girls played tag.

Once they were back at the apartment, Eliza asked if she could light a candle. Jared dug out one of Mave's from her pantry. It was a fat, creamy white pillar that smelled vaguely green, hinting of freshly mown lawns. He put a pie tin under it. Eliza stuck a marshmallow on a fork and said, "This is for Shu."

She let the marshmallow burn into a bubbling black mess. Shu grinned as a marshmallow the size of a head appeared in her hands. The smoke alarm went off. Jared waved a towel under it before he took the battery out. Shu pulled off chunks and crammed them into her mouth, happily bouncing on her toes. Eliza burnt some chocolate and Jared was glad he didn't have to clean up after Shu because she smeared it all over her face and hands as she ate.

"Hey," Dent said, floating down from the ceiling. "Share-sies?"

Shu closed her eyes and shook her head.

"She's too hungry," Eliza said. "Here. Have your own marshmallow. This is for Dent."

Dent's marshmallow was just as large. He sucked it in as if it was water and then smacked his lips. He solidified; the threads of him wove back together and you couldn't see through him anymore.

"Why is the food bigger on the other side?" Jared said.

"It's the land of the dead," Eliza said. "Day is night there. Summer is winter. A little food is a feast."

Jared went down to the nearby hardware store and bought a cheap propane grill. They sat on the balcony and fired it up. Eliza said they needed to put the food on real plates if they burnt food in a real fire, so they did until one of the neighbours shouted that barbecues weren't allowed.

After they'd eaten, the ghosts held hands and danced through the walls. They spun each other around, and then flew up, off the balcony.

He heard a hum, and then Huey the flying head zipped up to them, smiling his big, goofy smile.

"Let's burn something for Huey," Jared said.

"He doesn't eat human food," Eliza said.

"What does he eat?"

"I don't know. I've tried feeding him everything."

"Dude," Jared said to him. "That sucks."

Huey bobbled, shaking back and forth, before he followed Dent and Shu. Jared shut the propane off and closed the lid.

"Wanna watch *Frozen*?" Jared said.

"Shu talked to you," Eliza said.

Jared considered lying, because she was a kid and he didn't want to lay a heavy on her. But she heard Shu too. "She did."

"What did she say?"

He didn't want to lie. "She told me how she died."

They watched the ghosts playing on the top of the building, doing their weird hopscotch thing.

"Shu can be scary," Eliza said.

"Are you scared of her?"

Eliza nodded. "But she keeps the bad things away. When she's not here, it's scarier."

"Sounds like my mom," Jared said.

"Momma says you're our cousin."

"I am."

Eliza smiled up at him. "Good."

Olive brought home a bucket of KFC. She didn't seem to notice that the apartment smelled like burnt marshmallows. After dinner, she picked up the sleeping Eliza and carried her home, leaving Jared with the leftovers. Dent sat in the recliner.

"I think I passed my mid-terms."

"Told you," Dent said. "They dumb these things down so anyone can pass."

"Thank you for helping me," Jared said. "If you want anything to eat, I can burn it for you."

Dent considered him. "I'm good."

"Are you sure? You were looking kind of faint."

"I'm not sticking around forever. I wasn't put on this earth to tutor your sorry ass through remedial science. Don't get used to this."

"I respect your intellect," Jared said.

Dent's eyes narrowed. "Are you being sarcastic?"

"I'm trying to think of all the ways you aren't an ass. Positive thoughts. Be the change."

"You want to thank me? Shut up, Oprah."

Jared turned the TV on. He hoped Sophia wouldn't come up to the apartment tomorrow. He'd slipped lately with the magic stuff and things were sliding down to crazy-ville.

Cold turkey, then. Full commitment to ordinary human-beingness. A Day One for magic sobriety.

He glanced at Dent, who snickered along with the canned laughter on the boob tube. He supposed he could afford a living tutor now. But Dent was a good guy, despite the crank. And it wasn't like they were whipping up curses or dabbling in the dark arts.

He didn't want Sophia to banish Dent or Shu. Or Huey. They didn't do anything but hang out, really. Besides, they were here first, and he wasn't going to be rude and boot them out. He would just have to avoid all the other things that wanted to rip him apart or use him as bait for having a dink-ish father.

Huey returned, flying in the open balcony door. He buzzed around the room and landed on Jared's toes, smiling.

"Hey, dude," Jared said. "Want to watch TV with us?"

"Don't encourage it," Dent said.

Huey hopped onto Jared's legs and then his chest and then perched on top of Jared's head.

"Okay," Jared said. He didn't get any pictures from Huey the way he had with Shu. Huey began to bounce off Jared's head like an unruly toddler. The bouncing didn't hurt, but it was annoying.

"You really don't know what you're doing, do you?" Dent said.

"Okay, Huey. Okay. You can stop now."

Huey rolled through the air, smirking, looking pleased with himself. Jared planned on studying more, but he really was fried and went to bed. Huey followed him, disappearing into the wall to swim with the other floating heads.

Jared hesitated before switching off the light and then didn't. He lay down, listening to the planetary mobile creak while he sensed the thing watching him from inside the wall. The hairs on his arms and neck prickled. He was glad Huey was here. The thing stayed in the wall when Huey was around. Huey landed on Jared's toe, weightless as a feather. He was worried he wouldn't be able to settle his thoughts, but he drifted off effortlessly, sinking quickly into a dreamless sleep.

34

YOU SAY YOU WANT
A RESOLUTION

Sophia texted Jared a reminder for the pickup time, and to the second, a cream limo pulled up and double-parked in front of the apartment building. The driver leapt out and jogged to the entrance. Jared had worried about Sophia and Mave meeting up, but her bedroom door was closed and her light was on, which could only mean she was in writing mode. When the driver buzzed, Jared headed down.

"Madame is waiting for you at the restaurant," the driver said as Jared climbed into the empty back seat.

The pale leather was butter soft under him and the bar was loaded with every type of booze imaginable. Jared picked out a bottle of sparkling water from the little fridge and sipped it as he watched the streets roll by, the rain beading on the tinted windows, giving everything a soft focus. They rode the Georgia Viaduct downtown, the city sparkling against the dark sky.

The driver dropped him off in front of a restaurant called Hawksworth. A giant picture window showed him Sophia sitting at a white table in a white-and-gold restaurant, sipping a glass of white wine. Her finger-waved hair sparkled with tiny barrettes and she wore a long grey pantsuit and thin wool throw with a silver thunderbird clasp at her throat. She raised her glass when she saw him, but didn't get up.

"Hey," he said when he was led to her table.

"Hello, Jared," she said. "I hope you don't mind, but I've ordered the halibut for you."

He shrugged and sat. A waiter filled his glass with water. He unfolded the napkin and placed it on his lap. She studied him.

"Is something on my face?" Jared said.

"I'm so used to thinking of you as a child. And here you are, a man." She leaned forward and lowered her voice. "Who's making some very foolish choices."

Straight to it, then. "You don't have to step in. I'm not your problem."

"My darling, stupid boy, you don't escalate things with a psychopath."

Jared glanced at the other patrons around them but not near enough to hear them.

"Mrs. Jaks died," Jared said. "She visited, and I . . . I wasn't myself when it happened. I was kind of numb after she touched me."

"Numb?"

"It didn't last long. But I couldn't feel anything."

"Was that your neighbour? The one who looked after you that summer?"

"Yes, her."

"Ah," Sophia said. "I was afraid you were following your mother's path. Before she met my son, she was reckless with her power and her use of violence."

Jared couldn't imagine his mother being *more* reckless. He also felt weird talking about her with Sophia. They sat quietly until the waiter brought their appetizers, two small plates of seared scallops.

"Mrs. Jaks was a witch, you know," Sophia said.

"She didn't practise," Jared said.

Sophia rolled her eyes. "Right. Your sanctimonious Mrs. Jaks pushed all your mother's buttons, did you know that?"

"Mom mentioned it a couple of times."

"Be choosy with your magical dance partners. Don't invite creatures into your life if you don't understand their motives, and certainly don't participate in magic with them."

"I'm not doing magic," Jared said. "I've just got some protection things going."

"You have a 'glow' about you that says otherwise. I'm not judging, my dear. Just remember, the supernatural realm can be treacherous."

Jared wondered how much he could tell her. They weren't back to their old relationship, where he shared everything with her. They were still feeling each other out and he didn't want to break their fragile connection.

"Maggie would be here in a heartbeat if you asked her for help," Sophia said.

Jared wasn't so sure. Sober Jared was not her favourite flavour and Jared realized he didn't want to put her love for him to the test. He didn't want to know for sure that she was over him.

They ate. The scallops were fresh. The plate was full of arty sauce swirls and green garnishes.

"I'm leaving for Portugal tomorrow," Sophia said. "My island man has a long-stay arrangement near Lisbon."

"Cool," Jared said.

"David Thompson is heading into his fourth divorce and this wife is determined to make the domestic assault charges stick." Sophia pulled a card from her purse and pushed it across the table. "I think the best thing is if he gets put behind bars. I leave it up to you to contact her."

Jared left the card on the table, feeling his food churning. "I dunno."

"I can't change what he did," she said. "But I can offer you a pestilence of lawyers."

"Why?" Jared said.

She sat back. "I can't help liking you, you silly thing."

"Mom says you're dangerous and I should stay away from you."

"Has she suddenly become irony-impaired?"

No denial of the danger. Just a quirk of her well-groomed eyebrow.

"She doesn't like competition," Jared said.

Sophia laughed, a tinkling, warm sound. He felt the world was a better place then, with Sophia back in his life. He ordered a dessert he was too full to finish, and they both lingered in candlelight.

The limo dropped him off at his apartment. He changed into his grungy clothes and lay down to rest before his Friday night shift. He was a bit nervous about the walk. And exhausted from being on graveyard. Maybe he needed to simplify his life. Maybe he needed to focus on school and sobriety. Maybe it was Mrs. Jaks's death. Maybe it was all the transitions. Almost getting run over and then retaliating by torching an SUV. He felt raw. He wanted to curl up under his blankets and avoid everyone. Cocoon. Hibernate. Be alone and quiet and let his brain sort itself out and not be constantly sleepy from the late nights. Shu was a help as a lookout, but Jared didn't want to give David any more chances.

That night he gave his two weeks' notice at the Donut Hole, and thanked the manager for the opportunity.

The manager banged his coffee mug on the counter. "Yeah, don't bother coming back after tonight, you loser. And don't bug me for a reference."

"Okey-dokey."

"You and your smart mouth."

Jared was tempted to half-ass his shift, but finished his batches and the manager didn't make a further scene, just paid him.

Shu popped up beside him when he stepped into the alley as the sun rose over the mountains. A picture formed in his head of the neighbourhood as if he was looking at it from above. No David. She hopped over a Dumpster, adding a twirl.

Mave's light was still on and her door was closed. He burnt Shu some marshmallows to thank her for keeping watch. Dent popped in and Jared burned for him as well. They bounced off the balcony like hyper kids and he could hear them squealing as they started their leapfrogging game again. Neeka buzzed up.

"Really?" Jared said.

"Morning," she said.

Neeka made them tea and came and handed him a mug. She sniffed, following her nose to his bedroom. She came back, frowning.

"Marshmallows?" Neeka said. "You fed the ghosts?"

"They were hungry."

"When you become a Trickster, remember we want our skins back. We're good allies. You want us on your side."

Jared glared at her. "I'm human."

"Magic transforms," she said. "The more you do, the more you change."

"That's not even magic."

Neeka frowned. "I'm not sure why you're fighting your transformation. We've been human for two hundred years and we'd rather shit razors than spend another minute in these monkey suits."

"It's just a snack."

"You're living in a cauldron of magic. If you want to stay human, you should leave this apartment."

Jared looked around the living room. Without him, his aunt would go back to living on frozen burritos. Besides, he didn't really believe Neeka. It wasn't like he was dabbling in the dark arts. He'd just fed his friends.

"Don't say you weren't warned," Neeka said.

Neeka picked up his phone when it pinged, reading it as she lounged on the couch. Feeling his temper rise, Jared took a deep breath and held it. He couldn't concentrate on his textbook anymore.

"Kota met someone," she said. "He's a vet with ten years."

"I have eyes, you know. I can read my own messages."

"Keep studying."

"How long are you staying?"

"Until I have to pick up my nephews at Grandview and take them to aikido."

It was such a plain answer, so soccer mom-ish, Jared was surprised.

"Family is all," Neeka said. "Everything else is noise."

Neeka brought him to and from his meeting and then left him at the apartment entrance. Justice popped in to pick up Mave, they both yelled bye, and they were gone. Jared took a long shower then sat on the balcony scrolling through his phone.

Kota had put heart emojis in his text, which was so out of character, Jared wondered if it was really him. His mom had posted selfies, proudly straddling the seat of a Fat Boy, one of her favourite Harley-Davidson motorcycles, grinning ear to ear in someone's garage. Crashpad and Muriel were posting longingly about each other, heartache poems and sad-faced pictures, promises of unending devotion.

Děda stopped eating, Sarah had texted him late last night. *He has a no-resuscitation order. We're making arrangements to bring him home.*

Sorry, Jared texted back. *That's awful.*

He waited for a response, but Sarah went radio silent. Jared's feelings churned in an uncomfortable mess. He sat with them, wishing he could do something.

Later that Saturday, Jared defrosted two packages of ground moose meat. He cleared the kitchen counters and started a double batch of sugar cookies. He made three German chocolate cakes with egg replacer so Justice could guiltlessly eat them. He took all the tomatoes from the fridge and made a simple spaghetti sauce, letting it simmer on the stove. He carefully washed and dried two heads of romaine lettuce. He boiled some coconut icing for the chocolate cake. Late that afternoon, he sent out a text inviting a few people over.

Eliza and Olive showed up first. Eliza helped him roll out the dough and they baked until the counters were full of cooling cookies. He made a large bowl of frosting and split it into smaller bowls, filling several decorating bags with different-coloured icing. Eliza decorated the cookies with faces and suns, hearts and stars. She sandwiched cookies together with icing, adding layers of frosting and rolling them in coloured sugar and sprinkles. Her mouth became smeared with layers of icing and the cookies started disappearing. Mave and Justice walked in as Jared layered the cakes into a tower. Justice ate a slice the second she learned it was egg-free and Mave joined her.

Mrs. Jaks loved sugar cookies. She loved boiled coconut icing. She loved moose meat. She loved spaghetti. She loved home-cooked meals, made slowly and carefully. She loved dumplings. She loved sockeye. She loved watching her husband, Petr, working the garden. She loved hymns. She loved a clean countertop and a crisp shirt.

The Starr brothers showed up as Jared finished frying the moose meatballs. Olive ripped up the romaine and made a Caesar salad. Pat asked if he could bring Barbie and her gang. Jared said the more, the merrier. They helped him tip the vat of spaghetti into the sink and carefully drain it. He put aside some for Justice, with plain tomato sauce. The brothers helped him pour the rest into a large metal bowl, poured the meatballs and sauce on top, and shredded Parmesan into a small bowl.

"Help yourselves," Jared said.

Barbie and her family rolled in, and then Hank. Barbie wrestled her kids away from the cookies until they all promised to eat at least one meatball. They sprawled through the apartment. Hank and Barbie sat in the corner, heads close together as they talked quietly. Her husband and kids finished eating and grabbed handfuls of cookies from the counter. Eliza crawled into Olive's lap. Jared made tea. Olive smiled at him when he handed her a cup. Kota texted him that he wouldn't be showing, but thanks for the invite. It was nice that someone in the family remembered he existed, he added.

Jared could see why Mrs. Jaks cooked so much. He felt calmer. Or, at least, too tired to worry and overthink. The Starr brothers led the kids in a game of Monopoly, and they all argued over who was the biggest cheater.

He wondered how Mr. Jaks and Sarah were doing. He hoped Kota was okay. Roll with it or get rolled, as his mom liked to say. He had classes. He had a place to stay. He had this moment, when the apartment was full, everyone had eaten, and their laughter was probably driving the old lady downstairs completely bananas. Mave and Justice started the dishes, playing music and dancing around the kitchen.

After everyone was gone, Mave holed up in her room writing, and Jared flipped through his notecards. Restless, he got up and wandered around the apartment. It looked like he was going to have another long, sleepless night, he thought, wishing he could turn off his brain. As he went to sit on his bed, Huey flew through the open window and circled above him, landing on his toe again.

"Hey," Jared said.

The red flying head nodded hello back.

"Do you like spaghetti?" Jared said.

Huey yawned, and then closed his eyes. Jared felt sleep pulling him down, felt every muscle in his body relax.

35

WEIRD-ASS CHATS
WITH RABID DOGS

Shu woke him up early Monday morning, vibrating. She tugged his hand to sit him up and he went to throw on his shorts. He unplugged his phone, automatically tucking it in his back pocket. As he walked past the living room, Jared could hear someone banging. When he unlocked the apartment door and looked down the hall, some dude was pounding on Olive's door. He was tall, hefty and clean-cut, wearing dark jeans and a butter-yellow shirt. He had a fade, neat and groomed to the side. The guy banged and banged, loud. Annoyingly loud. He supposed this was Olive's ex, Aiden. Shu popped into existence in front of Jared, staring at him hard, confirming that yes, this was the ex, wanting him to hold her hand, wanting Aiden cursed and vomiting out his guts.

"Hey," Jared said, stepping into the hallway. "Hey!"

The guy stopped, and frowned at him. "Mind your own business."

Jared held up his phone. Gave it a waggle. The guy came down the hallway, suddenly smiling, jovial. Jared hit the Record button. "Let's make you Internet famous!"

"You think you're smart?" The man's face was shiny with sweat and his eyes were narrowed, but he was still smiling. "Stop filming me, you freak."

"I'm Jared Martin," Jared narrated. "I live in apartment 202. This dude doesn't live here and he's, like, banging on my neighbour's door super loud." Jared said to the guy, "What's your name, dude?"

"Don't fuck with me."

"Catchy. Is that your DJ name?"

"Are you a pedo? Are you sniffing around my girl, baby fucker?"

"Dude, so nasty."

"Answer me."

Jared kept filming as the guy towered over him. They were both breathing hard, not moving. The dude grabbed for Jared's phone, but he was slow and telegraphed his move. Jared stomped his ankle and ducked back into his apartment, quickly locking the door.

"Too slow!" Jared shouted through the door.

The guy punched the door. Shu zapped inside, flitting up and down the hallway. She wanted him cursed. She wanted Jared to help her. She wanted it now. Mave stood in her bedroom door in her nightshirt. Eventually, Jared heard receding footsteps and cracked the door open. Other people were also peering out. He sent the video to Olive's cellphone.

Mave said, "Jesus, Jared. You don't antagonize Aiden when he's high."

"Maybe he shouldn't antagonize me," Jared said.

She shook her head. "So cute. And so clueless."

"I've handled worse," Jared said.

The amusement fell from her face, and she flinched, suddenly finding something terribly interesting beyond his left shoulder. He wasn't sure how to read that. Was it pity or sadness?

She forced a smile. "Coffee?"

"The answer is always yes," Jared said.

Dent, who had been trying to help Jared with his studying, popped away when Hank arrived. Jared picked up his phone and crept Sophia's wall. She was spending her second anniversary near Lisbon, posting many arty food pictures to mark the occasion. She'd posed at a restaurant with a patio on a white sand beach, looking windswept and happy beside her sunburnt husband.

Hank ignored Mave in the kitchen and came to stand by the table as Jared shut his phone off.

"You did good, Jared," Hank said. "You gave us good evidence."

"But . . . ?" Jared said. "With you, I always wait for the 'but.'"

"Just film next time. Don't engage."

Jared said, "He was trying to break down her door."

Hank was instantly pissed. "I said don't engage."

Jared wished he'd just accepted the half-assed compliment. He stood to go to his bedroom. "Later."

"Did you hear me?" Hank said, grabbing him just above the elbow.

"Yeah, yeah." Jared yanked, but Hank had a solid grip on him.

"Jesus, Jared. He's unstable! You don't have your kind of weird-ass chats with rabid dogs. You call security. You call 911. You come get me. Is that clear?"

"Geez, you're extra shout-y today," Jared said.

Hank gave Jared a shake. "Don't engage with Aiden."

"You're dislocating my arm, dude."

"Henry-kins," Mave said in a warning tone.

"This is serious," Hank said. "I want you to take this seriously."

"I know. Okay? Got it. No more chit-chat with the 'roidy ex."

Hank released his elbow. "You don't handle this on your own."

"He's a giant asshole," Jared said. "But he's slow."

"He's a starving bear," Hank said. "And you are a squirrel."

Jared let the burn settle in. "Does that make you the moose? You know, moose and squirrel? The cartoon?"

Hank slammed the door behind him as he left.

"Yup," Mave said, handing him coffee and a hard-boiled egg. "Making friends and influencing people. That's you."

Olive and Eliza came to visit. Olive shyly thanked him, shoulders hunched, obviously embarrassed. Shu popped into the room, sizzling sparks. She stuck close to Eliza. Jared heard a hum, like power lines on a hot day, but no one else seemed to hear it, so he said nothing. Eliza handed him a quarter and asked him to get as many marshmallows as it would buy.

"For Shu," she explained.

After they left, Shu stayed behind, staring unblinkingly at Jared. She held out her hand to him. She still wanted him to curse Aiden. She wanted him dead. She wanted Jared's help. Jared got a picture in his mind of Aiden convulsing on the ground.

No, Jared thought at her. *Shu, no.*

His mom would do it, had done it. And he'd been tempted with David. But he couldn't. That was a step beyond. He wasn't ready to curse anyone. He might never be ready for that. Shu slapped his hand with a spark that was like touching an electric fence. Jared yipped and yanked his hand back.

"Are you all right?" Mave said from the couch.

Shu glared at him, radiating disappointment, before she popped away.

"Yeah," Jared said. "Muscle cramp."

Mave shut the TV off and came to the table, wrapping him in a hug from behind. "I'm glad you're here," she whispered.

He checked the mail on the way out to buy some eggs. He recognized Granny Nita's carefully sloped cursive immediately.

Dear Jared,

I'm happy you are safe. I'm so proud of you. Here is some coffee money. I'll write you again if you like.

Love,

Granny Anita

She'd included a twenty-dollar bill. He tucked the letter in his backpack.

He felt a little unhinged, and decided to hit a meeting before he grabbed the eggs. He googled the closest one and took a shortcut down an alley. His phone pinged. Sarah was waiting for her grandfather at the airport and feeling ambivalent about it all.

Danger, his nerves told him, as he heard heavy footsteps behind him.

Before he could turn, his skull lit up on the inside, pain opening like a gunpowder flower sparking against a dark sky. He felt his face thump the slick concrete. His nose burst, a red splatter and the tell-tale taste of copper. A part of Jared's brain hoped he wouldn't have a bent nose like Richie's, a crooked reminder of a brawl. He flailed, trying to stand, the ground tipped like a Tilt-a-Whirl ride, and he stumbled, coming to rest against a brick wall, barely standing.

David wore a baseball cap and sweats. He raised his length of pipe again and swung it like a bat. Jared couldn't move fast enough. The pipe connected with a thunk. Jared slid to the ground. David kicked him, and kicked him, and kicked him again. Jared stared up the alley, at the traffic zipping up and down the street. He managed to shout, but then David dragged him a few feet and straddled his head. David's knees clenched on Jared's ears and the world became muffled. David paused.

He can't kill me, Jared thought. He can't. It's daylight.

David produced a forty-sixer of vodka from his backpack. Not a great vodka, but a vodka Jared remembered, with a raw, medicinal bite. He held it up so Jared could see it. He cracked it open, then put it down beside them. He produced a red plastic funnel. Jared kicked, realizing what David was going to do and thinking, No, no, I have a year.

David shoved the funnel through Jared's clenched teeth. He could taste the plastic, felt the tip of the funnel hitting the back of his throat, triggering his gag reflex. The vodka burned. He held his breath as he struggled, he held it as the vodka splashed everywhere. He choked, couldn't catch his breath, couldn't breathe. He gurgled.

When David finally let him go, Jared rolled onto his side and vomited, his guts clenching while his lungs tried to suck in as much air as they could. David pulled out another bottle. While Jared retched, David splashed him, sprinkling him from head to toe with more vodka.

Sauce for the goose, a part of Jared's brain told him, and he crawled away, heaving. David kicked him until Jared was stuck on his back like a turtle, too dizzy and drunk to figure out which way was up. The sky, the grey sky, a bird, a pigeon cooing on a fire escape, the sounds of traffic, a girl laughing. The snap of a match being lit. David paused, looking down at Jared, his pupils wide and dark.

The match burned in David's fingers. The smell of sulphur. Jared's soaked clothes clinging to him. His backpack a lump beneath him. His phone was going to burn. His first good phone, the closest thing he'd ever had to new.

The slow arc of the match. David danced back, eyes meeting Jared's, and he would plead for his life, he would beg for it, but the match was already flying and he was soaked with alcohol.

Stop, drop and roll. Stop, drop and roll. Jared's brain suggested things that weren't going to work, panicked problem-solving, still confident that he could wiggle out of this. Scrambling, he jumped back enough so the match missed, but it hit the puddle of booze that Jared had left behind. The sudden flare of heat and the whoosh of combustibles realizing their potential.

I don't want to burn, Jared thought.

The fire trailed him like a wedding train as he hopped back. He heard his own panicked scream.

I want to live, he thought.

And he leapt, losing his clothes in an instant. He shed the ground. He startled the pigeon into flight when he landed on the fire escape beside it, his vision suddenly strange with colours he didn't recognize, the world acid-high intense. His arms were unwieldy, weighted with blue-black feathers. He flapped, confused, and realized his feet were claws and he needed to grip the iron grating, but he couldn't figure out how and he tumbled, croaking and flapping.

By the time he hit the alley floor, he was human again. David stared at him with wonder, even as he reached into the box of safety matches and pulled out another one, moving close.

I'm human, Jared thought. That didn't happen. Because I'm human.

He stumbled as he tried to rise, and he was naked, like an anxiety dream come true. David lit another match and Jared bolted skywards, his wings knowing what to do with the lazy breeze even as his brain scrambled to deny that he was flying. David ran below him, a shrinking, furious figure.

When he caught an updraft, he swooped. The ground was still there, but the air embraced him and he was overwhelmed by the kaleidoscope sky, its swirling shades of blue like the waves of an ocean, greenish where the air chilled and orange-tinged near the buildings where it was warmer. The sky above him was wide, beautiful and free.

36

THE RUPTURE

The continent of North America rides on a giant shell called a tectonic plate, one of the great slabs of mantle and crust separating all living things from the earth's molten core. The speed at which the North American plate crawls across the planet makes glaciers seem like rabbits on Red Bull. It is placid, taking millions of years to move negligible distances. But there are tectonic plates moving in different directions. Occasionally, at the edges, older, stiffer rocks gum up the gears of Earth's geological clock. The plates keep moving, but they bulge, like flood water piling up against a dam, ready to burst. Where the tectonic plates brush against each other as they travel in opposing directions, the world shakes itself free. At the places where one plate slides under another plate, the world shakes until it rips itself apart.

The San Andreas Fault is famous for causing quakes, but it has a quieter, more lethal cousin. The Cascadia Subduction Zone runs from the northern tip of Vancouver Island, British Columbia, to Cape Mendocino, California. The smallest of the tectonic plates, the Juan de Fuca plate in *the Pacific Ocean, slips under the North American tectonic plate. Every four hundred to six hundred years, North America catches and gets stuck. The tension builds until the plates burst apart, releasing all the pent-up energy instantaneously. During the rupture, these interplate earthquakes are the planet's most powerful. A magnitude 9.0 earthquake releases the same amount of energy as 500 megatons of TNT. For comparison, the atomic bomb dropped on Hiroshima in 1945 released 16 kilotons or 0.016 megatons of energy.*

On a winter's evening on the twenty-sixth of January in the year 1700, a magnitude 9.0 earthquake shook the northern Pacific coast of North America for five minutes and released a tsunami so powerful that when it reached Japan, the 600-mile-long wave churned the waters around the island of Honshu for eighteen hours.

Eyewitness accounts tell us that late on a dark winter's night, many years ago, Thunderbird fought a whale that had become a monster, killing other whales. As Thunderbird pulled the whale out of the ocean, the water receded, and then, when he dropped the whale, the water came flooding back, flinging canoes into the trees. When they fought on land, it shook with the epic battle.

The earth snapped, popped and rippled as the shaking moved from west to east. Sand became so loose, people walking on the beach sank into it. Trees whipped, making a strange rattling noise. Longhouses up and down the coast collapsed. Landslides buried villages. The elders warned the people to run into the mountains. Those who heeded them were chased by a wall of waves. After a few days, the salt

37

DAY ONE

He couldn't quite navigate the curve required to descend and swoop through the open patio door, so he hit the frame and squawked, tumbling into the apartment, naked and still smelling like a distillery. Jared sat up and cricked his shoulder and the pain went away. Then he was afraid of what that meant and the pain hit him again. He touched his nose, but his hand came away with no blood. His lips weren't split or sore from the funnel. The fiery slice of skull where the pipe had struck was gone or had never existed, as if he'd been dreaming about falling but woke before he hit the ground. He touched his sides. He reeked and he still felt hosed, and he wondered if he could change that, and then he became afraid that he could and of everything that meant. He picked up a throw blanket and wrapped it around his waist.

It meant nothing. He wasn't . . . he couldn't . . .

Crap, he thought. My backpack. My wallet.

Jared went to the kitchen to make himself a coffee. He laughed, because the grinder wouldn't grind. He had to plug it in. He knew he should phone the bank and declare his debit card missing—his loan, the money from work. He should phone his cell provider and declare *water sank back into the ocean. The survivors returned to their villages to find them scrubbed from existence.*

The shore had dropped six feet in an instant, long stretches of coast vanishing into the ocean. Stands of cedars and firs near the shore died as salt water drowned their roots. The resulting ghost forests can still be seen on beaches in Washington and Oregon, dead stumps and grey skeletons emerging from the sand.

The ghost forests witness this new age and these new people who don't understand what a thunderbird can do.

his phone stolen. He mourned the phone, but he didn't see himself getting it back any time soon, or his ID, his bus pass and his ten dollars and change. Then he caught a glimpse of his reflection in the microwave door and saw that he still had half a head of feathers. He wanted his stubble back, and with that wish the feathers shrank back into his head.

He took a shower. Scrubbed and scrubbed and scrubbed, but the crazy stuck to him, fed him sensations of reading the wind with his feathers, seeing the city from its rooftops. The ecstatic freedom of it. The tumbling pleasure of flight.

Feathers sprouted from his arms. His heart trip-hammered and he felt nauseous. He shut off the water and heaved, still dizzy and half-drunk. He vomited again, vomited and clutched the toilet like it was dear friend.

I forgot how this felt, Jared thought. Drunk and rolled.

He wrapped himself in a towel and peeked out the bathroom door. Mave was still working in her bedroom. He heard something screaming and went to check. The murals in the hallway popped to life as he came near them, the little figures dancing and eating, swimming and screaming. Terrible red smoke rose from the painted longhouse on the shore as the painted bear with a seal's tail started snacking on little chiefs in the war canoe. When he walked into his room, the floating heads blinked and yawned. Sarah's fireflies shot through the ceiling, forming a tiny figure eight of cold fire above his head.

Crap, Jared thought.

There aren't enough of us to go home, they told him. *We need your help.*

No, he thought at them. *No, no, I can't.*

His bedroom filled with ghosts he'd never seen before and an assortment of new spirits. He didn't know what they were, much less what to call them. They were piled up to the ceiling where Sarah's fireflies spun. The ghostly murmur reverberated through the apartment. The ghosts and spirits stared at him. The fireflies sparked and disappeared, then reappeared.

He steeled himself and walked through them to sit on his bed, his skin prickling, chilling. He felt himself getting shaky, anxious.

Go, he told them. *Get. Now.*

The ghosts and spirits all went silent. In the dark corner of the room, something darker tapped the wall. The fingers came through first, pale arms and a pale, bald head. Its black eyes scanned the room and it sniffed as it crawled out. All the other spirits puffed out of existence and the only sound was the television and the thing from the wall crawling towards him. Jared lifted his feet off the floor.

It curled up like a dog and waited just out of reach, still except for its chest rising and falling, eyes fully black and hopeful.

Jared could hear other spirits and ghosts surrounding the apartment, flashes of faces in the window, sounds above and below. Scratches. Scurrying. Children's giggles.

The faces painted on the wall were still as they watched the thing on the floor, suspicion etched in all their expressions.

"It's just me," Jared said. "Lil plastered, but still me."

The heads all turned to examine him. He received waves of love. He'd shifted and they knew it, but they didn't care. He was Jared, even if the body changed, and they liked him.

He *was* Jared. Jared and only Jared. He threw on a shirt, some underwear, his shorts. He grabbed his Big Book. He wanted to text Kota, he wanted someone to reassure him that he hadn't just cracked his skull open and let the crazy build a nest behind his eyes and tiny condos in his brain so all of crazy town could have free, affordable housing.

The thing from the wall slithered behind him as he went back to the kitchen to try to make himself coffee again. It stayed out of kicking range as he struggled with the Bodum. He heard the fireflies snapping in the hallway. Jared ignored the whispers, the cold flashes and the quick, darting things in the corners of his eyes. The water boiled. He tipped the water from the kettle into the Bodum, splashing hot water everywhere. He dropped the kettle and jumped back. The thing slid around like an eel, whipping in ways a human-shaped body shouldn't.

He clumsily cleaned up his mess on his hands and knees. He wanted to curl up on the floor, but he rinsed the dishcloths in the sink, gave up on making himself a coffee and stumbled out of the apartment, no keys, no wallet, and headed to the church where he knew an open meeting would be. David could set him on fire. David could kick him to death. Jared didn't want to see the shit he was seeing anymore. He wanted what he'd had before, as close to normal as he'd ever gotten. He was early, so he sat on the steps, hugging his knees, watching the thing watch him from the bushes, sad and resentful waves of loneliness radiating towards him.

He was afraid there was no path back to normal. Normal was a line so far away it was a dot in the rear-view mirror. A flyspeck as small as his remaining hope that once he sobered up, he could live in the world and have his biggest worry be bills and passing his courses with decent marks.

———

He turned his second white chip in his fingers, over and over, reflexively. He sat glumly near the coffee maker, and people came up and patted him on the back and congratulated him for getting back on the horse. They shared their own relapses until it was time to clear the room. He was tired, but any last bruises were gone, any breaks, any cuts. He'd healed himself without realizing it and that left him cold.

Jared didn't want to go back to the apartment and deal with the ghosts and spirits and the walls with their spells. Maybe it was time to strike out on his own. Maybe this was a sign that he needed to avoid all things supernatural. Everything. Find the most ordinary place to live and never, ever leave.

But he didn't feel like sleeping in the bushes. He downed his coffee before he walked home, not bothering to watch out for David. Dude had done his worst. The place where that fear had lived had been bulldozed over by a new fear.

You're a Trickster, a little voice reminded him. His own voice. No other.

I could be, Jared thought, if I wanted it. If I let go.

He still wanted to finish upgrading, though. And he still wanted a quiet life. Flying was okay, but the rest of it was annoying.

He clenched his chip. Death grip. Literally white-knuckling his first night of sobriety.

Mave's apartment was lit up. The windows were open and Jared could hear laughter. His aunt waved to him from the balcony. He waved back.

Ironic and typical. He'd finally found a place where people liked him, welcomed him, and it was the one place he should avoid if he wanted to stay sane.

———

Jared slipped in the front entrance when another tenant opened the door. He was going to have to tell Mave he'd lost the keys. God. David had the keys. He took a deep breath. Which, maybe, didn't mean as much as it used to now that Jared could flap away from him. God. He was such a freak.

Mave had ordered pizzas, which had attracted the Starr brothers. They avoided the vegetarian pizza but tore through the meat-lover's. Jared heard the thing in the wall slithering in the bedroom. He listened to the ghosts and spirits hiding just out of sight. He caught Mave watching him, and realized he must be acting odd. None of them seemed to notice the painted murals were alive. He wished they'd stop, and they did.

Normal, normal, I'm normal, he told himself.

"Are you all right?" Mave said.

He nodded.

Halfway through supper, Neeka buzzed the intercom. Jared said he'd meet her in the lobby, but she insisted on coming upstairs.

The guys hooted, pounding the table.

"Grow up!" Jared said, his heart rate increasing. He started to sweat, hoping, desperately, that she wouldn't see that he had become, he might be . . . non-human.

"Boys," Mave said, raising an eyebrow. "Behave."

When she knocked, Jared let her in. She was wearing her jogging gear, her hair in a high ponytail.

"Where is he?" Neeka said.

Meaning, of course, Wee'git. Jared wondered how much of the alley incident he'd been broadcasting. "Did you hear him?"

"He was close. I pray he wasn't tormenting some innocent."

Jared said, "Are you sure it was him? Maybe it was another Trickster."

"His energy signature is unmistakable."

"Hello!" Mave said, leaning over in her chair to peer down the hallway. "I'm Jared's aunt, Mave. Are you hungry? We have pizza."

"Hello," Neeka said. "No, thank you."

She pushed past Jared to stand near the table. Pat and Sponge stumbled over themselves offering her their chairs. Pat sat on the back of the couch so Neeka could sit at the table. Before she sat, Neeka held her hand out for Mave.

"'We hear the ocean in our dreams,'" Neeka said, "'our cages of blood and bone sing her songs. Exiled on shore, our tongues caress the lost words we no longer understand, her language of salt and surging.'"

Mave seemed flustered, but also pleased. "Thank you. I'm flattered."

"You found the words for what we feel. We curse your enemies, Mavis Moody."

"Oh. Well, then, um . . ."

"May they rot in hell."

Mave's smile grew strained. "Are you in school with Jared?"

"We're kin through his father."

"Who's your mother?"

"We haven't done any tests," Jared said, still uncomfortable with the lie. "It's not official."

"I'm Neeka Donner," she said to them, and then turned back to him. "Jared, I need your blood."

He let her lift his wrist, smiling as everyone watched them, completely confused, pretending he was okay with her flicking a Swiss Army knife and drawing a thin line of blood that she blotted with a handkerchief. Mave's eyes went even bigger. Sponge lifted his phone and took a picture.

"Do you want to be there when we confront him?" Neeka said to Jared.

Jared shook his head.

"Thank you." She kissed his cheek, and then turned her head to the others. "Lovely to meet you all."

After she left, Mave and the Starr brothers were momentarily silent.

Then Mave said, "Neeka seems . . . intense."

Sponge whistled. "That was the closest I've come to banging a supermodel."

"Dude," Jared said. "That's so wrong."

"She can bleed me any time," Pat said.

When the brothers had gone, Mave sat beside him on the couch. "Can I ask what that was about with Neeka?"

Jared shrugged. "She's . . . artistic."

"Ah," Mave said. "Are you all right?"

"It wasn't deep or anything. Just a scratch."

"Oh, sweetie. I mean emotionally."

"I'm okay," Jared said. "Just . . . lots of changes. And I . . . I had a slip. This is Day One."

Mave hugged him. He rested his head on her shoulder.

"What you're doing is hard and courageous," she said. "Tell me if I can do anything, okay? I'm here."

He fought crying. He fought breaking down. They held each other until Jared felt something easing in his chest, a kind of hope.

"I quit the Donut Hole," Jared said as he sat up. "I'm going to cut back on things. Refocus."

"Good," she said. She grabbed his hand and squeezed it.

"Thank you," Jared said. "For everything."

"You sound like you're saying goodbye," Mave said. "You don't have to leave. I'm not kicking you out."

"I'm counting my gratitudes."

"Then I'm glad I've moved over to your plus column," she said.

She made tea and they sat on in the living room in silence. He didn't know what was going to happen now. He had no experience with transforming. He thought then of Granny Nita, and her absolute certainty that he was Wee'git when he was little. She'd known before anyone else, and he'd bet that she could tell he'd shifted. Another relationship that was done. She hated Wee'git.

He didn't feel supernatural. But he remembered flying, and not like a dream. He still felt his feathers under his human skin. He was earthbound by choice. But he wanted to soar again. Once you tasted flying, how did you stop? How did you walk around on your legs?

Jared had gone to bed, but he couldn't sleep. He lay there watching his mobile spin in creaky circles. The thing was curled up at the foot of the bed, growling at the other things that tried to drift towards Jared. He recited the Serenity Prayer to try to calm himself.

Dent came through the ceiling, tugging Shu behind him. She was a wisp, a puff of steam, a suggestion of her former self. Her eyes were closed. Her expression, serene.

"Get," Dent said to the thing curled near Jared. "Go on! No one wants you here!"

"He's keeping the other ones away," Jared said.

"Damn. Blech. So creepy."

"What happened?" Jared said.

"She cursed Aiden," Dent said. "I don't know what to do. It was a big curse. It took the stuffing out of her."

Shu pulsed to an unseen current. Dent tugged her wrist, pulling her down.

"Maybe we should feed her," Jared said.

"Eliza tried. Shu's not eating."

"Oh," Jared said. "Is the kid okay?"

Dent shook his head. Shu vanished, and Dent went after her, but only Dent came back. Maybe it was her time. Maybe her family was waiting for her. But what about Eliza?

"Shu," Jared said.

Shu floated into and then out of view.

"Maybe Huey can help. Or the floating heads."

Dent moaned. "That's a really bad idea."

"I don't think the floating heads would hurt her." Jared struggled to get off the bed. Dent watched him, shaking his head. Moving hurt. Dent snagged Shu's foot and towed her towards the bedroom wall.

The painted faces mouthed, *Hello, Jared!* All cheery and bouncy, rolling through the walls like tumbleweeds.

"Hey," Jared said. "This is my friend, Shu. Do you guys know how I can help her?"

They stopped rolling and all floated to one wall. They stared at Shu, vibrating.

Shu sank slowly into the painted city in the floor. Dent tried to hold on to her, but she sank down until she was the size of an AA battery. Dent stuck his hand through the floor, then gasped and yanked his hand back as if he'd been stung by a wasp.

"Shu," Jared said. "Shu!"

Her tiny figure waved and she skipped through the streets. Dolphin people formed a ring around her and Jared wished she'd come back, but instead she started dancing with them.

"This is so much worse than before," Dent said, hand covering his mouth.

"She's alive," Jared said. "Or, you know. Less dead."

"The room, you idiot!" Dent said. "Do you understand what's happening?"

"Shu's okay."

"She's in another universe!"

"Relax. She's in the floor."

"Which is another universe! You have a pocket universe in your floor! Interdimensionality is not good, Jared! Not good!"

"Chill, okay? Shu's better."

"Oh, my God!" Dent said. "Jared, universes are separate for a reason! When the boundaries break down, you have chaos!"

"But she's dead," Jared said. "Aren't ghosts supposed to be interdimensional? I mean, I'm not sinking through the floor, right?" He stomped a couple of times. "I'm not floating through the wall, right? The rules are still there. Just not for you and Shu."

Dent studied the faces and then the city in the floor. "She looks like she's having fun."

"Shu!" Jared shouted. "Come back now!"

Jared had to sit on the bed, suddenly dizzy. The shadow thing tried to come through the wall, but the floating heads butted against it like angry goats until it slunk away.

Dent squatted down, his eyes following Shu as she danced through the city. The faces in the wall watched them quizzically. Jared felt the room do a slow spin. He wanted a glass of water but not enough to get up. His bed was comfy. If he could swing his legs up, life would be perfect.

"I don't want to leave Shu there," Dent said.

Shu floated up. The closer she came, the larger she got. By the time her hand came through the floor, she was normal-sized. She wanted to show him what she'd seen, what she was hearing. Dent swallowed loudly.

"Boldly go," Dent said.

"Dent! Shu!" Jared said. "Wait! What the hell! Both of you stay here!"

Dent took a loud, shaky breath then grabbed her wrist. She pulled him down and he squeaked as his head went through the floor. His body was sucked through with a whoosh. He turned and waved to Jared, excited. Dent tried to yell something at him, but no sound came through.

Dent and Shu spun down, holding hands, like a maple seed helicoptering through the air. They shrank as they descended. Jared watched them land, and then the dolphin people circled them and stuck them on a chariot, parading them across the city, out of Jared's sight.

He leaned over and wished them back. The dizziness increased, and he felt himself listing, but was stopped by a warm, gentle wind that lifted him up and laid him on his bed.

The faces in the wall assumed their positions and went still.

38

THE ANGRY BITCH
THAT LIVES INSIDE US ALL

Mave woke him up by shaking his arm. "Morning," she said.

"Mmm," Jared said, squinting at the window. "Is it?"

"It's almost noon. I'm going to Vancouver General Hospital. Aiden got into a bad car accident last night and the doctors called the family to discuss organ donation."

Jared sat up, reaching for his clothes.

Mave shook her head. "You have your own stuff to deal with," she said. "I just wanted to let you know I'll be there with Olive and Eliza. Don't feel bad about missing class."

"Damn," Jared said, struggling with his T-shirt.

"Jelly Bean," she said. "Focus, right? Sobriety first."

"How's Eliza?"

"Heartbroken. Just when they were finally free of him, too. Call me if you need anything."

"'kay. Bye."

She kissed his cheek and left the room. Dent and Shu banged on the other side of the floor, waving to grab his attention.

"Crap," Jared said.

He heard his aunt talking to someone on the phone and then he heard her heel clicks and, finally, the opening and closing of the apartment door.

Help, Dent mouthed.

Shu, at least, looked more lively than she had when she entered weirdoville. She hovered just under the floor, giving him puppy-dog eyes. The little universe below them was crowded with dolphin people. Jared sat on the floor and tried to stick his hand through. He met floor. Solid floor.

The thing crept close but stayed out of reach.

"Can you help them?" Jared asked it.

Jared sensed its pleasure that Dent and Shu were stuck in another dimension. He felt its smug satisfaction. It snickered, a sound like dry leaves being blown across the frozen ground.

"God," Jared said. "Take a hike, creep."

It crept back to its corner, glaring at Jared, radiating hurt and feelings of being unappreciated. It crawled through the floor and the room instantly filled with spirits, top to bottom, a crowd so thick the hair on his body stood on end. Jared sighed. He had no idea what to do. Sophia was enjoying Portugal. His mom would take care of this crowd if he asked her, which was great, but she did not like the dead. Period. Full stop. She was not going to help get Dent and Shu back. She was not going to understand that Dent was a good, free tutor or that Shu protected Eliza.

Instead, she would make sure the apartment was thoroughly purged, which would leave Dent and Shu trapped where they were. Or blasted out of existence.

Maybe Aunt Georgina could help them. Even if his guts didn't like her, she had written in her letter that she could help him if he got in over his head with magic. He watched Shu and Dent trying to push through the floor. It wasn't like he had a lot of options. If she turned out to be terrible, he could call in Neeka as a last, last resort. He dialed Aunt Georgina's number. She picked up on the second ring with a cheery hello.

"Hi," Jared said. "Sorry. I'm . . . having . . . I have, I mean, I, thank you, you know, for the money. Is this a bad time?"

"I'm old and bored," she said. "I'm glad you called, Jared."

He didn't know how to start. "I'm . . . I'm having ghost issues."

"Are you seeing them now? Is it serious?"

Jared hesitated and cleared his throat.

"Never mind," she said. "You wouldn't call if it wasn't. I'm babysitting Cedar today. I'll have my grandson with me. To be clear."

"That's okay," Jared said.

"What's your address again?"

Jared gave it to her, and she repeated it back to him carefully. He could hear something breaking in the background, the tinkling of glass. Aunt Georgina hastily said goodbye before the phone clicked off.

"Okay," Jared said. He looked down in the floor to Shu and Dent. "Hold on."

He was going to text his lab partner to borrow his notes from the morning class, but he remembered he didn't have his cell. It was gone. He didn't want to go there. Didn't want to think too hard about yesterday. He sat on the couch, and burnt as much cedar, sweetgrass and sage as he could find. A grating buzz woke him from wherever he'd zoned. He staggered to the intercom.

"Jared?" Aunt Georgina said. "Jared, it's me. Is this thing working?"

Something circled the floor like a centipede, arms and legs moving in a blur. It shook its head. It spat. The ghosts and spirits crowded into the living room, into the kitchen and down the hallway.

"Hey," Jared said. "I'm in 202. Come on up."

He pushed through the spirits and unlocked the door, leaving it open while he waited. He heard the elevator ding and the door slid open. Cedar clung to Aunt Georgina, who blinked through her thick glasses as the ghosts and spirits poured into Mave's apartment. She wore a long floral dress and a heavy sweater that poked out of her rain jacket. Jared shivered.

"My," Aunt Georgina said, hesitating at the door. She peered inside. "Oh, my, my, my. What have we here?"

"Hey," Jared said.

"Don't like you," Cedar mumbled.

"It's kind of weird in here," Jared said.

"Pish-posh," Aunt Georgina said. "We've seen worse. Come, Cedar. Be a big boy."

"Mmm." Cedar held her hand with both of his.

Jared backed up to let Aunt Georgina come in. She stopped just inside the door. She unhinged her jaw. The bottom half rested on her chest. Her eyes rolled back as she sucked in a deep breath. The ghosts and spirits bellowed as she swallowed them, inhaling them, and then the hallway was empty. Aunt Georgina's spine straightened and she pulled herself up, expanding until her head brushed the ceiling. Her large plastic glasses fell from her face and her human skin burst, her dress shredded, hanging from the thing that had been hiding under her skin. Jared slowly backed down the empty hallway. She touched the walls and the painted bird men in the painted landscape beneath the normal, beige wall blurred then flowed in an inky river to her fingers. She cupped the blood-coloured flood and drank hungrily.

"Better," she said, wiping her mouth. She patted Cedar on the head. "Take your skin off, dear heart. We're among family now."

Cedar plunked himself on the floor, scratching his ear. He studied Jared. "Do we eat him now, Gran?"

"Don't be silly, Cedar," she said. "We don't eat family. We're here to help."

Jared backed up into the living room as she came down the hallway, swinging her head back and forth, sucking in the dead and the otherworldly. She pushed open Jared's bedroom door. The painted faces in the wall shrieked and then went silent. By the time Jared got there, the walls were bare.

Cedar barrelled into the room in his wolf pup shape, shaking his fur and jumping up on the bed to lick his paws. Aunt Georgina studied Dent and Shu on the other side of the floor. She bent to touch the surface, unhinging her jaw again.

"Don't!" Jared said. "Wait! No! They're friends!"

"Ashuta," Aunt Georgina said, her mouth becoming normal. Ish. "And a stringy little ghost. My, but we have developed our talent since our last meeting."

"Can you get them out? And not eat them?" Jared said.

"Of course," Aunt Georgina said. "But we're going to join them first, I think."

She grabbed Jared's arm and yanked. He screamed. Cedar howled on the bed. And then the floor was gone and they were falling through the sky and Cedar's howls were gone.

The thing that had been Georgina Smith cradled him like a baby as the air roared past them. His arm was on fire. Jared shut his eyes in panic, then felt them slowing, felt them drifting, and he opened his eyes in time to see them land. Music, a thousand songs, all played at once, all rising and falling. The sound vibrated in his chest like the world's loudest rock concert. He tried to cover his ears, but his one arm wouldn't move.

The Georgina thing tucked him in a tree. Below him, dolphin people clicked and squeaked at them, their language a physical thing moving through them. They backed away from Georgina, creating a wall of grey faces with tiny black eyes. The city rose around them, echoing back the sounds in a way that made his head throb.

Georgina lunged. She shredded one of the dolphin people and then reached through its chest and pulled out its heart. She tipped her head back and swallowed it in one gulp, like it was a raw oyster. Jared watched them stampede away, heard their fear in their cries as they ran to buildings, ran to cars, ran. Georgina licked her fingers.

"Mmm," she said.

Dolphin police cars drove through the crowd and dolphin officers shot at her. The bullets bounced off her scaled skin and she laughed. She stomped towards the police cars and ripped them open, chomping on the drivers' faces.

The music was a constant blare. The street lights all went red. Dent and Shu circled him, saying things; their mouths were moving, but Jared couldn't hear them above the alarms and the screams and the music.

Dent touched Jared's arm. It wasn't ghostly; his hand didn't go through him. Shu willed something, and Jared's shoulder snapped back into place. He could move his hand. The pain became bearable, a dull ache.

Georgina flipped a cop car in the air. It crashed through the lobby of a nearby hotel. Sirens echoed off the buildings as more cop cars approached. Shu and Dent took hold of Jared and they lifted him up. They floated.

"No," Georgina boomed, marching back and grabbing Jared's ankle. She flicked Dent and Shu away and they arced through the sky, vanishing into the horizon.

"What a delightful little world you've found," she said.

Gran! Gran! Come back! Cedar's voice was frightened and Jared could hear his hiccupping crying.

I'm coming, Georgina thought at Cedar. *Calm yourself.*

Her breath smelled like blood. Her face was slick and red. She smiled as she pulled Jared close. A little bit of grey skin was stuck in her teeth. She wrapped an arm around him. They lifted up, floating.

Gran found us a new hunting ground, dear heart, Georgina thought at Cedar. *No gods. We can eat as much as we want.*

Want Mama, Cedar thought.

Shh, Mama's coming. Everyone is coming. We're all going to feast.

A black spot hovered in the sky and Jared could see Cedar peering down. They went straight to it and Georgina climbed through, carrying Jared like a football, tucked under her arm. Cedar jumped up and down, excited, wagging his tail so fast it blurred.

Come, Georgina thought. *Everyone. Come now.*

Jared could hear them all. Excited. Curious. Hungry. He could sense the ones that were near and the ones that were far away. They all dropped what they were doing to listen to Georgina promising them a banquet, a terrible feast.

Wanna stay here, Cedar said.

Dear heart, Georgina thought. *This world is dying.*

Is not.

Remember when I told you about the Quake and the Eclipse? The Year with Two Winters? The Flood?

Mama.

Your mama's coming, dear heart. Don't be frightened. Georgina tenderly stroked Jared's cheek. *We have our key now. The humans will kill their world sooner rather than later, but we'll be long gone. We'll be safe and well-fed. We'll feast on this little world beneath our feet, and then the next, and then the next.*

39

THE END IS NIGH

As midnight rolled around, Jared sat on his bed, cradling his arm. It still ached, but he could lift it. The floor was filled with flashing lights and helicopters. Dolphin people in uniforms. A barrage of missiles that exploded harmlessly beneath his feet.

He was glad Mave wasn't home. Coy wolves filled the apartment. Coy wolves wearing people skin. They came in one by one or as couples. They padded silently across the floor. Cedar's mother had stripped her human skin and suckled Cedar near Jared's feet. Georgina sat cross-legged on the bedroom floor, flanked by two men.

"I knew one of Wee'git's children would be the key," she said. "But I never thought it would be you, Jared."

He shrugged.

"We should bring his baby witch," Georgina said. "As insurance. In case our baby Trickster gets uppity. Go get her."

"No," Jared said.

The men glanced at him and then at Georgina.

"Go," she said.

As they left the room, she smiled at him.

"Don't," Jared said. "Please. I'm not fighting you. I'm not."

"We won't hurt her," Georgina said. "But as you grow more experienced, you'll get ideas. You'll turn against us. We know your kind. You're fickle."

Jared wanted to wake up. He wanted to wake up now. He wanted this to be a dream and he didn't want Sarah dragged into it. He didn't know what he could do. He wanted to warn her. He wanted her to run. He wanted a way to tell her what was coming. He wanted his mother. He wanted Nana Sophia. He wanted help. He wanted it *now*.

"That's enough," Georgina said, standing. "Go get his aunt. Go get his mother. Get his cousins. Quickly."

"No!" Jared said.

"Calm yourself," she said. "Or we'll make your friends and your family suffer. You'll watch us rip them apart, Jared. If you don't listen to me, everyone you love will suffer."

"No," Jared said.

The thing from the wall slithered through the ceiling and wrapped itself around Jared's feet. Wound and wound and wound itself like a snake.

"What the hell is that?" Cedar's mother said.

Help me, Jared thought. *Please, help me.*

The fireflies rose through the floor, faint. They gathered above Jared's head.

"Jared," Georgina said. "Stop. Now."

"Home," the fireflies said.

Tendrils of light wound down, pausing in front of Jared's eyes. He didn't want to, he really didn't want to, but the wolves would find Sarah, they would bring her here, and he didn't know what would happen then. He didn't know what they would do, and it scared him. He didn't want to go back to the dolphin world and watch the dolphins get slaughtered by coy wolves and the Georgina thing.

More fireflies came into the room and Georgina tried to grab Jared. But she couldn't grasp him as he shredded into wisps, and she roared in frustration. Sarah had been right. As he joined the fireflies, as he disintegrated into glowing threads, somehow he was still Jared, still had his own thoughts. But he could hear them now, their song like whale song, but high and sweet.

"Bring his family! Now!" she shouted.

Jared wanted *not*. He wanted them safe. He wanted Sarah safe.

"Sarah," the fireflies repeated, beginning to spin together, sparking.

"I'm warning you," Georgina said. "I will not have mercy if you cross me. If you run, if you get away from us, we'll hunt down everyone you love and slaughter them."

The thing that loved to wind around Jared's feet chittered, amused at the thought of bloody death for all the people who took Jared away from it.

The fireflies suddenly rang like a gong and he could hear them in his head again, their voices singing, tired of this universe and its clumsy numbers. Tired of monsters eating them when they had never, in all their remembered history, been subject to annihilation.

"Home," they sang, their voices full of longing.

He saw the dusty mountains and hot, barren plains of the world he'd visited with Sarah through his basement ceiling. He saw a sky full of bright, unfamiliar stars.

"Don't test me," Georgina said.

We should all go, the thing whispered. *Take them with us so they can't hurt anyone.*

All of them, yes, Jared thought. *All of us. Now.*

And they went.

The fireflies streamed up into the night sky, joining a river of other fireflies, merging and winding away, lifting out of reach, joyous. The stars were as bright as light bulbs, unnaturally close and vivid. Jared thumped as he landed.

Caught by the thing around his feet, Jared staggered and fell to the dusty ground and his skin burned in the heat, rocks sizzling like concrete after a summer's day. He sucked in a breath but couldn't get any air. All around him, coy wolves struggled to breathe, stumbled and fell to the ground, gasping. Georgina howled. Cedar and his mother ran in frightened circles, snapping at Jared.

"Bring us back!" Georgina shouted. "Bring us back now!"

Coy wolves. Hundreds of them, suffocating. Jared wouldn't bring them back because they would kill everyone he loved. One by one, they stopped moving. Georgina, though, didn't die. She howled. She shoved him down, put one large foot on his leg and snapped it. The sounds he made, the sounds, his leg.

"I have gold," she said. "I have treasures you can't imagine. Jared, bring us back. Please."

He wouldn't bring them back. He wouldn't bring them back to his family. She could make all the promises she wanted. He crawled. He felt his leg drag behind him as Georgina wrapped one hand around his neck and snapped.

———

Georgina stood on Jared's body as her family died around her. Jared hadn't expected to die, but here he was, hovering off the ground near his body. The thing slithered around, unhappy about the cold feet of Jared's dead body. Georgina was alive and he hadn't expected that either. He didn't know how she was still breathing when everyone else from their world had choked to death.

Jared heard the rattle of bones and turned to see hairy men with large, slanted heads and bared teeth creeping down a hillside, gingerly avoiding the bodies of the coy wolves as they came closer. Jared wondered if any of them remembered him, remembered being trapped in his world. He wondered if they could help him.

"You killed everyone I love," Georgina said to his ghost.

"I didn't mean to," Jared said.

"I'm going to resurrect you now," she said. "And then I'm going to kill you again."

No, Jared thought as he felt himself being drawn back into his body. *No, no, no.*

"Eventually," Georgina said, "you're going to bring me back to our universe and you're going to watch me kill everyone you love."

40

SOMEDAY

Jared was dead again. He moved as far away from his body as the ghostly tether would let him. He couldn't feel himself being eaten anymore, but he could hear the joints popping as Georgina ripped off his arm and licked the flesh from his bones, the crack as she snapped his humerus and sucked the marrow. The thing from his bedroom wall kept out of her reach but never stopped watching Jared's body, amused.

The ape men hadn't been any help. She'd chased them down and eaten a few of them, but she wouldn't let Jared's body go and he slowed her down, so the rest got away. The fireflies formed a cloud, glowing like northern lights in the night sky, blocking the stars.

"Can you help me?" Jared asked them.

He felt their attention, but they didn't move any closer. If they would shred him again, send him up to the sky in tendrils, he could shake Georgina's grip on his body.

You need to be in your body, the fireflies thought at him. *The ogress is demi-mortal like you, so she can't be touching you or she'll hitchhike. We don't want her back in your world with Sarah.*

"All you had to do was behave, Jared," Georgina said, "but you couldn't do that, could you?"

Jared was stuck in a dusty, rocky valley with an ogress who was picking through his corpse's torso for her favourite organs. Pain skewed his sense of time, as did being a ghost. He wasn't sure if they'd been here forever or a few hours, but this was the third time she'd eaten his body. She was hungry, endlessly hungry. And sad, underneath her fury. Although she was starving, she didn't eat the bodies of the coy wolves. She squatted beside one, nibbling on Jared's arm like it was a scrawny chicken wing. Whatever magic she was trying to work failed. The wolf remained dead. The thing that had claimed to be his aunt hit her fist against the rocky ground.

The ground was littered with beings he'd murdered. When he was in his body, he could smell the wolves starting to rot, wave after wave of smell, like driving past a slaughterhouse.

Kill or be killed, bucko, his mom used to say.

He'd never thought that could be him, that he could be as violent as his mother, but here he was, drifting along the ground, examining his handiwork. Obviously it was self-defence. But it still felt wrong. The coy wolves hadn't actually done anything. Yet. And now that possibility was over. All their possibilities were over.

Soon, he was going to be dragged back into his body as the ogress resurrected him again. And then ate him. And then brought him back. Rebirth was like being tasered. She would try to kill him slowly, but her hunger would overcome her and she'd begin ripping off things, crunching his bones between her teeth. The pain was vivid and erased all thought, but short-lived, and then he was here, floating around in a world without television or wi-fi. Or coffee. God. This world had no coffee. There was nothing here but the dusty wind. His cannibalistic fake-aunt cracked his bones and slurped the marrow.

Just to hear something other than his own bones crunching, he sang "Someday," one of his favourite songs after he'd broken up with Sarah.

"Stop it," the cannibalistic Georgina said. "No Nickelback!"

"Or what? You'll eat me?" Jared said.

Jared couldn't remember all the words, but he sang the bits that he could remember over and over, out of sequence, heartfelt, earnest. Cannibal Georgina threw his foot at him. It sailed through his non-corporeal body. She furiously mojoed his body back together and shoved him back in it so she could strangle him.

"Stop singing!" she screamed, her hands wrapping around his throat, throttling him like the brainless chicken she thought he was.

Jared sang louder. Mentally, in his head—because he was choking, fainting, and couldn't so much as squeak—Jared sang and sang and sang.

"You irritating thing!" she said, lifting him up and slamming him into the ground.

Now, the fireflies said. *Go*.

They sent a single firefly down and when it touched him, he dissolved into golden threads. He listened to Georgina screaming curses at him. The thing from his bedroom wall spun like a dervish on the ground, furious that he was leaving it behind, alone, alone, all alone.

The world shimmered and was replaced by an empty basement, a damp concrete room with moving boxes piled to the ceiling. Jared lay naked on the cold floor, breathing in the sweet, sweet air. Sunlight beamed through the windows. His old bedroom in Kitimat. His childhood house. The one his mother had apparently sold, because two movers in coveralls swore when they saw him. One of them discreetly covered him up with a moving blanket. They asked him who he was, but he couldn't even squeak because his throat was bruised.

"Buddy," one of them said, "are you stoned or drunk?"

"I told you it was a party palace," the other one said. "Poor suckers who bought it didn't do their research."

Jared felt fear surging through him, fear of himself, of what he could do, of messing up any more than he had, and that fear paralyzed him so he couldn't answer even when the movers asked him how he'd got there. And he couldn't get up.

Crap, he thought.

ACKNOWLEDGEMENTS

Thank you to my redoubtable editor, Anne Collins, for going boldly through the looking glass and guiding us both back. Thank you to everyone at Knopf Canada, and the larger company, Penguin Random House Canada, especially Emma Ingram and Sharon Klein. Thank you to my bionic-kneed agent, Denise Bukowski, and her lovelies, Stacy Small and Alex Keys, for keeping my career on track through the continual challenge that was 2017.

Thank you to the Writers' Trust of Canada, the Canada Council for the Arts and the Hnatyshyn Foundation for their generous financial support.

Thank you to Carla Robinson, Leenah Robinson, Sam Robinson, Blair Grant and Keith Freeman. Thank you to Jennifer Savard at the Kiuna Institution and her students, Tewashontake White, Kateri-Marie LeBlanc and Shawerin Coocoo Weizineau.

As always, thank you to the good people of Ci'mot'sa and Waglisla for being you. I appreciate the support, cousins! Much love, many hugs.

Haisla/Heiltsuk novelist EDEN ROBINSON is the author of a collection of short stories written when she was a Goth called *Traplines*, which won the Winifred Holtby Prize in the UK. Her two previous novels, *Monkey Beach* and *Blood Sports*, were written before she discovered she was gluten-intolerant and tend to be quite grim, the latter being especially gruesome because half-way through writing the manuscript, Robinson gave up a two-pack-a-day cigarette habit and the more she suffered, the more her characters suffered. *Monkey Beach*, a national bestseller, won the Ethel Wilson Fiction Prize and was a finalist for the Scotiabank Giller Prize and the Governor General's Award for Fiction. *Son of a Trickster*, the first installment of Eden's Trickster trilogy, was a finalist for the Scotiabank Giller Prize. She lives in Kitimat, BC.